CEM BILICI

THE MECHANICAL TÜRK

AN OTTOMAN STEAMPUNK ADVENTURE

www.debaclemedia.com.au

CONTENTS

Preface   v

Chapter One   1
Chapter Two   13
Chapter Three   25
Chapter Four   37
Chapter Five   49
Chapter Six   61
Chapter Seven   73
Chapter Eight   83
Chapter Nine   95
Chapter Ten   105
Chapter Eleven   117
Chapter Twelve   129
Chapter Thirteen   139
Chapter Fourteen   151
Chapter Fifteen   163
Chapter Sixteen   175
Chapter Seventeen   187
Chapter Eighteen   197
Chapter Nineteen   201
Chapter Twenty   213
Chapter Twenty-One   223
Chapter Twenty-Two   233
Chapter Twenty-Three   245
Chapter Twenty-Four   255
Chapter Twenty-Five   265
Chapter Twenty-Six   267
Chapter Twenty-Seven   271
Chapter Twenty-Eight   277
Chapter Twenty-Nine   287
Chapter Thirty   291

The Ward Series   298
The Ward Series   300
The Enlightened   301
About the Author   302

PREFACE

The Mechanical Turk is a culmination of many things.

It is an exploration of my Turkish heritage, which for many years I ignored or outright rejected.

It is also an exploration of a genre which I, at the time, knew very little about apart from the fact that characters and cosplayers seemed to wear goggles and corsets and whatnot.

Mostly, though, it is my own authorly curiosity and pursuit of that little white rabbit we all chase named What If.

As such — in case it needs to be said — it is to be taken only as a work of fantasy. I have taken *many* liberties with events, places and people from history. Any errors are just that, or were made to suit to the story's needs. The story is in no way meant to either erase or minimise acts which took place and still cause pain to this day for many.

In other words, it's all in good fun, and I hope you enjoy *The Mechanical Turk*. And if you do, please be so kind as to leave a rating or review — also for other authors' works. It means so very much to us.

— CEM BILICI

Damlaya damlaya göl olur.

Drop by drop a lake is formed.

— A TURKISH PROVERB

CHAPTER ONE

LONDON, ENGLAND: 1837

The gold coin rolled deftly over the back of her slender fingers, then was lost as she palmed it, only to emerge once more. It was a simple parlour conjurer's manipulation that fooled most, which was precisely where, and why, she had learnt the skill, along with other such tricks of prestidigitation.

Her hand pivoted to snatch the coin, which had barely moved from the air. So hard did she squeeze, she expected to find the solid gold bent when she opened her hand again. Gripping the coin, she inspected her surroundings.

The cell was small and sparse of furnishings, as most cells were wont to be. Though she was used to long periods within austere rooms spent in silent contemplation, she had not had to suffer one such as this for many a year. Apart from the two chairs and table at which she sat, the only other items in the room were a stained cot, and chamber pot and wash basin in the corner. Nothing of any interest whatsoever. Certainly nothing she would use.

She slapped the coin on the rickety table. "*Mon dieu! Tu me prends la tête!*"

The jangle of keys and loud, grating click of the lock on the sturdy door behind her signalled the end of her interminable wait. She slipped the coin into the secret pocket in one of the folds of her clothing, such as they were, as the cell door opened and someone entered. Her loud exclamation had done the trick and drawn them in. Her captors would have congratulated themselves on how they had brought her to the point of breaking upon hearing her outburst.

A plain-clothed gentleman came around the table to face her. To his credit, he paused but only briefly upon setting eyes on her. A brown paper bundle was under his left arm. He cast an appraising eye over her, as one might a book on a library shelf while attempting to discern its contents by observation alone.

"Very good," the man said, then proceeded to the chair opposite her.

Another fellow, this one in a constable's uniform, came alongside the table with a proud grin. His expression fell when he spied her lounging on the chair in her undergarments. "How in the blazes did you get out of your manacles?" the constable bellowed, rushing forward to grab at her.

"I don't think that will be necessary, Beechworth," the plain-clothed man—an Inspector from Scotland Yard she presumed—said, stopping Beechworth. "Why don't you and Miller go see to the other one?" He indicated to the doorway.

She turned to a second policeman loitering in the threshold, not crossing it as if too afraid to be anywhere near her.

Beechworth frowned. "But, Inspector Kaylock—"

"There's a good chap," Kaylock said in a tone that brooked no argument.

Beechworth glared at her before turning to the Inspector. "I brought her in, Inspector. I should—"

"Now, now, Beechworth." Kaylock gave him a thin-lipped grimace that held no small hint of a threat. "Best listen to my instructions, eh?"

With a curt nod, Beechworth made to storm from the room.

"You may want these back, Monsieur Beechworth," she said, her accent distinctly French, and tossed him the manacles she had removed a short time after he had locked her in the room. "I think you may need them more than me, *non?*"

Fumbling to catch them, Beechworth sneered at her. She watched the angry policeman as he backed out of the room, and waved with her fingers as he closed the door.

"So, Inspector Kaylock..." She turned to face the man. "To what do I owe the pleasure of a visit from the famous Scotland Yard?"

Kaylock grinned at her. "Oh, the pleasure is all mine, I can assure you... Mademoiselle Angelique Morreaux."

Angelique's mouth formed an oval in shock. She placed her hand demurely over it. "*Mon dieu*! Scotland Yard knows who I am? Am I in very big trouble, Inspector?"

Kaylock's lips widened, though his lips did not part. "Perhaps we should dispense with the subterfuge, eh?" He tapped the large brown parcel, now atop the table, marked with a ragged red EVIDENCE stamp. "Quite the cache the lads found on your person, wouldn't you agree?"

Angelique gave him a sweet smile. "Well, when one does something, one should always do their best, Inspector. Would *you* not agree?"

Humming, he methodically unfolded the mouth of the paper bag. "Quite." Opening it, Kaylock peered within, his lips pursing as he nodded. "Yes, quite a haul, Mademoiselle. We have, of course, been following the infamous Night Mare's thefts for some time. I daresay we even came close to catching you a few times."

Shrugging, Angelique crossed her legs and eased back into the uncomfortable chair. "Perhaps."

"A rather fitting name. Morreaux. Means dark-skinned, does it not? Though in your case, a misnomer." He looked over her pale skin.

She fluttered her long lashes. "I assure you, Inspector, despite your inference of it being a pseudonym, it is my true name." She drew a silver cigarette case from somewhere under the table. Kaylock didn't bat an eyelid. Angelique offered him one of the cigarettes, which he took. "But, of course, I would say that even if it were indeed a pseudonym, wouldn't I?"

"That you would," Kaylock said as he held the cigarette to his nose and took in its aroma.

He dipped his hand into the bag and retrieved a match box. With one finger, he deftly slid the container open, then picked out a match and struck it. Leaning across the table, he first lit hers, then his own cigarette. The match sputtered as he shook it and placed the matchbox on the tabletop, resting the spent match atop it. He slid the box to the corner opposite the bag, then ensured it was aligned with the edges.

"Hand rolled cigarettes. Very nice," Kaylock said, exhaling smoke. "You've expensive tastes." He indicated the bag with the cigarette, drawing a lazy arc of smoke in the air. "May I?"

She nodded, and flourished her hand, smoke spiralling to the gas lamp above them as he gingerly removed and placed another item from within on the table.

"One razor-sharp hairpin dagger," he announced, his thumb testing the carefully honed edge before withdrawing the next item. "What one can only describe as a diminutive pocket pistol." He pointed it at her, holding it with casual abandon. "I am assuming it is loaded. I'll put this somewhere rather more appropriate, hmm?"

Blowing smoke at him, she watched in faux fascination as he pocketed it.

"One black pouch." He tipped the contents into his palm. "Containing a locket." Kaylock pried it open with his thumbs. "Complete with a portrait of a fair-haired maiden." He lay the locket gently on the pouch, spreading the delicate chain above it. "A family memento, perhaps?"

She remained silent.

With a nod, he continued. "One black corset, removed by the constabulary for fear of further concealed arsenal or tools."

Angelique sat up straighter and smirked.

Kaylock grimaced. "Yes, that worked spectacularly."

"*Absolument*," she said, shrugging, her unshackled hands held wide.

Kaylock's hand crept toward the bag, then stopped. He considered an unseen object. "I'll leave *that* particular item in the bag."

"Dressed such as I am, you need not worry about my modesty, Inspector."

"Perhaps, Mademoiselle. But my morality trumps your ease, I fear."

"In my profession, Inspector, the moral are paupers." She eased back in the chair and drew on the cigarette.

"Of that, I have little doubt." He too now sat back, only to open the front of his jacket and remove an item from an inner pocket. He placed the object, barely contained in his fist, on the table and inspected her expression.

Angelique sat quite still. Her lips stayed fast, but her eyelids narrowed, her line of sight flickering from his face to the object and back again.

"Then there was this," he said, flicking the corners of a red velvet cloth back to reveal the large sapphire. "Recovered from within the... *décolletage*, as it were."

"Your Constable Beechworth was very gentle," she said, then pouted. "Such a pity I could not keep the pretty bracelets he gave me."

Kaylock ignored her, seemingly over with games now. "This," he said, tapping the gem, "was the only item stolen, despite the number of other priceless stones and artefacts in its vicinity. Most, I daresay, far more valuable. Why is that?"

She exhaled softly and fluttered her eyelids. "Blue is my colour."

The inspector smiled and stared into her eyes as he stabbed the cigarette out on the edge of the table and tossed the remainder away. "This alone would get you time in the darkest of gaols. Perhaps even sent to one of the convict colonies. I hear the war effort in Australia against the Chinese is always in need of able-bodied women to manufacture shot, and wash and sew uniforms."

She pouted again and lifted her hands, turned them about. "Do these look like the hands of a seamstress or factory worker, Inspector? They are made for far more... delicate work. Perhaps we could come to some understanding?"

Kaylock's teeth flashed. Standing, he removed his jacket. "Now, there's a capital idea."

Sitting straighter, Angelique's shoulders tensed and her nostrils flared.

"Oh?" he said in amusement. "Does the thought repulse you so much?"

"Where are your morals now, Inspector?" Her voice dropped to a low, accusatory tone.

"No," he said, smirking. "I did not think you would stoop to such a level. That's not altogether your cup of tea, is it, Mademoiselle?" He dipped into the brown bag once more to pull out another item. "Though you may well have to consider it given the amount of trouble you now find yourself in." Thrusting his hand out, a long cylindrical object wrapped in heavy fabric rolled across the tabletop.

She halted the heavy item with her free hand, the cigarette she had been raising halfway to her lips as she hefted it. Nestling the cigarette in place, she uncovered the thing, almost dropping both it and the burning tobacco from her lips in shock.

"This is—"

Kaylock nodded. "Indeed it is."

"But I didn't—"

He nodded again. "I know that. You know that. His Majesty knows that. Yet here it is. In evidence with the infamous Night Mare thief, caught red-handed robbing The British Museum. And of royal artefacts no less." The inspector tutted. "Very naughty, Mademoiselle Morreaux."

Covering the jewelled gold rod, Angelique set it down gently. It was not part of the crown jewels proper, merely one of a multitude of the monarchy's treasures. Belonging to the King, however, it made little difference. "What do you want?"

Removing a pipe from his jacket pocket, Kaylock set it down before pulling two leather pouches from another. As she watched him, Angelique made out a stamp ingrained on the larger. A square and compass.

"How is your history?" he said as he pulled the pipe apart. He opened the pouch to produce cleaning tools, and set to it with a scraper.

"I know what I need to know." She stubbed out her cigarette and dropped it without thought.

The inspector grinned, not taking his eyes from his task. "To better aide you in your acquisitions, eh?" She didn't answer. "What of the Ottomans?" He glanced up briefly.

"I suspect I know more than most," she said with disinterest, then leaned back, hanging an arm over the back of her chair. "But please, do go on. I am intrigued as to where this conversation is leading."

He nodded, ignoring her sarcasm, and blew black dust from the pipe's chamber. Peering into it and frowning with dissatisfaction, he began scraping again. "They formed at the dawn of the fourteenth century, a group of some few hundred horsemen led by a chap called Osman—from which the Anglicised name Ottoman is derived."

"*Fascinating.*"

"Quite." Kaylock blew out the bowl again. Nodding, he began work on the shank that connected to the stem. "No one quite knows how the blighter gained control. Anatolia of the time was an assemblage of states. From there, they set out conquering the region, taking land from the Byzantines as they went—Constantinople, Greece, Jerusalem, northern Africa. In a few centuries they grew from a spit of land to reign across three continents."

"Most impressive," she said, now not even pretending to be interested as she gazed about her. "How do you English say it? Bully for them?"

"Yes. Quite an enterprising lot. Do you know, one of their Sultans had Leonardo da Vinci design a bridge for him? Imagine? *The* da Vinci. Didn't use it, though. Perhaps that is why they were in decline in the early eighteenth century? They had the vision, but not the foresight to implement it."

Kaylock blew through the shank, the bowl turned sideways and away from himself, then put it down and began on the stem with a pipe cleaner.

"Perhaps," Angelique said. "Or perhaps they needed a female leader or two?" she said with some vehemence.

He chuckled as he ran the long, brushed wire through the stem tube. "In any case, the beggars discovered Greek Fire, and with it the steam power that led to their resurgence, if one could call their prodigious spread that."

She gave him a bitter smile. "Like the mythical phoenix."

"Hmm, quite." After blowing out the stem, he re-assembled the pipe and pulled a wad of tobacco from the smaller pouch and packed the pipe with his thumb.

Angelique crossed her arms and hung her head back. "As fascinating as the information I already know is, Inspector, I do wish you would make your point."

"I'm getting to that. My you are an impatient one." He lit another match and held it to the pipe until it began to smoulder. "One would have thought," he said around the stem, puffing to get it going, "in your line of business, patience would be a virtue."

"Were I about my business, Inspector, you would be barely conscious enough to breathe, let alone smoke a pipe."

Shaking the match out, he laughed heartily. "I do hope you carry that enthusiasm with you wherever you go, Mademoiselle Morreaux. You will be in dire need of it, I fear."

"And just where is it, Inspector, that I will be going for you and His Majesty?"

Kaylock stood, picked up the evidence bag, and replaced everything but the gold sceptre and the sapphire, which he pocketed. "All in good time, Mademoiselle," he said, and ushered her out.

Inspector Kaylock opened the door to another cell and stopped short. Angelique let out a chuckle as he pushed her in ahead of him.

Constables Beechworth and Miller were shackled back to back in chairs with socks in their mouths. Kaylock marched in and pulled Beechworth's makeshift gag, the man spitting and cursing at his unceremonious treatment.

"What in the devil happened to you, man?" Kaylock said. "Where's the prisoner?"

Beechworth spat once more, and his mouth turned down. "It was that damned Oriental, sir! We transported him from the carriage to the cell and... I swear, by God's teeth, he used some sort of witchcraft on us! One moment I was standing, the next I woke up in this chair."

"This was very amusing, Inspector," Angelique said, and chuckled. "Though I fail to see what I would want with two bound policemen. Although..." She made a show of looking the men over, causing Beechworth's already ruddy face to redden.

Kaylock found a key on the floor and worked on the men's wrists.

"Yes, quite enough of that thank you, Mademoiselle Morreaux. Though I am sure it is no coincidence that while Beechworth was arresting you, Constable Miller also apprehended a suspicious Oriental gentleman outside the museum. The Oriental is *not* who we are here for, however. Beechworth is."

The constable looked up sharply from massaging his wrists. "Come again, sir?"

"You'll be accompanying Mademoiselle Morreaux on her journey, Beechworth. Best pack your bags, old chap."

"The devil you say, sir! I'm betrothed to be married! I can't be seen galivanting about London with a woman in her undergarments. What would my fiancée think if she heard?"

"Ah," Kaylock said, clapping Beechworth on the shoulder. "Lucky for you then, Beechworth, that you won't be travelling within London." Kaylock strode from the room, passing the brown paper evidence bag to Angelique on his way out, Beechworth in close pursuit.

She removed her hairpin blade and slipped it between her teeth as she bunched up her hair then fixed it in place before putting on her locket. Tucking the jewellery away, she pressed it to her heart a moment, then took out her corset and pulled it on.

"Miss?" Angelique turned to face Constable Miller. "Why *are* you in your underclothes, miss?"

"My dear Constable, what else would one wear to rob a museum?" She turned her back to him, cinching in her sides. "Be a darling, *mon cher*, and do me up?" Angelique took a deep breath. "Then perhaps," she added, expelling as little from her lungs as possible, "you would be so kind as to fetch me a Hansom cab?"

By the time they'd released her, it was well on its way to daybreak, though still dark enough that the only person who witnessed Angelique exit the constabulary was a lamplighter extinguishing the street lamps.

"*Bonjour, monsieur,*" she said with good cheer as she sauntered to the awaiting cab, her short heeled black boots clicking on the cobbles and carriage steps as she climbed aboard.

As oblivious as she was to her outfit of opaque stockings, chemise and corset, the elderly man was more than aware. He eyed her with a lascivious leer that was extinguished like his lamps when the driver turned to glare at him. The lamplighter pulled his tattered cap down and turned to the next lamp post.

With a grunt and a sharp flick of the driver's hands, the cab pulled away.

Angelique sat in silent contemplation a long while, her fingernails digging into her palms. So intent had she been, she had not noticed the cab had come to a stop. As the door opened, she whipped a hand to her head and pulled the deadly hairpin free and lashed out.

With a soft slap, her hand came to a sudden halt.

The driver's eyes were wide, her wrist held tight in his gloved hand. "*Nanda kore?*" he grunted angrily in Japanese.

She dragged him into the cab beside her, slapped the soiled cap from his head and tore away a well-worn scarf to expose his face. "I could have killed you, Hideyoshi!"

"You would have tried, *nee-chan.*" Hideyoshi gave her a lop-sided smile and released her arm.

She stabbed the blade into the seat beside her so hard it lodged into the wooden frame beneath the upholstery. She unclenched her teeth. "You'd best keep to English," she said. "They are still searching for their escaped 'Oriental', and speaking Japanese will no doubt draw attention."

Hideyoshi put his hands on hers and bent to meet her eyes. "What is wrong?"

"I lost the sapphire."

"But we escaped, as we always do. That is what matters. Any victory is better than utter defeat," he said, echoing her adoptive grandfather's words.

"*We* did not escape. *You* escaped."

Hideyoshi gave her a puzzled frown. "Then how did you..." He closed his eyes, sighing heavily. "What did you do, *Tenshi?*"

He used the Japanese name he'd given to her as children. Angel.

That generally meant he was either very emotional, or very cross. She knew just which it was in this instance.

"I had to make a deal with the British empire."

"To do what? And in exchange for what?"

"Both are the same to me, little brother. Revenge."

"*Chikushō!*" he said, swearing. He tore her hair pin blade from the seat and waved it angrily. "This again? I assume that means we are to go home."

"In more ways than one, little brother."

Hideyoshi snorted through his nose. "You engineered all of this beforehand, didn't you? Our being *caught*, too. All of this so we had no choice but to go to Constantinople. As you've wanted to do since you were a child!"

Her lips pressed tight as she nodded. "I did not intend on losing the sapphire, however." Coiling her dark, wild hair once more, she took the hairpin from Hideyoshi and stabbed it into submission. "And, I believe they call it Istanbul, not Constantinople, now."

He picked up the felled hat and pulled it roughly atop his head. Hideyoshi flicked the stiff collar of his coat up to hide his face in shadows and gathered the scarf he'd pilfered along with the cab. "You would have made a formidable member of our clan," he said with a stern glare.

"If only the Iga would allow an outsider such as myself to train with and join them," she said, not hiding her contempt.

"Do not fear. Grandfather would have been very proud of you, *Tenshi*." There was not a single hint of admiration in his voice as he exited the carriage, slamming the door behind him. Soon after, the horses set off at a breakneck gallop.

As she rocked about, Angelique drew forth her locket and opened it to gaze on the portrait within. "Soon, *Maman*. We will have our revenge, soon."

CHAPTER TWO

The American privateer schooner was neither the biggest nor most luxurious vessel Angelique had ever been on, but it was, Kaylock assured her, safe, well-armed and, more importantly, fast. Despite that, she found herself doubting its suitability as transport from the British Isles all the way to Japan. Especially given the waters between were heavily patrolled by Ottoman ships.

She voiced this opinion as Kaylock gathered her and Beechworth in the captain's cabin.

"Oh, heavens no," Kaylock said. "It's not at all made for such a journey. And I'd wager the poor captain would have a thing or two to say about that, also."

"Then—"

"We're not headed to Japan," he said, cutting her off. "You'll be disembarking on American shores and conveyed to its western coast by an altogether more, shall we say, experimental conveyance."

She raised an eyebrow. "Experimental? That fills me with the utmost confidence," she said in a dry tone.

"You and me both," Beechworth muttered. He crossed his arms tight and turned away.

Beechworth was not the least bit happy about being strong-armed into playing escort for her, a criminal he had caught and then been instructed to release. Angelique was sure the fact she had allowed herself to be captured in the first place, and had carefully orchestrated this mission to be enacted, would not brighten his mood... had she been inclined to divulge that information.

She had chosen the *nom de guerre* of Night Mare herself, planting it in the head of a little newspaper man who was easily swayed by drink and pretty women. Then the police had been tipped off by an informant, who had in turn been handed anonymous information. And so on and so forth. She was so far removed from all said information, it would be nigh on impossible to pin her as the source.

"My poor, little Constable," she said, frowning at Beechworth. "I really do not mind if you are sent back to your beloved." In fact, she much preferred it. She had not counted on Kaylock anchoring her with such a weight.

Kaylock smiled. "I rather think not. And need I reiterate the terms of your release, and payment?"

Angelique rolled her eyes. "*Mais oui*. Constable Beechworth must accompany me at all times or you will not absolve me of my crimes, nor relinquish the sapphire into my possession."

Beechworth sat tall, head snapping to each of them in turn before resting on the Inspector. "Sir, surely you can't be serious? You're giving this... this... *reprobate* a precious artefact from the British Museum?"

"Reprobate?" Angelique gasped. "I much prefer the term *libertine*."

"Look here, Beechworth," Kaylock said, lighting his pipe." You were chosen for this task for just the very traits you now exhibit. Your unwavering loyalty and moral code."

"Thank you, sir," Beechworth said, his manner gruff but accepting of the complement.

"In this instance, however, do be a sport and shut it." Beechworth's mouth opened before he firmly clamped it closed. "There's a chap. Now, what I am about to disclose is of the utmost secrecy." He turned to the sullen constable. "Beechworth? This comes from the very top." Beechworth frowned. "The *very* top."

Beechworth sat tall and turned himself, chair and all, to pay attention.

"God save the King, eh, Constable?" Angelique said as she brought out her silver cigarette case. Pulling a lantern on the table nearer, she lit the thing from it, then held the case out to him.

Beechworth gave the cigarette case a disdainful look. "I tend to side with King James."

Snapping the case closed, she gave him a quizzical glance.

"King James the First," Kaylock said, "imposed a heavy tax on tobacco as he found it noxious to his senses. He went so far as to compare it to the fumes of Hell itself."

Angelique gave a gay laugh. "Here's to the devil then, Inspector." She held her cigarette aloft.

The inspector cleared his throat. "Yes, quite. It's rather apt, really, that you should say that. Given the nature of your expedition, you'll likely need to strike deals with many devils. The more allies you have the better. Wouldn't you agree, Mademoiselle?" Kaylock pointed his pipe stem at the window of the captain's cabin.

Angelique exhaled a stream of smoke with a long sigh. "Come inside, Hideyoshi."

Beechworth scowled at them both before jumping and knocking his chair back and drawing his pistol as a shadowy figure crawled in through the window. "What in the—"

Eyes locked on Beechworth's, Hideyoshi pulled the dark cloth of a sailor's scarf from his face one handed, the other tensed about his own pistol, barrel pointed at Beechworth's chest.

"Please sit, Mister Hideyoshi," Kaylock said, puffing his pipe calmly and not having moved an inch during the course of the activity.

"Sit, *otōto*," Angelique commanded sternly when he did not move, using the Japanese for 'little brother' to enforce her words.

Hideyoshi glared at Beechworth for several breaths before moving to a seat beside Angelique.

Beechworth shook his pistol. "Inspector," he said in a low tone. "That is the Oriental that incapacitated Miller and—"

"I'm well aware, Constable. Now, if the both of you could put your weapons away? We have much to discuss."

The captain of *The Fortuitous Maid* had graciously given over his cabin to Angelique, and she made the best of it. Hideyoshi, who had until that time been hiding aboard without detection, was made known to the crew, who gave both him and the other strangers a wide berth. They likened Hideyoshi to something supernatural.

"You do a good job of perpetuating the Iga clan mythology, little brother," Angelique said softly in Japanese, her eyes closed beneath her arm in feigned sleep.

"Whereas you seem intent on exposing me at every turn, big sister." His feet kicked through the very same window he had used earlier that day and he landed near silent on the creaky boards.

"You do know you may freely use the door now."

Hideyoshi sat cross-legged atop the table, back straight, chest puffed. He let out a breath, shoulders sagging, and fidgeted with the oil lantern beside him. "The crew do not like to see me, even though they know of my existence."

She sat up, eyes cast straight ahead. "Perhaps I should have not told them you could run on water and turn into a demon and would steal their souls in their sleep." Her voice held none of the mirth she had intended.

"You are troubled, Tenshi."

"When am I not?" she said, rubbing her temples.

"Good!" he said with vehemence. Despite his frustration with her, however, he went to Angelique and rubbed at her shoulders. "You deserve these knots in your muscles. I should leave them there for putting me in the position you are about to." He continued working her shoulders.

She did not respond for some time, the alleviating of her tension at the forefront of her mind. "Thank you, brother," she said, resting her hand on his. "I know this is more than I should ask of you..."

He snorted. "You did not need to lure me to England under false pretences for it. You know I am always glad to help you."

"I do. And that is why I did not want to presume too much. This puts you in a dangerous position with the clan should they discover me. But it means so very much to me that you are here."

"That is something we will worry about when the time comes.

What we need concern ourselves with now is how will we speak with the clan elders? And my father."

Angelique did her utmost to hide the anger in her heart, though her shoulders hardened under Hideyoshi's fingers.

He gave a final press, then took her hand. "For now, we must rest. This will not be an easy journey."

She knew he was right, but she could not think about sleep. As he said, they had a difficult path and an almost impossible task ahead of them.

Angelique turned to him. "I really cannot do this without you, brother."

Hideyoshi regarded her a moment, then climbed out the window.

She moved to the portal. A breeze heavy with sea spray met her as she pulled it closed, then pressed her forehead to the cool glass. Angelique lifted the small pouch Hideyoshi had pressed into her palm as he'd taken her hand. The black bag contained a powder to induce sleep. A small amount would render her unconscious. A precise amount would kill her. It was used on targets of the Iga, who generally were the enemies of the Ottomans they were allied with. But it was not uncommon for it to be self-administered for pain or sleep. The Iga, too, had their demons.

She was loath to use it. Users were prone to fever dreams, though the mountain monks it came from used the experiences to refocus their memories and minds.

Perhaps it would show her the revenge she so desperately sought. Perhaps it would inspire her.

The journey passed much the same for the following eight weeks. On that particular morning, on what was expected to be their last on *The Fortuitous Maid*, she had no more clarity than on the first night of their journey. She could recall nothing of use from the images brought on by the sleeping powder. There had been memories of the Iga village where both she and Hideyoshi had grown up, but nothing that would aide her.

At least, Angelique conceded, she had slept well and was reasonably refreshed to face the task at hand. Though the storm she had woken to that day was hardly conducive to her remaining that way.

She hurried below deck to the smaller requisitioned quarters the two policemen occupied, which normally housed the first mate and quartermaster. She led them to the captain's cabin with food they appropriated from the galley. They found Hideyoshi sitting on the bed within, his shoulders slumped and lips turned down, legs crossed and hands on his knees in deep meditation.

"Your friend is rather wan," Beechworth said. He turned to Hideyoshi. "I thought your lot were used to sailing, and had the best ships outside of the Ottoman Empire since throwing in with the Turks?"

He was certainly not well. Angelique could not recall Hideyoshi ever being that particular shade of green.

"We do," Hideyoshi said, not opening his eyes. "And if you are very lucky, Mister Beechworth, you may actually live long enough to see one." The ship rolled, throwing Hideyoshi aside. He thrust his hand out to the mattress to still himself, skin paling as he broke out in a nauseas sweat. "If the *isonade* do not claim us and drag our bodies to the bottom of the ocean first!"

Beechworth gave Angelique a questioning glance.

"The *isonade* are sea monsters, their bodies covered with hooks and spikes," she said.

"Lovely," Beechworth said. "Best I write to my betrothed and bid her farewell now then, eh?"

Marriage was not something Angelique could imagine for herself. Not that she was against the affections of a man or romance, but she could not imagine being tethered to one place, one person. Though she had to wonder what a stable life would be like. Not to have to fend for herself constantly.

"Eggs and pork, Mister Hideyoshi?" Beechworth said, holding out a plate.

Hideyoshi's eyes screwed tighter before flying open as he hurled himself from the bed and away from the food to void his stomach in the captain's chamber pot.

"Best tread lightly, *mon ami*," Angelique said as she cut her own food. "My little brother is not his usual amicable self when he is not well." Her fork laden with its dainty mouthful paused. "Though, what man ever is?"

Beechworth's moustache bristled as he gave her a thin-lipped smiled, the one he always did when she called Hideyoshi her brother.

Halfway through the meal, Inspector Kaylock grunted. "By Jove, I almost forgot." His tone did not in the least suggest whatever it was he was about to raise had slipped his mind. He drew a bag from within his jacket and dropped it with a familiar jangle on the table. Two more landed beside it.

Angelique hefted one in her hand. "Quite a tidy sum to simply 'forget', Inspector." Weighing the bag, she assessed it to be substantial. From the sound and weight, gold. The others, jewels in one, and an assortment in the other.

"Yes, and of dubious origins," Kaylock said, confirming her suspicions. "So they cannot be traced back to you-know-who." He tapped the side of his nose as he took out his pipe and stood. "Remember, once you leave American soil, you are on your own."

"Sir, I thought you said the Yanks would be assisting us?" Beechworth said.

"They will only be transporting you from one side of the country to the other, Beechworth. Outside of that, you are all *personae non gratae*." The Inspector tapped his pipe out the window and turned with a grave stare. "Should you be discovered, the British Empire will deny any and all knowledge of you. As, I imagine, would the Americans."

Angelique pointed at Beechworth with her fork. "Perhaps, Constable, you should steal into the galley to procure some salted beef rations for us?"

"I do believe stealing is rather your racket," Beechworth said. "Although I do think I might be utilising the least of your crimes and adopt a pseudonym."

"A wise decision, no doubt," Kaylock said with no little sarcasm.

Beechworth ignored him. "I think I shall use—"

Kaylock tore the pipe from his lips. "For heaven's sake, man! Don't divulge any of your plans to me. Any of you! Especially in such close quarters as this." His eyes shifted to Hideyoshi. "The Ottomans have spies everywhere."

Angelique set her cutlery down hard and turned to him. "I assure you, Inspector, my brother is loyal. Besides which, you've yet to disclose what it is you want from us exactly."

"As I said when we set sail, I can't yet say. Far too risky." Kaylock waggled the stem of his pipe at them, eyes wide. "But I make no small claim when I say that your mission may well impact the course of global history itself."

"How dramatic," Angelique said. "And how is it we will receive our mission?"

"The Americans. One of their lot will debrief you."

"The Americans?" Beechworth said in indignation.

"Yes, Beechworth, the Americans," Kaylock said. "They have a vested interest in this just as much as us, believe me. You'll soon see that for yourself. But for now..." He indicated the bags of gold. "Those will only get you so far, depending on what means of ingress you choose."

Having regained some of his colour and composure, Hideyoshi lifted his head from the pot. "We are to devise the method ourselves?"

"Indeed," Kaylock said. "And by any means necessary."

Angelique raised a brow. "Any?"

"Any," Kaylock said, grim faced.

The trio disembarked at the harbour in New York and separated, only to meet again at different intervals at a carriage stop where they were to be picked up. To any bystander, they were three disparate travellers waiting to ease their weary bones and move on to whatever their next ports of call may be. Beechworth blended in, and unless spoken to no one would be the wiser as to his origins. Angelique passed as a European lady, despite her mixed lineage. And the vast majority of the public avoided the dishevelled and stained sailor who, to all intents and purposes, was asleep against a wall and reeked of sweat and fish guts. It was a pity Hideyoshi himself had chosen that exact same disguise.

With surreptitious glances, Angelique watched as he dealt with the seated man, an obvious spy to the trained eye. Hideyoshi feigned tripping into him, then shifted his limbs into a semblance of seated slumber once more, hands across his belly to cover the wound. As Hideyoshi settled beside the man and adopted a similar pose, he identified him as Kōga by a hand signal. It would not be long before someone discovered his sleep was no longer false but altogether permanent, though they would be long gone by then.

The Ottoman agents were truly everywhere. She knew this firsthand. Many a time as a child she bore witness to the Iga village hosting Ottoman sailors, captains and, on the odd occasion, dignitaries. As a slave, she could only observe from a distance, however, though Hideyoshi always provided her with detailed reports, allowed to be present near the meetings as the Iga lord's son.

Outside of the village, Ottoman spies could be found anywhere a hint of advancement or investigation in the steam power that had brought them back from decline arose. And there would soon follow a fatal accident, or a murder by a jealous rival or lover, with the Iga or Kōga usually employed to carry out said assassinations.

The Ottomans were as unreachable as they were untouchable, unrivalled in power as the sole holders of steam technology. Many suspected Leonardo da Vinci, when he had been commissioned to design the bridge for Sultan Bayezid II in the sixteenth century, had played a part in their development of the Greek Fire-powered steam engine.

The clatter of a carriage and trotting hooves pulled Angelique from her reverie as it stopped before her. It was driven by a burly American who said nothing, not even to would-be passengers he drove away, doing so by his intense stare alone. Once in the carriage, Angelique stared Hideyoshi down until he relieved himself of the fetid clothing he had appropriated.

She was surprised when the carriage drew to a stop some miles from the port in a shadowy alley between tenements. Even more so when a lanky gentleman with a big hat, unkempt hair and matching moustache eased his way inside and settled beside Beechworth with surprising speed. Once seated, he sent the driver on with several heavy thumps of his boot on the floor.

"Afternoon, gents, ma'am," he said in a southern American drawl, doffing his hat and nodding at each of them in turn, a huge grin on his face that wrinkled his eyes.

Even as she took the man in, Angelique sensed Hideyoshi's movement.

"I reckon I wouldn't do that," the American said, returning her steely stare with a smile that no longer extended to his eyes.

Hideyoshi's hand stopped as two tell-tale clicks of flintlock pistols sounded in quick succession. The man had quickly drawn and trained the barrel of a pistol each at her and Beechworth.

"Just in case you're still havin' funny ideas," the American said, "these here ain't your regular flintlock pistols. Each has a revolvin' barrel capable of six repeatin' shots without reloadin'."

Beechworth and Hideyoshi lifted their hands from their jackets, while Angelique sat up taller.

"You may as well put those away, *Monsieur*," she said softly.

"And why might that be?" The American chuckled in earnest as she revealed her small pistol from beneath her skirts, aimed between his widespread thighs. "I like you, Mademoiselle Morreaux," the American said, then lowered the hammers of his revolvers with his gloved thumbs, and lay the pistols across his lap.

Angelique did not reciprocate, her pistol moving to train on the man's heart. "And what might your good name be, *Monsieur*?"

The man smirked as he eased his pistols into their holsters and pulled off his gloves. He offered his hand to Angelique. "Jonathan Wake, at your service."

After a moment of contemplation, Angelique uncocked her weapon and transferred it to her left hand. She held out her gloved right hand for Agent Wake, who took it up and lay a gentle kiss on its back. He gazed up at her as he did so, a mischievous smirk on his lips.

Hideyoshi scowled at Wake.

"Yes, well, if you've both quite finished with your dawdling..." Beechworth said.

"Who are you exactly?" Hideyoshi said, voice full of venom.

Beechworth waved at the American agent. "He is obviously our American contact."

Her brother turned his gaze on Beechworth. "Any fool can see that!"

From there, the two descended into gruff argument.

"These two peaches must have been a joy to sail with," Wake said, chuckling.

She rolled her eyes. "Oh, *mon dieu*, you have no idea!"

Pulling off her glove, Angelique placed her thumb and mid-finger between her lips and let out a loud whistle that silenced them and brought the carriage to a sudden halt. Speaking in rapid-fire Japanese, she snapped at her brother. Hideyoshi threw open the door and climbed the side of the carriage, slamming the door behind him with a kick of his foot.

"I think I've fallin' in love," Wake said. He slapped the roof of the carriage, setting it going again before letting his hand fall to his chest.

"Good grief," Beechworth said, turning his gaze to the window. "I may just join Mister Hideyoshi outside."

Angelique eyed him up and down. "I doubt you're quite as limber as my brother."

Wake let out a hearty laugh. "Besides which, if you fell and broke your neck, you'd miss out on ridin' *The Pony Express*."

Beechworth quickly turned his head from the window. "You can't mean to transport us across the damned continent by horse and carriage!"

"If he does," Angelique said, "his ponies better be very big and strong."

Wake's smirk grew. "Angie, darlin', you have no idea!"

CHAPTER THREE

After an interminable age in the carriage, there was a commotion from both above and outside, and the buggy pulled to a stop. Beechworth frowned at Angelique in confusion. Giving him a shrug, she threw open the door and climbed down. Ahead of them, a crowd of onlookers blocked the road, gawping at something, their intermingled voices washing over her.

"*Oi!*" a familiar voice called out from behind.

"Hideyoshi?" Turning, she placed her hands on her hips as she saw him standing high atop the carriage roof, much to the driver's annoyance.

"Damned fool's liable to kill himself!" the portly man bellowed.

Hideyoshi pointed excitedly over the gathering.

Beechworth let out a sigh of exhaustion and rubbed his face. "What the devil is going on?"

Angelique shook her head. "I have no idea, Mister Beechworth, but I intend to find out."

Placing her foot on the spoke of a wheel, she ascended, Hideyoshi reaching out to pull her up by her hand. As she stood taller, her eyes widened. "Beechworth?" He turned from the crowd to peer up at her. "I think you should see this."

He frowned deeply as he took in the crowd, then glanced to the top of the coach with concern. "Must I?"

"Go on, limey," Wake said. "You won't be disappointed, I promise."

Beechworth soured at Wake's use of the derogatory term, though was still unable to resist. As he climbed the carriage, his frown turned to an expression of amazement. "What in the name of..."

Not taking her gaze from the sight, Angelique leant him her hand and pulled him up to join them. "Did I not tell you?"

"My word!" Beechworth said as he took in the huge steam locomotive.

The machine hissed and spewed smoke like some great dragon of folk legend, but it was decidedly a thing outside of either fiction or nature. All hulking metal constructed of geometric shapes, Angelique could not even make out the whole of it. A tall wooden fence barricaded the locomotive, with armed men protecting the only way through.

"How on Earth..." Beechworth said, shaking his head.

Hideyoshi was less impressed, having seen Ottoman locomotives on the mainland and describing them to Angelique. He had talked at length on their ingenuity and snaking train of opulent carriages. But standing beside such a marvel in person... Beechworth was right. How had they come by it? Only the Ottomans had the means and the knowledge of Greek Fire to fuel them.

She turned to yell the question at the American, though stopped as she saw Wake motion to the driver, who nodded back. He stood in his seat and pulled a signal gun from beneath his long coat. Raising it high, he set it off, and the crowd shrieked and parted. He replaced the pistol with a large red kerchief, which he waved at the guards, who worked to clear a path for the carriage.

Wake called them down and ushered them back inside. The journey to the locomotive seemed to take as long as the one that had brought them to it, though they finally made it through. As she exited the carriage once more, Angelique was utterly captivated by the steam engine.

"This is amazing!" Beechworth said, forgetting his earlier frustration.

"It's not bad," Hideyoshi mumbled in Japanese, drawing a glance from Angelique. There were not even such machines in Japan, despite their being allied with the Ottoman Empire for decades.

"I've seen her plenty," Wake said. "But I still feel the same way you're lookin' at her now, every single time."

Angelique gawped at the feat of engineering before them. The steel wheels alone were as tall as a man, connected by beams so huge they could crush a person. The body of the locomotive was a massive barrel atop a box, both covered in an array of pipes and valves. Atop the body, a wide chimney belched black smoke to the sky even as steam as white as the purest clouds escaped from various other locations.

A man in a thick leather apron and matching cap and gloves climbed from an opening toward the rear of the machine. A pair of large, blacked-out glasses adorned his face, the lenses surrounded by brass cowling. His mouth and nose were covered with a blue and white spotted kerchief layered in soot. Spotting the party, he pulled down the cloth to reveal a wide grin, then lifted the darkened glass on a hinged panel to reveal clear windows.

The man waved as he hurried to them. "Agent Wake!" he said in a decidedly British accent.

"Tom," Wake said, raising his hand. "Lady, gents, this here is *The Pony Express*'s chief engineer, Tom Yardley."

"Greetings!" Yardley strode with excited purpose and offered his hand, still gloved and covered in soot and grease. He struck himself on the forehead, leaving a dark line on his sweaty skin. "Apologies!" Shaking his head, he worked to pull the thick gloves off. "I've become so accustomed to having them on, I now hardly notice. Thomas Yardley, at your service." He shook their hands excitedly in succession.

Wake looked *The Pony Express* up and down. "How is she, Tom?"

"In tip-top condition, Agent Wake, if I do say so myself."

Beechworth shook his head. "What in blazes—"

"Ah, a fellow countryman!" Yardley bristled with pride and patted the machine as if it were a horse. "Steam locomotive, old chap." He frowned at Beechworth's confused expression. "The Turks may have revolutionised the world when they developed the steam turbine with the use of Greek Fire," Yardley said in an excited tone. "And used

Greek Fire to their advantage in battle and turn about the decline of the Ottoman empire, but we'll soon catch up, what?"

Beechworth continued to stare in amazement. "I've seen pictures in the papers and read reports, but..."

Angelique finished the question for him. "How is it the Americans have an Ottoman steam locomotive when you British do not?"

"We don't either," Wake said, giving her a wink.

With an exasperated huff, Beechworth waved his hands at the machine.

"All in good time, Mister Beechworth," Wake said

Several men approached and Wake directed them to take the three travellers' bags.

Angelique inclined her head. "You may have been keeping it a secret until now, but it shall not stay that way for long. Enemy agents will soon have this reported back to the Ottomans."

Wake smiled. "Let them. As far as the outside world is concerned, the United States of America has now cracked the secret of the steam engine."

"But in truth," Yardley said, "we appropriated the machinery and fuel in a rather more cloak and dagger fashion." He tapped the side of his nose, blackening it.

"You captured an Ottoman steam ship," Hideyoshi said, his tone matter of fact.

Yardley frowned. "How the devil—"

Hideyoshi waved at the machinery before him. "I recognise the parts from several assignments in the Japanese navy."

Wake huffed in frustration as he pushed back his coat to put his hands on his hips, his repeating pistols in clear view. A practiced move, Angelique was sure. At any given moment, Wake could more than likely whip the weapons free and fire off multiple rounds. It would be akin to a skilled swordsman in the Iga village practising *iaijutsu*, as she had seen her adoptive grandfather do many times.

Yardley held up his hands in defence. "Agent Wake, I assure you I did my best to cover up the markings, but getting it running was of paramount importance, you said!"

"Calm down, Tom." Wake screwed up his face. "I ain't gonna shoot you. But you gotta get it done! If the Turk's spies get close enough to see—"

"I will take care," a deep voice said from behind the group.

Before them stood a tall, dark-haired, tan-skinned figure with a curled moustache, dressed in much the same manner as the engineer Yardley. He was a solid, imposing man, seeming to be of all muscle. His eyes were sharp, intelligent, and took in the three newcomers with a sweep, blinking as they met Angelique's.

Yardley flapped his hands at the man. "Ah, there you are, Sully."

Angelique returned the man's open stare, who turned away and scooped up a handful of mud from the side of the thick iron tracks the hulking locomotive rested on.

Sully slapped the mud on the exposed and suspect machinery. "Fix." He removed the excess mud from his fingers with a flick of his hand before wiping it on his apron.

Wake clapped the man on the shoulder. "Sully here is Yardley's cloak and dagger. He's the reason *The Pony* was possible."

"Sully?" Angelique said with a questioning turn of her head, her eyes unwavering from the man, a Turk judging by his thick accent.

"Süleyman Reis," the man said with a bow of his head, right hand on his chest.

"You were the captain of the captured ship," Beechworth said.

Reis. Not a name, but a rank, the Turkish word denoting Süleyman a military naval commander.

"Sully here didn't take too kindly to the way things were bein' run from the palace in Istanbul," Wake said by way of explanation.

Angelique shook her head. "I do not understand." It was unheard of, an Ottoman steamship captain defecting. While news exiting the Ottoman empire was not a common thing, relegated only to the earth shattering, something as crucial as this had to be in that realm. Had there been a coup she had not heard of?

"There is much you do not know about how things are in *Türkiye*," Süleyman said gravely.

Wake broke the confused silence with a clap of his hands. "Come on, let's get you all aboard. Plenty of time to talk in comfort with food and drink."

29

"Comfort?" Beechworth's incredulous tone rose as he walked to the cabin from which Yardley had emerged, taking in the juggernaut as he went. "There's barely enough room in here for all of us, let alone any sign of comfort! And I daresay it's as hot as Hades!"

"Hotter," Wake said before laughing.

Yardley beamed. "If you'll allow me?" He beckoned for Süleyman to follow.

Together, the two men entered the locomotive and soon after the machine began to slowly move. Chuffing and hissing, the heavy metal rails and thick slabs of wood beneath them creaked and groaned under its weight as the locomotive inched away in reverse.

Wake grinned as Beechworth, Angelique and Hideyoshi backed away.

Beechworth gave the man a scowl. "Is this thing safe? It's not likely to fall apart, or worse?"

"I assure you, *The Pony* is more than safe," Wake said, walking away. "Let's meet them, shall we?"

They followed the tracks to a nearby building. As they came alongside the structure, massive doors were opened to allow the locomotive within. Wake entered through a much more conventionally sized door, holding it open for them. Once inside, Angelique was greeted by three gleaming carriages the likes of which she'd never seen.

"My word!" Beechworth said as Wake led them up a set of black lacquered metal steps into the first.

They were indeed impressive. Each was as long as a house, painted and polished until they sparkled in the way something new that had never been used or exposed to the naked elements only could.

The carriages were lavishly furnished as a luxury hotel might be. Red velvet seats were within the cabins, which were all lined with varnished wood and gleaming brass fittings. The expansive windows were draped with curtains the same fabric as the seats, and even they shone in the darkness of the building. There were even tables and chairs for dining, along with a well-stocked liquor cabinet. One carriage was set solely for sleeping quarters, the bedding within far more luxurious than the captain's bed on *The Fortuitous Maiden*.

The last carriage was by far the least austere, essentially a warehouse on wheels, set aside for storage of equipment and food in a larder. There were crates of all sizes tied to the floor and walls. One of these crates was so large Angelique could not help but wonder what resided within. Glancing around to see how they may have gotten the crate in, she found large double doors each side of the carriage at the centre, and a large hatch in the roof.

Returning to the lounge car, Angelique turned about, taking in the interior. "This is all very impressive, Agent Wake. But so far, I have yet to witness the express in your pony."

Wake frowned at her for a change, perhaps taking umbrage at her comment. "While I admit she ain't at full capacity like the Ottoman *Silk Road Express*," he said, referring to the tracks that stretched from Istanbul to the Chinese coast, "I think you'll find, Mademoiselle, that instead of the usual months, she'll get you where you're goin' in little over a week." Wake's dour expression lifted a little.

Beechworth turned to the American, aghast. "A week? Just how fast does this damnable contraption go?"

Beechworth clutched at the doorway behind Angelique, watching her in open-mouthed horror. He had followed her to the rear of the storage carriage, but however seeing her standing atop the bottom rail of the safety barrier, holding her flying skirts in her hands, crying out like a child on a carousel at the speed with which they travelled... it all appeared to be a little too much for the constable.

"Isn't it fabulous, Beechworth?" she cried, but he did not answer.

As they passed a crossroad, an open buggy pulled by a lone horse stood well away from the tracks. A couple sat in terror as they passed, the husband lifting his head from calming the horse and his eyes widening.

The young wife's eyes also grew as she saw Angelique's hitched dress and bared legs, stockinged as they were. She slapped a hand over her husband's eyes and crossed herself.

Angelique laughed gaily, and blew the woman a kiss and waved.

"Oh dear lord," Beechworth said. "They must think we're a travelling house of ill repute!"

Beechworth staggered back through the car, leaving Angelique to enjoy the breeze, speed and view a while longer.

The Pony Express had been stopped in the middle of nowhere so the group could safely convene. They sat at a table in the main car, its surface laden with maps and documents as Wake prepared to brief them. Süleyman Reis stood to the side with Yardley, at Wake's request filling in information where needed.

The American rolled out a map and drew his finger in a large clockwise circle from Turkey to surround the Arab countries, northern Africa, and a narrow band of China, the area he indicated filled in maroon. "This is the Ottoman Empire's territory as it stands today." Pointing at Hideyoshi, he then dragged his finger eastward to the Japanese isles, spots of bright red on the yellowed paper. "And here's your folk."

Above the red was a stretch of brown, the Russian territories. He tapped at a tattered band of yellow beneath the maroon, what was the Chinese territories and India after the Ottoman invasions. The yellow spilled south through islands including Sumatra, Java, Borneo and Papua New Guinea into a ragged band stretching across the top-most third of Australia. If not for the inhospitable nature of the continent, the war for it would have long ago been lost.

At Wake's request, Süleyman Reis spoke at length of the Ottoman rebirth under the rule of Sultan Osman the Third, who had been the changing factor in the empire's decline, which was all the more fitting as he was the second sultan named for their founder. Süleyman Reis knew a great deal more than was publicly available, though, and outlined the history for them.

Osman the Third was famous—or infamous, depending on one's perspective—as having orchestrated the collection and implementation of steam innovations that brought the second rise of the Ottoman Empire. This he achieved during an internal coup to oust the

Sultan of the time, his uncle Ahmed the Third, with the help of the *Yeniçeri*.

"The what?" Beechworth said.

"What we call the Janissary," Angelique said.

"That's right," Wake said. "The Sultan's loyal, personal armed force. Practically a small army in their own right. Back in the day, they were made up mostly of captured Christian boys converted to Islam." Wake's face twitched and his nose wrinkled.

"Over the hundreds of years since they created," the Reis continued, "the *Yeniçeri*... Janissary, become more powerful. First, they obey to the Sultan, with no power. Then, they are given power that go from father to son."

"Quite a feat, really," Beechworth said. "Going from what amounted to slaves to being granted hereditary titles."

The Turk nodded. "Before Sultan Osman, the Sultan only listen to their family, usually number one wife, mother, other adviser. But Osman..." He shook his head.

Wake and Beechworth's brows furrowed in thought.

"The rumours were," Angelique said softly, "Osman hated women and music. Once he took power, he banished them all from Topkapi palace." Her face screwed up in disgust. "He sent many of the previous Sultan's wives— His *uncle's* wives, favourites, and all their children and staff, to allies as hostages to *appease* them."

"Is true," Süleyman said, nodding. "He take out the harem, music, wife and children. Before he was Sultan, when a boy and growing, *he* was prisoner in a small palace inside harem."

"What does this have to do with the present?" Hideyoshi asked. "That was a century ago."

Wake cleared his throat. "With no one else to listen to, as Sully has told it to me, Osman relied heavily on the Janissary. And in turn, he gave them more and more."

"Now there is Sultan in Topkapı, yes," Süleyman said gruffly. "But the *Yeniçeri* are ones ruling."

They all sat quietly for a few moments before Hideyoshi spoke up. "It was Osman that brokered an alliance with the then Emperor of Japan. Then, over time, the Ottomans provided ships and Greek Fire so we could maintain their hold on the mainland while they attacked from the west."

Angelique nodded. "With the backing of the Muslim Chinese population, the Ottomans were able to proliferate through Asia. Under the proviso that the Japanese were never given too much."

Wake rose from his seat, moving to the liquor cabinet. "What's your point?"

Angelique crossed her arms and pursed her lips in thought. "More than anything, we need allies on this mission."

"Can't any of you say what it is on your blasted minds?" Beechworth said.

Angelique rose to pace. "What I am saying is that the help we require will not readily come from within Japan. They are steadfast allies with the Turks."

Wake gulped down a measure of whiskey and raised his glass toward her. "Well, if the Brits chose you three for this task, I assumed there was a reason behind it."

"What exactly is America's involvement in all of this, Mister Wake?" Angelique's eyes narrowed as she took the man in.

"Simple, Angie."

"I do wish you would not call me that."

Wake grinned. "How about, Angel?" That annoyed her all the more, but she bit her tongue. "The good ol' U.S. of A can't sit by and allow the continuin' spread of such an empire."

Beechworth eyed the map. "You fear they will encroach on American soil?"

"Oh, they've been encroachin' plenty. On the high seas, Ottoman Corsairs and privateers have been interferin' with trade ships, interceptin' our naval vessels between here and Asia. Their spies and assassins from Japan and other places have been infiltratin' our offices."

"Piracy and spying is nothing new," Beechworth said.

"No, it's nothin' new." Wake poured himself another drink. "But usually when it escalates, it only means one thing."

Angelique frowned. "Expansion."

Wake nodded. "And we aim to be ready for 'em. Have been for some time. That's why we've had our own spies get the specifications of their rails and have been layin' them out for the past thirty or so years. In preparation for what's to come. Though judgin' by the fact they never did anythin' about it, they either thought we'd never make it—"

"Or they have something much larger planned." She turned to Wake. "Do you really think they would start such a war, though?"

"Not today," Sully said. "Maybe even not soon. But they will?" He turned his head to her with determined surety. "Yes."

"And that's why, Angie darlin', the countries of Europe, and America, would be ever so grateful if you kind folk could sneak us out the plans for their steam vehicles and formula for Greek Fire."

Hideyoshi scoffed. "Is that all?"

"That's all," Wake said, grinning. He held his glass out, index finger jutting as he waggled it side to side. "The fuel's the most important. Because without that... Well, you can be assured that we won't survive any war against the might of the Ottomans."

Angelique shook her head. "You are putting all of this weight on us three? We cannot possibly succeed."

"Well..." Wake shrugged. "If you can't get your hands on the plans and the formula, there's also a secondary mission you three are more likely to accomplish, given your... skill-sets."

"Which is?" Hideyoshi asked, eyes narrowing.

Süleyman Reis supplied the answer, his voice low and grave. "You must to find and assassin the *Yeniçeri ağa*."

Hideyoshi's eyes widened. "You want us to kill the highest military commander in the Ottoman Empire?"

Wake downed his drink in a gulp, then grinned. "Simple, huh?"

CHAPTER FOUR

Good to Wake's word, *The Pony Express* was well on its way to get them to the other side of the country in little over a week. Four days into the journey, they had now traversed over half the continent's length. It seemed hardly possible to Angelique, despite the tales she'd heard.

Her first experience with steamworks had been on her escape from Japan as a young girl. She had stolen away in a shipping crate on a Japanese vessel, an older and more inferior steamship than the Ottoman's. All the reports she had read since were mere hearsay when compared to the real thing. Most of the public thought them to be fanciful puffery. How little they knew.

They had fast become accustomed to travel by train, having found it was infinitely less disruptive than by sea or carriage. With neither the same movement as those other forms, nor being as tightly confined in an enclosed space, Angelique was certain it would fast become the most popular means of travel... *if* they could liberate the technology from the Ottomans. *The Pony Express*, however, as told by Agent Wake, would be utilised for the sole use of the President of the United States after this, its maiden voyage.

Late in the afternoon of that fourth day, something of a disaster struck when the great metal leviathan, as Beechworth called it, came to a screeching halt.

Cursing and blasting, Beechworth had emerged from his quarters, face half lathered and a razor in hand. He was in his undershirt, pant braces hanging around his waist. "What the devil is going on? I could have cut my blasted throat!" he yelled as he entered the lounge car.

The others were picking themselves and assorted items from the floor. Hideyoshi muttered something to Angelique that caused her to laugh.

Beechworth's eyes narrowed. "What is your *brother* saying about me now?"

"He says you are like the old oxen we had in our village as children. Loud and foaming."

Beechworth raised his hand, razor glinting in the sunlight. "Kindly tell your *brother*—"

Hideyoshi puffed up and bore down on Beechworth, speaking in loud, angry Japanese. Beechworth held his hands up and attempted hasty apologies, the razor nestled harmlessly between finger and thumb.

Angelique moved swiftly. Her hands fell on Hideyoshi's chest as he continued to lambast the man.

She shouted in Japanese at her brother. "*Why must you keep taunting him?*" she said in mock anger, just as he had been, yelling about lazy oxen while he kept a straight face.

Her brother could hide his amusement from the others, but not from her. His eyes shone with mirth. "*I'm bored. And it's fun!*" he answered as angrily as he could.

She shook her head as she left them both and moved back to the table where she had been playing cards with Wake before they had been interrupted.

"You know," Wake said in a lazy drawl, a grin on his face as he scooped up cards and poker chips, "you didn't have to cause a catastrophe to cover up the fact you were losin'."

"You did say this locomotive was for your president, did you not? Tell me, does he always used marked cards?"

Wake's smile became wry. "You noticed that, huh?"

"Next time," she said in a consoling tone, "do not try to swindle an *artiste*."

He cleared his throat and stood, dropping the mess of cards in his hands on the table. "Shall we, uh, go and see what all the fuss is about?"

Angelique shrugged and offered her arm. "Yes, and quickly." She glanced over her shoulder. "Before the children decide to play once more," she said loudly, drawing glares from both Hideyoshi and Beechworth.

As Wake leapt down from the carriage, Angelique took up a parasol from a holder by the door. Wake extended a set of steps, which she descended, holding out her hand for him to assist her. Instead, he placed his hands on her hips and gently lowered her to the ground.

Angelique pushed him away and slapped his hands playfully with the parasol, then opened it in his face before lofting it high. "Don't you know it is improper to manhandle a lady in public?"

He stretched his hands out to the wilderness. "We aren't in public. And I reckon, as this kind of transportation catches on, it will become the height of bad manners *not* to assist a lady down from a train."

"Next time, Agent Wake," she said with good humour as they walked along the car, "I suggest you keep your hands to yourself, unless you have permission."

"Next time, ma'am?" She was certain his eyes sparkled.

As they reached engine of *The Pony*, they saw both Yardley and Süleyman on the tracks clearing rocks.

"Apologies for the sudden stop," Yardley said between grunts and huffs.

Süleyman made no sound as he hefted a much larger stone and sent it rolling away.

Wake scanned the tight space between the front of the locomotive and the pile. "You came a might close." He indicated a wedge-shaped scoop close to the rails at the nose of the engine. "Wouldn't that have cleared the way?"

"Firstly..." Yardley said, standing straighter and arching his back.

"That is simply to ensure that cattle and other *vermin* do not get caught under the wheels and gum things up."

"I'm glad that was not the case." Angelique's lip pouted. "Poor cows."

Yardley frowned. "Er, quite. Secondly, it is only thanks to Sully's keen eyes and spyglass that we avoided this at all. Had it not been for him, we would surely have derailed."

"Is nothing." Süleyman shook his head, then grabbed Yardley by the arm and pulled him away.

With a rumble that travelled through the soles of Angelique's boots, a shower of rock, debris and dust undid what small amount of work they had managed, adding to it significantly.

Angelique waved her hand at the dust, squinting. "I shall fetch the others to assist you."

"You mean, you're not goin' to hike up your skirt and dig in?" Wake grinned. "More's the pity."

She spun about, ignoring Wake, but smiled once her back was to him. "No, *Monsieur.* You would enjoy that *far* too much, I am sure, and—"

She stopped short, frowning. An odd sound filtered over the baked landscape from a distance. Turning back, she walked through the men and climbed atop the rock pile to peer at the horizon.

"I was only pullin' your leg," Wake said. "This ain't no job for a—"

"Firstly, if you continue that sentence, I will show you just how deadly a simple parasol can be." Saying so, she blocked the sun with the dainty thing, but raised her hand to her brow when the lace did nothing to halt the sun's rays. "Is that a wagon train?"

Süleyman ran back to the engine cabin and returned with an ornate spyglass of Ottoman design, no doubt the very same one he had used on the vessel he captained. He held it up for Angelique.

She thanked him as she took it. Extending it to its full length, she brought it to her eye. "Yes. A wagon train."

"Agent Wake!" Yardley exclaimed. "No, absolutely not! Why, I forbid it!"

"Forbid? Really, Tom?" Wake said.

She lowered the spyglass as the engineer followed Wake away from the rubble.

Hideyoshi passed them, ignoring both men, Beechworth a short distance behind him, who nodded at them but was ignored.

"Where are they going?" Angelique said, closing the looking glass with annoyance.

Hideyoshi shrugged. "The American said something about a foal."

Süleyman smirked as he went back to work, muttering something in Turkish. He caught Angelique glancing at him and tapped the site of his forehead. "Wake... He crazy."

They did not have long to wait to discover what the Ottoman captain's hinted insanity was. Beechworth and Hideyoshi's expressions said they were in complete agreement with the once sea captain.

Wake came thundering toward them on a vehicle the likes of which she—and, she wagered, anyone else—had never lain eyes upon. "Do you like my goggles?" he said, lifting darkened eyewear similar to Yardley's from his eyes.

"Is that what you call them?" she said, admiring them. They were the perfect thing for this bright landscape. She shrugged. "I am far more interested in this foal of yours."

Sitting up straighter on the thing, Wake beamed with pride. "What do you think?"

The machine had two steel spheres for wheels, one each at the front and the rear and covered with round, flat-headed metal spikes that resembled large thimbles. The spherical wheels were joined to a frame of steel and wood laden with brass pipes and panels. At the centre of the thing was a seat that was more saddle than anything. At its rear, pointed at the ground, four large open pipes vented steam, two to each side of the contraption. This, Angelique surmised, was the contents of the large crate in the storage car.

"It has the looks of a velocipede," Angelique said, eying the thing. It did indeed bear a passing resemblance to the two-wheeled, pedalled vehicles popular in London and other European cities.

"Indeed," Yardley said with pride. He still appeared annoyed at Wake, and was casting him sidelong daggers from his eyes, but his interest in this machine quickly softened his resolve. "This is my aeolipede!"

"Aeolipede?" She was intrigued by the thing and examined it minutely. "How does it work? There are no external moving parts like *The Pony*. No fire to stoke, or means of adding fuel."

"This is all she needs to gallop," Wake said.

He twisted a wide cap and withdrew a wide glass container with brass rods spaced around its circumference. Inside the canister was a crimson liquid that shone as if lit from within, sparkling with an almost magical quality.

Angelique gawped at the mysterious fluid in awe. "Is that—"

"Greek Fire!" Wake's eyes widened as he spoke.

"See," Süleyman said as he continued working. "Crazy."

"But how does it work?" she said.

"No one quite knows how Greek Fire does what it does," Yardley said. "Due to its properties, when it comes into contact with water, it causes an explosive discharge of steam. That is what also allows *The Pony Express* to operate at the capacity she does. If not for the injected Greek Fire, she would be far slower and inefficient. Why, the power to weight ratio alone—"

Hideyoshi scoffed. "Explosions? Between your legs? No one would be stupid enough to—"

Angelique snapped her parasol shut and slapped it against his chest. "Hold that for me would you, *otōto*. I shall be back in a little while."

"*Oi!*" Hideyoshi barked before unleashing a stream of invectives.

"You sure you wanna take a ride?" Wake said. "Your brother doesn't seem—"

"Quite sure," she said, glancing at both men in turn. "I make my own decisions, thank you both very much."

"All right," Wake said with a shake of his head. "But you ain't exactly attired for—"

He stopped open-mouthed as Angelique bent to lift the hem of her skirt and thrust her hands beneath. She grabbed at a chord and pulled, which in turn caused the entire length to rise and bunch above her knees.

"My word!" Yardley exclaimed and turned about, the Turk and Beechworth doing the same.

As she attached two brass rings at the ends of the cords to two decorative buttons at her waist, Hideyoshi's voice rose, but she paid him no mind.

"Ready when you are," she said to Wake, reaching a hand for his hip, then stopping and cocking her head. "May I?"

"Oh, you may indeed! But be careful, the—"

Angelique placed her boot atop one of the pipes and kicked the other over deftly to straddle behind him. "You were saying?"

Wake chuckled. "Nothin'. I wasn't sayin' a damned thing. Though, if you feel the urge to take liberties from our close proximity—"

"Mister Wake!" Yardley bellowed over his shoulder. "The aeolipede has not nearly been tested enough! And now is hardly the time for a jaunt across the—"

With a sound like something that had fled Tartarus itself, the aeolipede shot forward, leaving the three men coughing in the cloud it left.

The Pony crept along in the distance as Angelique approached it alone on the aeolipede. She gave little thought to anything but the stream of air on her face and through her hair, whipping it into all manner of mess, no doubt.

The concerned faces of her brother, Yardley and Beechworth swung from the locomotive engine's cabin doorway and portal.

"Where the devil is Wake?" Beechworth shouted.

"*Where have you been?*" Hideyoshi yelled in Japanese at the same moment, climbing out to hang from a handhold.

"My aeolipede!" Yardley screeched, all but dancing a jig as he did his best to inspect the dust covered machine.

Angelique rolled her eyes—which were hidden by the dark lenses of Wake's goggles, as he called them—and sped deftly away from *The Pony* and circled back as it came to full stop.

The three men continued talking over one another and arguing amongst themselves as she slowed the aeolipede. All but Süleyman

Reis, who ran to her side and assisted in steadying the heavy machine and putting it up on a stand that folded out from beneath it.

"Thank you, kind sir!" she said, her cheeks aching from laughing the whole trip back, despite her face and clothes and stockinged legs being caked with dust and tattered in places.

"You good pilot," Süleyman said, nodding.

She had no time to respond as the three loud men approached, arguing still. With a shrill whistle, she silenced them.

"I know you have many questions," she said. "But calm yourselves. Both your aeolipede," she said to Yardley, " and Agent Wake are quite unharmed."

Yardley darted to the machine, rubbing dust and dirt from its surface. He let out a harumph. "Yes. Quite."

"What of Wake?" Beechworth said.

"At this very moment, Agent Wake is returning with our prize."

"Prize?" Beechworth said? "What blasted—"

"*And...*" Angelique said, raising her voice. "He will meet us at that bend, there." She pointed to the bottom of the hill. Hideyoshi made to speak, but she silenced him with a raised hand. "*And,* I am very thirsty and in need of freshening up!"

"I'll prepare some drinks then, shall I?" Beechworth muttered to himself when no one moved or spoke. Turning about face, he stormed away, still muttering as Angelique followed.

By the time she had cleaned herself, tidied her hair, changed her dress and sat down for a drink, *The Pony* was near the bottom of the hill she had indicated, and soon came to a screeching stop with a rattle of its couplings. Angelique made her way outside, heading for the shade of a tree. She rapped on Beechworth's cabin window with the tip of a fresh parasol to match her outfit, drawing him to it. He yanked the window up and pursed his lips.

"It is a lovely day outside, Mister Beechworth," she said. "I do believe I saw a picnic basket. If you would be so kind?"

"Madder than hatters. All of them!" Beechworth said loudly, slamming the window closed once more.

Agent Wake arrived a little while after driving a covered wagon and found them in the shade.

"Afternoon, all," he said, doffing a strange hat, an even stranger man sitting beside him doing the same as the wagon continued to the storage car at the rear of the train.

"Absolutely, stark raving mad!" Beechworth muttered, and tore a bite out of his sandwich.

Several days later, they reached the port city of San Francisco. It was the final stop for *The Pony*, in both that it was their journey's end, and that without more Greek Fire she would only be able to make it part way back across the continent.

They left the train in secret, Hideyoshi leaping from it before it came to a stop, landing on his feet running and blending in with the growing crowd. Not long after that, Angelique had done the same from the opposite side, leaving Beechworth flummoxed and alone as she found a cab to take her the rest of the way.

The docks were in chaos as she reached their appointed meeting place, a small shack on a pier owned by the harbourmasters, ships swaying and creaking a mere stone's throw from its very windows.

She knew for certain Ottoman spies would be watching. And even if they were not here to witness the monumental success of *The Pony*, news would soon reach them, and they would be absolutely livid. As was Beechworth as he arrived, harumphing, blasting and muttering to himself until he finally calmed enough for the American to speak.

"You gotta get us more of that magic formula, Angie," Wake said, his usual genial manner replaced with deep concern. "You get us the formula to Greek Fire, and we'll get *The Pony* to the capitol, and build more like her."

Beechworth crossed his arms. "And share it with us poor 'limey's', of course."

Wake's smile was small, almost nervous. "Of course, Constable." He took up Angelique's hand, stopped his lips short of it and looked up. "May I?"

She sighed as she returned his gaze. "Ah, to hear those words again."

"Perhaps when you return?" he said. The kiss was as gentle as it was longer than propriety dictated.

"Perhaps," she said. Pulling her hand gently from his, she turned about without so much as a goodbye and exited the shack.

"I really do think I have fallen for your sister, Mister Hideyoshi," Wake said, slapping him on the shoulder with gusto before snatching the limb back at the deathly glare he was given.

"Again?" The menace in Hideyoshi's voice touched his stare, making it icier still.

Beechworth balked, turning to the American, aghast. "You don't mean to say that you and she... She and you..."

Wake held up a finger and tutted at the two, shaking the proffered digit. "A gentleman does not speak of such things."

"Do come along, *otōto, Beechworth,*" Angelique called out as she headed for the wagon holding their possessions, the British engineer and Turkish captain already there, staring at a large crate.

"Do they really think that... that *contraption* is going to secure their path into the Ottoman palace?" Yardley said to Süleyman, his eyebrows dancing with indignation as he threw his hand at the crate the aeolipede had occupied.

"I have no doubt, Mister Yardley," she said, drawing the man's attention. "Especially with your... modifications."

As soon as she had clapped eyes on the thing in the wagon train, she knew it was their best chance, and worked hard to secure it at any cost, though it had taken almost all the gold and jewels Kaylock had given them, along with Wake's position, to convince its previous owner, who had been loath to part with it.

She caught sight of Beechworth, stood to one side with his arms crossed and a look of distaste written on his features.

"Whatever is the matter with you?" Angelique said.

His lips pressed tighter, turning down. "What Agent Wake intimated..." he said in a low voice.

"I'm curious, Mister Beechworth. Did you tell your fiancée you were travelling with a woman?"

He seemed taken aback. "I most certainly did," he said proudly.

"And what did you tell her of me?"

Beechworth stumbled. "Why... I told her the truth, of course. That I was to escort a criminal, and it was of utmost importance to the British Empire."

"And, did she ask if I was attractive?" He made no response, but for a slight twitch to his face. Angelique gave a throaty chuckle.

"She may have asked," he said in anger. "But that does not mean—"

"It means *everything* to a woman, you silly little man." Stepping close, she prodded him in the chest. "Society says that what I—a grown woman capable of taking care of myself since childhood—choose to do or not do is theirs to judge, and question, and constantly scrutinise. Simply because I was born with a different set of anatomy!" With a last prod, she stalked away.

"That, Mademoiselle," Beechworth said loudly, "is hardly my fault. Nor a facet of my character that is within my control."

Angelique turned and rushed back to stare defiantly into his eyes. "I disagree. But if that is what you truly believe, then I only have this to say to you, Beechworth. Keep your opinions to yourself, lest you infuriate me. And I promise, you do not wish to infuriate me."

"Right!" Beechworth said loudly. "Very well. I'll see to our belongings then!" Having said so, he walked away at a brisk pace.

Angelique watched him hurry away, her eyes narrowed.

"You'll make no friends behaving that way," Hideyoshi said in Japanese, grinning.

"I have no interest in making friends with Beechworth, little brother."

"No? Perhaps you are interested in sticking out, then?"

"That, my dear little brother," she said, switching to English once more, though now with a perfect British inflection, "is precisely the idea." She waved to Yardley and Süleyman to get their attention. Affecting her French accent once more, she called out, "Where might we find a fast ship with a *reputable* captain to carry us to Ise Bay."

Süleyman Reis nodded. "I know a captain who will help. And his ship?" He gave one of his rare smiles. "Is *very* fast."

CHAPTER FIVE

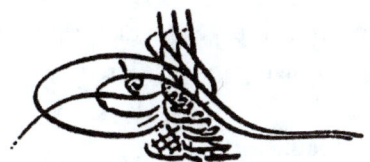

Ottoman sailors scurried across the ship, constantly busy and highly regimented, each of them moving in service of the ship. One of them had a clockwork arm from the elbow down, perhaps lost in battle or some deck accident. It was another marvel to add to an already fast-growing list.

The Ottoman ship moved faster than any seagoing vessel Angelique had ever been on. It was almost as exhilarating as riding *The Pony Express*, though once they were out at open sea and with no fixed reference point, it became that much harder to gauge their speed, and the novelty soon wore off.

They had departed the harbour of San Francisco in a much more conventional ship, setting north for a deserted stretch of Oregon coastline. The Americans had pre-arranged for the Ottoman ship to come in close to shore for a transfer, which was Angelique's first encounter with such a vessel and the beginnings of her amazement. The machinery the Turks commanded and their efficiency in merely transferring their belongings—especially the overlarge and heavy shipping crate—was phenomenal.

From there, they had flown from the shore, the ship's turbulent wake stretching behind them as they thundered away. She had watched until the pine trees visibly shrank, becoming indiscernible from constant bobbing. It had barely taken any time.

Though still part of the Ottoman fleet, the ship and its crew, she learnt, were rebel sympathisers, though there was no mention of what faction they might belong to. While the Japanese were allies of the Ottoman, they conducted some small amount of business and trade with Americans so, while rare, it was not uncommon to see such ships and Japanese sailors come and go. For a crew of Turks, however, it was tantamount to suicide.

"I miss the sea and the ship," Süleyman said, drawing her attention from the crew taking down Japanese standards and replacing them with Ottoman flags.

"It must be very difficult for you."

"Life is life," was all he said in way of response. "*Kısmet.*" He looked sideways at her. "Fate. It was not my fate."

"I do not believe in such a thing."

Süleyman regarded her with narrowed eyes a moment, then shrugged. "What you believe, or not believe, not make a thing be or not be."

"Truer words have never been said. But I make my own fate, Süleyman Reis. My own *kısmet.*"

He laughed at her not unkindly, then pointed skyward. "Only Allah —God—writes *kısmet.*"

"As you can see..." She held out her arms. "I am not a scrap of aged parchment to be either written upon, or read."

Süleyman smiled knowingly. "When someone know you, they can read."

"Not if you do not allow anyone close."

Süleyman pointed to her heart. "*Meyve ağacının dibine düşer.*"

As he walked away, she wondered if she had been imagining it, or if the man had instead pointed to her locket. Pulling it gently by its chain, she gripped the aged, lozenge-shaped gold in her hand and deciphered his words.

If she had it right, he had said, "Fruit falls at the base of the tree."

Now if she only knew what he meant by it.

The journey to Japan had been as quick as the one that had taken them across America. If only such travel had been readily available to all, she would have travelled more often. As it was, she had been luckier than most, having visited America, Europe and Japan long before this. Though her journey through the continents had hardly been leisurely. And as Ise Bay grew from a dark line on the horizon, it seemed to taunt her with fears of the past and what was yet to come.

Her formative years had passed under the skies and on the soils of this country. She had even spent some time in this very bay until she had found a way onto the ship that would steal her away. She had lived like the multitude rats that habited the docks, even preying upon them to survive. And it was they who'd inspired her method of egress.

Unlike their journey on *The Pony*, there was no greeting of bewildered masses. Neither was there subterfuge. The sailors and Hideyoshi dressed as they would be in every-day attire. And all too soon, she found their group winding up an all too familiar mountain track, led by Hideyoshi and a contingent of Iga men that were posted in the bay. Melancholic memories flooded her mind and Angelique felt something she had not allowed herself to for a long time. The sting of tears.

She blinked them away, and was glad for the distraction when Beechworth spoke to her, being mute for much of the journey.

"How was it you came to be *here?*" he said, voice full of awe and scorn. He took in their surrounds and the peoples as if they were in an unearthly landscape. And to him, they undoubtedly were. The mountain and road leading to the Iga village was about as far removed from the streets of London as one could get.

Of the fact that Beechworth had served in the military she had no doubt. Most men of lower social standing and his age had, especially those in the constabulary. She had no clue as to where he may have been posted, but it was clear it was not in what the Western world called 'the Orient'.

Angelique sighed. "You recall our discussion on *The Pony*, I assume?"

Beechworth frowned, then his expression became one which

Angelique hated most in the world. Pity. "You were... sent here as a slave?"

She shook her head. "No. However, I was the fruits of just such an endeavour. Thankfully, I was born in and lived under the protection of the then Iga lord, and was treated kindly. For the most part, in any case."

"No small miracle by the sounds."

"*Urusai!*" Hideyoshi shouted, using what Angelique knew was his battle voice. It almost caused her to cry out in laughter. Falling back, he brought his horse close to Beechworth's, leaning forward in his saddle with a menacing scowl.

Beechworth lowered his gaze, shoulders drooping. He had been warned to follow every command, however insulting.

The Iga men at the head of the group laughed and jeered, calling for Hideyoshi to teach the English dogs a lesson.

"Woman!" Hideyoshi shouted to her in English, his smirk clearly genuine. Angelique turned to him slowly. Her eyes fixed on him even as she cowed. "Lower your eyes, or I will have my men tear them out and have them cooked for your next meal!"

Angelique narrowed her eyes at him before lowering them, then said, "Yes, my Lord."

Hideyoshi sneered then looked to his men, who turned to face front, laughing between them. "We will be at our village soon! Speak only when you are spoken to, or you will be speaking to my sword next!" Urging his horse on, Hideyoshi joined the men at the lead and joked with them.

As their horses trotted through the Iga village gate, children gathered to call and run after them, laughing at the strangers. They were used to Turks and captured slaves, but real outsiders were a rarity. Especially those that came willingly.

While Beechworth had hair on his upper lip, he was nothing like the Turks with their tanned skin, curling moustaches, fezzes and turbans. And they would most definitely have never seen a European woman on a horse, let alone in a corseted voluminous dress of many layers riding side-saddle.

Angelique did her best to play the outsider. She waved and cooed at the children as she held the sun back with her parasol, smiling and laughing gaily.

As they neared the Iga village proper, its large fences and keep-like houses looming, the procession of children ran ahead of them chanting, "*Hideyoshi-dono ga kite iru!*" until they reached the gates of the vast mountain estate.

"What are they yelling?" Beechworth said softly, leaning across to her.

"Lord Hideyoshi is coming," Angelique whispered. "Now, hush."

Once the leading men had dismounted, a footman brought forward a set of black lacquered wooden steps and set it down for Angelique to dismount with some dignity. The display of etiquette was surprising. Perhaps there had indeed been some female visitors of note at some point. The thought was still on her mind as they were instructed to remove their shoes and ushered within the main hall and instructed to kneel and wait some distance from the head of the room, as all foreign visitors were. At least that had not changed, along with almost everything else in the village. She had fought to stem the memories as the sights and smells brought them crashing back like a veritable great wave from the ocean.

Seven men in various stages of advanced years entered the room. She knew them all. Hideyoshi had long ago advised there had been no change in the clan elders, but to be in the same room with the very same men so many years later...

Angelique fought her rage and stared around the hall like the naive, doe-eyed foreigner she was portraying. She stared ahead as her brother prostrated himself. One of the senior clan elders grunted, and Hideyoshi turned and motioned angrily for them to bow. She waited for Beechworth to do so before emulating him, making a show of awkwardness from her clothing.

After some further shuffling, a crier called out in Japanese that they could rise, and again, she waited for Beechworth to act first. She rose in spurts, gaze darting to and fro, deep in her subterfuge, though her heart pounded. That she did not need to feign.

Ishinari Hideo, Hideyoshi's father, had arrived.

Six elders were fanned out in an arrowhead formation around and to the rear of the lord, three to each side. Just as they had sat all those years before. And all of them in silent, assessing contemplation of the two strangers. Not a person in the room moved or made a sound, which only amplified Angelique's beating pulse in her ears.

Did Ishinari Hideo recognise her?

Hideo bellowed something so suddenly that she was sure Beechworth was going to faint, his shoulders flinching sharply. Hideyoshi bowed once more before approaching his father to kneel several meters away, where he spoke openly in loud Japanese. The elders turned their heads, now rapt in attention at their lord and his son.

For some time, all Hideo did was blink and grunt as he listened to the tale that was told to him. The tale that Angelique had constructed. Once Hideyoshi finished, he bowed once more, and awaited his father.

Hideo turned his head with deliberate slowness and stared at them. He then motioned to his side. Hideyoshi half-jogged forward and knelt, behind and to the side of his father.

"Why do you wish to broker passage to Constantinople for yourself and your wife?" Hideo spoke in a voice both deep and deeply accented, but wholly understandable.

"Aye, that we do, your lordship," Beechworth said in a thick Scottish brogue. His mother and immediate family on her side were all Scots, he had revealed one night, giving Angelique the idea for him to put it to good use. "I dinnae wish to tarry with your time so I'll keep it brief as can be."

As Beechworth spoke, a frown settled across Hideo's face that used every muscle beneath his skin. The shadows of its craggy surface grew deeper the longer Beechworth intoned. Hideo suddenly grunted at Hideyoshi, who shuffled forward, putting a stop to Beechworth's speech.

"Bailey," Hideyoshi said quietly to his father. "Donald. Fenella," he said, indicating Beechworth and Angelique in turn before speaking more quietly and indicating them once more.

Hideo's eyes wrinkled as he glanced at his son, then turned to blink at Beechworth. "Mister Bailey, please forgive me. I cannot understand your words. However, my son informs me that your wife can act as... mediator?"

Hideo chose his words carefully in order not to insult Beech-worth, his 'guest', despite his temper. Angelique's plan for Beech-worth to use a Scottish accent to incense the lord was working a treat. But it would not do for Hideo to show disrespect before gaining the knowledge he sought. That would be a sign of weakness. And despite him being quick to anger, one thing Ishinari Hideo was not, was a weak man.

But now, not only could Hideo not understand Beechworth, he had to resort to dealing with a woman.

"Aye, truthfully I cannae hardly ken your lordship's tongue maeself."

"Hush now, Donald," Angelique said without a touch of French inflection, sounding every part the London lady.

Beechworth's eyes narrowed in surprise, though recovered quickly. "I must warn yae, she can be wee bit feisty this'un."

With a playful slap on the back of his hand, Angelique bowed lower, then addressed Hideo. "I do hope you can understand my words more clearly than my husband's, Lord Ishinari Hideo."

"Yes. Please do convey my deepest apologies to Bailey-san if he is offended." He offered a small bow of his head. It was no more than a nod, and a forced smile that she knew he was not accustomed to. Diplomacy had never been his strength.

"Do not concern yourself, my lord. Donald does not offend easily, especially when matters of business are at stake."

She glanced briefly at Hideo. If he had recognised her, he showed no sign of it. And why should he? When Hideo had last seen her, she was a tan-skinned wildling running around dressed much as the village children who had trailed them to the estate.

Hideo had always made it a point to ignore the slaves, being beneath him other than for his 'needs'. The other elders were not so discriminating, though thankfully for Angelique, she had been a favourite of Hideo's wife. Had the man she now faced been her adoptive grandfather... Well, her plan would have been altogether different. For a start, there would not have been need of one.

Hideo nodded thoughtfully. "And what business does your husband have with the Ottoman Empire?"

"Your lordship, my husband and I travelled to America from England in order to procure cotton for a business venture. Unfortunately, that did not eventuate as there had apparently been some misfortune or predicament with this last year's crop."

Every part of their cover story was accurate down to the last detail, this last supplied by Agent Wake.

"He did, however," she continued when the man made no comment, "come into possession of an incredible machine by way of some good fortune. And he, being the shrewd businessman that he is, acquired it in short order instead."

"And what is this incredible machine you speak of?"

The lord's interest was now piqued, she could tell. The glint in his eyes was the same as ever. He may not have paid her any mind as a child, but she had most definitely had watched him, and seen enough to learn his mannerisms. She had made a point of it.

Angelique leaned in, widening her eyes as if about to speak of a great treasure. "The Mechanical Turk."

Hideo frowned deeply before his brow lifted. "The... Mechanical Turk?" He snorted. The snort turned into a chuckle when she did not react, and then became open laughter. The elders looked to each other in confusion. When he explained to them in Japanese, his words exploding between chuckles, they too laughed along with their lord.

"I dinnae ken," Beechworth said, concerned. "Why does the lord laugh?"

Hideo spoke to Hideyoshi, motioning at the two, far too amused to sink to the level of using English.

"My father says, the Ottomans have no need of a hoax chess-playing automaton, and already have many human puppets aplenty."

Angelique joined them as the elders continued to laugh. Her smile almost slid from her face as she was gripped by a memory, one that she had not recalled until that moment. Not a true memory, but one she had concocted upon seeing this same scene many a time.

The same room. The same men within it, though much younger, laughing and taunting a young woman. A young woman much like the hand-painted portrait within her locket that she had been told from a young age was her mother.

She pushed the vision from her mind. The current mission was all that mattered. If she failed, everything was done for. *They* would be done for. And her larger plan would fail.

"We are well aware of its nature, my lord," she said, grateful her voice had not broken. Any sign of weakness now could spell disaster.

Hideo forced out words full of scorn between his barking laughter.

"My father asks, what do you hope to achieve by taking that... *toy* to Constantinople?"

She waited for the right moment before making the revelation.

Hideo's laugh came to a choking halt. His face became so ashen that the men about him stopped still immediately lest they be punished. He blurted something in angry Japanese to Hideyoshi.

Hideyoshi gave her an uncomfortable glare. "My father says—"

"I said, Lord Hideo, that we converted it to a true automaton powered by Greek Fire."

The ruse had worked so well that Hideo ordered horses be immediately readied despite the hour. They rode to the waiting Ottoman ship so he could see the machine firsthand for himself.

Aboard the vessel, he paced in the hold as the crew worked to open the large crate.

It had been tremendously good fortune that they had happened on The Mechanical Turk as they had. As Angelique saw Süleyman Reis, toiling about the ship with the fez of a lowly crewman on his head, she could not help but think of his description of kismet. How nice it must be to so wholly believe in something as wondrous as fate.

But try as she might, Angelique could not.

It was not fate or a god that had made her and Wake take that trip. It was plain and simple human curiosity, and her own keen senses that had spied the wagon train in the first place. As serendipitous as it was, fate was only as great as the observer.

With a crash, the front panel of the crate came down, and she chose that moment to turn her attention back to the present.

In the dim lighting of the hold, Beechworth leaned into the crate and opened the polished wooden cabinet to expose brass clockwork within, gleaming in a red light and lighting Hideo's aghast expression.

Despite the Greek Fire glow, Hideo's face grew redder still. "Where did you get this? How did you come aboard an Ottoman vessel? Explain yourselves!"

Beechworth chuckled and tapped the side of his nose. "I cannae tell a lie, but I cannae reveal my secrets neither, if ye ken, my lord?"

Hideo gave a stare that would have frozen a lesser man to the spot, a stare he was infamous for. Angelique knew it was one developed in his many years of martial training. She also knew that once he and his men were in private, he would be frothing with anger at them all. This incident would go all the way to the shogunate, and from there to the Turks, and back again. To say that they would not at all be pleased with the Iga and their lord was a monumental understatement.

"Show me how it works," Hideo commanded.

"Begging your lordship's pardon." Angelique bowed her head in apology. "We cannot."

He seethed at being denied and barked at Hideyoshi, who translated, though she needed none.

"My father demands that you show him the machine operating, immediately!"

"I am sorry, my lords, but it is not at present operational. We had to disassemble it in order to ship it for safety reasons. Greek Fire, as you know, is—"

Hideo snorted in derision as he calmed himself, then spoke of the pair of outsiders in derogatory terms, calling them charlatans and worse before flicking his hand at Hideyoshi.

"Unfortunately," Hideyoshi said smugly, "my father cannot broker passage to Constantinople if he cannot verify your claims." He had translated his father's words as diplomatically as he could, which made the lord puff up and smirk.

He thought he had the upper hand.

Angelique did her best to keep the spite that bubbled within from her expression as she turned to Hideo. "That should not be an issue, I think, my lord. I am certain the Ottoman naval officers on the other more magnificent vessel we encountered during our journey here should have already conveyed the news to... Is your father quite all right, Lord Hideyoshi? He suddenly appears quite pale and most unwell."

"I hope you're pleased," Beechworth hissed under his breath.

Angelique smiled, despite that they both were prisoners in the hold of the ship, their hands shackled above their heads. "Am I pleased, *husband?*"

In all her years of living with the Iga, spying and plotting both her escape and revenge, she never recalled ever having seen Ishinari Hideo's face reach quite that colour in both rage and fear. Gazing at the crate holding their precious cargo affectionately, she sighed. It had either been the greatest of gambles, with their lives on the line as collateral, or a stroke of insane genius.

"My dear," she said in her perfect English accent, "I am positively ecstatic."

CHAPTER SIX

s hoped, Hideo charged Hideyoshi with overseeing their transfer into Ottoman hands on the mainland, where they held a constant presence and offices. The local *Bey*—the chieftain or governor of the province—even had a small palace, which from her knowledge had been quickly erected after the Ottomans had swept their narrow stretch across China.

Thankfully, Hideo did not appoint any additional men for the short trip from the Japanese islands to the once Chinese-held city port, so their journey was in reasonable comfort. Certainly as much comfort as one could expect shackled in a vessel's storage hold.

Once there, however, Hideyoshi had to bid them farewell, and wished her luck as best he could, disguising his concern as distaste as he handed them over to Ottoman soldiers. "My only regret," Hideyoshi said before turning away, sneering though his eyes were soft with concern, "is that I will not be there to see what becomes of you!"

The captured Chinese port city was the first Ottoman settlement she had seen. On fleeing Japan, the ship she had stowed away on had been bound for the Hawaiian archipelago, though she'd not known it at the time. From there, she had boarded the first vessel she could find with sailors speaking neither Japanese nor Turkish and landed in America, then quickly on to France and England.

Her thoughts now were firmly in the present, however. The port was awe inspiring, replete with steamships of varying size and shape, of both Japanese and superior Ottoman design. Steamworks were in evidence at every turn. Hoist and pulley devices lifted and carted loads far bigger than any human or beast could manage. Horseless carriages ran about everywhere spewing steam, powered by Greek Fire much like Yardley's aeolipede Angelique suspected, though nowhere near as thundering as that fantastic invention. In fact, there was nothing the likes of it anywhere.

The horseless steam cars, and other vehicles like them, were far more advanced than the aeolipede however, their wheels coated in a thick, dark red material. As vehicles hissed passed them on the road, their wheels created hardly a sound compared to traditional carriages. She mused how much the aeolipede would benefit from the same.

The Ottoman guard behind Angelique prodded her in the small of the back with an equally unconventional weapon. "*Yürü!*" the man grunted, telling her to move and waving a pistol glowing with Greek Fire.

The pistol held two small glass canisters atop it, one filled with the magical fluid, the other with water. There was no indication of its workings, though by all reports it was more than capable of multiple shots, many more than Wake's revolvers, infinitely surpassing it. Soldiers that had gone up against the Ottomans had learnt that the hard way.

Her curiosity earned Angelique a harder shove and she fell into the back of a uniformed man talking to another. The man stopped in annoyance and turned about face.

The man, an officer by the insignia on his fez, looked kindly. Rugged and handsome in a way that she would never have thought possible. His eyes spoke of both kindness and resoluteness. She found herself oddly taken by him.

"Pardon?" she said as she realised the man had been speaking.

He inclined his head to her. "My man? He is not very polite. I was apologising for his rude behaviour."

"Yes, well..." Beechworth said in his affected Scots brogue, frowning at her. "You're very generous, Mister...?"

"Captain. Hasan," the man said.

"Captain?" Beechworth nodded in respect. "Now, if you couldae unlock these shackles...?"

Hasan smiled. "As rude as he is, we are both under orders, Mister Bailey. Though you'll find you will not meet any such further roughness as you are taken to the city commander for questioning."

The captain nodded to the two soldiers, and they were loaded into the rear of a carriage that was essentially a cage atop a steam car. As they waited, two new vehicles, one a large flatbed steam carriage, the other a much smaller, utilitarian machine thundering along on metal wheels and forked mechanism at its front. The forks lowered as it approached the massive wooden crate now housing The Mechanical Turk.

"Be careful with that!" Beechworth shouted as the crate was dropped on the long metal prongs. "You're gonnae damage mah propertae! That wee thing willae never—"

With barely any trouble, the crate was hoisted aloft by the forked lifter, then moved and placed gently on the flat carriage.

Captain Hasan nodded to Beechworth with a small smile and walked away to oversee the transfer of their other belongings.

"Are you quite all right, *Fenella?*" Beechworth asked her quietly.

"Eh?" she said, eyes on Hasan. "Yes, of course, Donald. Why would I not be?"

"What the blazes is wrong with you then?" Beechworth scowled at her, then followed her gaze. "Egads, woman, not here of all places!" he whispered in his natural accent, the din of the machinery all around them giving them some privacy.

"Remember that little conversation we had about your opinions, *husband?*" Her voice held a hint of menace.

Beechworth sat back. "If I recall correctly, that particular conversation was with a certain French mademoiselle, who now seems to be conspicuously absent!"

She turned to him with a grin. "I'm beginning to like you more and more, Beechworth."

"I shall try to take that as intended. A compliment."

She tutted. "Be careful, *Donald,* we may just become fast friends at this rate."

Beechworth raised a brow. "You're absolutely right. I *should* be careful. Something tells me being your friend may be hazardous to one's health."

The questioning by the city commander had been brief, and their stories consistent enough that he believed it wholesale, or at least enough to warrant further investigation. And that story, as they told it, was that Donald Bailey had purchased a small amount of Greek Fire and sketches of steam engines from an American sailor, who had in turn traded it from another sailor who was in the employ of the United States navy. Where he had gotten them, they did not know, and would not venture to guess.

Along with the Mechanical Turk giving their story credence, it hopefully ensured the Ottomans would be at least intrigued enough to warrant shipping them to Istanbul.

They also made sure to slip into their story that there had been a great hullabaloo in the port of San Francisco when a steam locomotive had appeared as they were leaving. From there, they had arranged to pay a captain with flexible morals to rendezvous them with an Ottoman ship, which was in no way far-fetched. Money was money, after all, and the Ottomans were well known to utilise pirates.

The city commander paced, muttering to himself in Turkish once they were done. Angelique listened intently to make out what he was saying, catching a great deal of the one-sided conversation.

"*How did these British get it? ...Americans... ...how have they... ... a defected ship?... engineered a locomotive... How much Greek Fire do they have? ...danger... We must alert the Sultan at once!*" The commander motioned to Captain Hasan. "*Yüzbaşı,*" he said, calling him by his rank. His voice was then too low to discern.

Hasan nodded, indicated the guards to follow him, and they were quickly marched out of the commander's office.

"Where are you taking us, Captain Hasan?" Angelique asked.

"Your 'gift', along with you and your husband, will be receiving the audience you wished for."

"Gift?" Beechworth asked, confused. "I dinnea ken," Beechworth said to Angelique

"Captain?" Angelique batted her eyelids. "What gift are you speaking of?"

"Your machine, of course. You will, all three of you, be carried to Istanbul and presented to the Grand Vizier, where you will be guests of the Ottoman empire. Now, if you'll excuse me, I have preparations to make for our transport."

Beechworth shot the man a look. "*Our* transport? Ye're tae come with us, then?"

"That is the city commander's wish." Hasan nodded curtly, then departed.

Sooner than either of them would have thought practical, they were aboard one of the many trains that made up the infamous *Silk Road Express*. More surprising to them, it was far larger than *The Pony* and faster again, despite that it pulled well over treble the number of cars, which were themselves also larger and longer than the American locomotive.

They were quickly confined to a tiny cabin in one of the cars to the rear with soldiers standing guard outside. The cabin was austere, but as prisons went it had to rank among the most comfortable in the world. Without a doubt, the carriages to the front would be of a more comfortable variety, much like *The Pony*, and likely reserved for higher ranking officers and dignitaries.

They spoke little on the voyage, and when they did, they maintained their assumed identities rigorously. There was no telling who was listening, or to what degree. Their captivity apart, it took rather more adjustment than travelling on *The Pony*. For one, the train was crowded, and all those aboard the vessel spoke Turkish or, in few cases, Japanese or Chinese. They were also woken early every morning by a mechanical clock that was in synchronicity with others like it in every cabin. Each played a wax cylinder recording of the call for prayer, and this was repeated on four other occasions throughout the day, much to Beechworth's annoyance.

"Cheer up, husband," Angelique said when later that day he was crestfallen as the call to prayer echoed through the train. "We shall be there soon. Think of the heroic stories you can regale your *friends* with."

Beechworth no doubt realised she had been inferring to his fiancée. He became all the more sullen.

She gave his arm a gentle squeeze. "I know this is not what you imagined, but you *will* return to Merry England again."

With a nod, he gave her as genuine a smile as he could manage before turning to take in the view from their cabin.

As much as the Sino-Japanese port city had been a marvel, Istanbul was an entirely different level of civilisation. Even Beechworth's mood lifted when he took in the spectacle from the high, arched bridge the train travelled on, much like the aqueducts of old Rome. It had only taken them fifteen days, despite the circuitous route and distance of the Silk Road.

The city gleamed with polished brass domes of mosques and their minarets, the buildings throughout painted and maintained to almost match their lustre. As they neared the Bosphorus Strait dividing Europe and Asia, another great bridge came into view, and further along the waters there was another in construction.

With a knock at the cabin door, Captain Hasan entered. "We will be arriving at the station soon. This way, please." Hasan held his hand out.

As they emerged, their guards stood more alert, clutching their Greek Fire rifles. At each man's belt was a pistol in a holster and several pouches, which must have held ampules of Greek Fire and water. Given the explosive nature of Greek Fire coming in contact with water, they would no doubt be in separate pouches.

"Please," Hasan said, showing the way again and prompting Angelique.

They walked the narrow corridor the length of the carriage as it jostled to a stop, people peering from their cabins as they were led to an outer door and steps. They had not left the train once in the two weeks it had taken to reach Istanbul, despite several stops. Angelique took a moment to stretch and take in the sights.

Throughout the inner city, science shone, without blotting out the historical strata upon which it was built. In fact, the reverse appeared to be the case. The Turks had put their stamp on everything wherever they went—that was the way of all empire builders from time immemorial. The chief and most infamous example being the conversion of the Hagia Sophia from church to mosque once the city had fallen from Byzantine grasp.

Steam ships worked their way up and down the Bosphorus, ranging from the smallest vessels—which appeared to be converted row boats —to mid-sized sloops. The water itself shone like the sapphire she had stolen from the British Museum.

The streets were likewise filled with vehicles. To one side of the Silk Road rails, there was a road with space enough for both pedestrians and conveyances. There was what appeared to be a horsecar tram, though there was nothing evident pulling it, the steam engine built somewhere into its body as the vehicle worked its way up a busy thoroughfare on sunken tracks. Everywhere the streets were busy with people of a variety of shape, size, colour and nation, all used to the traffic and pace.

London, in comparison, seemed antiquated.

Whichever way Angelique turned, the spectacle only grew in magnificence. But as much as beauty and wonder surrounded her, Angelique's heart was filled with malice and dread. She was finally here.

Angelique turned back to Hasan as she saw that the train rails continued on despite the fact the train had stopped. "Are we not going on to the Palace?"

"Only the Sultan and Janissary can go further," Hasan said.

"Forgive mah ignorance, Cap'n," Beechworth said in a gruff grumble. "But I thought you said we were tae present The Tur— The *machine,* tae the Grand Vizier hisself."

"And you are," Hasan said. "But not at *Topkapı* Palace. You will see him in the Vizier's private residence, *Yıldız Saray*. The Star Palace. Now, if you'll come this way..."

They were led out of the way of the carriage doors so others could exit—dignitaries and soldiers first. Angelique looked over the men, paying special attention to those with a uniform altogether different than the soldiers, their fezzes made of brass. Even the soldiers gave these men a wide berth, allowing them to disembark first and collect their belongings.

The Janissary.

Hasan led them to a lushly fitted steam car, which he and another man boarded along with Angelique and Beechworth, the other soldiers moving toward a far less ornate machine.

Beechworth peered from its large open windows, clapping his hands and rubbing them. "Definitely an improvement over thae first mechanical carriage ye had us aboard in China."

"With security, one can never be too careful," Hasan said, giving them an apologetic smile.

As they pulled away, what few passengers who had alighted were already filtering out, and the train began to reverse. A flat vehicle similar to that at the Chinese port followed close behind them, loaded with their belongings and the Mechanical Turk, and also a number of soldiers.

As they were driven through opulent gardens, Angelique wondered whether this was simply the path to the Vizier's palace, or could this be the palace gardens. Then the trees gave way to a clearing and a view of what had to be Star Palace.

It was a far more modern construction than the city they had viewed, though what she had seen of Istanbul had only been at a distance. The grounds were a mix of natural woodland and geometric gardens with varying plant species. She did not have long to admire it, though. If there was one drawback to travel by steam car, this was it. They moved far too rapidly to take in such a view at leisure.

That also meant, of course, that they were now to confront the Grand Vizier of the Ottoman Empire.

As they drew to the bottom of large steps leading into the palace, an imposing man stood at the top, hands behind his back in a military posture. He watched with a keen eye as footmen and soldiers alike ran about, making preparations for their arrival and forming an armed escort around the Vizier.

Instructing Angelique and Beechworth to stay within the steam car, Captain Hasan and his man stepped out to oversee things, saluting the Vizier as they did. As the Vizier spoke at length with Hasan, the loading vehicle moved past them, bearing their belongings away.

"What in the devil do you suppose they're doing?" Beechworth whispered. He tapped on the glass to get Captain Hasan's attention, who approached with an apologetic salute to the Vizier.

"It will not go up the steps and through the doors," Hasan said to him, and pointed by way of explanation. "Do not be concerned, it will be waiting for you both inside, where you can present it to the Vizier himself."

Beechworth hemmed and hawed, but otherwise remained silent.

As the box had disappeared, so too had the Grand Vizier. Shortly after, a soldier ran down the steps, saluted Hasan and quickly spoke to him.

Captain Hasan opened the door to the steam car, beckoned Angelique and Beechworth out and motioned for them to follow him up the steps and within. There, in the opulent and cavernous foyer of Star Palace, they found both their crate—which was opened—and the Grand Vizier, who was examining it, his hands still firmly clasped at his back.

"Welcome to Istanbul, Donald and Fenella," the Vizier said without taking his gaze off the Mechanical Turk.

He was dressed in a highly polished brass fez with a thick, silk-padded edging, a large gold pin at its front emblazoned with the crest of his position. He wore a dark blue jacket, and a sash cut diagonally across his torso. It held several insignia stitched and pinned upon it, the meaning of which Angelique had no idea about—nor the inclination to learn. White gloves covered his extraordinarily large hands, and as he stood taller, one of those hands came to rest on a sword hilt at his hip, the weapon decorated beautifully. She knew the steel would be from the finest Japanese swordsmiths. At the opposite hip, a Greek

Fire pistol, though decorated with the gold, jewels, and Ottoman script.

The Vizier turned from the Mechanical Turk and gave a forced but amiable enough smile. "I am Ali Pasha." He gave a shallow bow. "Grand Vizier of the Ottoman Empire."

They returned the gesture. The man's English was almost as good as either of theirs. Were it not for his accent, they would have been hard pressed to be any the wiser.

"This is grand work, your lordship," Beechworth said in his thick Scots. His neck craned to take in the surrounds in genuine admiration.

"As is this," Ali Pasha said, gesturing to the machine. "A fine work of both craftsmanship, and sleight of hand." He smirked almost slyly. "However did you convince Herr Mälzel to part with it? I hear he was making quite the living touring the machine since he purchased it from the original inventor's son. Most recently in Central America."

"Fenella," Beechworth motioned to Angelique, expression uncomfortable. "Please explain tae his lordship. I fear he may not ken my tongue as occurred in—"

"I can understand you quite well, Mister Bailey." Ali Pasha held his hand out with a slight nod. "Please. Indulge me."

"You'll have to forgive my husband, Ali Pasha," Angelique said. "He lacks certain social niceties, which is why my presence has been a boon to his business."

Ali Pasha shrugged. "Very well. Please, continue, Mrs Bailey."

"Herr Mälzel— Have you met the man himself, Pasha?" He shook his head, swiftly losing patience, she could see. "Herr Mälzel was in the American mid-west, as you said, when we encountered him and—"

"Yes, yes! I have had all this from Lord Ishinari Hideo's account, and that of his son, Ishinari Hideyoshi." The Vizier was making a definite show of both the extent and reach of his knowledge. But he was also showing his true nature. His face gained colour as he became more animated. Tendons in his neck stood out. "What I am most interested in, as you well know, is how you came by the steamworks within that charlatan's box. The steamworks and Greek Fire that you claim to have acquired and fitted yourselves!" He was almost yelling by the time he finished.

"Ali Pasha, I am attempting to explain—" Angelique began anew, keeping her own temper in check, which for her was no easy thing when confronted with men such as this.

She had dealt with their ilk all her life. From Ishinari Hideo and his men, to the men from the various ships and ports as she had made stops at after her flight from Japan at the tender age of fifteen. Men in France, the birthplace of her mother and where she first went, and then in other countries. She usually dealt with them in short order, and despite that she knew she and Beechworth were lying—or perhaps because of it—all she wanted to do was put this man in his place also.

Ali Pasha surged forward with surprising speed and gripped her by the throat. Spittle foamed at his lips, which trembled across his clenched teeth. The muscles in his jaw bulged.

Beechworth took a running step, but the Vizier's hand whipped and his Greek Fire pistol was in his face, bringing him to a stop. Janissary soldiers ran forward and gripped Beechworth's arms tightly.

"You are a liar!" Ali Pasha spat words and spittle both in Angelique's face. "You are both liars! There is no Donald and Fenella Bailey. You are spies sent by the Americans to steal our secrets. Admit it now and your lives might be spared."

Angelique blinked into the madman's eyes, unable to speak.

"Oh, thank the heavens for that," Beechworth said in his natural accent, his shoulders falling. "I really was getting quite tired of feigning that Scottish accent."

CHAPTER SEVEN

The Grand Vizier paced in silence, hands behind his back for the most part. When they were not clasped behind him, he stroked and tugged at his moustache, or rubbed his bare chin.

A Janissary walked in briskly, his uniform and general air far different from that of others that guarded Angelique and Beechworth. He walked with self-assurance, head high. *"Paşam,"* the man said, using the Vizier's rank to both announce his presence and gain Ali Pasha's attention as he approached. The Janissary muttered something into the ear of the penultimate leader in the empire.

Even though she watched them carefully, Angelique could not discern what they were discussing, the man clearly trained in the evasion of lip reading. She did note the way Captain Hasan was also watching both men, his eyes gaining a steely quality that was not present earlier.

She strained to catch any word the Janissary and Ali Pasha might drop, but only managed to catch the word Sultan. Whatever it was the Janissary guard was conveying, Ali Pasha was becoming increasingly irritated.

"Söyle Sultanımıza," Ali Pasha growled in an explosion of words,

Angelique's mind rushing to translate them. "Tell our Sultan," he had begun, "that I am, at this very moment, far too busy to stop what I am doing and entertain whatever whim is upon him now!"

She blinked and glanced around nervously. Keeping up appearances was the best subterfuge and disguise in the world. She had learnt that both from her years with the Iga clan observing their training, and in the real world. Misdirection and misinformation were also chief amongst those essential skills, the best of which—also employed by the Iga's rival, the Kōga clan—was the dissemination of both their so-called powers and skills. Also, owing to their quickly spreading infamy aided by the Ottomans, their now infamous all black clothing.

She knew the story well, told to both Hideo and herself by their grandfather. Some enterprising Kōga assassins had carried out a mission while working as kabuki stagehands, and thus the legend of the shadow warriors had been born. Hidden, but in plain sight, that was the essence of the ninja. And oh how the Kōga had spread that story! And, by way of association, it now applied to the Iga also.

While certainly not perfecting them, Angelique had become quite adept at those three skills with painstaking practice. Also, at distracting her mind with facts when faced with danger in moments such as this and in doing so not allowing herself to give away her true intentions or thoughts.

The Janissary saluted Ali Pasha and promptly left. What Süleyman Reis had said about the Janissary controlling things in the heart of the Ottoman seemed to be holding true. And from the look of things here, the Grand Vizier was heavily involved.

Ali Pasha turned back to them. His open hand thrust toward the chess playing puppet. "That you obtained the materials in America is quite clear to me. Also, that this is the very same machine paraded around the globe. Do you deny it?"

They stayed silent.

With a nod, he continued. "We have known for some time that the Americans have been working toward their own derivative of our technology, of course. Laying their tracks for decades in hopes of replicating... or *stealing* our inventions." His eyes hardened and turned to his two captives. He undoubtedly knew of *The Pony*. "And, I am certain, they are cognisant of our awareness." He resumed his pacing. "What I cannot fathom is, just who the two of you are." He cocked his head, indicating that he expected a response.

"We—" Beechworth said.

"What are you doing?" Angelique shouted, starting a quarrel between them so loud that the guards had to intervene and silence them at gunpoint.

"Enough testing my patience!" The crimson flush returned to Ali Pasha's face. "Answer my question, or I will have you both beheaded, here and now."

Angelique shook her head slowly at Beechworth, who looked back and forth between her and the man holding their fate in his hands.

The Grand Vizier shouted at the guards, who pushed them to their knees as Ali Pasha drew his sword, the steel flashing.

Angelique's eyes widened at Beechworth.

"We're inventors! We're inventors!" he yelled, eyes and face screwed tight.

The Pasha stayed his hand. "Inventors?"

Beechworth blinked rapidly, nodding almost as fast, pleading with his eyes. "Yes! Our names are James and Katherine Farnsworth. We are brother and sister. I design, my sister is the engineer."

Ali Pasha seemed nonplussed. "We have designers and engineers aplenty. And I am unimpressed with your..." He sneered at the Mechanical Turk. "Work." Raising the sword higher, her stepped forward, the Janissary pushing them down to expose their necks.

"No, wait!" Beechworth implored.

"That is because you have not seen it in motion, Pasha," Angelique said loudly. Her chest rose and fell as real fear gripped her. At any moment, the Grand Vizier could end her life, and plans.

But he held.

The guards let her up into a kneel, Beechworth still held down. He smirked at her. Then his face turned into a snarling frown. Drawing his left hand back with speed, Ali Pasha slapped her backhanded. Though the strike had been slow, it spoke of the hulking man's restrained and incredible strength.

Angelique's hair flew loose, and she was only stopped from falling to the floor by the men holding her in place. Face hidden by her hair, Angelique's fingers balled into aching fists. She turned her anger inward and dug her nails into her palm. The pain was the only thing that prevented her from taking the nearest man's sword, and then as many heads in the room as she could before they shot her down.

Instead, tasting the blood on her lip, she turned her defiant gaze up.

Ali Pasha met her defiant stare. "I will summon our chief engineer. He will discern if this *contraption* of yours is of any value. Until such time, you will make yourselves comfortable in our cells."

With a wave and snapped orders at the men, they were dragged away.

The cells they found themselves in were certainly no dungeon. The out-building was of a stone construction, white-washed within, with many high, barred windows allowing light and fresh air inside. If anything, it was a little too bright for their gloomy demeanour.

They dared not speak as several guards were posted both within and outside the walls. Angelique could hear them traipsing about on duty. She could even smell the tobacco smoke that wafted in at regular intervals. Angelique wished she could pick the locks to go through their confiscated belongings and join them for a cigarette to settle her nerves. Given the circumstances they found themselves in, she might just have two to calm herself.

As the guards changed shift, a younger man took the position inside who eyed her up and down constantly. He was the one, she decided and, leaning on the bars, she asked the man if he might give her one from the case atop the table not far from the cells.

Leering, the man shook his head and shrugged.

Passing her hand through the bars, Angelique pointed at the case, smiled and batted her eyes at the man. "Please, kind sir?" she said.

The lascivious grin on the man's lips growing, the guard opened the case and took one out. But he did not pass it to her. Instead, with a constant leer fixed in place, he lit the thing and held it out for her to take it, but not within reach.

Pressing her chest tight against the bars, Angelique knew his game, but played it in any case. Should she get out of this mess and enact her plan, he would be the first to pay.

The man grunted in smug satisfaction and took a puff from the cigarette, then handed it to her, and returned to his post, all without a single word.

"They'd give our Queens Guard a run for their money," Angelique quipped to Beechworth, who was supine on the cot in his separate cell, faced away from her.

He played the part of scared Briton aristocrat to a tea, the role continuing with his sulking. In truth, she could tell from his tensed shoulders that he was wide-eyed and alert, counting the steps of the guards outside and timing shift changes. Beechworth had assuredly been a soldier.

Their confinement continued for the better part of the day. The only respite for Angelique when she had refused to relieve herself in a filthy pot in front of men and was taken within the palace to staff quarters and then promptly returned.

It was late afternoon when they were finally moved, in prison vehicles once more.

"I do hope you are bringing our things along," Angelique said as they were being led out.

She had no idea if they had or not, but forgot all about them as they entered an expansive space that boggled the mind. There was equipment of all shapes and sizes strewn about, and men at work who were promptly sent away.

There, in the middle of the room on a thick canvas tarpaulin, sat the Mechanical Turk, in pieces. With it was the Grand Vizier and a man they had not yet met. Given his attire and stature, he was not Janissary and had to be the master of the Ottoman steamworks.

"Our Chief Engineer," Ali Pasha said, indicating the man and confirming it. "Abdulrahman Selim Gazi."

The man stopped boggling at the pieces to give them a cursory nod before returning to the puzzle with a shake of his head and scratching his grey bearded chin.

"Abdulrahman Efendi..." Ali Pasha said, using the title of respect which essentially meant sir. "He has been in this role for a decade and is still baffled by your machine and its purpose."

The man spoke to the vizier in quiet, broken Turkish. His name and appearance suggested him to be of Arab descent.

"He believes it may be used for the purposes of mining, or digging, due to the two spheres he discovered hidden within the cabinetry. He cannot, however, decipher why there are two of these spheres. He believes one is a replacement should the first fail. He also cannot decipher how to re-assemble the device, nor how a single man would lift such a machine."

"One could not," Angelique said, smiling. "And both the spheres, as you put it, are utilised at once."

An angry vein crept down Ali Pasha's temple from under his fez, so red it almost seemed to glow. "I give you until the morning to have this assembled and make a demonstration." He strutted away with his hands tightly held behind his back, growling at the chief engineer to watch over them. He stopped and spun on his heel, his rage no longer held back. "But make no mistakes! I *will* have your heads if you fail to impress me! You may have fooled Ishinari Hideo and his village of spies into getting you here, but you will find me to be far less impressionable!"

With that, he stormed out.

The Chief Engineer blinked at them, unaffected by the Vizier's outburst, more than likely used to it.

They stared back at the man.

Beechworth thrust his hand at the man. "A pleasure to make your acquaintance, Mister Gazi."

The engineer regarded the hand. He lifted his gaze, and pointed at each of his eyes with a stiff index finger, then shot the same digit at them both before thrusting it at the parts on the floor. With that, he walked to a set of metal steps that led to platformed area on high that oversaw the workshop.

"I do not believe Mister Gazi knows English, brother," Angelique said with as much sincerity as she could, and loud enough for the man to hear.

"I know little," the man bellowed through a speaking-trumpet that amplified his voice far more than its size accounted for. It boomed to fill the entire space, though distorted heavily. "I know work."

They stared up at the man.

"Work!" he shouted. "Or—" Lowering the horn, he drew his thumb across his neck making a choking sound which the horn picked up.

Angelique scowled at Beechworth as she saw the engineer turn the trumpet, which was mounted on a tripod meant for a large spyglass. The narrow end now point at them. "You heard the man, brother."

"Do you think he is using that device to listen to us?" Beechworth whispered.

"I listen," Abdulrahman shouted. "Work!"

They kept their talking to a minimum as they set to the combined parts of the Mechanical Turk and the aeolipede. Beechworth implored her with his eyes whenever she stopped to look over the multitudinous pieces on the floor, to which she would nod reassuringly, though after several occasions of Angelique having to refit a part, he did not at all appear optimistic or convinced of her skills.

Having observed and listened to Yardley intently as he had carefully and lovingly dismantled the aeolipede, then refit those pieces within the Mechanical Turks cabinet—adding to the thing where needed with cabinetry from *The Pony*—Angelique had been certain she could piece it back together. Now, that task seemed daunting and not at all helped by the limited time she had. Yardley had assured her it was the simplest of things and given her the design drawings for her to pore over on their journey.

"Why not just glue them within the woodwork?" Wake had asked Yardley in jest.

The engineer had been utterly aghast at the mere suggestion.

By the time they had reached San Francisco, she knew the thing's workings and theory behind its propulsion intimately. A cylinder of compressed air, that would need priming by hand pump as the machine had not been operational, would push both water and Greek Fire into the wheels, which served as aeolipiles—also called Hero's engines, invented centuries ago by Hero of Alexandria. A hand lever on one side of the vehicle's body worked a valve that determined the amount of water and Greek fire, and so too the speed. Another lever on the opposite side worked as a brake by basic friction. At the end of this lever was a metal foot with an old boot sole, which pushed into the ground. It was crude, but effective enough.

The trick of it, Yardley had said, was ensuring the right mixture of water and Greek Fire. "Too much water and you'll flood the engine and will have to drain it. And Greek Fire is nasty business when not properly handled."

"And what if you have too much Greek Fire?" she had asked him.

He had given her an uncomfortable smile. "Let us say that they do not call it Greek *Fire* without reason."

Angelique and Beechworth worked well into the night on assembling the machine, and were not surprised when the man began snoring.

"A good thing he hasn't got that thing turned about," Angelique whispered.

The engineer started, having heard her words through his listening horn. The nasal sound continued a few seconds later.

Beechworth lowered his hunched shoulders and gave her a stern look.

She waved him off and leant forward to hitch up her skirt by its inner drawstrings. She had been testing the man to see how deeply he slept, and he appeared to have a heavy head.

Beechworth made to turn away, then stopped himself, face stony with determination.

Angelique gave him a grin. She had asked him not to treat her in such a manner, and he was doing his utmost not to be bested. She made a note of his competitive streak. It's manipulation could come in handy at some later point.

From her garter, Angelique removed four decorative silk flowers on strings. Beechworth gave her a quizzical frown. Leaning down, she tied the flowers to the soles of her boots. Standing, Angelique skipped silently from foot to foot to demonstrate, then held her hands out in a theatrical gesture.

Beechworth made to applaud.

Angelique shot forward and caught his wrists before he could do so, glaring at him.

He balled his fingers, wincing and lowering his head. He raised his face, frowning, and gave her a questioning shrug.

She swept her hand about to encompass the interior and mimed walking with her fingers. Pointing to him, she made a few motions of her hands of tinkering.

Beechworth tapped the side of his nose with a nod and picked up several items to tap and scrape them gently together. With absolute silence, Abdulrahman may well also wake, sensing something amiss. With some expected sound, however, he was more likely to sleep on.

Angelique moved with silent footsteps to a nearby work bench and examined the items atop it. Picking up a ball of yellow material, she sniffed it. Rubber, much like that in the sound dampening roses on her soles. A large glass vat full of the raw material sat on a corner of table. The India rubber tree sap was as white as milk and would stay that way so long as it was not exposed to the air.

There was another, much smaller vat on the table that cast a glow. Greek Fire. From what she had learnt of it from Yardley, she dared not touch it. Though she would have to once she had completed the aeolipede. If, in fact, she could.

Her eyes were drawn to another item and she dropped the ball of rubber, ignoring it as it bounced and rolled away. It was a dark red square about the thickness of her finger. She examined it in the light. Like the rubber ball, it too was malleable, though far stiffer and stronger. It had an altogether different scent, sharp and pungent. Then it dawned on her. This too was rubber. The same rubber she had seen used on the wheels of the Ottoman steam cars. It was far stronger than any rubber she had dealt with. No matter how she twisted and bent the red square, it did not crack or stretch.

She turned to the India rubber vat. Then the red glowing Greek Fire beside it. The two added together somehow produced this, the red variant the Ottomans used. Processing it with the combustive material somehow made it into a much hardier substance, perfect for use on the wheels of vehicles.

Turning about, Angelique slunk off silently, only to run back to the aeolipede as an enormous clatter echoed about the workshop, amplified by the speaking and listening device.

Abdulrahman Selim Gazi sat up with a loud snort and wiped his lips with the back of his hand and a wet slurp. He glared at them with suspicion as they worked diligently, or at least appeared to.

He snorted, this time in derision, turned the horn sideways, pulled his fez down over his eyes, and crossed his hands over his belly.

After waiting some time for the man to get back into a deep slumber, Angelique gave Beechworth a steely glare before resuming her investigation.

With no little embarrassment, Beechworth took a much firmer grasp of the pieces in his hands.

CHAPTER EIGHT

"A bbie?"

Beechworth followed after his fiancée Abigail, who ran through the streets of London, laughing gaily. But try as he might, even picking up his pace, he could not catch her.

"Abbie, wait for me!" he called, arm outstretched as she turned a corner, her hair, dress and ribbons floating behind her.

As he turned the corner, heat and light struck Beechworth in the face.

London was awash with flames.

The Grand Vizier, Ali Pasha, was at the heart of the conflagration, holding the thief Angelique by the throat in one hand, brandishing a sword high in the other.

A scream drew Beechworth's attention. Turning, he saw Abigail— his Abbie—trapped in a corner behind a wall of fire, unable to flee as the flames clawed closer to her, consuming everything in their path.

As he made to run to her, unnaturally bright red flames leapt in front of him, as if alive and blocking his path.

Somewhere, the hammering of metal pounded, his head throbbing with the crashes of an anvil.

Behind him, a growl of a demon creature sounded and he turned to the beast. It was a brass mechanical monstrosity with glowing eyes of Greek Fire. Its feet were metal spheres with massive, spiked claws covering them. Roaring, it drew closer.

Abbie screamed for him.

Angelique choked and gagged and began to fall limp in the Vizier's hand.

And the demon machine bore down on Beechworth and raised a spiked metal foot high.

"Abbie... I'm sorry," he said as the demon fell on him.

Beechworth awoke with a shuddering gasp and found his breath ragged, and brow wet. "Wh... Where am I?" he said, struggling to open his eyes and rise.

A figure in shadow shushed him and pressed a cold cloth to his skin. Her golden hair shone from behind, lit by the sun blazing through a window on high. Her long lashes fluttered as she dipped a cloth in a silver bowl and wrung it out, unaware that he had awoken.

"Abbie?" he said in a croak. "Oh, Abbie! I had the most frightful nightmare!" He rose, and reached to stroke her cheek.

The woman gasped as she jumped away and ran from the room shrieking unintelligibly, sending the metal bowl clattering.

It was not Abbie. It was not any woman Beechworth knew, and she was most certainly not attired in the fashion of London.

As a man came running into the room, Beechworth sat up to defend himself, though he could not speak for coughing and trembling. The man was dressed in finery, the fez atop his head emblazoned with a floral emblem of silver and inset with jewels. In the army, Beechworth and the other men had been trained on the most common symbols of Ottoman rank, though that only extended to military insignia. This man's was most certainly not one of them.

The man came on with his hands flapping, chattering in Turkish and adding to Beechworth's confusion. The stranger yelled out and several young boys of similar appearance and garb, though far less sublime, rushed in. One cleared the mess while the other mopped the water. Having done so, they both ran out.

The stranger stared at him, a delicate smile on his lips.

Beechworth attempted to sit up, without much luck. The man ran forward and helped him, tutting like a matron and pushing pillows into his back before returning to almost the exact same spot he had previously stood to stare again, in almost the exact same posture.

Licking his lips, Beechworth parted them to speak, which caused the man to lean forward expectantly. Beechworth paused, mouth open, and the man straightened. He pursed his lips, and the man again reacted. "Where am I?" Beechworth finally managed, deciding if he let the man continue in the same fashion, they would be there all day. "Who are you?"

The man smiled wider and nodded. "I am Kerim *Ağa*, the Harem Master." Having said so, he placed his hand upon his breast and gave a short bow of his head.

Beechworth was open-mouthed once more. "H— Harem, you say?"

Kerim gave a slow, solemn shake of his head. "There was a time when a man in the harem would have been *undreamt* of, let alone heard." He gave Beechworth a sad nod. "And the Chief Harem Eunuch—*Kızlar Ağa*—was the third highest rank in the empire! Though that was an age ago. A hundred years gone, before all this *steam* nonsense began."

"Eunuch?" Clearing his throat, Beechworth was unsure what to say to the man. "Your English is exemplary."

"Little consolation, but thank you." He touched a smooth hand to Beechworth's forehead. "You are still a little poorly, but seem well on the way to a full recovery, Mister Farnsworth."

Beechworth frowned, almost correcting the man. He cleared his throat as he remembered his character's name. "I fell ill?"

Kerim nodded. "Very much so. Probably from working all night in that terrible, draughty steamworks. We feared for a time you may have consumption, or some other affliction brought from more tropical climes."

"A time?" He sat up more fully, his body aching. "How long have I been here?"

"The better part of a week."

"A week?" Beechworth exclaimed, sitting taller. "Whe... Where is my—" He almost said associate.

"Oh, poor Fenella." Kerim Ağa shook his head, a pained expression on his face. "Alas, your sister..."

Beechworth hobbled out of the steam car, thankful it had not been another prisoner transport. The ache in his body was already impeding him, he did not think he could have withstood the rattling of a cage. As it was, when he stood a white-hot blade of pain lanced across his vision as the sun assaulted him.

He had been taken to a stadium nearer the city of Istanbul proper. Beechworth noted that the architecture was of old Romanic design, or at least influenced by its architecture. Given the rich history of the country, he imagined that at some point in time, gladiators might have done battle and trained here. Perhaps even charioteers. Now, an altogether very different, though familiar, vehicle disturbed the soil.

Angelique raced at frightening speed about the open space on the aeolipede. He knew it had to be her, despite the leather armour she had adopted as protection, and the goggles and cloth across her face. No other person would have been mad enough to ride the thing.

The aeolipede slid to a stop in front of Beechworth and the guards leading him, throwing up a shower of sand. He could not be certain if it was a result of the space they were in, but the machine was even louder than it had previously been. Its rumble had permeated the very ground. Now still, it was silent save for the hiss of still escaping steam from its rear venting pipes. It appeared some changes had been made to its design, though he could not be sure what.

No wonder the thing was the inspiration for the creature from his nightmare. He gripped the bridge of his nose as frightful images of Abbie and London brought fresh agony to his head and heart.

Angelique kicked down a stand and dismounted the aeolipede. Leaning the machine to stand on its own, she rushed to his side, shedding her armour as she came, which appeared to be constructed of thick leather and patches of the red rubber she'd discovered in the steamworks.

He almost expected to see her underclothes again, but instead she was wearing some sort of pant that flared at the thighs and cinched at the waist, constrained like thick stockings from the knee down, her boots still on her feet. On top, she wore a blouse-corset combination over which was some sort of short, tailored jacket. It was obviously designed for such riding, though he'd never seen the like.

Pulling down her mask then goggles to hang around her neck, Angelique embraced him. "Brother!" she said, then kissed him on both cheeks. "You appear much better." Her wide grin appeared quite genuine as she hooked her arm in his and led him toward the aeolipede.

"As do you," he said, as puzzled as he was relieved.

"The Grand Vizier has been quite amicable since Abbie's unveiling."

"Abbie?" he said in confusion. She waved at the vehicle. "You've made modifications to... er, my design."

She pulled a rag from a pocket and buffed lettering hewn from polished brass now affixed on the body of the machine until it shone. "I did. I hope you do not mind."

"Not at all. But... Abbie?"

"When you fell into your fever, you were muttering her name in your sleep. I thought it a befitting homage to you both. Hope, as it were."

Hope. Had she succeeded?

"A very touching gesture," he said. "Thank you. But however did you—"

"Your sister is a very skilled engineer," the Vizier said from the stadium entrance behind them.

Angelique cleared her throat in a suggestive manner. "And, of course, dear brother, you are aware of my keen intellect and capacity for remembering every small detail of things."

"Of course." Beechworth shook his head. "But still, this..."

"While you were incapacitated," Ali Pasha said, approaching, "Abdulrahman Efendi was *gracious* enough to allow your sister to peruse our workshop library. There, your sister was able to both broaden and implement her new knowledge, greatly improving upon the design of your aeolipede."

"A good thing too," she said with some nervous mirth, her fingers spreading across her throat.

Beechworth nodded, contemplating all this. "Well... Of course, Ali Pasha, we knew there was a risk when we undertook this adventure. But we deemed it, and our skill, worthy."

"Indeed. And I am glad we do not have to call it a *mis*-adventure." Ali Pasha's smirk and eyes were full of scorn.

"As am I," Beechworth said, hoping he managed to sound both relieved and appear nervous all at once.

"The best news is yet to come!" Angelique said, eyes widening with excitement.

"Yes," the Vizier's eyes and lips drew thinner at her behaviour, drawing into a frown. "I have extolled your skills to the Sultan, and he, too, was most impressed. He has decided to commission you to design further such inventions. Though with perhaps a more practicable approach?"

"Are you quite certain the Sultan does not want a fleet of aeolipede, Pasha?" Angelique said. "I find it rather..." She narrowed her eyes and pursed her lips, taking in a deep breath that filled her bosom, releasing it with a shudder as she finished the thought. "Invigorating."

The man visibly grimaced. "Yes, we are quite certain, Miss Farnsworth. Thank you."

She bowed her head gracefully.

Ali Pasha clasped his hands at the small of his back. "I shall make arrangements for your travel. Tell Abdulrahman Efendi what you require, and he will ensure it is taken with you if it is not already there."

"Travel?" Beechworth frowned.

"You *are* well enough to travel, are you not, Mister Farnsworth?" the Pasha said, annoyed. "I gave strict instruction to Kerim Ağa that you only be sent if and when you were in fit condition to do so."

"Very much so, sir," he said quickly, not wishing the Harem Master to find himself in trouble. "But I do not understand where it is we will be going, nor why."

"James!" Angelique smacked him on the arm. "We go wherever our patrons wish us to go. Be grateful that we have such esteemed employment."

"I did not mean to—"

The Grand Vizier waved his hand, and screwed up his face in impatience. "It does not matter. I am not easily offended. Abdulrahman and Hasan *Yüzbaşı* will explain."

Having said, the man stormed away.

"Captain Hasan?" Beechworth cocked an eyebrow.

"Yes, he has been most helpful and will be accompanying us," she said.

"I did not think he would be staying."

"Nor did I. And, apparently, nor did Hasan," she said, grinning.

"If I did not know better, sister mine, I would think you were rather taken." Beechworth chuckled, then began to cough violently.

Angelique grabbed him by the arm and pulled him in close. "Are you quite all right, James?"

He whispered into his cupped hand. "Did you find it? The formula for Greek Fire? The plans?"

Shaking her head, Angelique continued to fuss over him in concern. "Don't be silly. We'll pack soon enough and be there, James! First, let us have some lunch so you can rest and recover some energy."

He nodded more openly now, a slow bob of his head.

She seemed to be saying that she suspected what they sought would be at their destination. All things considered, it should serve to make their task that much easier outside of Ali Pasha's hawk-like eyes, and immediate influence. There was little doubt, the man was a predator, pure and simple.

"Yes, lunch. Capital idea," Beechworth said.

They sat within the stadium, in the shade of its tall wall as the guards went about their duties. Angelique still had her mask and goggles draped around her neck, seemingly not wishing to part with them. Now that they were in effect employees of the Ottoman Empire, the men had no need be so vigilant around them. That relaxed attitude gave the pair the first real chance to speak in weeks.

"How the devil are we going to design actual steam vehicles for this madman?" Beechworth did his best to speak in genial tones even though he whispered, but even he heard the desperation in his voice. She had gotten them into another impossible situation with her ruse.

"Please do try to relax, *James*," Angelique said, pouring tea for them. "Incidentally, what is your name? I've been calling you... *other* names all this time."

"James *is* my name." He took up his teacup roughly and added a sugar cube. He stirred it with a little too much vigour, spilling it into the saucer, though ignored it. He was hardly in esteemed company, or in the mood, to worry about tea etiquette.

Angelique giggled behind her hand. "You used your actual given name?"

"I was on the spot!" he said, then made to sip his tea.

"James and Abigail. Well, now I know how to monogram your wedding gifts."

His lips stopped short of the cup. "I hardly think now the time for your misplaced humour." He took a gulp of tea and was surprised by its wonderful taste, realising he shouldn't have been. The Turks controlled a good portion of where the stuff originated. "I wanted my last cup of tea to be when I was quite a bit older and beside my wife, children, and grandchildren. Not in the heartland of—" He started as someone walked around him to lay several trays of food on the table.

He had not realised just how hungry he was until he smelled the fare. There were meats and rice, bowls of fruit, dates and other dried goods, as well as nuts. The servant began to serve the food, but the two excused them with thanks until the man left, and Beechworth helped himself to a hearty plateful.

"I promised you would get back to your Abbie, and I will make good on that. As to the how?" Angelique served herself a dainty portion of stewed lamb with dried fruit and a side of rice. "We will be getting a step closer. Their engineer, Abdulrahman, told me he is in constant fear for his life. Most of them are."

"Yes, I got a bit of a sense of that," he said, his mouth partially full. He was so hungry and anxious that he forgot all about good manners, tea or otherwise, realising he had not had a proper meal for as long as he had been ill.

"Well, he now owes us a debt. I saved his neck as well as our own, and he knows it. Since you have been resting, Sleeping Beauty, he has been the most supportive and helpful soul one could imagine, sharing his work area *and* information with me."

"I'll bet he has," Beechworth said, scoffing.

Angelique raised her eyebrows. "Why, dear brother, do I detect a hint of impropriety in your demeanour? Are you implying that the gentleman's behaviour has anything to do with my appearance?" She tutted as she laughed. "I do believe my influence is finally having an effect on you."

"One might even say taking a toll."

She laughed louder and looked up from her spoonful. "It's quite all right, James, I'm more than used to being told I am attractive." She winked at him as she took the food.

"You are without a doubt the absolutely most infuriating person I have ever met!"

She lifted her eyes again, now with a frown. "Do close your mouth when eating, James. I know you're in need of it, but Mother would be so ashamed."

He scowled at her, red faced, swallowing before continuing. "So he'll help us? Abdulrahman?"

"He has already agreed to it. His coming with us is a demotion for his failure in ascertaining the purpose of the components within the Mechanical Turk. Ali Pasha was apparently quite livid and almost ran him through. He is grateful he still has his life, let alone any position."

"Yes, well, I suppose it could have been a weapon." Beechworth sat up. "You plan to use the engineer to stand in for us."

"Why, James, you are learning fast. That is indeed my exact thoughts."

"Do you not think the Turks will know his work by now? His

colleagues and subordinates, one of whom will more than likely be the person to take his position, will see what we give them is nothing new."

She finished her own mouthful, carefully chewing, before she answered. "I merely intend on using Abdulrahman Efendi to do the manual work."

"You— Are you completely insane?"

"Quite the opposite. Are you forgetting who put together the aeolipede and improved on the design?"

He blinked at her in shock. "You actually believe you can learn all there is to know in order to keep our skulls firmly attached, as well as hatch your plots of intrigue, don't you?"

She picked up a jug that had been left and peered into it. She proffered the jug to him. "Wine, James?"

"No! I do not want any blasted wine!"

With a shrug she poured herself a goblet.

Sighing, Beechworth picked up his own goblet and held it out. "Prudence be damned. If we are to die... Pour away." She leaned across and filled his cup. He took several generous sips. It was good stuff. "So where is it exactly that we are being sent to die?"

"We're to go to Pergamum—or Bergama, as they call it."

"What the devil for? Do you think they suspect us?"

She shrugged. "According to Abdulrahman, there is a great library with volumes documenting steamworks that date back to Alexandria and the discoveries made there. Also, original copies of their research and plans, in case Istanbul should ever fall under attack."

Beechworth grimaced. "With the way they've been going, I don't see that as a possibility any time soon."

She shook her head as she drank more of the wine. "Although," she said, raising a finger from around the goblet, "should we succeed, that will all change."

He let out a bitter chuckle. "Do you really think that we two can make that much of a difference?"

"We two? No." He nodded in accordance with the thought. "But we are not just we two."

"We are not?"

"We have the might of Europe and America behind us. We are making allies here already, reluctant or not."

"I hardly think one aged engineer—"

"That aged engineer, as you call him, has a mind like a diamond the size of your fist. Each glint and gleam filled with ideas, knowledge, and years of experience. With him, we can accomplish far more than you give both the man, and ourselves credit."

He picked up his goblet and swirled the wine within, deep in thought. "I would still much prefer to have someone on the same side of the battle-lines as us for once."

She smirked. "Well, that would be a most useful thing to have. Unfortunately, my dear James, if wishing and making a thing so were possible, then there would be no—"

An almighty boom rocked the very ground, sending mortar and dust from the wall to tumble to their heads and table, soiling their food and wine.

"What the devil?" Beechworth shouted as he jumped to his feet, only to be knocked down again as another explosion sent him reeling.

His head rang from the sound. He could not see what was happening about him from the blinding dust, and the throbbing whiteness the pain in his head caused.

"Angelique?" he called out in his confusion, realising too late. He doubted that anyone would have heard him in any case as new thunderous peels assaulted the area, sending fresh plumes of dust into the sky.

CHAPTER NINE

The world became dark and thunderous as explosions rocked the stadium, throwing up clouds of dirt, dust and smoke as sections of it burnt. Over the sounds of battle, cries of the wounded and dying filled the air.

Angelique left Beechworth to fend for himself as she ran into the dense cloud toward the screams, pulling up her mask and goggles. While they did their job in keeping the material in the air from her lungs and eyes, they did little to increase visibility. Her training allowed her to navigate the stadium acting on memory and instinct alone, however the cacophony of battle and fire hampered her ability to detect approaching enemies.

As a shadow appeared before her, Angelique slipped into the smoke and dust, pressing against a low inner wall that circled the stadium field. Vaulting the barrier, she ducked low and continued on. While the majority of the walls were stone, the seats and support beams were wooden.

She glanced over the barrier, then turned to head up the levels of seats, only to fall back and leap into the stadium arena as a flaming bottle arced over the outer wall. Flames burst high as glass crashed.

The seats instantly caught fire, the flames bright red and so hot the heat licked at her exposed skin.

The enemy, whoever they were, was using Greek Fire.

Another explosion, then another, set the billowing smoke and dust alight. A man's pained howls drew her in panic, thinking it could be Beechworth. Military trained or otherwise, no one could predict the fall of these infernal weapons, and the manner in which the liquid spread as it exploded was as wide and blistering as it was unnatural. It seemed to move with a mind of its own, making it wholly unpredictable.

As she drew nearer, the voice fell silent and she doubled her speed. She soon came upon a felled section of the outer wall, a severely burnt figure pinned beneath it. It was not Beechworth. A scorched fez with a Janissary crest sat to one side by the disfigured and still steaming head, and clutched in the man's hand was an Ottoman sword.

"Forgive me, *Monsieur*," she said, crouching low. "But I need this far more than you."

Prying the dead soldier's fingers open, she took the blade and his fez. If she was to venture further, she could not be recognised. Her mask and goggles would hide her face, but her hair was another matter, not to mention her corseted blouse. Gathering her hair and pushing the fez atop it, she then buttoned her short jacket. It would have to do for the moment.

Ahead of her, smoke billowed and swirled as it exited the stadium. She followed the stream to the street and stepped into chaos. Steam cars were stopped up and down the road at angles, several of them on fire. Those that were not, harboured people behind them, soldiers among those seeking shelter, what little they would provide. They did, however, provide her with much needed information. The soldiers were all pointing their pistols and rifles in the same direction.

Fresh screams filled the air.

A body lay on the ground nearby, a soldier's coat lain over its face. As she broke into a run toward the sounds of distress, she bent low and took up the coat, quickly throwing it over her shoulders and slipping her arms in, swapping the sword as she did. She rounded a steam car burning brightly, spitting Greek Fire from its engine, and faced a man.

The man saw her and hunched down, baring his teeth and grunting as he flexed his bare arms, which appeared to be painted red. An animal fur wrapped his torso and ran atop his head, which he inclined. A wolf head stared back at her. The furred man drew his own sword and came at Angelique with a wild battle cry in his throat. Deflecting the poorly swung blade, Angelique pivoted and slashed the man across the back, causing him to stumble. Any man would have fallen from the wound, but there had been a resistance that spoke of armour beneath the fur and the man stood taller and span on his heel. Sneering, the man growled almost like the animal whose pelt he bore.

Angelique frowned as she held her blade higher. Blood, and not an insignificant amount. As she looked the man over, it became apparent that his skin was not painted. It was indeed bright red, as if the man had been in the sun far too long, or burnt by the fires around them.

The man came again, slicing down on the diagonal, then turning and raising the blade in the opposite direction. Angelique quickly parried both cuts. The strange attacker had some training with the sword. But nowhere near enough.

She sent a swift front kick to the man's kidney, which again should have brought any man to a spluttering stop, but he stood his ground. While baffling, it made her sidelong strike that opened his throat and ended the altercation all the easier.

Angelique ran on, fire and smoke raging from all quarters. She lifted her goggles to her forehead as three more of the wolf-furred and red-skinned invaders came into view on the road and turned to her, the goggles posing a hindrance. She would require her full field of vision, especially given each man was similarly dressed and, she presumed, armoured in whatever manner the first had been. She suspected the furs hid some form of light chain mail beneath.

She ran at the first of the men, who proved to be more skilled than the one she had dispatched, his stance and form refined. Over their years of occupation and support, the Ottomans had adopted many of the martial techniques from both China and Japan, and Angelique recognised some of that in this man's style. The Janissary and Ottoman soldiers, she knew, much preferred the many styles from Japan, and the rebel forces, what few of them there were, leaned toward those from China. This man's—however loosely—resembled the former. Possibly a *Kōga-ryu* derivative.

Angelique stopped the man's blade with the flat of her own, then slipped under her opponent's leading arm, sliding her sword across his blade and drawing it up sharply and cutting into his underarm. She stumbled as she again felt the same resistance against her steel, the sword coming to a stop. The underarm was a weak point in any armour, or should have been. Blood gushed, as expected, from the near severed limb, though the blade should have continued through. She yanked her weapon free as she slipped past the man and moved on to the second and third.

They came at her as one, swinging wildly and kicking. Despite their obvious training, they almost seemed like drunkards in the way they moved, though they were not slowed from drink. Far from it, they were invigorated. As each moment passed, that unusual flush to their skin deepened. They were under the influence of some substance. It was certainly not unheard of, but she had never seen anything quite like this.

The first of the men, a sword in one hand and an inverted knife in the other, raged as he ran at her. He brought the larger blade up high and chopped at her one-handed, as if wielding an axe. It was a clumsy move. The sort of move a man made when infuriated and frenzied, not one a trained soldier would make.

Angelique blocked the sword, and was again surprised. His strength was prodigious. It was all she could do to not drop her blade. Nothing about these attackers made sense to her, and she would have to adopt altogether new tactics.

He lashed out with his knife, thrusting at her stomach. Pivoting to bring her abdomen out of reach, she brought her sword hilt down on his wrist, trapped the man's arm and twisted the knife from his grasp. Clasping the handle of the knife, she thrust the under his chin then pulled the long blade free, and the man gagged, clutching the wound, though his body spasmed from the blow to his brain.

As the last man leapt in, Angelique used his movements against him, deftly batting away his blade with twists of her own rather than attempting to block the attacks. Finding an opening, she drove the hilt of her sword to his temple, knocking him sideways.

The man stumbled, clutching the split skin on his brow. He lowered his hand and stared at the blood. Enraged, his fingers bunched into a fist. He reached for his belt and produced a squat glass and metal tube. There was a flat brass cap on one end, and a ring on the other of the same metal, almost like a syringe. Within the glass tube, tiny as it was, a bright red spot of Greek Fire stood out, emitting a crimson glow even in the sunlight. With a grunt, he stabbed the tube into his outstretched forearm.

Angelique gasped as the man drew his blood into the tube with a quick movement of the metal ring—veins of red lightning sparking in it—then thrust his thumb down. Throwing aside the syringe, the attacker reached under the wolf pelt and pulled a Greek Fire pistol from his belt. He held his arms out wide. An array of angry previous puncture marks stood out as his veins inflamed and brightened with a soft glow. The light crept through his now vermillion flesh, slipped under his furred armour, and up his neck. He shook his head, blinking rapidly like a wolf driven mad with mange. Eyes widening like a madman, he fixed his gaze on Angelique, and bayed like a wolf before sprinting at her.

He was all the clumsier and enraged after injecting himself, but he was also that much stronger and faster. The Greek Fire in his blood—in all their bloods, she now realised—somehow fortified his body while robbing him of his mind. The speed and ferocity of his blows was unbelievable, even single-handed. Her sword rang as they clashed, and her bones were jarred with each blow. Angelique fought to maintain her defensive stance and to safely deflect his attacks. That task was made all the more difficult and treacherous as he brought his pistol to bear.

Cursing in Japanese, Angelique side-stepped the first deadly shot by mere inches, sizzling past her ribs. She had since learnt from Abdul-rahman how the weapons functioned, steam from the initial reaction sending a highly corrosive ball of Greek Fire from its barrel. It was not a fate she wished to contemplate, let alone suffer.

Continuing her spin, she trapped the man's weapon hand with her sword and dagger and twisted her hands to wrench it free. She may as well have attempted to rip an oak tree from the ground barehanded.

With a self-satisfied grin, the attacker drove his forehead at hers, attempting to knock her senseless with the blow. Managing to dodge the attack, Angelique grunted and fell back in pain as his forehead connected with her shoulder, though she had to abandon her weapons to do so. Blades clattering to the stones, she stumbled back momentarily before regaining composure. It was as if she had been struck by a boulder.

"*Demek kadinsin,*" the attacker said, a grimace on his lips. So you're a woman.

Angelique's cloth mask draped from her chin. Pulling it free, she twisted the cloth in her hands until it was a rope. She shrugged and smirked at the man. "*Evet,*" she said, answering the man in his native tongue. "Yes. I am a woman. A woman who bested three of you mangy dogs. And now, I will do the same to you, with nothing but this cloth."

"Try your best, *woman*! After I am done with you..." His eyes roamed over her. His lascivious manner was made all the more terrifying by his red, veined flesh. "I will enjoy feasting on your body."

"You are not a wolf," she said, sneering. "You are just another pig."

Gritting his teeth, the man shook at the insult, amazingly his face reddening still. Even the whites of his eyes, now wide, were shot through with the same veins that covered his body. And it was those bulging orbs she aimed at as the man surged toward her.

As he neared, she flicked the cloth in her hands, whipping him across the eyes. The man clutched his face bellowing. Whatever the Greek Fire did to strengthen his flesh, it apparently did not extend to those sensitive organs. It was no killing blow, but it had allowed her to twist the cloth once more, ready to fend him off. He lowered his hand, and tears streamed from one of his eyes.

"Do not cry, Mister Wolf," she said. "You will join your friends soon enough."

"Witch!" he screamed, and attacked once more.

He fired shot after shot, and swung wildly with his sword. He was nowhere close to striking her as she danced about him, the ends of the cloth rope wound around each of her hands. Staying close to the enraged invader, Angelique used the makeshift rope to push his hands as he fired the pistol, sending the shots wide, and to also stop his hand as he attempted to bring the sword down on her skull, or stab her with it. She would not make the error of attempting to trap his limbs again, instead using her skills to wear him down. However, as she felt her own limbs burning, his energy seemed endless. She had to end the fight, now.

Angelique seized her opportunity when the man stepped awkwardly, his leg bending. She kicked him swiftly behind his knee. The man barely stumbled, his muscles so hardened by the Greek Fire. But it was all she needed.

She leapt forward, looping the cloth rope around his throat, and twisted her body and pulled, using her full weight. His back pressed against hers, the cloth creaked as she hauled with all her might. The man let out a gasping choke as he whipped his head, then body about, twisting and dropping to a knee in an attempt to reach her.

Angelique swung with him and was face to face with the man, though her cloth rope was still wound about his neck, turning with her. She pressed her heel to his chest and hoisted. The man's neck corded and his eyes bulged. One of those bulging orbs was reflected in his sword, the blade now trapped by the cloths second twist around his throat and pressed to his cheek. The sword edge was aimed at Angelique's face, angled and behind his ear. With a grunt, he thrust the blade forward, severing his own ear, skin from his cheek, and shearing through the cloth.

She was already off the man as he lurched forward, his balance thrown from the effort. Angelique kicked the heel of her boot into his wrist and snatched the sword from the crazed man's hand and swung. The man blocked with his pistol, then swung it with a victorious sneer as he aimed it at her face.

Angelique took a step back and took in his weapon and the deep cut on it near the glowing Greek Fire ampule. "We'll meet again in Hell, Mister Wolf," she said in Turkish, grinning.

He pulled the trigger.

Angelique threw herself to the ground as he turned into a ball of red fire. Screaming in agony, a rush of bright red flames over his skin, the invader ran at her. Angelique's hands and feet scraped at the cobblestones as she attempted to escape, but the man slowed, then fell to his knees. His body sat aflame before keeling onto his face on the stone flags.

She observed what was left of the still burning man as she caught her breath, whose chest had sunk into itself. She had no time to ponder or rest, however.

The cries of men sounded from somewhere, though she could not tell their origin. A crowd of terrified voices intermingled from every direction, echoing from the walls of the stadium.

Then the voice of a child cried out.

"*Anne!*"

Before she even knew it, her feet were flying over the stones, carrying her in search of the frightened calls.

"*Anne, nerdesin? Anne! Korkuyorum!*" Mother, where are you? Mother! I'm frightened!

Angelique was on the child, sweeping the girl into her arms. Tears had etched lines of clean skin on her soot laden cheeks. Angelique clutched the girl to her, memories of her own tearful, lonely nights filling her mind.

"*Ne crains pas, petit,*" Angelique said to the girl, using the words she longed to hear from her mother. Do not fear, little one. "We will find your mother," she then said in Turkish. "Do you know which way she went?"

Nodding, the girl pointed to a space between buildings. "The wolves. They took my mother there."

Nodding, Angelique gently pushed the girl's face into her shoulder. "Do not look until I tell you to, understand? No matter what, or who, you might hear."

"But we're just girls. What are we going to do?"

Angelique stood tall and tightened her grip on the girl. "When you open your eyes, you will see what girls can do. Now... onto my back, and hold tight."

She swung the girl behind her, the child clutching for dear life as

Angelique took off. The child hardly moved at her back as Angelique put her training to full use. Silent running with a load, target, or comrade was a required skill, though rarely utilised. Angelique had never been allowed to formally train, and certainly had anyone found out she had been taught at all, serious questions would have been raised of the then Iga lord, at the least. More likely, had any of the Iga elders known that her grandfather had taught their secret skills to a slave, he would have befallen some accident or died in his sleep of 'old age'.

The two wolf-men had no idea what befell them, Angelique's sword swift and silent, first taking the head of one, then the other, despite their Greek Fire-bolstered flesh and blood.

The woman on the ground looked up at her without seeing, her eyes on the bloodied blade.

"Fix your dress," Angelique said to the woman quietly, turning to show her the child on her back.

The woman blinked in shock, then took in her saviour's face. "My daughter!" she said, lip trembling, pulling her dress down and struggling to rise.

"You may open your eyes now, little one," Angelique said over her shoulder when her mother was decent.

The girl gasped at the bodies around them. "Who did that?"

Angelique smiled at her. "Just some girls."

The woman flew to Angelique, first embracing her, then the girl who leaped into her arms. "May Allah bless you," the woman said. "If you had not come in time, I—" Tears streamed from her shimmering eyes.

"I need no blessings," Angelique said. "Only that you say a brave soldier saved you from these beasts. Is that understood?" The woman nodded, the fear in her eyes becoming a resolute, unspoken understanding. "Now go, take your daughter home."

The woman covered her face, and fled with her daughter held tightly in arms.

The girl stared over her mother's shoulder, eyes locked on Angelique and the ghastly scene.

Angelique covered her own face and disappeared into thick black smoke. Soldiers were now streaming across every road, and Angelique could do no more without being caught.

Turning back toward the stadium, she stopped and lifted her eyes to the sky as a fantastical sight greeted her. With a sound like the deepest war-horns she had ever heard, a glimmering thing of legend swam through the sky.

"An airship..."

Angelique allowed herself a smile and moment of respite as she watched the long egg-shaped balloon and its gondola move gracefully through the sky, its engines swirling a thick bank of smoke that trailed on high as it passed through. It was absolutely magical in its dream-like flight.

Then the dream became a nightmare as something lit the sky. Like a falling star, but in reverse, a ball of flaming Greek Fire shot from the ground. It streaked through the smoke, lighting it from within. And like some hell-born thing, it emerged once more, bursting forth and striking the gondola.

"No," Angelique said, shaking her head as the flaming airship rocked and slowly fell toward the heart of Istanbul.

But her fear was unfounded. The ship listed, cutting a slow arc of fresh black smoke as it fell faster and faster. It would miss the populated areas of the city, she saw, as its nose turned to point at a far closer location. A large, open area with high walls that might contain the calamitous fire that was sure to spring forth.

"Beechworth!" Angelique said, and sprinted toward the stadium.

CHAPTER TEN

The drone from the airship at her back turned to the screaming of banshees as Angelique flew into the stadium, her mask long gone. Her lungs were fit to burst, and her legs burned like the fires that still raged around the stadium, belching smoke.

A wolf-skin clad man appeared in front of her, raging in victory as a soldier went down in red flames. But the invader did not have time to celebrate as he turned to the sound. Angelique could tell from the man's widening eyes that the airship was upon them.

Slicing diagonally up, she cut the man from belly to chest, and he fell atop the burning soldier.

"James!" Angelique called as she went.

Over the roar of the falling airship, she heard a sound. It might have been Beechworth or another person, or the crackling sizzle of blazing wood. She had no real way of knowing, but had to believe that he was still here.

It was as if they had descended into the pit of Hades himself, the flames of the underworld come to claim them. She had trained to find her way around in near darkness if required, and quickly navigated the space, though Beechworth was gone.

Cursing, she ran to the only other point of reference she had.

The aeolipede started with a roar that challenged the falling airship, and Angelique turned it about, kicking up dirt as she raced back the way she had come.

At that moment, the once magnificent airship broke through the smoke.

The *Piri Reis*. Abdulrahman Efendi had extolled its marvel and his own work on it, as had the news and reports the Ottomans had circulated.

Named for the long dead Ottoman admiral and famous cartographer, even failing as it was, it was every bit as miraculous as the engineer had said. Word of the *Piri Reis* had captured minds and imaginations across the world and, as the Ottomans had planned, struck fear in their hearts as they imagined fleets of aerial ships attacking from on high, like dragons of yore. Though their fear would never be so immediate as Angelique's was now.

With a flare, the balloon of the airship bloomed like a deadly red flower and burst of fresh heat, quickening its descent. She raced forward with little time to spare, hoping that her mad dash into the storm of detritus would not result in a life ending collision, for herself and Beechworth. Tears streamed her face as dust and smoke assaulted her eyes, not daring to take her hands from the reins of the mechanical beast for a moment to don her goggles.

The *Piri Reis* hit the top of the curved stadium wall, crashing through it with a deafening roar. She spied a hunched over figure in the smoke as metal screeched and flew toward it. A mighty explosion rocked the aeolipede as she pulled the figure behind her, the *Piri Reis* crashing to the stadium's field, bringing a rain of stone and scorched earth.

Through the flaming deluge, the aeolipede raced out of the arched stadium gateway, Angelique hunched down on her metal steed, Beechworth clinging for dear life at her back. His hands trembled about her waist as she slowed to a more respectable speed and brought the machine to a stop well away from the blazing stadium.

"Are you all right?" she asked with urgency.

"Nothing a stiff brandy wouldn't fix."

"Make that three, eh?" Her own hands shook on the handles of the aeolipede.

He let out a laugh that had more to do with his elation at being alive than mirth. "Thank you," he said after getting the laughter under control, though his body still shook.

"Thank me later." She turned the machine about and headed back to the centre of the destruction.

"What are you doing?"

"We must see to any survivors."

"You're right, of course. But..." He indicated the inferno.

The flames from the felled airship rose high, reaching for the sky.

"Nevertheless, we must try."

They arrived back at the entrance to the stadium and surveyed the destruction. The wall the *Piri Reis* had destroyed held for the most part, but there were cracks evident through it, huge portions of brick and stone hanging precariously. Through the broken section, the smoke and heat haze rising from within had increased immensely. It would be in no way bearable.

"Anyone still within the stadium walls would have surely perished," Beechworth said, voice low.

Angelique nodded.

She circled them around the structure at a slow pace as they searched for survivors outside, but either there were none in their general vicinity, or they had fled. All they found were bodies, or what was left of them.

Dejected, Angelique turned them around and made her way toward a grouping of steam cars and trucks setting to the fire, hoses pumping a strange smelling concoction at the Greek Fire, which frothed like freshly fallen snow. Wherever the white foam touched the crimson flames, it fizzled out.

A smaller steam car arrived, and a man emerged to yell at the fire fighting men to stop what they were doing and turn their attention to the burning neighbourhoods.

Beechworth tapped her shoulder and pointed to the yelling man from the new vehicle. "Is that Captain Hasan?"

It was indeed the captain. Stripping herself of the fez and soldier's coat, she moved them closer and they dismounted to join him.

"James! Katherine! Thank Allah you are both safe. When I heard what had happened and where..." Hasan shook his head.

Angelique gave him a grim smile. "Thank you for your concern, Captain. It has been most terrible. Who on earth did this?"

Confusion crossed his face before Hasan grit his teeth. "A rebel group has claimed responsibility. They call themselves Asena, after the legend of the grey wolf mother." They both gave Hasan equally quizzical stares. "The myth is that she is the mother of the Turkish ancestors, giving birth to ten children who— It does not matter," he said angrily. "Asena believe they serve the *true* Turkish people and are pure, and have been setting about to cleanse the empire."

"Cleanse them of who?" Beechworth said.

"The Janissary, who they believe are usurpers."

"Are they?" Angelique asked openly.

His face was a mix of emotions. "If you ask the sultan? No." Clearly Hasan did not believe that, though seemed loathe to voice it. "This attack though..." Hasan shook his head, viewing the destruction, his expression deeply pained, and more than a little confused.

"How have these Asena managed to get their hands on Greek Fire?" Angelique said. "More to the point, if they believe they are pure to the empire and its people, how is *this* any way to make their point?"

"My sister is right, Captain. There were Janissary in and about the stadium, but the city and its people..."

"You are both right. I cannot explain it. And on top of all that tragedy, we have also now lost Ali Pasha."

"Ali Pasha?" Angelique said. "What do you—"

"He was commanding the *Piri Reis*, as he always does."

Angelique narrowed her eyes as she turned to the stadium and the hole the airship had made. "Was he their true target, then?"

That would certainly have made their task all the easier, if he had indeed been the Janissary leader. And if these Asena were behind it, had the men she faced been former soldiers? If that were true, happenstance had eliminated their secondary target for them.

Captain Hasan's brow furrowed. "Not that we believe. The Sultan, perhaps... What reason would Asena have to target the *Vezir*, though?"

Beechworth appeared just as perplexed. "Well, surely he is also the Janissary Commander?"

"No. Whatever made you think such a thing?"

Having finally had opportunity to wash and change, Angelique and Beechworth sat in public parkland, having requested an outing to calm their nerves after their ordeal. Captain Hasan, having seen the devastation for himself, had arranged for it personally.

"I still do not quite know what to make of it all," Beechworth said in a low tone.

They sat on the edge of a fountain, its babbling waters assisting to confuse any would be listener, whether they used a listening horn or not. They simply could not trust anyone in the empire.

"Nor do I," Angelique admitted.

She had been certain the Grand Vizier Ali Pasha was behind it all. His demeanour and the way he spoke of the Sultan certainly suggested it. Quick tempered or not, perhaps she had been wrong about the man. And she now had no idea what to make of this Asena, and the men she had fought.

"What are we to do now?" Beechworth said.

She turned to the fountain and ran her hand through the cool waters, then lifted her wet hand to dampen her neck. "What to do, indeed. There's really nothing we can do but continue with the plan."

"Off to Pergamum, then?"

With a nod, she opened her cigarette case and removed the last one with a sigh. She would need to source more.

"Do you think Ali Pasha's death will make things easier, or harder for us?" Beechworth said as she lit it.

She shook her head before she did the same with her match, extinguishing it. "It is far too early to say, but it could well be a blessing in disguise."

Beechworth nodded. "My thoughts exactly. Now that they have

these wolf blighters to contend with, they will have their hands full, and not be so intent on us."

"Or," she said, taking a deep draught of the cigarette. "They may intensify all suspicions outright and simply execute us and be done with it."

He screwed his face up with a grimace. "Must you be so dispirited?"

She let out a snort of laughter. "I thought that was altogether your game? Where has this newfound conviction come from?"

He pursed his lips and looked about, lifting his hands finally. "Perhaps it was my convalescence. Either way, I am still here, despite the challenges that have been put before us."

Angelique blinked in thought. She took a puff. "Now I am absolutely certain that by the end of this expedition, dear James, we will be lifelong and steadfast friends." She dropped the cigarette to the ground and stamped it out.

"That was your last. Why ever did you not finish it?" He stood as she did and walked apace with her.

"I've had quite enough smoke for one day, I should think." She gave him a smirk before becoming solemn. "There is far more happening here than we were led to believe."

Beechworth harrumphed in disdain. "I've half a notion to go back to America and give that Wake a piece of my mind."

She twirled her parasol as she let out a small laugh. "As would I." His expression soured. "Whether by intention or ignorance, I don't think we can blame the Americans. We have our lot, now, and must deal with it."

"Well, I cannot say I am altogether happy with that, nor your devil-may-care attitude. I, for one, will be working to discover whether Wake, the Americans or, God help me, my own empire has indeed left us in the dark!"

"As will I, dear brother." Stopping, she turned to him. "All in due course. One fire at a time, eh James?"

He considered her a moment then gave a nod. "Agreed."

"And do try to maintain your new disposition, James. We're going on another exciting trip."

"Oh. Bully for us. And so soon after we arrived."

People around the park turned with open curiosity as they walked past. If only they knew what they were really about, Angelique thought, her grin widening.

Beechworth cast his gaze at her sidelong. "I really am learning to become quite fearful when you smile in that manner."

"Hush, James. I am plotting."

"That, my dear sister, is entirely what I am afraid of."

When they returned to the recently departed Vizier's palace, they were met by Captain Hasan, who was now dressed in the far more formal attire of an Ottoman officer's dress uniform.

"Ah, there you two are," he said upon setting his grave gaze on them. "My apologies to you both. This is very short notice, but we have been summoned to the palace to attend the Sultan. He will be appointing a new Grand Vizier and chief engineer given... recent events."

"Quite all right," Beechworth said. "We can attend to ourselves and gather our belongings for our journey to—"

"You do not quite understand me, James. When I say we, I mean the both of you also."

Angelique turned to Beechworth and the question on her own mind was clearly written across his face. Why would the Ottoman Sultan wish to see them in person, especially on such an occasion?

The Captain waved a hand, then shrugged. "Perhaps the Sultan wishes to meet the new stars of the empire's engineering division? Some good news amid all the darkness? I do not know. It's all very unconventional. All I know is, I have orders to bring you."

"Stars?" Angelique had known that there would be talk, especially after the dismissal of Abdulrahman Efendi, but to have been so elevated when they had yet to produce any results?

"The news of your daring escape on your fantastical machine from the stadium reached to Sultan's ears. I believe—but this is only assumption on my part—that he may well wish you to design something new upon your arrival to the Bergama steamworks."

Beechworth paled, his moustache rippling as he swallowed. "D-Design? Something new?"

"The loss of the *Piri Reis* is not only of military importance, but a blow for morale to the entire empire. Now, please do prepare. We are to leave shortly."

A multitude of thoughts tumbled through Angelique's mind on the journey to the palace, which were consequently all forgotten when they stepped foot within its walls. It was as splendid as she had imagined from the brief glances of its exterior. It was not as contemporary as the glimmering white Star Palace, but everywhere about it, the modernity of steam industry was visible, married with the romanticism of architects long gone.

Greek Fire lanterns adorned walls and chandeliers, their flames burning brighter and whiter than any candle or oil lantern, and cleaner judging by the noticeable lack of the tell-tale black soot that came with those more conventional light sources. Though the number of slaves and workers busying themselves about the palace halls also no doubt had much to do with the cleanliness.

The western world was awash with stories of such people. The Turks were satirised in the papers with caricatures, and in art, depicting them as evil, and ignorant devils and monsters, lechers and satyrs, stealing away women and children. And here in their heartland, they themselves would have you believe that the people who toiled away, making themselves scarce before soldiers and members of office, hiding in whatever nook or cranny they could, were freemen. If one could consider that a person who, at any slight to the echelons, could be put to death as free.

More than the bright lights of Istanbul, Angelique would much rather witness the conditions under which these people lived, especially the slave women. Were they maids and workers, such as her mother had been? Or had they been sold to be used for whatever sordid pleasures of the Janissary and officials, even the Sultan himself, under the guise of names such as concubine or wife? It was abhorrent.

Captain Hasan broke her brooding thoughts as he led them within.

Beechworth's face reddened as they entered through an ornate portal patterned with gilded lines and surrounded by ornately decorated blue-and-white tiling. His expression flashed contempt and horror before becoming impassive. He was either of much the same thought as Angelique, or was thinking about his fiancée, Abbie. He was difficult to read at times, and as much of a mystery to her as she was no doubt to him.

Angelique allowed herself a laugh. If he had appeared to her a few scant months ago, she would have thought anyone stark raving mad to suggest she might be companions with this policeman. How funny life was.

"Something amusing?" Beechworth whispered.

"I was simply ruminating on our many differences and similarities when confronted with all this, brother," she said, waving a gloved hand about them.

"Well, we are brother and sister after all," he said with a lopsided smile.

"I was very much the same with my siblings," Hasan said from his place ahead of them.

"Past tense?" Beechworth asked hesitantly. "Were you... taken? As a child?

"You're referring to the *devşirme?*" He searched for the right word. "Tithe? Some call it the blood tax." Hasan laughed. "That was mostly abolished by Sultan Osman the Third."

"Mostly?" Beechworth said.

"Now it is more of a... conscription? Still something of a tax, and it retains the same name. Each region must supply a certain number. Most are poor families."

"But yours was not," Angelique said, matter of fact.

Hasan's shoulders sagged. "Some are volunteered for hopes of family advancement. The same with the harem, to a degree. Boys and girls are sent to appease their local leaders, and through them granted favour should their children find a high enough position."

"Bribery? With one's own children?" Beechworth had a hard time keeping his voice down.

"Incentive, as they like to call it." Hasan's sadness was replaced with a bitter smirk. "It does not matter. I am happy to be where I am. Far more so than I would have been in the family business."

"But you would have been with your family," Angelique said.

"Have you ever been to a tannery, Miss Farnsworth? Not a pleasant environment, and not easy work. They are happy enough for me that I am a captain, and in return they are flourishing. As am I." He glanced about their surroundings, eyes narrowing. "No. I would not choose to be anywhere else but here."

Angelique's jaw hardened. "So, your family was fully satisfied."

"Not quite. Not until I have a wife and family."

"Surely a man in your position would not be in want of suitable prospects?" she said, teasing.

Hasan's eyes slowly narrowed. "Perhaps. But I've other... ambitions I need to first achieve before I can consider such things."

She observed him closely, and the captain turned to meet her gaze.

Beechworth cleared his throat. "Leave the poor captain alone now, Katherine. You've asked him quite enough personal questions, I believe."

Hasan chuckled. "It's quite all right. I must leave you here to attend to the Sultan in any case, and assist with other preparations required. Excuse me."

He left them with a bow of his head, walking briskly down a hallway to enter the space beyond a massive, arched door ahead leading into what Angelique assumed was a state or throne room. She had no idea just what to expect within, though the area outside it was full of stately, elderly men. In fact, Angelique had not seen another woman beyond a certain point as they had neared this antechamber.

Angelique proffered her head around them with a show of discomfort. "I confess to feeling somewhat outnumbered, James."

Almost to a man, the pashas—or aghas, or whatever their respective titles on their ornate fezzes might have represented—stared at her with great confusion and open animosity.

"I can't imagine why," Beechworth said, smiling genially and nodding at one of the nearest men, who merely sneered and turned to his colleagues to mutter. "They don't seem well pleased with either of us being present, least of all you."

"No. I had best watch my pretty little back, lest someone attempt to stab me in it."

Voices of dissent grew in the rank and file until several guards approached them.

"Madam," one said, his accent thick. "If want, you we take from here?"

Angelique fanned her face with her hand. "While it is getting rather warm with all the hot air being vented—" Beechworth gave her a scowl, shaking his head, "—I do believe I would rather stay with my brother. After all," she said, projecting her voice, "the Sultan did request *both* our presences here."

The men around the room coughed and grunted and slowly quietened, averting their gazes, much to her amusement. Bowing, the guards left.

Beechworth rolled his eyes. "I'm not entirely sure I will ever grow accustomed to your *unique* mannerisms, sister."

"My dear brother, if you have not become used to me by now, then you have absolutely little—"

With a booming crack and deep creaking, the large doors they all waited in front of swung open. A page—or the equivalent of a page—called out in deep boom that filled the space.

"*Destur! Sultan Orhan Han Hazretleri!*"

Angelique blinked as the men in the room parted to quickly form two lines and bowed at the waist.

Beechworth reeled about in confusion, attempting to take in what was happening. "What in the—"

She made her translation all too late. Make way! His royal highness Sultan Orhan approaches!

Guards with spears filed out and thrust the points to bear on their hearts.

CHAPTER ELEVEN

The room was silent despite all the sabre rattling. The Janissary guards stood their ground and motioned at Angelique and Beechworth to bow their heads and step aside. As she complied and lowered her gaze, Angelique noted the spears, like the swords the soldiers used, were also of deadly Japanese steel.

Someone grunted in dismay as she backed into them, and she had to hold in laughter at the thought of some elderly man's discomfort at the sight of her posterior making its way to him. The man did not have long to hold, however. The thumping of booted feet came to a halt as the same booming voice from earlier called out, and she stood tall once more as the men surrounding her did so. Her surprise, she was sure, was not well hidden as the Sultan strode before her.

He could not have been more than sixteen years of age and had not even developed a decent amount of facial hair. The down at his top lip, what was meant to be the approximation of a moustache, was more laughable than her brush with the gentleman behind her.

What was not as amusing, and what kept the smile from her face, was the way that the boy was openly ogling her, a lascivious smirk playing across his lips as the announcer called out the vast and various titles that was the full standard of the Ottoman Sultan.

Once the page finished, the room stood in silence once more until the boy—she could not think of him as anything but—waved the page away with a dismissive hand, then another man forward with almost the same motion.

Angelique affected the same curious glances Beechworth gave the procession, head flitting side to side like some curious bird. She listened to the man the Sultan called on as he spoke of the recent attacks, the tragic loss of Ali Pasha and numerous men, women and children. While the expressions of many about the room changed to pain and horror, the boy Sultan's gaze did not once remove itself from her person, or change one iota.

Unable to resist, she returned his gaze with cold indifference, though this appeared to please him all the more. Fighting a losing battle with her anger, she sought out a friendly face. It was when she realised Captain Hasan was not among the line of men behind the boy, as he said he would be. She wanted nothing more than to ask Beechworth if he had seen the captain, but she feared that she would be run through by spears and contemptuous gazes alike. Now was not the time for her to be worried for a relative stranger, but she could not help but fear something had gone awry given recent events. Captain Hasan had been, if nothing else, a sympathetic supporter.

Was that perhaps why the boy had called for them? Did he suspect them in being complicit with the attacks of this rebel group, Asena? Was Hasan being held to fault for not stopping it? Or worse? As her heart boomed in her bosom, she was not long in waiting to discern his fate as the report on the attack to the Sultan ceased and the page stepped to the fore once more.

Angelique blinked and attempted to fathom the words that followed as Captain Hasan was paraded out.

"*Vezir-i Azam, Hasan Paşa!*"

Grand Vizier, Hasan Pasha.

It seemed inconceivable both to her and to those in the room, who showed their surprise as openly as Angelique and Beechworth did. Through utter silence and wide-eyed stares.

The Sultan viewed the congregation with a steely glare and crooked smile as the page announced the new chief engineer and several other edicts before he and his newly appointed men withdrew.

The crowd did not move or make a sound until well after the doors had closed, at which point they milled into groups—more than likely factions—and gossiped amongst themselves.

"At least our presence is long forgotten," Angelique said in a breathless whisper.

A guard approached Beechworth and bowed, muttering something before bowing and motioning at a side door. He nodded and the man retreated.

"Though not by all, it appears," Beechworth said in a grumble, and she gave him a questioning glance. "I've just been informed... that we are to dine with his majesty, Sultan Orhan, and his new Grand Vizier and Chief Engineer." Beechworth swallowed and shook his head. "Well..."

Angelique regarded the men around them and grinned. "Well, indeed."

The air was stifling, despite being on an open terrace that would put most dining halls of well-to-do Londoners to shame. The breeze was fresh with the tang of sea salt and a soft thrum of Oriental music. When Angelique had enquired as to whether the performance was a recording, much like the call to prayer on both the *Silk Road Express* and many of the minarets around the city, the boy sultan had laughed.

"No," he said, his face full of amusement as he lounged and chewed his food. "Women from my harem are playing for us." He pointed with a flippant wave of a hand at an ornate wall that had to all appearances been solid.

Upon closer inspection, Angelique saw it to be a well painted cloth screen, the music emanating from behind. She seethed within at her own inattentiveness, but most of all, the boy's words.

His harem.

She did not think raising the subject of the Ottoman ruler joining the nineteenth century would be received overly well, so instead she settled for tightly gripping the closest thing to hand.

Beechworth choked on his wine in shock from the pain inflicted on his hand, but recovered quickly enough. "Apologies, your highness," he said, coughing as the Sultan turned to him and frowned. "My throat is still somewhat smoke ridden. Not to mention being flustered from such tragic losses. Poor Ali Pasha. How goes the investigations?" Beechworth turned to Captain— No, *Grand Vizier* Hasan. Angelique still had to remind herself of that fact.

Hasan nodded gravely. "I'm afraid the investigation has come to a standstill. We have no missing Greek Fire inventory. Either Asena have somehow obtained the formula for it, or we have a traitor. And as unlikely as both scenarios are, the latter is the is the most prevalent hypothesis."

"Not an easy position to be in," Angelique said, finally able to control her anger.

"Yes. A rock and a hard place, as you English say."

"Precisely why I appointed you as my Grand Vizier, Hasan *Paşa*," the Sultan said, his voice as effeminate as his English was exemplary. "Your military field experience, and undying loyalty."

Hasan's expression was uneasy, to say the least. The man was in no easy position, having been handed such a coveted seat as he had. How many of the men who had waited on the Sultan, with experience measuring in the decades, had been overlooked for the much younger Hasan? He, too, now had a target on his back.

Hasan's lips were pressed tight as he bowed his head deeply. "Your beneficence is most gracious, *hünkârım*."

She'd heard the word bandied about during the night. *Hünkârım.* My sovereign. Any time it was uttered, the Sultan would puff up and hold his head higher. As divine as her meal was, Angelique quite lost her appetite upon seeing the boy do it once again.

"Sallettin *Ağa*," she said, turning her face to the new Chief Engineer. "Is there any indication as to when we might be on our way to Pergamum and resume our work?"

The man turned his tanned, hide-like face to the Sultan. His mouth was barely visible below a bushy moustache, but his thick lips writhed in a dance as he stammered to find words.

"Oh do be quiet, *Ağa*," the Sultan said, not bothering to even look at the man, instead taking in wine and Angelique with a smile. "Sallettin *Ağa* is a brilliant engineer, but his public speaking skills leave much to be desired, do you not think, *Mademoiselle?*"

An ice-cold blade pressed to her spine. Why had the boy chosen to use that word? "Does his highness speak French?"

"*Oui, je parle un peu,*" the boy said, smirking.

Angelique grinned. He knew nothing, was only attempting to impress her, as one would expect a child to do. "You will have to forgive me, your highness, but I do not have your way with tongues. I was always far too busy with other things."

"A pity," the boy said. He turned his head slightly. "Hasan *Paşa*, do we have any reason to believe that Katherine and James will be at any risk in *Bergama?*" Sultan Orhan tore his eyes from Angelique's person long enough to seek out his new vizier.

"Not that we can ascertain, *hünkârım.*"

The boy gave the impression of great contemplation, though Angelique did not see any real thought behind his beady eyes. "Have my troops there bolster defences around the workshop, then. We have been set back enough as it is with the destruction of the *Piri Reis.*" Angelique and Beechworth bowed their heads in gratitude. "Speaking of my airship..." He turned to the two of them. "I wish for you to design something in that regard for me. Something faster. Grander. I have been told at great length of your aeolipede and was most impressed." He waved his hand in their direction. "Build me one of those too while you are at it."

"As you wish, your highness," Beechworth said, bowing his head.

Unable to bring herself to make the utterance, Angelique inclined and held her head longer than etiquette required.

"It must be resplendent," the boy added. "The reports I have of yours, while fascinating, paint it as something rather... rustic. I'll have the necessary gold and jewels sent across so you can make something worthy of a sultan."

Angelique sat up. "Oh, I can most definitely guarantee his highness that she will be the single most resplendent and powerful thing he could ever dream to have between his royal thighs."

All eyes turned to her. What sounded like giggling quickly turned to coughing emanated from behind the music screen.

Beside her, Beechworth clenched his jaw and pried his lips apart to grin sheepishly. "My sister really does get overly exuberant where her work is concerned, your grace."

The Sultan stared at her with open lustful desire. "As do I. I do think, however, speaking of work, that I must end our festivities here."

Waiting for him to stand first, as the protocol described by Hasan Pasha before the feast dictated, the party rose and bowed from the waist, turning to follow him, ensuring they never showed their backs to the Sultan.

Angelique was reminded of sunflowers, the way they inclined toward the light, and how she may never be able to now enjoy the sight of another if she did not curtail her anger. That became all the more difficult as she stole a glance and found the boy muttering audibly to a Janissary at the door to fetch Kerim Ağa, all the while staring at Angelique.

The Harem Master, who escorted girls to the royal bedchamber at the Sultan's whim.

In that moment, Angelique was sure that Greek Fire itself pumped through her veins.

In the following week, Angelique was thankful that she had not been forced to set eyes on the boy Sultan once more, and did her best to remove him from her thoughts, though it was no easy task. Wandering in a part of the palace gardens reserved solely for the Sultan, his wives and children, she could not help but refuel that anger as she saw young women walking about and lounging.

She turned on her heel and returned to their quarters, resolving to find whatever information she could before they were scheduled to leave. And she was not without recourse.

She waited until well into the night, then unshuttered the window of her room, the candles and lamps within long since snuffed out. Pursing her lips, she made a bird call, and waited until a dark figure appeared from above it, hanging and then turning over to fall through the window and landing in a silent crouch on the floor.

"Is it safe to speak?" Angelique whispered.

The dark figure gave a single nod.

"What news?" she said in Japanese.

"I've not been able to uncover anything of use," the figure said in a muffled voice.

"Do take that off so I can understand you." She tore the cloth mask from Hideyoshi's face.

His expression was ill-tempered, though not directed at her. "These Janissary are impregnable. They keep the tightest of leashes on their men, and their ranks tighter still. Thankfully, we have many Iga here, or I would not have been able to ensure we can speak securely."

"There is always a chink in armour, brother. One simply need know where to find it," she said, quoting Ishinari Hanzo, their grandfather.

"That is my next port of call." He turned his faraway gaze to her, and frowned. "Take care, Tenshi. I grow more fearful for you as each day passes." He stood slowly and moved to her side, stopping briefly before slipping away.

Tenshi.

Angel.

She did not feel at all angelic. But he had called her by that name since childhood, in reference to both her name and appearance. What she would not give for her own guardian angel now to light their way and provide much needed divine assistance.

She really did regret she had no belief in such things at times such as this. Though that made her victories all the sweeter when won, hers and hers alone. A pity the reverse was as intensely true, as she only had herself to blame for her failures.

She exited her room to find Beechworth laying on a divan and reading through a book. They had found that the Ottomans libraries were quite diverse, with volumes in all languages.

"I thought you had gone to sleep," he said, voice low and casual.

"Hideyoshi is attempting to—"

Beechworth sat up as if he had been stung. "What?" he said in a whisper. "He..." He glanced about the room. "He's here?" he said lowering his voice.

"Do calm yourself. My brother has assured me we are quite secure... for the moment. We'd best continue our ruse even in private, though. As I was attempting to tell you, he has been prying into the Janissary without much success. I've instructed him to exploit the failings of even the strongest of men."

He stared at her. "You are waiting for me to ask, aren't you?" He let out a sigh, falling back on the divan. "Fine. And what, pray tell, is that weak link?" He slammed his book shut. "Happy?"

She gave him a triumphant grin. "Quite. That weak link, dear brother, is a man's belly and bed."

Beechworth conceded the truth of the matter with a slight raise of a brow and a nod. "And by belly, you are of course referring to drinking establishments. And..."

"And by bed—"

"Er, yes! That was rather self-evident."

Pillow talk was the great undoer of men dating back millennia. It was as tried and true then as it was here and now.

"Meanwhile," Beechworth said, stifling a yawn and putting up his book, "we're off to Pergamum tomorrow. Best we get a good kip, eh?" She nodded, half listening. "Do you really intend to attempt building the Sultan an aeolipede and airship?"

Her face creased in a deep frown before she focused on him. "Attempt? No. I will most *definitely* build them."

"But that's utter madness! Why on God's green Earth would you do such a thing? Apart from the fact you have already given one such machine to the Ottomans, you clearly dislike like the... fellow."

"You were about to say 'boy', weren't you?" He shrugged. "Because, James, I'm fairly certain we will one day find ourselves in desperate need of a quick departure. And having not one but two such fantastic means to do so at our disposal seems prudent, do you not think?"

"Two? Have you forgotten he intends to take them for himself?"

"You really do need sleep, don't you? The royal brat has no idea how long it takes to build an aeolipede, much less an airship and have them gilt and bejewelled."

"More to the point, do you?"

"No. But it will be jolly fun to find out, won't it?"

They were awoken, as usual, by the clockwork prayers emanating from the various minarets about the palace and city, but were quite used to it by this stage. Beechworth had even commented, as they broke morning bread, that he was rather curious how the things were managed and stayed in such synchronicity.

She casually told him that the current Ottoman chief engineer, while being a most poor conversationalist and apparently afraid of his own shadow, was a most excellent designer of clockworks and as worthy of the post as Abdulrahman.

"And how did you come by such knowledge?" Beechworth sipped his tea and closed his eyes. "Dear heavens, however will I go back to my regular fare when I return to Abbie."

Angelique let out a laugh. "Perhaps you'd best not tell her of your daily riposte of the finest teas and foods from golden plates, and bone china with gilded paisley."

"Oh, but I must. Though it seems cruel to do so, I could not keep any part of this mis-adventure from her."

A slight pang of envy washed through her as she gave him a small smile. "Do as you must. And as to the information, do not underestimate... our mutual friend."

Beechworth looked up sharply in confusion. "Eh?"

"Why, my *dear brother*... you know the chap well." Beechworth frowned. "Your friend from the ship and the train... *brother*!"

"Ohh!" Beechworth grinned and tapped his nose. "Quite." 'Hideyoshi' he mouthed.

Angelique rolled her eyes. "In any case, *he* has managed to dig up a great many facts, though none as can be currently applicable in our grander tasks."

"I can assure you I in no way underestimate our *mutual friend.*

Though I do wish, given the sudden revelation of your meeting and his being here, that you would invite me to your meetings." He glanced up from his tea. "And the information shared with me was somewhat less limited, perhaps?"

She stifled a laugh, the humour not as containable in her expression. "Why, James, are you feeling a little left out?"

He put his cup in his saucer quite firmly. "I do, as a matter of fact." She waved at him with a stern expression and pressed her finger to her lips. He leaned forward sharply. "I am putting my life on the line as much as the two of you. While I may not be as adept at your... particular skills, I was nonetheless chosen for this task for mine. And there is some overlap, I might add."

She sipped her tea calmly. "I've never doubted it for a moment."

He sat up and blinked rapidly. "You haven't?"

"No. Why should I have?"

"Well... You've never once asked."

She blinked over the top of the teacup. "You did not share." They sat in awkward silence. "Did you wish to—"

"No. No, that's quite—"

"Are you sure? Because I am more than happy to—"

"No." He lifted his teacup. "Unless..." His eyes narrowed, then widened. "If you wish to hear my story, and are genuinely interested..."

Angelique cocked her head slightly, then pressed her finger to her lips once more.

He put both teacup and saucer down with a rattle. "Typical. Just as I am about to—"

There was a firm knock at the door that caused Beechworth to jump and almost spill his tea.

"Come in," Angelique said in a chiming sing-song.

A guard entered to advise that their transport was waiting for them when they were ready. She sent the man away with thanks then turned to her sulking colleague.

"I am very much interested in your story, James. Perhaps you may even have a more *convenient* chance to relay it to me while we are on the road?"

He nodded sharply. "It is not a story I have told before," he said, eyes softening. "And—"

"And you know I will be more amenable to receive it than others, given my own experiences. I understand."

He appeared taken aback by her words. "When said out loud, it sounds rather churlish."

Angelique placed her napkin on her plate neatly after dabbing her lips, then stood from the table with a chuckle. She stepped behind him and placed a hand on his shoulder. Had they been amongst others in London, there would have been talk of impropriety and she had no doubt he would have balked. But he was strangely at ease.

"You well know by now, James, I'm neither prudish, nor will I faint away. I've heard many a war story, and become the subject of more than a few I imagine. My personal battlefields may be entirely removed from yours, but you'll find they've been no less bloody and... unsavoury." She patted his shoulder firmly, and affectionately.

"Perhaps, then, you might tell me *your* story, also." His hand lifted and found hers. "I can be equally a good listener."

His grip was not soft as a lover's, but firm. Reassuring. Almost brotherly. And she was indeed reassured. While she had called Hideyoshi by the name almost her entire life, she knew that he thought of Angelique as far more than a sibling.

"Perhaps," she said. Slipping her hand from beneath Beechworth's, she moved to her bedroom door. "But for now, we must pack for Pergamum."

CHAPTER TWELVE

Bergama was a small district in the province of Izmir, to the south of Istanbul, some three days travel in the old times. Now though, explained Abdulrahman Efendi as he drove their vehicle to the port with Beechworth seated beside him at the front, they would travel via steamship across the Marmara Sea. They would sail south-west to the port city of *Bandırma*—known as Panderma to the rest of the world, by its old Greek name—and from there onward to their destination by steam cars once more. There was also a train that went on to Izmir, and it was on this the aeolipede and other equipment would be sent.

Due to the expansion of the empire and the need for expedient travel south from the capital, the small coastal township of *Bandırma* had grown significantly, becoming a bustling port chosen for its protection afforded by a large outcropping of land and islands just before the inlet from the Aegean Sea, which was heavily protected by fortresses along its length.

The engineer took great pride in describing the might of the forts with their many Greek Fire cannons, which were well known in the history books from an attempted incursion in 1743.

Ships had patrolled back and forth along the inlet and stopped any approaching vessel for travel documents and tolls. The day of the incursion, the attack on the patrol vessel had been fatal. The response to the attack, far more so.

"So much Greek Fire, the waters was fire!" Abdulrahman said excitedly. "Only the one enemies ship was left, and she limp away. No one knowing who command the small fleet of ship. All of them different design and age, and no flag. And after, nothing or no one left to inspect from the Greek Fires burn."

Eventually, once security was no longer a concern, a tax was raised for passage. Many chose not to do business with the Turks, but to others the risks were outweighed by profit.

"Of course," Abdulrahman said with a chuckle, "no one try to ever take the Ottoman water again."

"Why would they?" Beechworth said with a grimace. "Most prefer to dine *on* fish rather than feed them."

That made the engineer laugh and slap Beechworth on the arm. Abdulrahman Efendi had been somewhat maudlin at the start of their journey, but had quickly turned around and warmed to them, taking James' dry, sarcastic wit with good humour, which caused him in turn to speak with them openly.

Angelique wished the man would be a touch more like his earlier self, as he now spoke almost incessantly.

"Ah, but war," Abdulrahman said, wiping tears of mirth away as he shook his head. "Such terrible thing to live."

"You've seen battle?" Beechworth enquired with interest.

The man nodded solemnly before his sad eyes looked up. "I see from your eyes, James, you too."

Angelique raised her voice quietly from the rear divan-like seat, fanning herself from the warm weather. "My brother does not like to speak of such things."

"You must, my friend." The engineer shook his head once more. "Holding such things inside is not good. Like the pressure in steam car." Abdulrahman held his hand out toward the fore of the vehicle, which hissed and chugged in a staccato rhythm. "If pressure build too much—" The fingers of his free hand sprung open.

"Yes, well..." Beechworth arched his eyebrows. "Just as well I am not full of such volatile material as your vehicle."

The old man shook his head, changing hands at the controls to grab his passenger by the shoulder. "That feeling..." He thumped his sternum, face dour. "It is worse. Like Greek Fire and the acid." He gave a curt movement of his head, almost a nod and shake at the same time. "It burn you insides first, then others outside. The people you love." He threw his hand behind them to indicate Angelique.

Beechworth's lips pressed tightly, then he unburdened himself, talking at length of the things he had witnessed, and done, during the Napoleonic Wars, which Angelique only knew of on a cursory level— variously formed European coalitions, mostly led by Napoleon, had attempted with little success to take over others in an attempt to bolster their power in case of Ottoman incursion.

Beechworth's story, which no doubt had minor changes to protect their true identities, continued until they were well aboard the ship and on their way across the waters. Angelique was unsure if it was his sharing of the details or the fresh sea air, but Beechworth seemed to breathe easier when he finally fell silent. He turned sharply to his companions to search their faces after they remained silent, as they had done all throughout his telling.

The engineer grabbed a boy, perhaps a ship-hand, and spoke firmly. "*Oğlum, söyle bize bir rakı sofrası getirsinler. Derhal! Abdulrahman Efendi emretti de!*"

Beechworth sat up in alarm. "What...?"

Angelique grinned as Abdulrahman wagged his finger at Beechworth, causing his consternation to build until the boy returned with several men, one of which set a small fold-out contraption before them. Beechworth eyed the wooden device as if it were an iron maiden until a large tray was placed atop it. It was a table, low to the ground, and shortly spread with food and drink.

There was a salty white cheese, bread, something that appeared to be small portions of sizzling unskinned sausage meat, watermelon, and two carafes that appeared to be of water, though one looked and smelled like anything but.

"*Köfte,*" Abdulrahman said of the meat dish. "*Rakı,*" he then said of the jug that was not water. "*Aslan sütü*, as the Janissary call. Milk from the lion. *Very* popular with them." He poured a small measure of the liquid into a glass.

Beechworth frowned. "Why do they call it—"

As Abdulrahman topped the glass up with water, it became clear why. The liquid turned almost as white as milk. The engineer held the glass out to Beechworth before offering one to Angelique also. Taking the glass, Angelique sniffed at it and took a small sip, and found it to be strongly anise.

Sniffing at his own, Beechworth tilted his head before shrugging. "To both your health." He held aloft the cup.

"*Şerefe!*" Abdulrahman said before taking a large dose.

The guards around them glared with envy, who, unlike their charges, could not partake as they were on duty.

She held her cup up to one of the men. "*Sheh-re-fe,*" she said, imitating the engineer before drinking.

Several hours later, a procession of steam cars pulled out of the *Bandırma* port. Onlookers seemed to be quite interested in one of the cars in particular, the middle of the three, from which raucous laughter emanated. Their car.

Angelique noted they seemed to be quite used to the drunken laughter. What they were not at all used to, she also noted, was that the driver of such rowdy passengers would be a foreign woman.

She gave as regal a wave as she could so the spectators would have more to gossip about later.

Also of note to her was that the Janissary in the other steam cars did not much care for her mischief. So much so that she could have sworn their commander's death stare would rival Ishinari Hideo's itself.

"Let them all stare," Abdulrahman, shouted when she mentioned it. "You are with me!"

His words did not seem to soothe the soldiers' demeanour.

Better men than them had given Angelique worse looks, though.

And some had even lived to regret it.

The next morning, Beechworth emerged from his room to the smell of food and Abdulrahman Efendi's radiant face.

"I feel as wretched as when I had been ill and insensible for a week."

"You do very good." Abdulrahman sounded almost proud as he slapped the seat nearest to him.

"I'm not at all sure his Abbie would be happy about that," Angelique said, giving Beechworth a wicked grin.

"Aaah," the engineer said. "A girl, yes? Girl always not happy." He turned to her with an apologetic shrug.

"Indeed, Abdulrahman Efendi," Angelique said. "It is one of our only small pleasures in life, to ensure that men do not have too much fun without us."

He gave her an uncertain frown, then guffawed when she smiled.

Beechworth inspected the food and lost some of his colour. "Yes, well, after that, I am entirely unsure as to whether I will ever drink again." He sat and poured himself tea. "What is our itinerary for the day?" he asked after he'd drunk almost half the cup and regained his colour.

Abdulrahman leaned in, eyes narrowing. The man had himself volunteered to ensure they would not be listened to, going for a morning walk about the property to get the lay of the land. He had come back to report the number of Janissary guards, their posts and routes. "We will go work," he whispered.

"This great library of *Bergama*..." Angelique said, opening the topic.

The man nodded and took a sip of his own tea. "Is not original library."

"No, I thought not. The original was almost two thousand years ago, and I believe most of that collection was gifted to Queen Cleopatra."

"Ah, you are knowing your history. Yes. But no book in that library to help us. This library was make after *Osmanlı* take *Konstantaniye*.

Many book and papers was move here to make safe, only copy kept in *İstanbul*, and other place."

"Why in the world did we have to come all the way here if there are copies in Istanbul?" Beechworth said between mouthfuls, now attacking the food with vim and about to take seconds.

"Firstly, brother dearest, we need to operate in secrecy." He nodded to her in concession of the point. "Secondly, copies are rarely ever as good as originals, especially when made long before full understanding of the contents."

The engineer nodded vigorously. "People make mistake. Or stupid."

Beechworth feigned not being able to decide to take more food before putting almost the same amount again. "Perhaps what we need to build then is an instrument that can copy something verbatim."

"While I've no doubt that such a copying machine would net us a tidy fortune, unfortunately here it would be utterly useless."

"Oh? And why is that, *sister*."

"Because, *James*, such a machine would not be able to copy any secret text impregnated in the pages and binding, or hidden in the spine or cover."

He gave her a dubious glance. "Surely after all this time any such things would have been discovered?"

Abdulrahman ripped a piece of bread from a loaf, and taking a large bite waved it at Beechworth. "Many of books do not be touch since they copied."

"Which," Angelique said, "would more than likely have been at least almost a century ago from the time of Osman the Third. And any subsequent copies would have been made from those readily available."

"Namely, the copies themselves," Beechworth said, nodding knowingly. "I see what you mean."

"Hence why we are here, to examine the originals ourselves."

"And how many dusty tomes and scrolls are we to investigate, exactly?"

Beechworth stared agog at the sheer amount of paper and vellum before them, only a small percentage of it visible to the eye. "Where would one even begin?" he cried, voice echoing about the cavernous space.

"Good job you will not have to, then." Angelique would free him from the task, though felt guilty that she was to give him an altogether harder one. "Your job will be to make it appear we are actively working on the sultan's requests."

Beechworth tensed visibly once more. "I thought we had established that deception is not one of my stronger character traits."

"Engineering is not the Janissaries, also," Abdulrahman said with a grin as he strode away, searching the stacks.

"There you go, James." Angelique handed him a book that was an obvious facsimile, perhaps even a surplus or flawed copy. "Here is the first piece of your disguise, *mon frère*."

Beechworth snatched the tome. "I thought you had altogether finished with your feigned Frenchness," he muttered

"You forget yourself." She leaned in closer. "*Je suis Français*," she whispered before kissing him on either cheek in the European fashion. "*Bon courage*," she said, offering her well wishes before turning about face and walking with purpose to dive into the fray.

"Yes, well..." Beechworth called after her. "You appear to be '*Je suis Français*' when it suits, and otherwise when not!"

Weeks passed with little progress, and with each passing day, Beechworth became as ill-tempered as Angelique became excited. As she walked into the workshop on that particular day, he commented on the same.

She made no quarrel with him, openly admitting to being thoroughly enchanted with the world of steam engineering, hitherto an unthought of endeavour for her.

"Of late, it dawned on me that the only excitement I drew from life was in the thrill of the chase." Her lips pulled into a smile and a flush rose on her skin of their own accord. What was more surprising to her was, she did nothing to hide it.

"I am going to imagine you are speaking entirely of your *previous* activities."

"Oh, do grow up, James," she said in jest. "I shall begin to seriously fear for poor Abbie's honeymoon night if you continue in this vein."

James coughed in indignation. "Abbie's honeymoon night, and mine might I add, is none of your blasted concern!"

She giggled gaily at his response. "You are altogether far too easy to rile. I almost feel guilty."

"Whilst I am elated that you have found a second calling in life, I wish that your third would not be to amuse yourself with my endless torment!"

She scowled. He was agitated and not quite himself. "I apologise, James," she said in earnest. "I know it cannot be easy for you to hold the fort while it appears that I amble through books merely enjoying myself."

"I do so hope you are not mocking me, as I am hardly in the mood!" His bleary eyes turned to her from the anvil he had been hammering as she had entered the steamworks.

"Not in the least." He eyed her warily. "I swear it on my honour as a woman."

Several months ago, she would have risked it all to be where she was now, perhaps even her 'honour'. But it was not several months ago. Much had changed in that time.

"I've worn so many masks for so very long," she said in a slow, quiet tone. "I have come to a point that I almost forget that I do so. And I am afraid I no longer know myself. Let alone anyone else."

Beechworth gave her a nod. "Knowing what little I do of your life, I can fully understand why. But I am not your enemy, sister. We are allies, trapped here together in a foreign and dangerous land. And if you let me... If you lower your masks..."

"I know," she said, raising her eyes to him.

"Good. And let it be known..." He raised a finger. "I am under no allusions as to how much of your true face you have shown me. But of this much, I would stake my life on. That you... *Katherine Farnsworth*, are an honourable person."

She smiled. "Thank you, *James Farnsworth*. You have no idea how much that means to me." He returned her smile, albeit weakly. "You're rather wan, are you unwell again?"

"As would you be if you had been cooped up for weeks on end with a splitting head from the repeated blows on a damnable piece of steel!" He hit the anvil in anger to make his point, then clutched his head.

She placed a gloved hand upon the metal to quiet it, the other on his shoulder. "Take heart, James." She pulled a large cloth-bound object from her skirts and held up a hand at his questioning brow. "Do not ask how I kept it there."

"Perish the thought."

She unwrapped the thing to reveal a dusty volume and eagerly held it out for him. He put the heavy hammer down and perused its pages, the edges of which had long since crumbled. It was filled with ancient Greek, smatterings of Latin and Arabic around intricate drawings and symbols.

Beechworth's finger traced the lines. "What the Devil is this? It looks like some sort of alchemists' journal."

"Indeed. A work journal. And look there." She pointed to a bent slip of paper marking a spot deep within the tome.

He opened the book gingerly to find the marked location and pulled the slip of paper out. "A page has been torn out!" His voice was indignant at the crime.

"Several in fact." She toyed with the frayed edges left behind from the defilement. "But look here." Her finger traced across the paper to tap upon a symbol.

It was a drawing of a gear, filled with intricate scrawl and lines in varying colours.

He blinked, then gave his head a vigorous shake. "I... don't follow. It doesn't appear particularly functional. Am I missing something?" He rubbed his eyes, then stared at the symbol. "There's writing and designs hidden within the design!"

She smiled widely as she took the book from his grasp and hurried to a drafting table, where she inked a pen and set it to blank paper. Done, she sat up.

Beechworth gazed over her shoulder and read her translation. "Iron Clockwork?"

"Iron Clockwork," she repeated, a sighing lilt to her voice.

He shook his head.

"Go and get some rest, James," she said, before letting out a heady laugh. "We shall discuss its meaning when you've half a mind with which to do so."

He seemed to be about to argue for a moment, but his shoulders fell. "A quick nap, perhaps?" he said before stumbling away to a cot in a side room.

Angelique sat for hours, studying the journal and grinning until her cheeks ached. So much so that she had been wholly engrossed until sounds drew her attention.

She cursed herself for an idiot when she recognised the soft scrapes and crunches as the tell-tale sounds of multiple people sneaking about outside.

CHAPTER THIRTEEN

S leep was in short supply in the days following Angelique's abduction.

Beechworth had awoken from a deep slumber to find the workshop in utter chaos, and Angelique gone. He had run about searching for any sign of her, calling her assumed name, which was when he found their Janissary guards outside. Every single one of them, dead to a man.

Along with the bodies, he had also found another item which led him to believe she had been taken. Her locket. It had been neatly placed atop a low wall near the dead guards. Tracks from a steam car led to and away from it. If the locket itself had not been a message, the formation its chain had been lain out in brooked no argument. The profile of a howling wolf head.

Asena.

Beechworth jumped to his feet as Abdulrahman Efendi returned from again petitioning the Janissary to do more for the missing girl.

"Well?" Beechworth said.

The engineer shook his head. "I am sorry, James. They only say same thing. They doing what they can, but not hopeful."

In all likelihood, the Janissary thought she was dead, or better off that way.

"We will find her," he said to Abdulrahman.

The man nodded. "Still, I send message to Hasan Pasha with bird. Maybe he can be helping more."

Beechworth clapped him on the back. "Good man. While we wait, I want to show you something. I didn't get a chance in all the commotion. What do you make of this?" He pointed out the drawing of the gear in the book Angelique had shown him.

"Hmm?" Abdulrahman leaned in and squinted. "*Demir Düzenek?* This I have never hear. And when it was write in book, I not know."

Beechworth trained a large brass rimmed magnifier on the symbol and cast his eye about the intricate etching intently, as if prognosticating. He stood from it and ran his hand over his jaw, set firm in determination and bristling with stubble. "If only there were a way to separate the elements," he mused aloud.

"You thinking there is something hiding in the drawing?"

Beechworth stabbed the page with a finger. "This is the only thing we have to work from. Whether coincidental with Ang— My sister's abduction or otherwise, I feel there is something within this to lead us on."

Removing his fez, the engineer scratched at his thinning hair. "When I younger, and start engineer, I was copier of such things."

"Can you copy this? Perhaps make it larger? Separate out its parts?"

"I think... Yes!" The man said with a determination to match Beechworth's.

"Good man! Maybe by the time we are done, we will have word from Hasan Paşa."

"*Inşallah.*"

By the grace of Allah.

Beechworth knew the meaning of the words, and as alien as the concept was to him after his Christian upbringing and years of war and crusader stories against such peoples, he could not agree more.

Beechworth returned from the Janissary post with a letter from Hasan expressing his, and the Sultan's assurances they were doing everything in their power to find 'his sister'.

"Dash them and their assurances!" he said, slamming the door to the workshop.

Abdulrahman Efendi turned to him in a ruffled state, striding back and forth, his soft felt fez wrung into a misshapen knot in his hands.

"Whatever is the matter?" Beechworth could hardly fathom what could have happened in his short absence. "Is it my sister?"

"Sister?" The man sounded appalled at the very mention, and began muttering to himself in Arabic and shaking his head.

"Then what is it, sir?"

The man shook his fez at the large sheet he had been working on. "This!"

Beechworth scowled as he made his way to the worktable, eyeing Angelique's locket where he had placed it above the drawing. Abdulrahman's facsimile was a beautiful copy of the original symbol, expanded in every detail. In each corner of the map-sized scroll, was a different element, as Beechworth had requested.

In the top left, there was the gear itself. Opposite that was Ottoman script with its Arabic based calligraphy, which Beechworth could not decipher. Below this, in the bottom right, were patterns and shapes of the typical Ottoman artistic calligraphy-work seen all about the palaces. The last image was the only one that had any discernible meaning to Beechworth. A crossed pen and scimitar.

It had all the trappings of an insignia. Given the ramblings of this Asena group, Sully and Wake, this could not be a mere coincidence.

"What does it mean?" Beechworth said.

Abdulrahman ran his hands through his sparse hair, looking for all the world as if he had only recently torn at it from worry. "The sword is soldiers. Pen is..." He waved his hand about. "The state! Only one in whole Ottoman empire, control both things."

"The Sultan?"

"No! This writings... Is Janissary!"

They'd had it right, then. A secret order of Janissary who controlled the Ottoman empire. But this image had to be decades old, if not older and in no way connected to the kidnapping he could discern. Why would Asena take Angelique? None of it made a jot of sense.

Beechworth slammed the heel of his fist on an enclosed shelf above the desk. Items rattled and small vial of Greek Fire tipped, running from the shelf across Angelique's locket. He thrust his hand forward.

"No!" Abdulrahman yelled, reaching for a vial of blue liquid from the same shelf, and carefully administered it first to the locket, then to the rest of the spill.

"If not careful—" The engineer made a hissing sound.

Beechworth nodded. "Is that the same solution used to douse the fires at the stadium where the *Piri Reis* fell?"

"Yes. We use here also for when accident happen. Is safe now."

Deciding to err on the side of caution, Beechworth picked up the locket in a rag and took it to a barrel of water, immersing and washing it thoroughly. As he pulled it out, Beechworth winced. "As if things could not become any worse!"

"What is wrong?" Abdulrahman asked.

"My sister's locket, it's ruined."

The engineer pulled a face, motioning with his fingers for Beechworth to give him the thing. He took the cloth and opened it with a puzzled frown as he inspected the melted surface. Abdulrahman dropped the locket, muttering under his ragged breath. "No! No more!" he said, making hastily for the door. "I cannot. I am sorry, James."

"Wait!" Beechworth shouted, snatching up the locket and running to the door as Abdulrahman jogged up the road.

Beechworth frowned as he examined the locket. The melted portion had been rubbed away, revealing a symbol in Ottoman calligraphy, perhaps a signature. It was almost like an egg on its side, lines running vertically through it and sweeping strokes off to the right of it.

Several days passed and Abdulrahman Efendi did not return to the workshop. Just as Beechworth was contemplating whether he should report the engineer as being missing to the Janissary also, the Grand Vizier instead himself came with news.

Hasan's expression was pained as Beechworth invited him inside. "James, I am afraid... A body was found in a nearby river, in a very bad condition, but we have managed to identify it."

Beechworth pressed his fist into the table he was standing at. "Tell me."

"I'm sorry, James. Abdulrahman Efendi was murdered."

He opened his eyes sharply. "Not my sister?"

Abdulrahman? Murdered? What in the seven hells was going on? His mind raced with the implications.

"Was it Asena?"

Hasan grimaced. "We do not have any evidence to either support or discount their involvement, but we believe it was *whoever* took your sister."

Beechworth did not share his own alternate theory. This was the Iron Clockwork. Had Abdulrahman spoken to someone of their discovery? What did that then mean for Beechworth's own safety?

He need not have wondered.

"With everything that has happened, the Sultan has ordered that you return to Istanbul at once. I will make arrangements, if you can gather your things. We will of course continue our search, however..."

Beechworth nodded. What was he to do now?

Beechworth held the small china cup by its diminutive handle between thumb and finger, and stared into its murky depth. Kerim Agha stood before him, lashes fluttering above his wide nose, but otherwise as unmoving as the mannequin that sat atop the Mechanical Turk that had brought them here.

"This is coffee, you say?" Beechworth said.

Kerim bowed his head. "Considered by many as the *original* method for preparing it." The aroma was stronger than any coffee Beechworth had ever sampled, though he did not usually partake in the beverage. "I had it prepared medium sweetness, as I do not know your preference," he said, flourishing a hand.

Beechworth drank, if only to please Kerim. The flavour and aroma immediately hit him. It was as potent as he had imagined, but not at all unpleasant.

Kerim finally eased and sat to drink from his own cup. He let out a satisfied sigh. "Do you like it, James?"

"Very much so." He was earnest, yet the man did not appear satisfied with the response, likely reading his agitation as aversion. He placed the cup down. "As much as I *love* your coffee, Kerim Agha—" Kerim smiled, "—I am far too concerned for my sister to be truly happy with anything."

The man's expression shifted, discomfort lining his face. "Of course. You must forgive me, James."

Beechworth shook his head and waved a hand. "There is nothing to forgive. Think nothing of it."

"No, sir, it is unpardonable! I did not once ask. For something so terrible to slip my mind... If there is anything I can do, ask it, and it is yours."

Beechworth nodded and picked up his coffee, drinking idly as he thought. Try as he might, he had been unable to find or contact Hideyoshi, though he had been more than discreet out of necessity. Nor had Angelique's brother attempted to contact him, however.

"I simply cannot believe the inaction!" Beechworth said, drawing an askance look from Kerim. "The... Janissary, they have been unable to do anything!"

Lines of contempt etched Kerim's face. "The Janissary!" He snorted in derision. "Nothing but ruffians and scoundrels."

"I did not wish to say anything," Beechworth said in a low voice, "but I am of the same opinion."

The hard line of Kerim's shoulders eased. "It is so hard to know who to trust these days." He nodded as he finished his coffee, then picked up his saucer, covered the small china cup with it, then after waving them around deftly turned both over. Placing them on the low table, he smiled sheepishly. "A superstitious custom. Fortune telling of the coffee ground."

"We do much the same with tea leaves." Beechworth emulated the Harem Master and turned his own cup over, which seemed to please the man. "Were I in London, I would instead consult public records, libraries, or assistance from the constabulary."

"Records and libraries?" The man scowled. "How would such things help locating your sister?"

Beechworth leaned forward. "Asena left behind a sign to ensure we knew it was they who took her. I believe it could lead me to her, but I do not trust the Janissary with the evidence."

"Because of... Abdulrahman Efendi?"

"You've heard, then?"

"I... That is to say, *we* have only had rumours. Nothing specific. It is all being kept very secretive."

"He was murdered."

Kerim's eyes widened with both shock and fascination. "Yes, as we'd heard. But why?"

Beechworth leant further yet. "I showed him what I had found, and the very next day—"

"No!"

"I'm afraid so. I feel *utterly* responsible. As I said, I dare not reveal this to anyone else."

"But, what of yourself?"

"I've no choice but to shoulder the burden alone for dear Katherine."

Kerim nodded in contemplation before crossing to sit beside Beechworth. He lifted Beechworth's cup and saucer and touched the base of the cup with his little finger. With a satisfied nod, he lifted the cup and gently wiped its lip on the edge of the saucer, then turned it over to peer into its dark depths.

"Your fortune tells of many great deeds, success, but also great loss. But here—" Kerim pointed with his little finger at a lump of mud-like ground. "A friend, who holds your confidence, tells you he will aide you in your quest." Kerim looked up at Beechworth, dark eyes hooded.

"Thank you," Beechworth said with sincerity, then listened as the Harem Master outlined his plan.

"Thank you again, Kerim Agha," Beechworth said as the man led him through the darkness. "I don't yet know how, but I will repay this kindness somehow."

"I am happy to be of service to someone in need," Kerim said, his face lit red by a small vial of Greek Fire he had pilfered from somewhere. "Now come, but quietly. The walls are thick stone, but there are some areas that we can still be heard from."

Kerim had told Beechworth all about the secret passageways in the walls of the palace, used for generations by the Harem Masters to lead concubines to and from the harem, and that information was passed from Harem Master to Harem Master. Sometimes, he had said, despite the Sultan being the supreme ruler of the empire, there were other rulers behind the throne. Beechworth could not have agreed more, and he was all the gladder Angelique had insisted they maintain their assumed names so steadfastly.

They finally arrived at their destination, and Kerim apologetically asked for Beechworth's assistance. "This door is behind a very heavy bookcase," he said, and he was not wrong. Beechworth was sure he could have opened it himself, but it was much easier with the both of them.

Once opened, Beechworth found himself in a large library, lined with volumes and occasional scrolls. Artworks and other such things decorated walls and shelves. The space was easily as large as the one in Bergama, but where that collection was dusty, gloomy, this was bright with Greek Fire lamps and marble floors. It was not a room made for storage, but artful display.

"I will keep watch at the main doors," Kerim whispered, pointing. "Use this if you need better light." He pressed the Greek Fire vial into his hand. "If anyone should come, they will not suspect me. If I cough twice, you must hide in the passage and wait. More than two, flee, and I will come find you later. If you are caught, ensure you do not have that with you or..." Kerim's eyes widened dramatically.

Beechworth nodded, only to stiffen as something caught his eye.

Within a large, gilded frame was a portrait of a man, obviously a former sultan from his stature and garb. "What is that?" he said in awe.

"Ah, you have a good eye, James. That, my friend, is the original Titian portrait of Sultan Süleyman the Magnificent. It, eh... may have gone *missing* at some point."

Beechworth shook his head. "No, not the painting itself. That." Beechworth pointed at what had truly held his focus. "The gold symbol below the frame." It was the same as the one on Angelique's locket, or at least similar enough.

"Ah, the Sultan's *tuğra*. His signature. That is—" Kerim grunted.

Beechworth turned to see what held the man's tongue and jumped back. The tip of a bloody sword protruded from the man's chest.

Kerim fell to the floor, revealing a masked and hooded assassin with a sword, its edge glinting as the figure moved toward Beechworth and lashed out, cutting his arm. As the assassin made to attack again, another similarly garbed figure flew as if from nowhere to tackle the murderer to the floor. The two assassins fought for the blade, their hands lashing and striking at each other with unnatural speed.

Beechworth stopped momentarily at Kerim's body before making his escape to the open bookcase passageway and pulling it after him. As it shut, the library door crashed open and booted feet and voices filled the space.

It was impossible for the Janissary to have been alerted so quickly. The only way they would have known to come at that precise moment was if they were complicit in Kerim's death. Which would have meant they knew he was coming here.

Head reeling with the implications, Beechworth stumbled from the bookshelf door.

Kerim Agha came to Beechworth's dream with heated accusations, his still flowing blood an unnaturally bright, glowing red. "See what you have done!" the spectre said, lifting a stained hand from his chest and turning it over to expose his smoking, eaten away palm.

"I am sorry! I am so very sorry!" Beechworth beseeched and apologised to the spirit of the departed man, but still Kerim came.

"Know my pain!" Kerim cried, and pressed his still burning hand to Beechworth's chest.

The corrosive liquid scorched through his shirt and skin alike, causing him to cry out in agony. He struck at the ghost and ran, mind reeling and vision blurred from pain.

He entered the secret passageway behind the bookshelf, slamming it shut and careening off the walls as he ran, like a pain-drunk roly-poly children's toy, teetering as he went. As he ran, the walls around him caught alight with Greek Fire. The cracks between the stonework oozed the stuff, lighting his way, but also presenting him with a deadly obstacle.

To make matters worse, the Greek Fire then became a living thing, a creature of flaming liquid, reaching out for him with extensions that bubbled and formed into human hands and wound around his ankle.

Beechworth loosed a cry of agony as he pulled his burning leg from its grasp and retreated, the Greek Fire creature clawing after him. His back hit a wall, but he did not stop, instead falling through it as it gave way like wet paper.

As Beechworth recovered, he found he had fallen through the Titian painting of Sultan Süleyman, the canvas in ragged pieces. He watched in terror as the canvas re-stitched itself, closing on the red nightmare, containing it.

He sat on the floor, panting and gulping, throat burning as he swallowed. His eyes fell on the tile below the painting. The Tuğra.

"Did you wish to get something off your chest?" a voice called out.

Beechworth blinked in confusion and sought out the speaker. The words had been said aloud in Turkish, but he had somehow understood them. Then he found the owner of the voice.

The painting of the long dead sultan, his face in profile, turned to Beechworth. Only it was not the portrait he had seen in reality. It was now Süleyman Reis—Sully—from *The Pony Express*.

"You have much on your chest, Constable James Beechworth," Sully said. "You should avail yourself of it before it kills you."

"I don't understand. What—"

Sully's hand shot out of the painting, his arm stretching incredibly as it dove into Beechworth's chest. Beechworth cried out in terror and agony as smoke issued from the wound. Then the hand withdrew as swiftly. Beechworth sobbed at the cessation and fell to the floor, only to have something fall on his unharmed chest through the hole in his shirt. Something hard. He reached for it and held it up to the light, the object glowing through the tears streaming from his eyes.

"Angelique's locket."

He sat up and held it high, the locket spinning on the chain momentarily as he reached for the *tuğra* on the painting. He stopped its movement to inspect the sigils, comparing the locket to the tile below the portrait of Suleiman the Great.

"It's... not the same," he murmured.

"They rarely are," a voice from the painting said.

He jumped at the voice and raised his eyes to it.

And immediately wished he had not as a large, curved scimitar rushed at his face.

Beechworth started awake instantly with a great gulps of air, fingers clutching at his chest before pawing at his face. It was drenched, but as he lowered his fingers, he found it was sweat and not blood.

The shadows in the corner of his dark room moved as a masked figure in black emerged.

"What in all the damned blazes—" Throwing his head about in search of a weapon, Beechworth fell from the bed. He attempted to rise, but his limbs were slow to respond to his commands. From his place on the floor, he could only watch through blurred vision as the assassin rushed toward him.

To his relief, if confusion, the masked figure lifted him back to the bed and made him comfortable before moving away.

Beechworth worked at controlling his heart and breathing as whatever afflicted him subsided. He played the events of the night through his mind, teasing out truth from nightmare. He attempted to move his hand, and it twitched. He turned his head to the figure. "I was poisoned, wasn't I? The assassin's blade?"

The masked figure cocked their head.

Now the trouble was, which assassin was this? His saviour? Or Kerim's murderer?

He eased his shoulders with a sigh of relief, then smiled. "No," he said. "If you had wanted me dead, I would be already. And, I know who you are... don't I, Mister Hideyoshi."

The masked figure sighed. "Do I really cut such a manly figure, Beechworth?" Angelique tore her mask free.

He attempted to leap up in excitement, almost falling to the floor once more. She ran to his side and propped him up, then pressed the back of her hand to his forehead.

"Still a little warm. You're lucky I got to you when I did. If I had given you the antidote any later..."

"Never mind that, where the devil have you been!"

She reached into her black robe and pulled out a plain case of cigarettes and lit one. "All in due time. Tell me, James. Whatever have you been up to in my absence?"

Beechworth gave her a glum stare.

CHAPTER FOURTEEN

During the night, they discussed at length the events that had occurred since they had last been face to face. Angelique, of course, insisted Beechworth go first, despite his insistence ladies should take the lead.

Once she had pried him of all information, only then did she finally agree to tell her side of things. Not without making Beechworth attempt at guessing what had happened, however. He had, after all, made the assumption on her entrance that she was Hideyoshi. And he was just as incorrect on what had transpired.

"Mister Hideyoshi... That is, your brother rescued you from those brigands," Beechworth said proudly.

"You should know by now, James Nathaniel Beechworth, that I am no damsel in distress. The longer you spend with me, the more you will come to know that fact."

"Yes, well, I've seen it firsthand several times now. I shan't even ask how you came to know my middle name." He glanced sidelong at the still open secret door she'd revealed in his quarters as she smiled at him. "Whereas I am the maid in the tower, once again. I don't believe I thanked you, speaking of..."

"A woman's promise is a promise kept. I will ensure you get home to be thoroughly put in your place by Abbie yet. Though if you wish to grace your knight," she indicated herself with a flourish of both hands, "with a favour, she will not say no."

"I am afraid I am all out of silk scarves. You will, however, now perhaps grant me the favour of *your* tale?"

"Very well. Though it may bore you after the eventful and harrowing time you seem to have had."

Beechworth, body and faculties all working to full capacity now, settled in as she recounted the events of that night...

"Iron Clockwork?" Beechworth said in confusion, eyeing the symbol on the paper.

"Iron Clockwork," she repeated. "Go and get some rest, Beechworth. We shall discuss its meaning when you've half a mind with which to do so."

"A quick nap perhaps?" he said, and left for the sleeping quarters.

She paced about in excited agitation, hardly able to sit still. She went through items on the shelves, delved in boxes, sat on Abbie, but nothing would dull the glow of the new fire ignited in her belly. So much so that she had not detected the altogether clumsy approach of the men outside. Had they been skilled assassins, whether from the Japanese clans or otherwise, she might have really been in trouble.

When she went to investigate, she found the Janissary guards posted by order of the Sultan missing.

That was when they took her.

Or at least, that had been their plan.

Angelique closed the door quietly and searched for her would-be assailants as she moved swiftly up the path toward a steam car at the top of the road that had no business being there.

There was a sudden crunch of gravel at her back. She reacted without thought, stepping aside and driving her elbow back. An explosive exhalation of air was her reward. Spinning on the toe of her boot, she hoisted her skirt and delivered a kick betwixt the thighs of the man attempting to catch her by surprise, felling him with a grunted outburst and invectives.

Other men ran from all around the workshop to surround her. They were all dressed in plain clothing, though had Ottoman swords in hand. She had little doubt these men would have had no issue in killing her and her companions. But it was the thought of them murdering Beechworth in his sleep that incensed her.

Angelique swept her hand low and hoisted the downed man's blade. As he made to grab at the scabbard, Angelique hit him sharply on the forehead with its end. The man went down again, though silent now, as solid iron struck flesh and bone.

"Good evening, gentlemen," Angelique said in Turkish as she bent forward to lift and secure her skirt by the cords hidden beneath, then set her feet apart at the ready for battle. The sword flashed as she pulled it free. "Are you here to dance with me?"

"The woman speaks," one of them said to his compatriots, smirking and drawing guffaws of laughter.

"If your swordsmanship is anything like your capacity for stating the obvious," she said, "I might just break a sweat, Asena dog."

"We are not Asena," one of them said, grinning wide.

"Do you need me to teach you how to handle that thing, little girl," said another, leering.

"You've obviously not had enough experience with real women, or real swords," she said. "If you had, you would realise you are presently in grave danger. Of course, you would also have to be real men. Never fear. I will enlighten you all presently."

The man's leer turned to a snarl and he came at her in a half run, swinging wildly. She quickly dealt with the man, giving the others pause as they glanced at one another. With a grunt, one of them pulled a Greek Fire injector from a pocket and stabbed it into his thigh. These were of the same men that attacked the stadium cloaked in wolf skins.

She had no time to ponder it though as the injected man ran at her as his skin reddened, his neck bulging as he let out a short-lived battle cry. She batted his sword aside with her own, slipped past him, turned and slashed and was momentarily facing the other crimson fleshed men even as he fell. The others took up the charge, enraged and red faced, though they were no more of a challenge. She had learnt how to deal with them, and did so swiftly, dispatching them like the wild animals they were, Asena or not.

Inside, she found James still fast asleep in much the same position he had first been. She saw no reason to wake him. In fact, she now had more reason than earlier not to.

That was when inspiration had struck.

By their own prideful admission, thinking they had the best of her, the attackers marked themselves as not being Asena. That could only mean they were Janissary in plain clothing. That also meant the conspicuously missing guards were part of the plot.

With some effort, Angelique manoeuvred their steam car closer to the building and loaded the bodies of the attackers into it. Moving the steam car out of sight, she waited for the return of their Janissary guards.

"*You* killed the guards I found outside?" Beechworth said.

"But of course. After having questioned them, though to little success."

"But what did you do with—"

"The bodies of the others?" She smiled grimly. "Coincidentally enough, on the same day I went missing there was a tragic steam car accident. The machine spontaneously burst into flames, killing all the men within and burning their bodies terribly."

He sat in stunned silence for a moment. "But why?"

"I couldn't well leave those Greek Fire injecting men out in the open, Beechworth, could I? Whoever they truly are, it would have given the jig up."

He nodded, then was in deep thought once more. "That means... *you* placed the necklace for me to find. And fashioned it into a wolf head."

"Well, I did hope you would. It *was* put it in a rather conspicuous location and configuration. I would have been disappointed if you had lost it." His silence was telling, his discomfort evident. "Beechworth?"

"You must understand when I say it was a serendipitous accident—"

"Accident? What have you done, James?"

"It... Oh, you may as well see for yourself and then I will explain." She did not move. "It's in the secret compartment at the bottom of your luggage. The book is there also."

She quickly moved to the case and threw it open to access the compartment. "But not all of my belongings, I see." She stood with the wrapped book in one hand and her pendant in the other.

"I had to get rid of your weapons, I'm sorry. I could not risk Hasan or the Janissary searching it and finding the Greek Fire pistol, *wherever* you got that."

Humming, she put the book down to inspect the jewellery. Her heart ached as she found the marred surface. "How did this happen?"

"I was in search of a clue after your disappearance when some Greek Fire fell and... Well you can see the result."

Her eyes locked on the scarred face of the locket, then opened wide as she saw past it. "I can hardly believe it!"

"No, nor could I. Poor Abdulrahman assured me it was impossible! And yet..." Beechworth turned his eyes to her, frowning. "You're not angry?"

"Angry? Far from it! Do you know what this means?"

"That you have a hidden Ottoman treasure on your hands?"

She stared intently at the thing. "So much more than that. A clue."

"How so?"

"Really, James. This was obviously covered up for a reason."

Beechworth grinned. "About that... I believe I may have the key."

"Oh? Do go on."

He picked up the book from the library in Bergama. "As you said, I had a vision in my poisoned state."

"Of course you would have. That powder is used to induce hallucinatory sleep by mountain dwelling monks in small doses for that very reason. What of it?"

He scoffed in scorn. "But it was so much more than that! I had a moment of clarity and... exposition." He pulled a folded sheet of paper from within the book, his eyes taking on an intensity. "What do you make of *this*?" He opened the sheet, laid it on a tabletop smoothing it out, then slapped it, beaming.

She gazed at the illustrations. "It is not the same."

"They rarely are," he said in a mocking tone.

"I do wish you would make sense, Beechworth. Are you quite sure you're feeling entirely well? Perhaps the dose you received was greater than I suspected."

He chuckled. "Your locket! The *tuğra*... The symbol on its rear?"

"Of course." She placed the locket beside the drawing. "And, again, they are not the same."

"Eh? What do you mean not the same?" He looked at the drawing, then the etching, repeating the motion several times over. "They're... not the same," he said slowly.

"Shall I repeat the phrase once more," she said in open annoyance. "Or, perhaps, you might make the point you were attempting to?"

He sat, downcast, and threw out his hand. "I was certain that the two were tied. The answer to the Iron Clockwork... everything!"

Angelique eyed the sketches. "You may be on to something."

"No," he said dismissively. "You said it yourself. They are not the same."

"Perhaps not directly, Beechworth. But indirectly... Yes. I believe you have hit on something," she said with optimism. "Chin up. We now have new clues to both our quests."

He frowned. "We do?"

"First thing first." She folded the drawing and put away the book, packing away her things atop it. Then she returned to the hidden door. "I must dispose of *this*," she said of the body. "Then, I make my grand re-entrance."

"And what am I to do?"

She smirked. "Perhaps work on your expression of surprise?" She began pushing the secret door. "After all, you will be making a miraculous reunion with your dear sister."

She was questioned at length by the Janissary as Hasan *Paşa* watched. While she was, she kept a wary eye on the men that interrogated her. She had no usable information to give them. None that would not forfeit her life, in any case, but they made her repeat the story over and over.

She ensured that she appeared the part when 'found' by the guards. Her clothing was dirty, torn and singed, reeking of a Greek Fire inferno. She told them that the steam-carriage the men had stolen her away in had suddenly caught fire. That her escape had been one of pure serendipity. That while the men had fought to escape the flames, she had leapt free as the steam car burst into flames.

That last was almost true. The steam car had indeed become a Greek Fire inferno. She had engineered it to be so. And as unbelievable as her story might be, she had known the Janissary were so entrenched in the belief they were the pinnacle of strength, they would never suspect that she, a lone petite woman, had bested their men.

"I was *so* afraid," Angelique sobbed. "The way they all looked at me, I was certain they were going to... to..."

Hasan sneered in contempt. "Animals!"

"But your virtue is intact?" a Janissary captain asked, sounding impatient, even bored.

He was to be her first target, or more correctly Hideyoshi's.

Hasan saved her from having to respond to the man, glaring and growling at him in Turkish that he was being an insensitive fool. The man shrugged, as if such a thing was below his consideration.

The door burst open, and Beechworth was suddenly rushing in and dashed to embrace her. "Katherine! Oh my dear, sweet sister, Katherine!"

Whether through fatigue or to spite her—she could not tell which, but thought the latter—Beechworth's performance was more full of drama than a London stage play. Chagrined as she was, she continued her own role. Thankfully, none of the men present thought his emotional outburst suspicious. If anything, they did their utmost to ignore it, uneasy with such an open display of affection.

"I believe we have all the information she can give us," the impertinent Janissary captain said. "You may take her to your rooms. My men will accompany her to the *hammam*—the baths—so she may clean herself if she wishes."

"Thank you," she sniffled. "I would like that very much."

She allowed herself to be led away. Guarded or not, she very much looked forward to a good, thorough, luxuriating wash.

"You really must try the hot baths, Beechworth," she said in the safety of the hidden passage "It's tremendously soporific at first, but leaves you quite invigorated."

Beechworth eyed the dark blood stain on the raw stone in the passage. Under the guise of rest, no one would disturb them. They had decided, however, not to take anything to chance and to only speak of their plans inside the thick stone walls, and even then, in hushed tones.

"I know the blighter was a murderer and deserved what he got, but must you be so cavalier about death?"

She blinked in response. "It makes you uncomfortable."

"Quite so." He relaxed his fists to flex his fingers and toyed with his collar.

"As it should," she said, even-toned.

He frowned. "Well," he said, giving her thin-lipped smile. "As long as you are not laughing maniacally."

"We have plenty of time yet for me to become a despot. For now, however..."

"Quite." Beechworth grimaced. "What are we to do?"

"As I said last night, our discoveries lead me to believe that while the two *tuğra* do not match, they do still provide us with essential clues." She held out the late Abdulrahman's drawing, a vial of Greek Fire lighting their faces.

"Do I dare ask where you procured more of that damned stuff?"

"No." She waved the vial over the sketch. "This was an ingenious idea, having him enlarge and separate the elements."

Beechworth swelled with pride, then quickly deflated. "So ingenious it got two innocent men killed."

"You must stop blaming yourself. As you also no doubt suspect, I believe Abdulrahman must have gone to someone with the finding, which then alerted the Janissary. Then they engaged their assassin."

He hummed. "Yes, I was of much the same opinion. I still cannot help but feel responsible, however."

"No, James. The men who killed Abdulrahman and commissioned the Japanese assassin are responsible, not you."

He sighed. "I know these assassins do a great deal for the Ottomans, but is it common for them to work within the walls of the palace itself?"

"Japan owes an insurmountable debt to them. And in turn the Iga and Kōga to the Emperor and shogunate. If the Sultan requested it, or they believed he did, they would do anything."

He cocked a brow. "Anything?"

"Without the Turks, the Japanese would still be contained on their islands. A faltering empire, much as the Ottomans would have been had they not discovered the secrets to steam power." Angelique sighed. "Which brings us back to our main task at hand."

"Our own insurmountable debt, you mean?" He let out disdainful snort. "Just where are these damnable Turks hiding these plans?"

Abdulrahman's drawing rustled as Angelique tapped it. "This is the key, Beechworth. I am certain of it."

"Iron Clockwork? That's all well and good, but what does it actually mean?"

"The meaning is irrelevant. Their motivations however..."

"Very well. And what might *that* be?"

"Why, that's simplicity itself, surely? Merely to continue their existence and grow their power."

Beechworth hummed, frowning as he tugged on his moustache.

Angelique sighed. "What do all secret orders and societies seek? To remain covert and carry out their business. Correct?"

"Well, of course. These blighters are not exactly Freemasons, however."

"Oh, really? There have never been any machinations among and within such fraternities?"

He opened his mouth to speak, but held. He nodded. "Very well. But again, we are speaking on something far more insidious. If we are correct, they control the most powerful empire in the entire world, for Heaven's sake."

"Quite right. An empire with the most sophisticated technology and deadliest weaponry the world has yet seen..."

"And in order to find our prize, all we three need do is crack the perhaps centuries old order holding the reins." He barked a single, derisive laugh.

"Not an easy task, granted. But we have something none of the others do."

"And that is?"

"Why, the truth, of course. We know they exist."

"Oh, jolly good. I expect we shall have them bested in no time at all."

"You forget, Beechworth, there are already extant murmurs and speculation. And now we know their name. Names, just as in myth, hold power."

He laughed. "If only we could defeat them simply by uttering their name."

"Ah, but we only have the one. But that is a crack in their armour. And in time, cracks become fissures. We have the head of the snake, so to speak. All we need discover now are the names on its belly. Once we have but one, we will be one step closer to taking that serpent's head."

He grimaced, the red light from the Greek Fire casting his face in scarlet tinged shadows. "This is altogether too gloomy a location for such morbid conversation."

Angelique pulled the vial closer to her chin, and grinned. "Let us then depart, James."

Beechworth took in her visage and swallowed. "I wager All Hallows is your favourite time of year."

She laughed lightly and opened the door, speaking over her shoulder. "As much as I do not put any stock in them, I always did so enjoy a good ghost story. Although in Japan they are altogether more—"

"My God!" Beechworth exclaimed, thrusting out his hand to point past her.

Angelique spun, ready to fight. Instead, she gasped and ran into the room. "Hideyoshi!"

He half lay across the bed, battered and bloody. "I'm... sorry, Tenshi." He gave her a half smile, his ashen skin slick with perspiration. He glanced at his hand where it clutched his side, blood seeping through his fingers. "I've... stained your sheets." His body trembled as he chuckled, then with pain as his face furrowed.

Angelique caught him as his fingers loosened and fell to his side as he slipped into unconsciousness.

CHAPTER FIFTEEN

Angelique ensured that Hideyoshi was comfortable on the makeshift bed she had arranged within the hidden passage before closing him in. She left her vial of Greek Fire with him in case he awoke, though having given him the spirit sleep powder, he would not wake for some time.

"That is an arrow wound," she said to Beechworth, her fingers tightening.

"After your disappearance and the murders, they increased the number of men on the ramparts. I'm surprised they still use arrows, though."

"Well, lucky for us they appear to, and he is safe for the moment. Some food and rest will do him good." The loss of blood had been the worst of it. She would deal with his wounded pride and temper later.

"The rotation of guards has also been increased," Beechworth said.

She hummed in thought. Angelique knew that well enough, having taken the lay of the land to both enter the library and save Beechworth then escape once more.

"What do you think the symbol and covering up of your locket means?" Beechworth asked. "For you personally, I mean."

She blinked rapidly, caught unaware by his question. "I am still trying to make sense of that."

"How did you come by it? I assume it was given to you by someone, but how did they receive it?"

She smiled, fighting back the shimmer and sting of tears. "That would require I tell you my story."

"Well, you have listened to some of mine. And as I've said, I am more than happy to hear yours and provide my counsel. Should you want it, of course."

He was right, she knew. She had hidden enough from him, and he had proven to be a loyal ally.

"My mother left me this locket." He sat up intently. "It is the only thing that remains of her."

Clutching it in her hand, she prepared to unburden herself. It was a very rare moment for her, indeed. She was not at all sure where to start. So she began the tale the only way she could.

"My mother's name was Marguerite Morreaux."

At the tender age of fourteen, Marguerite Morreaux had been travelling with her mother and father for America from their home in France. Her father had business there, and her parents decided it would be better instead for the family to move there temporarily.

Marguerite had excitedly bid farewell to her friends, promising to regale them on her return with tales of travel to this new land that she would write in her diary. They had laughed and made up all the wondrous things she was sure to see. One of them had joked about pirates. How little they all knew.

Her diary sank to the bottom of the Atlantic along with the ship, most of the crew, and her parents. Only she and a few others were spared, if one could call it that. Spanish corsairs had attacked and looted what they could, made captives of those on board they could make use of, then slaughtered the rest and scuttled the ship.

Marguerite and the other prisoners were taken to Morocco and sold to the Ottomans. One of the pirates had joked she would be taken to the Sultan's harem, where she would be taught to be a "real woman". Another had quipped that he would have started their education on the journey if it would not have meant less gold for their purses. She was not so young and naive that she did not understand their meaning, and was almost debilitated with fear of what fate would meet her in Tangier.

Stories of the barbaric *Turcs*, and their staunchest allies, *les Japonais*, raged across France and the continents, much like the Ottoman Empire itself. They had threatened the very borders of France in the past, and were in control of so much land and power due to their dreadful red fire and steam machines. Parents would scare their children into behaving, telling them the Turks would come for the girls as slaves, and the boys made eunuchs. Even grown men would warily whisper that they would be taken as soldiers and converted to Islam serving the caliphate Sultan.

As it was, Marguerite was never fated to set foot in Turkey. Barely leaving the corsair ship, the prisoners were loaded on a steamship and shuttled to Egypt and through what had come to be known as the Suez Canal—a channel the Turks had carved through the land from Damietta to the city of Suez, connecting the Mediterranean to the Red Sea. And from there, on to Japan as a tributary to the 'savages' that served their Ottoman masters.

Arriving in Japan, Marguerite was surprised to find the people there were, for all their differences, merely that. People. She had found the same of the Ottoman men on the steam-ship that conveyed them.

Soldiers with horses met them at the Japanese port, and behind those, caged carts that they were then loaded into. Marguerite held a girl she had befriended who cried, eyeing the unfamiliar landscape and men.

"Even their horses are strange," her friend said through snivels.

"They are smaller, yes. But horses still," Marguerite told the girl. "And these are *only* men."

And in truth, that was what scared her the most. They were men, and she had witnessed firsthand what men were capable of. She had known in the moment that the Spanish corsairs had captured her, her life would never again be the same. Now in Japan, that fact was driven home as sharply and swiftly as the Japanese soldiers' swords.

The fear of being held captive by these strangers was compounded by the fact the region was in the midst of feudal war, which the Ottomans did not concern themselves with. If there was a change in power, as long as the new lords capitulated, they were tolerated and given the same means the previous rulers enjoyed. For the most part, they only dealt indirectly with these clans. All official business was conducted through the Japanese Emperor, which was merely a ceremonial title. The Tokugawa Shogunate controlled all, and they ensured relations with the Ottomans went smoothly, despite whatever upheavals in the Eight Islands.

All this Marguerite would only learn later, though it impacted her life in Japan from the moment they had made landfall.

Tumultuous as things were, she had fallen asleep with her new friend in her arms, only to be awoken by the sounds of death cries. She rose to find her friend cowering in the corner as she watched.

The men transporting them fell all about them and, for the briefest of moments, she allowed herself to become excited at the prospect of rescue. But it was not to be. The men who had slain their captors were also Japanese, from two separate factions who had banded together. Some wore armour fashioned in frightening designs, curved swords flashing from atop their mounts as her captors were slain, but barely engaged in the skirmish.

The fighting proper was carried about by men who appeared to be peasants and fought with farming implements. While they may have held the outward appearance of farmers, they fought more like the demons the armoured men on horseback portrayed, making short work of their foes.

Once the attackers had dealt with the men, one of the peasant fighters spoke defiantly to one of the armoured soldiers, who had remained at the rear, his sword never having left its sheath. The armoured man, probably a general of some description judging by the fact his armour was the most decorative, gruffly answered the dirt-covered man. He sneered at the caged cart carrying Marguerite and the others. Having said but a handful of words, he turned his horse and rode off without further discussion, the remaining armoured soldiers following close behind.

Marguerite's life had yet again been bartered.

She could not know it then, but the men dressed as peasants were Iga and would lead them to their village. She had already surmised they were anything but farmers, and was soon to discover just how little she knew.

As they passed farmhouses, the men, women and children they encountered greeted the men with glee and pride, and they responded in kind. Eventually they arrived at the clan house, which was as grand in its construction as the Iga men and villagers were proud of it.

The captives were released within the grounds and Marguerite was moved into a line with the others by strong but not unkind hands. Not all of the Iga men were to be as gentle, though. Marguerite's new friend was manhandled terribly by a stern and sour-faced young man.

"Hideo!" a gruff, booming voice resounded through the court of the Iga stronghold.

The young man grunted as he shoved Marguerite's friend, and that was her first encounter of the then Iga lord's son.

The older man berated Ishinari Hideo from where he stood, ordering him to his side with a sword-like flick of a plain, folded fan in his hand. Once Hideo joined him, the lord looked over the captives before his voice boomed once more. Once he finished, he flicked his fan at another man who bowed to the lord before facing them and translating in French, English and Spanish.

"This is Lord Ishinari Hanzo of the Iga village clan! You were sent here to Japan to be the slaves of another lord, who is no longer on this Earth! Henceforth, you are now property of the Iga!"

Beside her, Marguerite's friend sobbed as they were told what was expected of them, and also what they could expect of the Iga.

The two of them were put to work straight away in the household of Lord Hanzo. Marguerite worked diligently, both at her given tasks and in learning their tongue. This last was aided by her befriending of a young Japanese girl, who was a servant from a nearby village rather than a slave proper.

Through her time in the Ishinari household, Marguerite found the

Iga to be a proud people, as were most of the Japanese she saw. They did not marry outside of their own race, her new friend told her, though they did *make use* of the girls in their possession at times. Luckily for Marguerite, Lord Ishinari Hanzo protected his own slaves, treating them much as he treated the servants as long as they performed admirably and listened to orders. He also brooked no... tampering with any of the girls in his care, Japanese or not.

"If anyone does such a thing," her Japanese friend said, "the penalty is severe."

Marguerite had certainly found the man had been kindly enough in their rare encounters. Once, she had almost walked into both him and his men in a hallway. His son, Hideo, had yelled and made to strike her, but had been stopped by the lord, sending him and the others promptly away as she cowered.

Alone with him then, she had feared the old man's words would be proven to be nothing but talk, and all but expected he would lure her into some room to see what lay beneath the rude robes that had replaced her fine French clothing ruined so long ago.

"I am very sorry, Lord Ishinari," she had said in Japanese with downcast eyes, bowing low.

"You have learnt our language well," he said, surprised. "What is your name?"

"Marguerite, my lord."

"Do you fear me?"

"No, my lord." It was the truth. She did not fear the man. Only what the man might do, or have done to her.

"Look at me," he said.

She raised her blue, unwavering eyes.

Hideo nodded. "You have strong eyes, despite their paleness." He turned his light brown eyes from her towards the gardens in contemplation. "Tell your superior that you are to be promoted to the top floor, by my orders. Understood?"

"Yes, my lord." She bowed, not rising until the lord had left. Only then did she tremble.

The top floor.

There were three storeys in the building, and anything above the ground floor had been forbidden to her and the others. She had been told who and what occupied each. The topmost floor was the domain of Lord Hanzo and his wife.

Her Japanese friend could hardly believe it. "It must be your pale skin and strange eyes and hair," she said, touching her golden curls. "You must be very proud." The girl seemed slighted.

"I did nothing to be proud of," Marguerite said, taking the girl's hands. "You are my truest and only real friend here. I will work to have you promoted also."

"What of your other friend? The girl you arrived with?"

Marguerite was pained. "I'm afraid there is not much I can do for her. All she does is cry and make mistakes. I heard they would be moving her to another household. Possibly the lord's son, Hideo."

The girl's eyes widened at mention of the name, but she said nothing. "Thank you, Marugurito."

The way her friend pronounced her name always filled her with cheer, despite her circumstances. And true to her word, Marguerite worked at, and succeeded, in getting her friend a promotion. They worked together in attending to the lord's wife, assisting her with dressing, brushing her hair, tending to her younger children and other tasks.

Life continued much in the same manner and, as things sometimes happen, Marguerite eventually fell in love. That it was a visiting Ottoman soldier pained her, but she had learnt in her time there at the Iga village that the heart craved what it craved.

Ottoman soldiers and other officials regularly came to employ the services of the Iga, and as she had learnt, their rival the Kōga. Though she did not know the specifics of the Ottoman commissions, she had quickly learnt what it was the Iga did. She would always look on the Ottomans in contempt when they came, imagining the floor she was scrubbing, or whatever task she was at, were the faces of their men.

That was until she was besotted with the handsome young man the likes of which she had never seen before. And he in turn was taken by her.

He had been stationed on the mainland, he told her, and had previously been an envoy for slaves from Europe, and spoke some French, broken as it was. Over the course of months, their conversations grew from his inquisitive jests and her short responses—which she hoped both he and the Japanese would take as timidness—to longer exchanges during stolen moments. Each of his visits was short, a night or two at the most, but the two would meet in secret, Marguerite now having some level of independence since her promotion to the top floor. Before he arrived, she would chance to sneak away for quiet respite when she could. Now, more than anything, all she could think about was never being alone again.

"I will make arrange so that we can wed," he had told her one night in his broken French, which at first she had found abhorrent, but had somehow become endearing.

"How will you accomplish such a thing? I am a slave to the Ishinari. To Lord Hanzo himself, no less!"

"You are forgetting, we Ottoman are holding the true power here," he said proudly. "Without us, they are having nothing. I make it happen."

It was then he had gifted Marguerite the locket, her likeness painted within.

"How did you manage this?" she said, amazed and delighted.

"We have a commissioned Italian artist with us, chronicling our journey. I instructed him."

"But how?"

"How? You must know, Marguerite... I fall in love with you the first time I see you. I know your face more than my own. I see your face in my dreams."

As much as she had sworn to herself she would never do such a thing, in that moment she wanted nothing more than to be with this man, and they succumbed to their passion. She had never felt her heart in such a grip before, and he had given her such a romantic gift, and words, and promised her the world.

That night he left, promising on his next return he would spirit her away if required. But he never returned. He was either dead, a liar, or both. She never so much as uttered his name again, though he had left his legacy with her.

As Marguerite's stomach grew, soon so too did her Lord and Lady's daughter-in-law, who was moved to the residence as Hideo, now a senior rank among the Iga himself, was called on to attend diplomatic matters and high profile missions more regularly. And as his status grew, so too did his temper, which was in stark contrast to his wife.

"You have been a most loyal servant," Hideo's wife said. She was the most kindly and beautiful woman Marguerite had ever met. "No matter what, man or no man, Japanese or not... you have the strength of the Iga in your spirit, and I will do my utmost to protect you and your child."

"But I am just a lowly slave, your ladyship."

"You forget," Hideo's wife had said, smiling kindly. "One day my husband will be the lord of the Iga."

"Marguerite Morreaux died in childbirth," Angelique said, eyes downcast. "The story of how she came to be in Japan was relayed to me by her Japanese friend, who raised Hideyoshi and I as our nanny. This is the only face of my mother that I know and remember." She held aloft the open locket, then snapped it shut with a shake of her head.

None of it made sense. Why would her father, such as he was, have a locket with a hidden seal of an Ottoman Sultan etched into its back? And why hide it? Had he even known? And if not, how had it come into his possession?

"So..." Beechworth said, blinking in thought. "You had ulterior motives from the very beginning. I mean, I knew as much. But the degree... Of course, now that I know you, I'm not at all surprised. You orchestrated all this, didn't you? The very beginning. Long before we ever met."

"I'm sorry, James, but you never arrested me. I allowed you to catch me so I could be precisely here."

"But... however did you know this was where you would end up?"

"I have been planning this for years. Since before I fled the Iga, little older than my mother was when she arrived there. After grandfather Hanzo's death, even at a young age I knew that I would not be treated so favourably by Hideo, despite his wife and Hideyoshi. He is a cruel man and, as my mother's friend had rightly feared, he was not kind to the girl my mother arrived with. To say the least. And, much like my mother before me, I had fostered a deep hatred toward the Turks for their sending my mother to Japan. For sending that unknown sailor there and stealing her heart. For her death. And my becoming an orphan.

"Hanzo treated me as family, and taught me in secret along with Hideyoshi. Whether he pitied me, or planned to use me as an extension of the Iga, I will never know. But I honed my skills nevertheless and used them to escape and put my plans into action. Once I came to Europe, I targeted Ottoman treasures as a thief. Like that jewel in the British Museum. Seeking out men of influence in London, I planted the seeds of thoughts in people's minds as I went, all in the hope that I could one day exact justice for my mother."

Beechworth appeared to be in shock. "I must say, despite my being here under your subterfuge... Well, that you have realised your goals to this extent... It's all rather astounding. And it also reveals far more about you than even I had ever suspected."

She stood from her seat and walked across the room to the window. "I understand why you might be upset. Please believe me when I say, I truly had no intention of you, nor anyone else being with me when I came. Though I must admit, I have grown rather accustomed to your presence. And more astonishingly, likewise your assistance." She returned his glower with a small smile, which he did not return.

The furrow of his brow increased with the gruffness of his voice. "Yes, well... I've little recourse now knowing the truth about you."

"You cannot stop me, Beechworth. I won't allow it. Not that you would be capable even if you were to—"

"Oh do for once be quiet!" Beechworth's anger was palpable. "I have a solemn *duty*." He stood, jaw and eyes set firm. "A duty to ensure that you do not fail in your justice," he said more softly, then smirked. "Not to mention getting me back to my dear Abbie before she ups and marries someone else!"

Angelique gave him a stunned glance. "You'll continue helping me?"

"There are two... No, *three* things I have now sworn to do. Uphold the right, always assist those in genuine need, no matter their circumstance..."

She almost hesitated in asking when he did not proceed. "And the third?"

"To make damned sure that for once *I* am the one to be saving *you*."

She laughed. "A most noble cause."

"My word it is. And also..." he smoothed his moustache as a light sparked in his eyes. "I do so love a good mystery. Now. Where do we begin?"

CHAPTER SIXTEEN

With no other firm clues on the whereabouts of the steamworks plans and Greek Fire formula, Angelique and Beechworth had little to do but search for other signs of the mysterious *tuğra* and pen and sword symbols hidden within the Iron Clockwork design. With limited access throughout the palace, however, they made little headway.

They used the hidden passages as much as they could, but all knowledge of any other such hidden paths had died with Kerim Ağa. They could find no list or map of them anywhere in his quarters. Even with Hideyoshi joining them when he recovered, it provided no advancement in their quest. Of what few sigils they did find about the palace, none matched the drawing, nor Angelique's locket.

"Why do we not simply concoct some ruse to get the Turks to do the work for us?" Beechworth suggested one night during their secret meetings in the walls. "We could tell Hasan Pasha that we found a clue we suspect will lead us to Asena or some such. Why, the man might know the answer himself, or simply order others to search for the blasted thing for us."

"A worthy enough idea," Angelique said quietly. "But also one I have already thought of. If the corruption of this Iron Clockwork is rife within the Pashas, as I suspect, it could trigger more assassination attempts, aimed both at us and any other persons investigating the matter. Or a full stop to subterfuge altogether and they'll simply be done with us." She pursed her lips in thought. "No. At the moment, whoever it was that sent the assassin has refrained from any further such action. That means they either suspect we are far more formidable than they first believed, or there is another party at play. I suspect the latter."

Hideyoshi grunted from where he was leaning in a squat against the cool walls, tossing an apple from hand to hand. The apple stopped in one hand as he snorted. "Now they will resort to other methods." He took an angry bite.

Beechworth frowned. "Could they even utilise more underhanded chicanery than they have thus far? How much dirtier could they possibly get?"

"That was the quiet approach," Hideyoshi mumbled around his mouthful.

"Yes," Angelique said. "The far more rowdy tactics now begin." She gazed into an imagined distance deep in thought, attempting to foresee what it was that their enemy might do.

"Such is our lot, it seems," Beechworth said.

Her eyes refocused and she turned to him with a frown. "You do so whine like a baby at times, Beechworth."

"Baby?" He turned to her brother, who averted his gaze, taking another crunching bite from his apple. "Please remind me when we return to England that I need to ensure I lose both of your wedding invitations when the time to send them comes."

Frowning, Hideyoshi's eyes darted up to the man.

Angelique smiled. "You intended on inviting us to your wedding?"

His cheeks turned crimson. "Well... we have all been through rather a lot. It would only be polite, wouldn't it?"

Angelique smirked. "I look forward to it. However, right now I'd much rather an invitation back into that royal library."

Beechworth frowned. "I don't see how. The beggars have it locked up and under guard after the grisly events there." His brow crept lower.

"What are you thinking?" she said.

"Eh? Oh, just that the whole bloody thing in the library drew quite a bit of attention to that one spot."

"My, my, Mister Beechworth. Are you thinking what I believe you to be?"

Hideyoshi drew their attention with a deep sigh. He tossed the remainder of the apple into the dark passage. "Since I have been away, you two seem to have formed a much closer relationship." He stood, wiping his sticky fingers on his rump. "Where, and how big?"

Angelique turned to Beechworth, who shrugged.

"Quite big, I think?" he said.

"Yes, I concur." She nodded. "*Very* big. And *very* loud."

"I will need to obtain a new uniform then," Hideyoshi said, eyeing his still dirty and blood-stained clothing.

"Yes, you do. You look positively awful," Angelique said, teasing her brother. "We'll let you know the details, *otōto*. And while you're about that, we will make ourselves useful and see if we cannot regain access to this new workshop of ours. I should be very interested to speak with the new chief engineer."

Beechworth's smile faded. "I see no reason why not. They've had plenty of time to set the thing up. And while they're at it, they could—"

Hideyoshi sighed loudly, interrupting the conversation. "I will leave you two to plot. That is, unless, either of you might know where I would best obtain a clean Janissary uniform, the use of a bath, and how I might cause a big, loud distraction on demand?" He glanced between them. "No? Very well then." He turned to Angelique. "I will speak to you later, Tenshi."

He did not wait for her to answer before he hurried down the dark path. She watched until he melted into the shadows, her heart heavy.

Hasan blinked in deep contemplation. "I do not know if it is a good—"

"Please, Hasan Pasha," Angelique said, using his new rank, which confused the man somewhat, his eyes narrowing momentarily.

It was exactly as she had intended. She knew he was still unused to the title, his body tensing every time it was used aloud. Pasha was something only very high-ranking soldiers of members of the Ottoman ranks gained, akin to a British knighthood.

"We are not in any danger here, Pasha," she said. "And where could we be any safer than in the heavy walls of the workshop within the very palace itself?"

He began to pace, brow deeply furrowed.

"My sister is right, Pasha," Beechworth said. "From your description of the place, it is a veritable fortress in itself. And no doubt guarded."

He stopped at that. "No, it is not. And we cannot spare either soldiers or Janissary to guard the workshop."

"Perhaps not," Angelique said, taking up the argument once more. "But the palace itself is now fortified. You've said as much yourself. And we can cook up our own... tricks?" She waved a hand gently in the general direction of his Greek Fire pistol.

He glanced at it, eyes widening. "Are you aware of the implication of your words?" he said in a low voice.

Angelique nodded. "But... Surely being commissioned engineers of his highness, the Sultan, that affords us access to Greek Fire now?"

Hasan gave pause at that.

"And we're hardly about to go into the public with the stuff," Beechworth said. "Especially given the current..." He cast his eyes about, in search of the appropriate word. "Climate."

Hasan's face relaxed, and in that moment, she knew they had his consent before he even spoke.

"Do not speak of this to anyone. *Anyone*! Do you understand? The Janissary are forbidden from interfering in the workshops, but that does not preclude them from entering it. If they should find you with weapons of any sort, even I will not be able to stay their blades, which fly swift and often as it is."

"You previously mentioned the Vizier does not command them," Angelique said, then took a risk with her next words. "But, surely you command their commanders, Pasha?"

His smirk was derisive. "I may issue them commands, but their commanders are many and wide-spread."

"Who then commands their commanders?" she said in surprise.

Anger flashed across his face. "That is not something that concerns the two of you. You have what you came for. I suggest you leave with your victory before I change my mind."

Beechworth's hand fell on her shoulder.

"Come, Katherine," he said. "The Vizier is right. Let's not pry into matters that don't concern us."

She cast her eyes downward with an apologetic shake of her head. "I'm sorry, I— I did not mean to..."

Hasan's face softened and he waved his hand to dismiss them. She let herself be led out, her head slowly rising as they walked, back straightening until she was fully erect once more.

Beechworth did not attempt to hide his frustration. "Not an entirely subtle approach that."

She cast a sidelong glance at him. "No use attempting to drive a nail with a rose when only a hammer will do."

"No, but it would be a damned sight more fragrant." Beechworth turned to her when she did not respond. "You seem agitated and impatient."

"Hmm?" She waved him off. "I wonder, though, if your Abbie would approve of your new attitude?"

His nose wrinkled in annoyance. "Your assumption that your influence has somehow wrought a change in me is as erroneous as it is false."

She adopted a more demure demeanour at the approach of some men, pulling a fan from a fold in her clothing to flit it before her in mock discomfort. "The only person making assumptions," she murmured in a tone to match her stance, "would be your kind self. I neither made nor thought such a thing."

He took her arm and leaned closer. "Then just what are you suggesting?" He gave a nod to the men who returned the gesture stiffly, barely moving their heads.

"I do not suggest, my good fellow. I manipulate others to impart what I wish to know."

He snorted a laugh. "And what is it that I have imparted to you?"

"That there are only certain persons you make privy to your true nature. Such as Abbie, and now myself."

He laughed openly. "Really? You're very sure of yourself."

Angelique stood to full height again as the footfalls of the passing men faded, though kept the fan in hand. "Only partially, but yes, indeed you have."

Beechworth stopped in place and tilted his head in thought. He shrugged at her, then strode to come in line with her once more. "I'm big enough to admit it... Yes. You are now one of the privileged few." Leaning toward her, he whispered, "And what of you, dear sister?"

"What of me?"

"Who knows your true nature?" He leant in closer to whisper. "Who has seen the essence of Angelique Morreaux?" She did not answer. "Mister Hideyoshi?"

It was her turn to laugh now. "I'm afraid my dear brother is somewhat smitten with me."

Beechworth pulled a face to say he found the very though abhorrent. "Surely not."

"Oh come now, James. Don't tell me you never had a pretty cousin or other relative you were drawn to? You well know it's not uncommon for such things to occur, and we're not of the same people let alone blood."

Beechworth opened and shut his mouth before speaking again. "I draw no judgements," he said tersely.

Angelique gave him a rueful grin. She very much doubted it, but he held his tongue. "It's quite tragic really," she said after a moment, the heaviness in her chest returning. "He should have married by now, at least by the standards and expectations of the Iga. I've done all I can to dissuade him without acting in such a way as would sever our kinship forever. I do so treasure him truly as family."

"What were you saying of roses and nails earlier?"

"Touché," she said as they reached the doors of the workshop. "Though I had hoped to spare him the indignity of a hammer to the heart."

Beechworth heaved one of the heavy doors back. "Well..." he said with a grunt, looking around the space. "We've certainly plenty of those now, whatever it is you decide."

They peered about the workshop in wonder as they walked through its massive doors. While the dungeon-like room no doubt would have stood in murky darkness upon a time, now it was resplendent. Greek Fire lanterns adorned the walls and ceilings, chief of which were several large chandeliers hung from tree-sized rafters on high. The windowless walls were constructed from massive stones, and the huge double doors behind them appeared to be of solid cast-iron and could be barred, though any such bar was missing. The whole building itself was disconnected from any others in the palace. Should anything go amiss within, it was the ideal containment. It also meant there was no hope of any secret passageway or other means in or out, especially with the place surrounded by Janissary and other guards.

The heaviness Angelique had felt lifted as her eyes fell on a workspace set out with tables, desks and shelves of books and other odds and ends. To a rear corner was a large, brass vat with a narrow glass window that glowed red. But it was the object in the centre of the workspace that she ran to, placing a hand on it as if it were a beloved pet.

She turned and smiled at Beechworth as she caressed the crate holding the aeolipede.

"Not so disenchanted after all," Beechworth said, grinning in return.

They worked tirelessly for a time, disturbed by only physical needs, and sometimes not even that.

"Eat! And rest!" Beechworth cried out again through a mouthful of hot bread and mutton. "If nothing else, simply eat! We are fed like royalty without having to leave this space, and yet you ignore it. Not that I can recall if you actually *have* left." She ignored him. "And you really should join me in one of my several daily constitutionals."

"One does not maintain a waistline such as this by overindulging," she said in little more than a whisper, distracted by her work.

"I rather thought it was those tortuous corsets you and all the women seem to wear."

"I'm not wearing one."

Beechworth choked on his wine, though she hardly noticed, far too busy on drawing a design that she had been, admittedly, obsessed with.

"Dear lord, woman!" he said, spluttering. "Why on Earth would you tell me such a thing?"

She shrugged, then looked up from her work. "I don't believe I've worn one since my 'disappearance', actually."

Beechworth shook his head. "As open-minded as you might wish me to be, I can't fathom this line of conversation."

"Why?"

"It— It's unseemly. Speaking of a woman's underclothes so openly."

"Why? Who decides such things? Because some person somewhere decided it is *de rigueur* to wear something under ones dress it becomes law?"

He shook his head again, blinking rapidly. "Why not simply be done with it and parade about without undergarments altogether!" he said, red-faced. "Go ahead and condemn me for pontificating if you wish, but—"

"Who said I was wearing undergarments?"

He stopped his glass short of his lips, eyes wide.

She took the wine from his hand. "You really are an easy mark, James," she said, smirking and drinking her prize.

He huffed in exasperation and poured himself another. "By all means, steal my drink. I half expect you're telling the truth, though."

"Why are you so interested in what's under my dress?" She laughed as his face reddened and he stuttered.

"Y-You really are insufferable!"

She nodded and held up the faceted glassware. "I'll drink to that."

As he sliced more meat, he questioned her about the design she had been working on. She had discovered illustrations and instructions for the doomed airship, the *Piri Reis*, and put it in her mind to redesign the thing. Her argument had been twofold, that they were expected to produce results, and that they were currently idle. Whilst she had been deep within that work, Beechworth had been tasked with sourcing any readily available parts for both the airship and another aeolipede.

"It really is most fascinating and ingenious," she said as she strode about, almost spilling her wine as she gesticulated. "It was well known that when Greek Fire comes into contact with water it reacts. But an Arabian gentleman discovered that it creates great quantities of hydrogen, which is what they believe also makes it so formidable in maritime warfare, feeding the fires."

"You don't say?" Beechworth said drolly. She knew she had told him this already, but he humoured her, nonetheless.

"Quite so. He then found a way to harness the gas, and in turn used it for a balloon. Of course, it took them almost this long to culminate all the discoveries into a fully realised airship. But then, they did not have access to—" She stopped as he chuckled. "What?"

"You. You're quite amusing when distracted. Normally, I dare say I would not be able to sneak up on you. Now, I could very well have left the room, had a nap, and I do believe I would have returned to find you much the same, walking about still talking to yourself at length."

Her free hand fell to her hip. "If your implication is that I am without all of my senses then—"

He raised his hands with a fervent shake of his head. "Quite the contrary. I find it endearing when I encounter someone with such a passion for something."

After a liberal gulp of wine she glared back. "You're mocking me."

"Damnation, woman. Why on Earth would I mock you?" He put the carving knife down gently after folding several pieces of meat onto a fresh plate and setting it down for her. "I've seen what you can do, after all."

One of her shoulders hitched slightly. He had a point. On both counts. "Then, I suppose... I thank you for the compliment."

"You suppose?" His eyebrows arched and he flourished his hand at the food.

Angelique sighed as she made her way to the battered table and sat on a worn stool. "I'm not in the habit of receiving praise."

"I find that quite hard to believe."

"Because I am beautiful?" Her tone was even and unwavering. "I know I am attractive, and therefore cannot accept any words relative to that as compliment. Is that so difficult to fathom?"

"The surety you have of your own physical appearance—true or not, and somewhat unsettling by the by—" He sighed. "Be that as it may, I was not commenting on your... aesthetic qualities."

He took up an apricot, making a show of inspecting and brushing it off on his sleeve to cover his abashed countenance more than having any genuine concern over the fruit, she thought. As they both well knew, it would be perfection itself, as had been all their food.

"What then?" she said, unblinking as she waited.

"Your very nature." He counted off on his fingers as he listed. "Intellect, skill, forthrightness and, damn it, yes even your moral compass, such as it is."

Her knife and fork quietened. "Most only see the exterior, and the shell I've meticulously cultivated. Or, of course, my *actions*."

"Then they are—and I say this with the utmost experience—the worse off for their presumptions. You are an extraordinary person." He stood and walked to gaze from the doorway, hands clasped at the small of his back, apricot still held in one. He stood in the bright sunlight, casting a long shadow.

He was, of course, right in his earlier summations. She had almost forgotten what it was like to simply enjoy the open air and natural warmth after her new-found passion for engineering. Even she needed to take time from the work every now and then.

Just when she thought she might join Beechworth for his next walk, a man strode brusquely around the corner of the heavy doors, almost knocking both himself and Beechworth over.

On instinct, Angelique slid an old drawing of the *Piri Reis* over her own design.

The stranger looked Beechworth up and down with a sharp nod, then did the same with Angelique. "You are the British?" he said, his accent light and tongue forming exact, clear wording as if he had practised at great length.

"What of it?" Beechworth scowled suspiciously at the man.

"Remzi *Ağa*." The man thrust his open hand at Beechworth, his fingers and thumb rigid, almost mechanical in their placement.

Beechworth offered his own before realising the apricot was still in its grasp. As he fumbled it to his offhand, the man grew impatient and instead marched around him to Angelique and repeated the motion.

She was already standing and at the ready as Remzi reached her, which appeared to please the man greatly. "A pleasure, sir," she said, nodding sharply and giving a small curtsy.

Beechworth approached quickly from the doorway. "That still does not explain—"

Remzi turned on him. "I am the new chief engineer."

"New chief engineer?" Beechworth said, puzzled. "What happened to, uh..."

"Sallettin Ağa," Remzi said. "The Sultan decided I would be better suited. How is your work progressing on Sultan Orhan's aeolipede and airship?" Remzi's gaze came to a rest the drawing of the airship she had covered her own with.

The man was more mechanical than the machinery in the room, his head darting about as if clockwork. Indeed, from the few astounding mechanical limbs she had seen, he could well be.

Her smile, as small as it had been, grew smaller yet as the man rotated his grip so his hand was dominant to Beechworth's, as men of power were often wont to do. As much as she despised the manoeuvre, she was far more focused upon a large ring on his finger. More rather, upon the ornate gear and sword engraved on its face and emblazoned with jewels.

"A pleasure, indeed," she said to herself, grinning.

CHAPTER SEVENTEEN

"Well?" Remzi Agha said, glancing back and forth as he waited for an answer? "Your progress?"

"Remzi Agha, we—" Beechworth said, stopping and raising his brows as he spotted the same Iron Clockwork ring Angelique had. "I, err... That is to say... We are still in the planning phase of both vehicles, and—"

Remzi's face finally showed some emotion as his features twisted into a barely restrained sneer. He turned his hawkish face to Beechworth. "You are only starting?"

Beechworth made no attempt to hold his own emotion in check as he bit back in annoyance. "Yes, we have only just started. Again. Perhaps you may have heard of my sister's abduction? And the deaths of several people, your own predecessor included?"

Remzi's face went through a series of changes as it attempted to find an expression to settle on. Before it could do so, or the man utter another syllable, Angelique interceded.

"It's quite alright, James." Remzi turned from Beechworth and trained his dark, beady eyes on her. "*Ağa*," she said, tone soft yet devoid of emotion, much as the engineer himself spoke. "I had been devising the most grand designs in my mind before my abduction, but in truth I cannot quite bring my mind to stillness after my... ordeal." She fluttered her eyes closed, her lips pressing tight as her chest hitched.

"I imagine that it was quite..."

The man seemed to not have the words for it. Not because he was lost in empathy, she suspected, but totally devoid of it. If Angelique did not know better, she would have thought the man to be more a Mechanical Turk than the chess-playing puppet she had acquired.

"Harrowing," she said, nodding, then changed tack. "But not because my... *person* was in jeopardy." She watched the man keenly and noted that, as she suspected, he did not react a jot to her allusion of lost chastity at the hands of brutes. "More than that, my mind was in peril." She congratulated herself as she saw the man's eyes narrow and his head cock.

"How so?"

"Forgive me. I did not make my meaning clear. Not my mind, per se, but rather its contents. My greatest fear was that all the creations I had in mind, and those yet to be conceived, would be blotted from the pages of time and lost forever." The man frowned deeply. "Oh, I know this makes me sound terribly conceited, to speak of myself as if some grand master, however—"

"No," Remzi said. "I know this fear greatly. The thought that you will not be able to complete your work, that there is not—"

"Enough time in the world. Yes!" Angelique nodded, her eyes wide now in fervour, matching the man's.

Beechworth watched the two of them in silent awe before raising a questioning brow at her. She made a small motion with her hand, hoping he would stay quiet.

Remzi gave a single curt nod, followed by several softer motions of his head, and she knew that she had his measure. Or at the least enough of it that she could work her way into his graces, perhaps, and learn something of this Iron Clockwork.

"While I was serving on steamships," he said, his voice not so much softer, but less intense, "I had this fear many times in battle." He stepped to her then and put a hand on her shoulder, as if she were a fellow comrade.

She shook her head and put on a plagued expression. "How does one move past such fear to continue working?" She glanced up at him.

"Every man has his own way."

"I wish I had map... Or schematic to such a solution," she said, giving a weak smile.

He smiled in return. It was a strange expression on his face, as if someone had pulled the wrong lever and not quite moved his features into the correct configuration.

"How did you find yours, *Ağa*?"

"The same way most men do," he said, giving her shoulder two hearty thumps. "At the bottom of a bottle." He pulled his hand away to his waistcoat and slipped an ornate watch with Ottoman artistry from its pocket. Thumbing the release on its crown, the chain tethering it giving a soft rattle, he checked the time with a quick glance before snapping the timepiece closed and slipping it away with practiced precision. "Speaking of which, I must bid you a good night, Miss Katherine." He gave her a sharp nod.

She returned the gesture. "I do so hope it does not take many bottles to quench the flames of these thoughts. I'm afraid I don't have quite the constitution for it and rarely take drink."

"Yes," Beechworth said, clearing his throat softly. "A little tipple and I'm afraid our Katherine is away with the faeries."

"Quite apt," Remzi said. He frowned and waved his hand in the air when they both frowned. "Faeries. You are working on a flying ship. Many see that just as magical, and cursed."

"Yes. I suppose it is apt," Angelique said, giving the smallest of smiles to which Remzi merely nodded as if he again approved.

"I shall return in a week's time. May Allah guide your hands." He nodded to them both and left the workshop.

Beechworth waited a good while before opening his mouth to speak, only to be silenced by Angelique's raised index finger in the air. He waited while she moved to the doorway and let out a bird call which echoed through the room.

Beechworth opened his mouth, and she repeated the earlier motion. A return call came, the same she'd made but in reverse.

"May I speak now?" He said tersely, to which she nodded. "First, what the devil was all that bird calling about?"

"I was signalling to Hideyoshi, or one of his watchers, that he is to be marked as a target." Beechworth paled and she cut him off once again with a raised hand. "For pursuit, not assassination."

Beechworth harrumphed in response. "I was not suggesting you were going to have the man killed. You saw his ring?"

She smirked. "How could I miss it?"

"Are you going to start talking about hammers and flowers again, or tell me what you are thinking?"

"No, but if I were, then I am very much the rose and he would be a very large nail in that simile."

Beechworth arched his brows and sighed, nodding. "You're not wrong there. The man was as immovable as a statue."

"But a statue that likes his drink," she said as she moved to her workbench

Beechworth grinned.

She briefly wondered when she had moved from thinking of it as *the* workbench to hers. As temporary as it was to be, it was indeed hers. She had set everything up just how she liked it. A pity it would have to end, she mused as she uncovered her sketch. She looked it over with satisfaction and beckoned Beechworth.

"It's quite magnificent." He shook his head. "Though I have to wonder how such a thing, of metal and wood and whatnot, can possibly be capable of flight."

"Science, James. Science."

"Damn science," he said. "You'll not catch me flying about in such a contraption."

"I am afraid, brother dearest, as a purported man of science in this endeavour that you will more than likely have to."

Beechworth sighed. "I was rather afraid you were going to say that." He took a bite from the apricot still nestled in his hand, and shook his head. "So, what are we to do with our new target?"

"We? *We* continue to do what we have. We work, and wait for news."

True to his word, Remzi reappeared a week later to see their progress, of which Angelique had made great strides but was still unwilling to share and had again hidden. The Chief Engineer was so bound by the strictures of time that she correctly predicted the man would visit at precisely the same hour.

"How come the designs?" he said, wasting little time on greetings, and none on pleasantries.

"We've made great progress," she said, and laid out a drawing.

"Very good," Remzi said, inspecting the design. "Sultan Orhan will be most pleased. To that end, he has ordered that a contingent of workers be made available to begin construction immediately."

Beechworth's eyes grew wide. "Construction?"

"Is something the matter?" Remzi turned to him, face wrinkled in distaste. "First you tell me you are on track and now—"

"No," Angelique interjected. "We simply wish to ensure that everything is meticulous."

"Yes!" Beechworth said, enthused now. "And I can scarcely believe that such a day has come. I know we did not invent the airship, but to build one for the Sultan—"

Remzi's eyes creased in annoyance as he shook his head, waving Beechworth silent. "Yes, yes. It is an absolute honour for you. I understand. Ensure everything is in order by Friday."

"Friday?" Angelique did her best not to sound overly curious. "May I ask why then?"

"Because Fridays are an auspicious day. And the Sultan wishes it. There is no higher reason than that in all the empire." Remzi turned on his heel. "Friday," he said over his shoulder, and promptly took his leave.

"Whatever is the matter?" Beechworth asked Angelique when she had remained in deep contemplation after Remzi's departure.

Angelique started a Greek Fire engine powered mechanical hammer to cover their words and feigned working a piece of brass.

"That man is very odd, Beechworth," she said in a low voice, looking up to see Beechworth scowling at her.

"He seems a dangerous fellow. That's probably it."

"No. I've known many a truly dangerous man, and he does not strike me as one of them."

Beechworth's brow furrowed in surprise. "No? He's very much like all the dangerous blighters I've ever met. And I have met a few myself, you know. Some even before I'd met you."

"No doubt," she said, grinning. "But I agree with your comment wholeheartedly."

"Eh?" His brow creased. "For heaven's sake, please do make sense. Do you agree with me or not?"

"Yes."

He nodded in triumph.

"But only your expression of him *appearing* to be a dangerous man."

"God's blood, woman. You'll be the death of me by vexation if not by action. Do, please, explain."

"Something about the man is completely off. For one, he acts very stiffly when in our company, yet Hideyoshi and his spies report he drinks like a fish and cavorts quite raucously."

"I've known many a man who was the same, also. That is no indication of his being good or otherwise."

"Perhaps, but what of his perusal of the plans for the airship and aeolipede?"

"What of it?" Beechworth shook his head, rubbing at his eyes, his voice drained of energy. "This one is new," he said, tapping it. "I saw you draw it myself."

"The aeolipede design is a wholesale replica of the same thing we showed him a week ago, with only minor changes. The one of the airship, the exact same one."

Beechworth let out a hiss of air from his nostrils in a sigh. "Either I am overly tired or you are not explaining yourself properly."

"A man that knows his business, as the paramount engineer of an empire should, would know at a glance that no progress has been made at all. Yet he stood here, before us, pleased as Punch." Her words gave Beechworth pause and she knew that he finally understood.

"And..." He spoke slowly, hesitant. "What are we to make of this?"

Angelique sighed. "If my assumption is correct, that he is every bit the puppet as the Mechanical Turk that allowed our passage to Istanbul."

"Well, how on earth are we to determine whether that is the case while cooped up here? All your brother has been able to learn of the man by having him followed is that he enjoys women and a tipple. A military man? Little mystery there."

"Perhaps, then, it is time we broadened our search area."

"Eh? I don't follow."

"You will soon enough, my dear Beechworth," she said, grinning.

Beechworth sighed. "I am entirely beginning to dread that smile of yours."

Well into the night in the middle of the week, Hideyoshi slipped into the workshop through one of the vented windows on high. He dropped near-silent to the floor.

Beechworth watched him open-mouthed. "If I hadn't seen you with my own eyes and now been somewhat used to it, I think I would have died of fright!"

Hideyoshi grinned.

Angelique hurried to his side. "What news, little brother?"

"Nothing tangible, I'm afraid," Hideyoshi said, his voice almost as soft as his footfalls as he took position hiding behind a bookshelf and she perused the tomes.

"Well, tell us anyway," Beechworth all but snapped. He frowned. "Apologies. I'm rather at the end of my tether."

"What's wrong with your... *partner*?" Hideyoshi said tersely in Japanese.

"James does not deal well with little rest," she said, replying in English with a smirk. "Much like yourself, brother." She stopped Hideyoshi with a raised hand before he could further protest. "Despite his rudeness, do please tell us what, if anything, you've found."

Another frown creased Hideyoshi's brow. "I always find something. What that is in this case though... I'm afraid it may amount to no more than simple gossip. Remzi does little work. The majority of his time is spent meeting other Janissary at coffee and drinking houses. The latter more so."

"He frequents them, then?" Beechworth asked.

"Frequents?" Hideyoshi said with snort. "He never seems to leave."

"A very cautious fellow then," Angelique said. Her lips pursed in thought.

"What do you mean?" Beechworth looked to her for answer, then back to Hideyoshi when none came.

Hideyoshi shook his head. "He lives in the larger establishments, moving from one to the next, never visiting the same one constantly. It's very odd."

"How is that odd?" Beechworth said. "I've known men who moved from inn to inn for a spell, all of those attached to drinking establishments."

"You're forgetting, James," Angelique said, still in thought. "This is not Britain. There are no taverns with sleeping quarters. And why, even if there were such a thing here, would an officer and chief engineer of the Ottoman Empire choose to stay in such a place when he has access to palatial housing?"

Beechworth frowned. "No. I take your point." He pulled at his moustache. "He's in hiding then. There's nothing else for it."

"He is the bait in a trap," Hideyoshi said without interest, staring at her prone face, the way he always did when he was trying to decipher her thoughts.

"Let us leave that aside for the moment," she said after a time, then turned to Hideyoshi. "Tell us the rest."

He let out a deep sigh, which she ignored. "I started to ask about after Remzi, and watched from afar as he cavorted with woman after woman. The drink always flows freely for him and his companions, wherever they go."

"Do we know any of these companions?" Beechworth said.

Hideyoshi shook his head. "I have seen them about, but they are not involved in palace affairs. They are lower ranking Janissary soldiers of little importance."

"Well that certainly makes little sense," Beechworth said. "Any officer or official worth his salt would not be caught dead fraternising with those lower than their office. I'm certain it's the same here."

He was right. It was unseemly. It was the same everywhere she had been, and she was certain the Turks were no different.

His thoughts on the matter were moot though as Angelique pushed on. "Women you say?"

"Many," Hideyoshi said. "Despite what you told me of him and suspected."

"Eh?" Beechworth said, glancing at her. "You've told me no theories on his womanising."

"Because, dear James, I thought perhaps our dear Chief Engineer rather had leanings in the opposite direction in regard to such matters."

Beechworth's frown deepened before his brows elevated in understanding. "Ah."

"Indeed. But it seems that idea is without merit."

"Perhaps not," Beechworth said. "I have met officers, who were purported to prefer the company of young gentlemen, and many of them did their utmost to exhibit their fondness for the feminine form. Even going so far as to marry. Allegedly, of course."

"Of course," she said, giving him a wry smile. "And well done for managing to speak on the matter without any discomfort." Beechworth harrumphed and turned from her. "That may well be a possibility. But something tells me his subterfuge is far more sinister. I am certain he is Iron Clockwork, in whatever small degree."

"Could he be their leader?" Hideyoshi said. "Remember Sanada San?"

Angelique rolled her widening eyes. "How could I forget."

Beechworth cast them both a questioning gaze.

"Sanada San was an old drunk in a nearby village," Angelique said. "A feeble looking, foolish old man. Or so everyone thought. As it happened, he was a highly trained assassin from the Iga's rival, the Kōga clan."

Beechworth cocked an eyebrow, crossing his arms. "The devil you say."

"Yes," Hideyoshi said. "That was the exact name we gave him after he killed half a dozen of our men less than half his age, then escaped without a trace after being discovered. The Devil Sanada."

"Apparent age," Angelique said, correcting him. "I still submit he was younger, though probably not by much. A master of disguise."

Beechworth sighed, uncrossed his arms and leaned forward. "All very interesting, however..." He rolled his hand in the air.

"Quite right," Angelique said, and turned back to her brother. "Is that all?"

"The only other things I could find out were stories about this Iron Clockwork. Rumours of Asena and a plot to discredit the Janissary and the Sultan in order to take over. And those that had even heard the whisper of the name were few and far between."

"Well," Beechworth said. "If *I* were plotting to overthrow an empire from within, that would be the path I followed. The blighters have the means and access to Greek Fire and all."

"Perhaps," Angelique said. She sat in thought, biting her lip. Then, without warning, she leapt to her feet and beckoned them to follow.

"What are you about now?" Beechworth said, looking to Hideyoshi, who merely shrugged.

"Why, did you not wish me to go for more constitutionals? We're simply going on an evening stroll."

Hideyoshi sighed and scratched out something on a piece of paper and handed it to her before climbing into the rafters. "I'll find us some disguises and meet you there."

Beechworth's moustache rippled as his mouth turned down. "I do not think this a wise move."

"I agree," Angelique said. "I must change my attire accordingly."

He harrumphed as she returned from the small ante-room they used for changing. "Blasted if I know why," he said under his breath. "You appear much the same as when you left."

"I needed to... accessorise. One never knows when there will be a to-do. Now, do come along, James." She shot him a smirk.

"And there it is. That blasted smile again." Letting his head fall back, he sighed, then followed her out of the workshop.

CHAPTER EIGHTEEN

Beechworth followed Angelique, casting furtive glances about as they made their way through the dark Istanbul night. They found Hideyoshi precisely where his instructions said he would be, in the tree darkened courtyard of a house nearby a *meyhane* —popular drinking establishments used by the soldiers and Janissary— that Remzi had purportedly entered. Hideyoshi handed over a bundle to each of them.

"What in the devil are these clothes?" Beechworth said as he unpacked his.

He raised his eyebrows as Angelique held a threadbare green costume aloft and spat angry Japanese at her brother before she strode into the shadows to change.

Beechworth turned to her brother. "Need I ask?"

"Best if you don't," Hideyoshi said. "But it was the only way I could find to get all three of us inside."

Angelique let out an angry tirade of invectives in Japanese, French and English as she changed, not quite hidden by the darkness.

Hideyoshi assisted Beechworth. The both of them did their utmost to ensure their gazes did not fall in the darkened corner where she angrily threw both limbs and clothing about. Once done, they stood in silence with their backs to her, waiting.

A little while later, Angelique rounded them in a huff. She had left the shadows, though her expression remained dark. "Not. One. Word!" she said as she led the way around the courtyard.

Beechworth fell back and glanced at Hideyoshi, who was smirking. "Why is she so angry?" he whispered. He assumed it had nothing to do with the attire, such as it was, given her thoughts on such things.

"You will soon see." Hideyoshi chuckled as he made to catch up to her.

"I'm not entirely sure I wish to," Beechworth muttered then hurried after him.

Sound and light grew from the drinking establishment as they neared. Beechworth was quite used to raucous taverns from his time in the army, though the music... it was all rather more exotic, to say the least. Not to mention the smells.

Angelique led them to a darkened back entrance, and Hideyoshi hefted a box onto Beechworth's shoulder before taking one of his own and hiding his face behind it. In the dark and shadows, one might mistake him for a Turk, but up close and lit, he clearly was not.

Angelique looked them both over, then with a frown, dipped her hand into an amphora of sorts and rubbed a liquid on her fingers, then grabbed Beechworth's moustache.

"What the devil—" he snapped under his breath.

She hissed for him to be silent as she worked the oil into, then curled the ends of his moustache. "There. You are much more the part now."

Beechworth grunted in indignation as she picked up and cradled a melon of some sort, hunching over it as she carried it away. "One simply does *not* touch another man's facial hair without permission!"

Hideyoshi shrugged as he passed. "If I am ever able to grow one, I will let you know whether I agree."

Clenching his jaw, Beechworth followed.

They slipped into a line of several other similarly dressed men entering the building from the side. As soon as they were through the door, Beechworth was hit by the aroma of charcoal fire and grilled meat—which served to overpower that of the oil in his moustache—laughter, clapping, and music.

Hideyoshi unburdened himself of his load and Beechworth followed suit, gazing around in awe. The air was thick with smoke, both from sizzling meats and vegetables, and exhaled by the men all around them. They sat on the floor on cushions and rugs, tall, coloured bottles filled partially with water at their feet. It certainly was not the first time he had seen someone smoking tobacco from a hookah, but the sheer number of them surprised Beechworth. Some of them, he now noticed, were women.

They were all dressed much as Angelique, though the majority of them were on their feet and not sitting with the soldiers. A great many of them tended to the men, serving food and drink, talking with them. But a great many were at an altogether more energetic activity.

"Dancers?" Beechworth said, doing his best not to gawp, and admittedly failing.

The dancers gyrated and twirled, shaking their hips, which set golden ornamentations on golden belts swaying. He was mesmerised by the display, so much so that he became uncomfortable and had to force his gaze elsewhere. He turned back to his companions.

Angelique was gone.

Hideyoshi moved to a dark corner and beckoned him to follow, and Beechworth slunk to the same position, attempting nonchalance as he went. Upon reaching Hideyoshi's side, he searched the area.

"Where is—"

Hideyoshi pointed to a figure in green, a diaphanous veil covering the lower half of her face and a head dress and similar veil draped over her hair, much like the majority of the women in the establishment. And much like a great many of them, she was dancing.

"Good Lord," Beechworth said, his eyes widening of their own accord.

Hideyoshi nodded slowly, his expression as disbelieving as Beechworth felt. "I told you, you would see."

Angelique moved lithely through the crowd, hips swaying, shoulders dipping and rising as her arms swayed to the music.

At least, Beechworth assumed, she believed she was. In reality, her movements were as awkward as Beechworth felt watching her attempt them.

"Does she not know how to..." Hideyoshi shook his head. "But... she has all those skills!"

"Tenshi could slay half the men in this room like a demon in under a minute without soiling her clothing and look like an angel while doing so. But ask her to dance..." He waved a hand in her direction. "Thankfully, she is more adept at the deadlier arts, and subterfuge."

As Hideyoshi had said, no one had noticed. It was either that, Beechworth thought, or they were in high enough spirits as to ignore her. In any case, she was a vision, which clearly helped her situation. Before he could feel conflicted about finding her attractive, Beechworth was led by Hideyoshi's hand on his shoulder around the room to a darkened position behind some barrels under a mezzanine.

As he once again located Angelique in the busy, smoke filled room, he saw she was moving straight for Remzi. He prayed her disguise would be sufficient enough to protect her.

CHAPTER NINETEEN

Angelique had little time to remain angry with her brother at his choice of disguise. They were soon within the establishment and both she, and everything around her, was moving too fast.

If she thought of it as a battle, she should be able to cross the room to the new Chief Engineer Remzi—such as he was—without drawing too much attention to herself. She hoped. There was no way of knowing but to try, though she had never once needed to gyrate her hips in such a fashion in any battle. With the number of foreign women around her, however, she need not have worried. Some of them were as equally out of place as herself, if not more. At least, she conceded, she had chosen to be here and was more than capable of defending herself. What she would not give to train them in the ways of the *Kōga*.

Feigning tripping from her own clumsiness, Angelique fell at Remzi's feet, laughing raucously and grabbing his thigh as she listed to the side and fell to a kneel. One hand fell to her chest.

Remzi smiled at her. Though to call the lecherous expression he wore a smile was far too polite. Curling his moustache, eyes and face red with alcohol consumption, he smirked. "And who might you be?" he said in slurred Turkish, staring with desire.

Thankfully, among the more deadly of the 'accessories' she had thought to bring on this mission was also a small container of face cream and powder, and a rouge and lip stain. With her hair worn down, and the veils and beauty creams, he would hopefully not recognise her. Then there was the matter of her voice.

Laughing into the back of her hand, Angelique looked away. "Melek," she said in a falsetto, using the Turkish name for angel and affecting an accent.

"Melek!" Remzi said. "How appropriate, then, that Allah had you fall from heaven to my feet."

Nauseated, Angelique repeated her coquettish laugh, turning her head in the other direction.

"Here we go then, little angel," Remzi said, and passed her his glass of *rakı*.

Taking the glass, her stomach churning once more, she raised her veil enough to put the glass to her lips and mimed drinking. His eyes narrowed as he watched her. Angelique quickly took the hose from a hookah—*nargile* as the Turks called it—imbibed an amount, and lifted her veil to blow a ring of smoke at the man, which greatly amused him. He laughed uproariously and bade her repeat the trick several more times.

This, Angelique noted, was most definitely not the same man that had visited her and Beechworth in their workshop.

They shared more words, more drink and smoke—thankfully from a fresh glass, and a pipe of her own—before a strange expression came over Remzi.

He straightened, his eyes hooded and lips pressing together then quivering slightly. His brows creased as he attempted to focus on her face. "I cannot help but feel I know you from somewhere, my little angel."

She saw Beechworth and Hideyoshi tense. With another practiced glance away and girlish chuckle behind her hand, she signalled her brother to stay where he was, and he held Beechworth back.

When she turned back, Remzi was once again casting a lustful gaze on her. "You are the most beautiful creature that Allah has ever created to grace this soil," Remzi said, all but muttering.

"You are too kind, *Ağa*," she said with good humour, though her fingers clenched.

How many times had she imagined similar words being used on her mother all those years before to get into her good graces, and more. Had her father been a man such as Remzi?

She stood and grabbed Remzi's hand, tugged on it. "Dance with me," she said, grabbing a carafe of fresh liquor from a passing serving girl and filling his glass as she did so.

He was all too happy to oblige her, his body and head swaying and teetering drunkenly, his hands dancing to their own tune as they roamed over her. But this was the sort of dancing she excelled at and she easily deflected his drunken advances and manoeuvred him around the room toward the barrels her brother and Beechworth had taken position behind.

"I will end him," Hideyoshi said close to Angelique's ear.

"Later," she said with cheer, keeping her voice low, but loud enough that Hideyoshi would hear.

"Oh, indeed!" Remzi said in answer. "Though not too much later, eh, little one?" Without warning, Remzi lunged at Angelique wrapping one arm about her lower waist while the other held her torso. He lunged his wet, puckered lips toward her face.

Her evasions had worked for a time, but he had now grown tired of the game, and as much as she would have delighted in knocking him senseless and could have done so dozens of times over, she had to persevere.

Unfortunately, Remzi had other plans. Using brute force, he dug his fingers into her hips and pulled, then slipped an arm behind her to lock her to his groin. Before she could feign surprise and escape, he did the unexpected and tore off her veil.

His hand tightened on the gossamer cloth as recognition came and he pushed Angelique away. "You?" Remzi said, sneering.

As Beechworth and Hideyoshi sprung to action, the doors to the meyhane burst open and sent up a clamour through the place. Women went screaming and drunken Janissary bellowed as the musicians threw down their instruments to replace them with daggers and swords. Chaos ensued as more men tore through both the *meyhane* and the Janissary, baying like wolves as their enemies fell.

"Asena!" someone shouted, the cry taken up by others. Steel clashed. Red death hissed. Men fell. Angelique lost sight of Remzi in the ensuing chaos, and then Hideyoshi as he availed himself of a sword from a fallen man, and Beechworth as he took up a Greek Fire pistol, both of them disappearing into the fray. Dressed as they were, in the same garb as the Asena insurgent musicians, Angelique lost them in the mayhem. They, too, were now targets for the Janissary, who fired indiscriminately at anyone not in uniform or a dancing girl.

A man fell mid-charge as Beechworth appeared and discharged his weapon into an Janissary's chest, then trained the weapon on the back of another soldier who had taken a dancing girl as a human shield. But Angelique beat him to it. Her own recovered sword flashed and the Janissary fell off the woman, who turned to thank her saviour, only to stop in open-mouthed shock, more than likely at finding a woman wielding a blade.

"Run!" Angelique yelled at the woman, who did not hesitate in doing so.

Where before the air was aromatic, now it hung with the reek of blood and acrid stench of burnt human flesh from Greek Fire shot. The melodic sounds of earlier had been lost to the painful cacophony of war.

Angelique spun as someone pressed to her back, stopping her blade when she found it was Beechworth.

"I thought I had left such battlefields behind!" he shouted.

"You!" came a shout from the crazed Remzi as he ran at her, breaking them apart.

The man had clearly never been an engineer, but he was most definitely a soldier, trained in swordsmanship. What he lacked in her speed and finesse he made up for in ferocity and strength, though he had also consumed a prodigious amount of drink.

Angelique kept apace of the man and was clearly his better, keeping him occupied more than battling him so as to potentially capture and question him. But in the bedlam, a man fell to her rear and crashed into her legs, knocking her down.

Remzi did not waste the opening.

Thankfully, neither did Beechworth.

He lined up Remzi for as brief a moment as it took to extend his arm, and pulled the trigger. The Greek Fire pistol let out an explosive hiss and jet of steam from its barrel.

Remzi bellowed as the shot hit its mark and he dropped his sword to clutch at his forearm. Just as quickly, he released the wound as Greek Fire scorched his palm. He turned on Beechworth with a snarl, forgetting his battle with Angelique and intent on his new target.

But both Remzi and Angelique's plans were quashed as Asena surrounded them all, pistols and blades pointed at their chests and heads.

Remzi turned and spat at Angelique. Her foot lashed out with a swift kick to a knee and he buckled. As he fell, she kicked once more and caught him in a far more tender spot. Remzi bent double with a whoop as his hands fell to his groin and he dropped to kneel, struggling to catch his breath. His trembling face was beet red as he attempted to turn it to Angelique as she stood, and spittle stained his lip as he attempted to speak.

"You—" he managed.

Angelique took his head in her hand, then wrenched it toward her with a cry as her knee flew forward and caught him in the face. He fell instantly, groaning in semi-consciousness and bleeding from both nostrils and lip. Angelique straightened what little there was of her clothing, then turned a circle to take in the Asena men, who stared at her with a mixture of confusion, admiration, and no little fear.

"Well then," she said, grinning. "Take us to your leader."

Angelique swayed about, her eyes closed in silent meditation as the covered horse drawn caravan bumped and shook at every stone in the road. Conversely, Beechworth had shifted about at almost every jolt and complained about his rump.

"How it can both hurt and be numbed all at once I simply cannot fathom! Nor how the two of you can sit so impeccably calm."

"Unspoken words are the flowers of silence," Hideyoshi said, causing Angelique to let out a small laugh.

It was one of their grandfather's sayings when they had spoken too much or fought.

"You two and your blasted flowers," Beechworth said. "You do realise who has us."

She let out a sigh, her eyes still shuttered. "We are well aware, James."

"Jolly good, then. I thought you had perhaps forgotten given your calm natures."

"I have not," she said. "Perhaps you have, though?"

"Eh?" Beechworth said. "What are you—" He let out a huff. "I suppose I will find out soon enough."

"Sit by a river long enough," Hideyoshi said, "and your enemies bodies will float by."

"Well..." Beechworth said. "I suppose I should be thankful, at least, that there are no flowers involved in this saying. Though sitting and waiting for your enemies to simply drop dead into a river hardly seems prudent."

Angelique chuckled and opened her eyes. "No. I much prefer to be the one causing their prone corpses to fall in. But for now... look and listen, James. Perhaps you, too, will see what we have seen."

Beechworth opened his mouth. Then shut it and nodded. Returning the nod, Angelique closed her eyes once more.

They sat in much the same manner for the rest of the journey. Angelique allowed herself to lilt like grass in a soft summer breeze, as she knew her brother would. She also knew that Beechworth would be doing his best to emulate them, his knuckles white as he gripped the edge of the wooden bench beneath him to ensure he didn't slide off, and would attempt to listen.

Would he be capable of seeing though, she wondered?

"These men..." Beechworth said after a time, his voice barely above a whisper. "They're a tired and sorry looking lot. In the heat of things, they appeared the very picture of the vicious warriors we encountered in the stadium. Now, though..."

Now, they were a rag-tag group of broken men. No furs secreting armour, or quality Japanese steel. And, more importantly to Angelique, no Greek Fire syringe devices that caused them to become berserkers. Whoever they were, and wherever it was that these men were taking them, she had little doubt they had no relation to the men that had attacked the stadium and brought the *Piri Reis* crashing from the skies.

Just as importantly, they were most assuredly Asena.

Eventually, one of the Asena men keeping watch from a small window on the lone door to the cart hastily threw the door open and jumped down to walk, stretching as he did so. Another man followed, but none of the others. They were obviously senior, which was why they rode by the door so as to leave all the quicker.

When the caravan came to a stop, Angelique and the others were gruffly prodded to move out, a guard between them as they exited single file. Once outside, another carriage came alongside them. The guest of honour within was revealed as the canvas over the cart was yanked away.

When she had last seen him, Remzi had lay unconscious on the floor of the cage, gagged and bound by both his wrists and ankles behind his back. Now, he was awake, and only his hands were tied and affixed to the bars. He flexed his hands, eyes transfixed on Angelique through the bars, their dark pits boring into hers.

Angelique blew him a kiss. "I do so hope you enjoy your new quarters, Remzi *Ağa*."

"Yes, by all means," Beechworth muttered to her. "Let us further anger the captive bear by prodding it."

Ignoring him, Angelique took in the Asena encampment. It was set in a clearing before a rock outcrop, several small fires lit around them. In the rock face itself were dozens of caves that also emitted firelight.

"This hardly seems like the headquarters of a highly organised revolutionary army," Beechworth said.

"Finally, he sees," Hideyoshi said.

"I believe I saw quite some time—" One of the men guarding them yelled. "I assume that means he wishes me to be—" The man yelled again, pulling his sword a fraction. "Right then. Jolly good."

Several shadows withdrew from the murkiness of the main cave and moved towards them. Three men, leaders judging by their stature and the way the other men stood taller as they approached. They quickly spoke to the man who had first exited the caravan, waving his hand at them before drawing the men's attention to Remzi.

Nodding, one of the men, resembling a bear more than a wolf, neared. He was the very personification of the creature. His hulking arms and chest, where it was visible, was covered with hair. Nothing in his weight suggested a hint of rotundity, however, his arms solid as carved oak, his height also harking to that giant of trees.

"You *Ingliz*?" the man said. Beechworth nodded. "Why you fight *Yeniçeri*? And look *Romani*?"

"Are you the Asena leader?" Angelique said, boldly stepping in.

The man turned to her. "I Yunus. I leader." The man placed his closed fist against his chest. "Who you?"

"My name is Angelique Morreaux, and—"

Hideyoshi took a step forward. "*Oi*, Tenshi!"

"Now steady on—" Beechworth added.

Angelique put up her hand to quiet them. "We were sent here in secret by the King of England himself, and by the United States of America, to put an end to the tyranny of the Iron Clockwork. *Demir Düzenek*."

Yunus's eyes widened at the last words, then narrowed. "How you know *Demir Düzenek*? I no believe you!"

Remzi yelled at length to Yunus from his wheeled cell in Turkish.

"If my Turkish is correct," Angelique said, "Remzi is telling you that *we* are in fact your enemies and from the Iron Clockwork, and not he. But believe me when I say this, Yunus... That man is *Demir Düzenek*. He openly wears a ring with their symbol. Like you, we believe the Janissary, through *Demir Düzenek* and whoever their leader may be, is in control of the Ottoman Empire. And I believe Remzi knows who that individual is."

Yunus' eyes moved across the three of them before settling on Remzi. After several moments, he motioned to the caged man with his head and two of the Asena men ran to retrieve him, cutting the ropes at his wrists and the bars, then manhandling him toward Yunus.

Remzi stood tall to stare into Yunus's eyes, though he had to look up to do so. Yunus stared back before moving aside to speak to the commanders of the attack at length.

Remzi turned to sneer at Angelique. "I will make sure you lose your pretty head and make it a prize for myself."

"And that, Remzi, if that even is your real name, is—"

Remzi turned in anger, she thought to lash out, but instead his hand went to his ring. He was stopped suddenly by a lightning fast strike from Hideyoshi. One moment Remzi was standing there, full of anger, and the next he fell to his knees, his already split lip bleeding afresh.

The guards grabbed Hideyoshi to contain him, but he stood calmly and eyed the man on the ground as he scrambled, again for his ring. Angelique dashed forward and brought her heel down on his wrist. He made to fight back, but Yunus and the other men ran over to interject. Yunus gruffly called out for his men to take Remzi away, and she stepped back as they picked him up by his armpits and began dragging him away.

"Wait!" Angelique said. "His ring!"

"You stupid whore!" Remzi shouted in Turkish.

"*Durun*," Yunus called, the men stopping. He grabbed Remzi's hand and lifted it to stare at the ring on Remzi's finger, face twisting in disgust. With a sharp yank, Yunus pulled the ring free and flicked his head at the cell.

The men dragged Remzi away, kicking and screaming the whole way in protest.

"You are not *Demir Düzenek*," Yunus said to Angelique, showing her the ring. The Iron Clockwork insignia had been pulled back on a hinge, and within a hollow was a small needle, and an all too familiar red glow. "You I believe."

"It's one of those blasted injectors!" Beechworth said.

"Indeed," Angelique said. "And, I believe, Asena has men in the palace, and Yunus here must have been informed that we are in fact the Sultan's foreign engineers."

"Yes," Yunus said simply, snapping the lid of the Greek Fire injector ring closed. "My men say you are." He pointed at Hideyoshi then and wagged his finger. "But this *Japon*—"

"Hideyoshi is my brother," Angelique said.

Yunus frowned. "Brother?"

"It is a very long, complicated story, Yunus *Efendi*. However, I can assure you that he is with us and not aligned with either empire. He arrived at the same time we did but has been in hiding, assisting us."

Yunus eyed Hideyoshi warily. "We are knowing of the things the *Japon* do for *Yeniçeri*. Their magic assassin."

"Then you must know, too, that if he had wanted to either escape, or kill you all, he could have easily done so." Yunus nodded, conceding the fact. "Splendid. We are all on the same page then. Now... What are we to do next?"

"Next?" Yunus frowned. "You, no next. Asena will break Remzi and *Demir Düzenek*, and bring real Sultan back to *Topkapı*."

"You and whose army?" Beechworth muttered, drawing Yunus's ire.

"I'm afraid Beechworth is correct," Angelique said. "You simply do not have the manpower to overthrow the Janissary and their Iron Clockwork. If my guess is correct, you were lucky when you obtained that Greek Fire to perpetrate the attack on the city and destroy their airship. However, luck won't always be on your—"

"Attack city? Airship?" Yunus snorted in derision and his men chuckled and shook their heads. Yunus threw up his hands and turned them around their encampment. "We no attack. We no have Greek Fire."

"Are you quite certain?" Beechworth said. "Because, many men claiming to be Asena brutally attacked Istanbul."

"We are protect people, not hurt!" Yunus said to Beechworth in anger, puffing with pride and indignation. "This... This is *Yeniçeri* trick!"

Angelique nodded and closed her eyes as her head fell back, her hands balling at her sides. "I had suspected as much, but I am very glad to hear it confirmed."

She let out a hiss of frustration before lunging at one of Yunus' men at her side and snatched his stolen Greek Fire pistol from his belt.

The men reacted, but too slowly. By the time they had pulled their weapons, though, they saw what she was about and relaxed somewhat.

Angelique marched to Remzi's cell atop its cart, stepped up and threw open the door and stepped within. She pointed the barrel of the pistol squarely at Remzi's face. When he screwed up his face and opened his mouth to bark something at her, she jammed the end of the weapon into the dark hole. She raised a finger to her lips, and waited until he had stopped simpering.

"Good boy," she said, smirking. "Now... You are going to be an even better boy by telling me everything you know about Iron Clockwork. Their command structure, your contacts... and every little detail you know of the attack they staged in Istanbul. Aren't you?"

Remzi, his eyes lit by the Greek Fire, very slowly nodded.

CHAPTER TWENTY

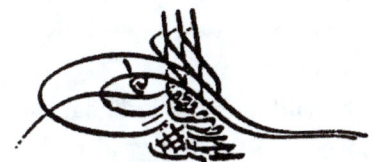

I t had been weeks since their meeting with Yunus and Asena—
who had secreted them back into Istanbul and allowed them to
steal back into the palace via the only hidden passage they had
found leading in and out of Topkapi. Since then, the metal workers
promised by the Sultan had been sent to assist with construction of
the new airship and newly designed aeolipede, and had made short
work of Angelique's designs. They continued work on the near
completed airship, and had handed over the body and parts of the two-
wheeled vehicle for Angelique and Beechworth to complete the finer
work required.

This also allowed Angelique to make modifications that had not
been on the plans, both to the new and existing vehicles. With little to
do in the time the workers had spent modelling and casting and weld-
ing, she had pored over every tome and manuscript she could get her
hands on. There was an abundance of information the Ottomans had
perfected or otherwise appropriated since discovering the secrets of
Greek Fire. Luckily, the large workshop had its own library, and the
volumes held there were all of the latest advancements. Through her
years of preparation for this day she had learnt what Turkish she could,
piecemeal as it was, and she utilised that knowledge to best effect.

Now though, as she strode excitedly about the large open area within the steamworks, her nose constantly in some book or scroll, all plans of her revenge had taken secondary consideration.

"By my stars, James!" she said, returning to Beechworth's side, a rolled copy of a plan in hand, sputtering as she swung to point it at the airship. "Do you even see what they are about?"

He sat up from where he was slouched in a chair and lifted his head. "Oh, you're speaking to me now, are you?"

"These so-called experts," she shouted the words over the loud hammering, "are attempting to use the entirely wrong gauge and brass alloy on the Greek Fire feed!"

"The philistines," he said in mock indignation.

"Quite so!" She turned to see him still reclined, feet outstretched and arms crossed over his chest. "This is no joking matter, Beechworth. A mistake like that and we won't need any outside influence to blow up our airship. Not to mention ourselves."

He pulled his legs in quickly and sat up, continuing the movement to stand and taking a firm hold of her arm. "Calm yourself, *sister*. You just used my real name aloud."

Heat crept into her face. "Apologies. I believe I may have become rather invested in this project of ours."

"Yes, I do believe you rather might have." He led her to his vacated seat and set her down. "I understand. I truly do. You're very excited about something for the first time in your life. But—" She made to protest. He ceased her argument with a single raised finger. "You think I do not know, but I do. You grew up dreaming of revenge and had no opportunity to be either a little girl or young woman. Now you have been given more toys than you know what to do with."

Angelique thought on that, conceding with a shrug. "Perhaps."

"Believe me, I have seen it before." He took her hands and gave the back of them a well-meaning pat. "Count your blessings that you came upon your passion so young and that you're not..." He searched for something tactful.

"A doddering old maid?" She gave him a grin, slipping a hand free and returning the affectionate gesture on the back of his own hand. "How lucky I am to have such a wise and protective older brother."

"That you are," Beechworth said, standing from his squat. "And your wise old brother also prescribes sustenance to keep your strength up, as he is positively famished."

She gave a curt nod and stood. "I'll send one of the lads to—"

"The devil you will. You need some fresh air. Yes. Food and a constitutional."

"But what about the—"

He caught her as she was turning to fuss over the work. "They'll manage. Or, send them away as well. I'm sure they'll listen to you and be appreciative of the rest. They almost treat you like you were the blasted Sultan as it is."

Angelique hoisted a heavy rusted wrench and gave him a smirk. She hammered the tool on the topmost railing of the platform that had once belonged to the poor Abdulrahman and yelled at the men to down tools and go for some rest until their return.

"I must admit," Angelique said, her pace and voice languid as they walked arm in arm through the gardens in the sunlight, "I really was quite hungry and had not noticed."

"I should think so. You've hardly touched a scrap since you started work on that blasted airship." Beechworth pulled a leaf from a nearby low hanging tree and spun it with his free hand by the stem. With a sharp twist, he released the leaf and watched it flutter to the ground. "I'm still not at all convinced about this flying business, you know."

"Where's your sense of adventure, James?"

"I rather think even you've had more than enough adventure for a lifetime here in Istanbul."

She laughed, her spirits also refuelled by the food and walk. "I rather think you're right. Not about adventure, no, but finding my passion."

"Ah. I was rather hoping you would say we could pack it all up and go home now."

Her hand playfully swatted at his arm. "I've decided I'll continue working in this same fashion once we've successfully finished up here. Set up shop. I have a goodly amount hoarded away—"

"Please do not tell me where or how it was obtained."

"—*and*, I will make an honest life of it."

"Well, I am jolly well pleased to hear it. Perhaps you'll set up shop in London? Come by to dinner once in a while with Abbie and I?"

"You know, James, I think I may. Since escaping the Iga, London always was my—"

A commotion ahead preceded by a booming voice left the both of them in momentary confusion until Angelique realised what was happening and pulled Beechworth back, telling him to cast his gaze down.

A procession of Janissary about him, Sultan Orhan strode up to the two and bid them to look up. "How goes my airship and..." He waved his hand in the air, prompting them.

"Er," Beechworth said. "Aeolipede, your highness?"

"Yes. Aeolipede. When will I be able to ride her?" The sultan was gazing at Angelique as he said the last and heat instantly flushed her chest and swiftly made its way to her head.

Beechworth jumped to answer before she could react. "Soon, your highness. We are making the final adjustments and necessary finery befitting the Sultan of the Ottoman empire."

"Excellent. I look forward to the first time on her. After many firsts, you would think a man would tire, do you not, Mister Farnsworth?"

The corners of Beechworth's eyes wrinkled as his mouth turned down. "I would not presume to know your high—"

"Come, join me in the gardens," Orhan said with no pretence of it being an offer.

"As you wish, your highness." Beechworth bowed his head as they awaited the procession to move ahead of them.

Angelique's fingers tightened around the imagined dagger in her hand as she stared intently on the spot on Orhan's back she wished to plunge it .

"Behave yourself," Beechworth said quietly.

She forced a smile. "Whatever do you mean? I am always well behaved."

Upon reaching the end of the path, they arrived at a section of the gardens they had never before been allowed into. The snake-like coil of people ahead of them slithered off the stone path onto grass. As they reached the garden two guards at the rear of the retinue turned about and stopped them. Or, more to the point, stopped Angelique. One of the men pointed to her then around a hedge while the other ushered Beechworth to follow the line, all of them men.

Beechworth stopped to glance over his shoulder.

"It's all right, James," Angelique said. "I'm sure I'll have a much lovelier time by myself."

He nodded, and mouthed '*be careful*', as he was led away.

Angelique ambled along past the hedge, and was surprised to find a colourful group gathered behind a translucent wall of what appeared from a distance to be silk. This was clearly where she was to go. She would have continued on back to the workshop instead, but the voices of women, children and music intrigued her. She had seldom seen either about the palace, other than slaves.

The moment of curiosity was replaced with awkward silence when all parties stopped to stare first at one another, then Angelique as she stepped into the enclosed area, attempting to stare back at multiple sets of eyes of varying ages. The moment was broken when a small girl walked to her, her large dark eyes staring up at Angelique. An odd sensation filled her chest with a grip on her heart when she realised the girl's features and colouring were a mirror of her own.

The girl lifted her hands toward Angelique.

Angelique's mouth slid open. "I'm... not at all sure what you want," she said to the girl in English, causing her to cock her head in curiosity. "Children have never been my strong point. Though you appear to be the only one interested in giving me the time of day." She decided to err on the side of caution and do nothing.

The girl attempted to climb her skirts.

With a smirk, Angelique hoisted the girl up, off-kilter at first before righting the child with what she hoped was the proper grip.

"You're a persistent and brave little one. I like that, *ma chère*. You remind me of myself. Perhaps we are even distantly related?"

The music resumed. A woman beckoned from the seated group. As she did, she told Angelique to join them in Turkish. Feigning not understanding and smiling politely, Angelique nevertheless walked across and did her best to appear every bit the odd Englishwoman as she handed the child back to what she assumed was the mother.

"What a darling little thing," Angelique said, again in English, before doing her best to sit demurely on the floor cushions and fussed about with her skirts. Any other time she would have hoisted them up or done away with them altogether. She ate a little food, sipped at tea prepared in the local style, clapped out of time to the music, refused to dance—though the last was not a feint. She'd had more than enough dancing to last her a lifetime. All the while, she listened intently to the women. Though their conversations were of no tactical importance, she found herself hanging on their every word.

Shortly after, another woman walked into the area and joined them, sending her son off to play. She smiled and spoke to Angelique in broken but passable English. "You are the *İngliz* woman?"

"Yes. I am."

"I Yasemin," the woman said.

"Katherine. Katherine Farnsworth." The woman smiled again and nodded awkwardly. "Are you all... wives?"

"Wife. Yes," Yasemin said. "And mother." She indicated the women around her and the children with a slow, sweeping arc of her hand.

"To... To the Sultan?"

Yasemin grew uncomfortable at the line of questioning. "Yes," she said, her tone non-committal. She fell silent after that, her expression as bereft of her initial warmth as her words had been.

"It must all be very exciting," Angelique said after a lengthy silence. "Living in a palace and treated like royalty."

Yasemin's eyes held pain and loss. Eyes that quickly flitted to her son. The corners of her mouth turned down ever so slightly before she turned and smiled quickly once more. "Yes. We very lucky." She stood. "Please. Excuse."

Yasemin did not speak to her again after that. She saw to her son, feeding the child though not eating herself before they snuck away.

Something was very odd here. And it was not solely with Yasemin. The children played gaily enough, and their mothers doted on them. Despite the cheery dispositions and music, however, Angelique could not help but feel it was all an act. But for whom? Her? If so, for what purpose?

There was a flash of heat in her chest, as if Greek Fire had been poured down her gullet.

Did that little insect of a would-be emperor seek to make her part of his harem? Was this all to impress her? It was common knowledge that women were compelled to be consorts to the Sultan, and not only those under Ottoman rule. If it came to that, at least she knew that she, Beechworth and Hideyoshi would have more than a fair shot at escape once she gutted the boy. Hideyoshi would more than likely take his head to ensure it did not even come to that. Beechworth would argue diplomatically before joining the fray.

"Bless them both," she said to herself.

She stood and made to leave. The guards that had been posted at the edge of the lawn, their brawny backs to her and the women, had other ideas however, and blocked her path. Foregoing her previous act, she sat in a most unceremonious manner, grabbed up a large bunch of grapes and began plucking them with vehemence.

She would likely be here a while.

"You have completely and utterly lost your senses. You do know that, don't you?"

Angelique waved Beechworth off. "If you were a woman you might understand, Beechworth. But as you are clearly not—"

"Absolutely stark raving mad!"

"You've seen the way he looks at me."

"Surely not. He wouldn't possibly dare."

"Why? Because we're a diplomatic envoy? The leaders of some foreign nation? Allies of the Ottomans?"

Beechworth made to speak, his mouth closing as his eyebrows quickly rose and fell. "You've a point."

"Or several."

"Nevertheless, you're risking your life, not to mention mine and Mister Hideyoshi's, as well as the plan."

"Oh, take your plan and—" Calming herself, she let out a sigh. "Please, James... If my brother turns up, do not make mention of this to him."

"You're afraid he will exacerbate things."

"If you think our plan will be in jeopardy from my skulking about the palace dressed like an assassin, wait until you see my brother on a sullen rampage."

Beechworth smirked, the line of his mouth becoming grim when she did not. "Do be careful."

"You're not going to argue with me further?"

"There's no bloody point. You're going to go either way so... Go. But be safe."

She nodded and climbed out the window.

The night air was still, yet cool, which was a boon considering the stifling black outfit Angelique wore. With thoughts plaguing her of the boy Orhan making designs on her or any other woman he pleased, she had made up her mind to go hunting when sleep had not come. One way or another, she would find a way to stop the boy and the Iron Clockwork who had put him there.

Entering the harem quarters, Angelique found them oddly empty. Half her body was through the opening on high that served as a window when she saw a young woman hurry out in an outfit made for the Turkish baths, various bathing paraphernalia in hand.

Slipping out again, Angelique padded swiftly across the rooftop, stopping several times to skulk in shadows from guards on battlements and various other vantage points. She knew where the *hammam* was. She was also fairly certain no guards would be allowed anywhere near it. That same burning anger she had felt when she thought of Orhan, returned. It would not be to protect the women, but to protect the Sultan's property.

One battle at a time.

Contrary to her belief, she found four men guarding the rooftop, and each seemed to be as wary of the others as they were of themselves. All four men were so intent on the other three, their eyes flitting back and forth in fear, that she was easily able to find a means of ingress. She wished she hadn't when she emerged from the tight space some time later. Nothing had been learnt apart from what she already suspected, and that dressing so heavily in a steam filled Turkish bath was ill advised. The late-night air was all the cooler as she crept away, the sweat and steam on her skin bringing a chill.

She made her way to her true target, the Sultan's private quarters. He was a braggart, so he may well be talking of any plans he had at length with whatever advisers counselled him on such things. She was not even sure Kerim Ağa had been replaced, but it was more than likely given what she had seen of the boy. Perhaps such things were not widely and publicly announced as a new vizier.

From the information that Hideyoshi had provided, Angelique knew the Sultan's quarters were palatial in themselves, containing room upon room and varying offices. She also knew that the area was tightly guarded. Her best option was to sneak in and through an adjoining area.

She perched herself in a dark niche like a gargoyle and observed the palace for a good thirty minutes. Her muscles had been conditioned by the exercises she had learnt in Japan as a young girl, a practice she had kept up over the years. It was one of the primary reasons she had been so successful in her short but illustrious career as a thief. The others, of course, were her keen intellect and instinct.

Using all of those facets now, she chose the perfect moment to emerge and run near-silent across a fairly precarious wall top with a vertiginous and fatal drop. She dropped to lay flat on her stomach moments before the guard she knew would be coming back appeared on a rooftop. Then, just as quickly, she was up again when the man continued on his rounds. She dropped from the height to grab onto a ledge and kicked through sheer curtains into an office, dropping to a crouch and seeking immediate cover. If one was quick enough and the room dark, most people would fool themselves into believing they had seen nothing. As it was, the room was empty, but voices from nearby echoed about it.

Hasan strode into the room and was in a heated but whispered argument with another man. She could not make out who the other party was without giving herself away. Examining the room, and given it was Hasan who had entered, this had to be the Grand Vizier's office.

There was a rumble through the floor and the scrape of stone. Was it a hidden passage? Or perhaps a hidden compartment.

Hasan muttered something. The shifting stone sounded again. Hasan's voice became more animated, and Angelique more brave—or foolhardy, if one asked Beechworth.

Hasan slapped a wad of papers into a Janissary's hands as the hidden safe behind him closed. He held his finger up at the man. "Make sure you get this to the men on the double. I want no more stupid mistakes! And make sure you take care of the English."

The man saluted and the two exited the room after Hasan made the man repeat his orders.

Long after they had departed, Angelique stood and inspected the hidden compartment, concealed beneath blue and white ornate tiles, though she could not locate a mechanism to access it.

What would Beechworth make of their luck now?

CHAPTER TWENTY-ONE

"Y ou went where?" Beechworth said, positively fuming when Angelique told him over breakfast what she had witnessed.

"Did you not hear me? Shall I tell you again?" she said, casually pouring herself tea.

"Oh, I heard you. I simply wanted to ensure that I was not still asleep, or perhaps as insane as you appear to be!"

"Do calm down and have some bread and cheese, James."

"Bread and—" His face was a blank, almost as white as the cheese she offered him.

"It's quite delightful, though I must warn you, a little on the salty side. Your thoroughly British palate might not tolerate it."

"I take it all back. It is clearly *I* who is addled of the mind."

"I'll have my tailor craft you a resplendent straitjacket when we return to England, monogrammed with your initials. But for now, do try to keep up." She proceeded to refill his teacup. "Hasan. Janissary. Clandestine meeting. Secret compartment."

With an indignant harrumph, Beechworth adjusted his waistcoat and crossed his arms. "Yes, well, it all rather makes sense doesn't it."

"In hindsight, you mean? Certainly. But I take your point. They most certainly would have engineered things in the background to put him where he is, as close to the Sultan as possible. Though I fail to see how he could possibly have coordinated affairs from abroad."

"Perhaps he was looking in on their troops in China? A routine inspection? If you leave men in far-flung places alone too long, they begin to get ideas."

"Perhaps. It's all rather too coincidental for me, though. And I don't believe in such things."

"Much like your coming upon this information, you mean?"

Tapping her spoon on the brim of her cup, she smiled. "*Touché.*"

"Whatever the case, we finally have a prime suspect." Beechworth played with the cup on its saucer before lifting it. "You seemed to like the fellow. If it comes to it will you be able to..." Skirting the subject, he took a lingering sip.

"Without question." She stared at him over her own drink, unblinking. "I know my speaking of death is... unceremonious to you, however—"

"Unceremonious? My dear, if the beggar is all we suspect, then by all means, dispatch the fellow. These Clockwork blighters have been behind a great many deaths, quite a few of which have been around our persons."

"I'm glad to hear you say that. If my brother and I should fall—"

He raised his tea. "You need not fear. I was a soldier, remember? I will do my level best. Though I may only be making a valiant attempt to avenge your deaths by throwing mine away."

She gave a laugh. "What more could a lady ask?"

After they had consumed their breakfast, Beechworth poured more tea for himself, Angelique declining his offer with shake of her head and fingers covering her cup.

Taking his seat once more, he stirred in sugar. "So," he said, spoon still clinking on the china. "We've yet to confirm that Hasan is indeed our culprit. Did you at least uncover anything on whether the Sultan has set his eye on you?"

Her previous jubilation faded. "I'm quite keenly aware of his eyes on me, thank you for the reminder. As to your question, no. I spent more time in attempting to access the hidden compartment, which I deemed to be a far more pressing matter."

Beechworth frowned. "Still, it would be quite an... inconvenient distraction."

"Quite," she said, glaring at him.

Clearing his throat, he finally pulled the spoon from his tea. "So then, given you were unsuccessful in opening this compartment, any thoughts as to how we go about catching Hasan? Force his hand perhaps? Set a ruse to catch him red-handed?"

She stood to pace and pursed her lips in thought. "We may well have to. From what I could make out, Hasan is not at all amused by our antics and is ready to make his own move, and soon. We will have to be far more vigilant."

"Easier said than done when in the heart of enemy territory. If only we had further allies close at hand, or somewhere we could fortify."

Stopping in her tracks, she turned to him, grinning. "You are a genius, James."

"Blast. There's that look again." Beechworth took a large gulp of his beverage. "No use wasting tea if I am to die in one of your schemes."

"No need for that just yet, I should think."

"Oh? What should I do then? Take up crochet?"

She shot him a smirk as she made briskly for the door. "If you like. But it would be far more useful if you packed our bags while I made preparations." She stopped in the doorway. "Oh, and do try not to rifle through my belongings this time."

Beechworth woke with a start from his dream, or more correctly nightmare if his fitful movements and mutterings were anything to go by. Angelique was quite certain he had mentioned something about trenches and called for a Brigadier. He picked himself up from the floor, recognition dawning as he blinked away the visions the calamitous thundering in the workshop had no doubt inspired.

"Rise and shine, James," Angelique said from where she stood, arms akimbo at the railing and surveying the work continuing on the airship.

He palmed his face and rubbed at it. "Why on Earth I let you convince me to take residence here in the blasted steamworks—"

"Because, dear James, you knew as well as I this is by far the most secure location, at least for us."

From up on their perch in the centre of the steamworks, they could survey all entrances, and Hideyoshi had taken to resting in the massive rafters above. They took watch in shifts, which was something Beechworth said he had become accustomed to in war time. That, too, had more than likely brought on his nightmares.

Grunting, Beechworth sat up from the uncomfortable seat and stretched then stood. "True enough. But could we not have arranged some civilised bedding?" Picking at some bread, he pulled a face. "It's gone stale," he said, complaining. "Well, it takes the taste of metal and oil away, I suppose. Marginally. When will the young lad—"

"Timur."

"Whatever his name is, when will he be fetching the food?"

She turned about, grinning wide. "He shouldn't be too long, I should think. Here. Let me brew you a tea."

Angelique all but dashed to the workbench that also served as their dining table. Atop it, she had set up an urn of copper under which she had constructed a burner. She picked up a lump of coal over which she dripped a small amount of Greek Fire. The dark rock was then placed within a heavy mortar and crushed to a coarse powder which she scooped into the burner. With a drop of water, the burner began to smoke and sizzle, then emit a jet of orange-red flame which she concentrated by closing or opening an adjustable brass cowl by a rod.

"Shouldn't be long," she said.

Half an hour later, Beechworth finally had his food and another tea.

"I do feel sorry for your Abbie," she said, smirking as he drank his tea and sighed.

"And why is that?"

"You're an incorrigible curmudgeon first thing in the morning. At least until you get some food and tea."

"Yes, well... I'll be the first to admit I am more in spirits after a good cup and—"

The large doors to the steamworks groaned and squealed as they were opened. Angelique and Beechworth leapt to see what was going on, his good cheer quickly evaporating as men filed in. It was Hasan and a small contingent of Janissary. Beechworth strode quickly behind her down the steps to the floor, Angelique telling the men to continue working.

"To what do we owe this pleasure, Hasan Pasha," she called out, her voice carrying. High above, a shadow among the rafters shifted closer as Hasan strode with purpose to meet them.

"So good to see you, Pasha," Beechworth said, being as cordial as he could. She noticed him glance to the rafters also, a mere flick of his eyes. Was Beechworth thinking as she was? Here, standing below a highly trained assassin, was the penultimate power in the Ottoman Empire. Or most powerful, and their true target, if their hypothesis proved true. How easy it would be to snuff him out.

"Sultan Orhan bade me to check on the progress of your work," Hasan said, inspecting the airship. "Splendid."

"Thank you, Pasha," Angelique said, her voice flat.

"But I thought it would be more finished by now."

"We are working on installing the balloon and Greek Fire chamber today," she said, eyes as unwavering as her words.

"Why has it taken so long?" The man turned on her now, eyes narrowed. "Is that not why you both relocated to the steamworks?"

He had come to interrogate them. Perhaps in response to Remzi's disappearance since they'd had no solid information as to his whereabouts. Could he know they were responsible, or suspect?

"I'm afraid that's all rather my fault," Angelique said.

"Oh? Explain."

"I'll do better. I'll show you." Angelique strode past the man.

"After you," Beechworth said, showing the way.

"I'll follow you, James, if you don't mind," Hasan said, sounding rather irritable.

With a nod, Beechworth followed after her, around the airship to a large wooden crate that stood as tall as her waist. She reached in pulled forth a deep red material and held it out for the Vizier.

Intrigued, Hasan stepped forward and took the material between finger and thumb. "What is this?" he said, frowning.

"Rubberised silk," Angelique said proudly. "I had intended on it being a surprise gift for the Sultan."

"Rubberised silk?" Hasan said in awe.

"Indeed," Beechworth said, giving the Vizier a grin. "This material is far lighter and stronger than the heavier stuff that the *Piri Reis* had been held aloft with. It is also a resplendent red due to your amazing Greek Fire vulcanised rubber."

Hasan nodded. "Yes. Sultan Orhan will be *very* pleased with this. But he does not like surprises." He looked up at the both of them. "And neither do I."

Angelique shrugged and nodded her head in resignation. "So be it."

"Speaking of our ruler, Sultan Orhan wishes you to re-double your efforts to finish the machines."

"Re-double?" Beechworth said, indignant.

Hasan flashed him an angry glare. "Is there an issue? Can you not do as you are commanded? Is my English not to your standards, Mister Farnsworth?"

Beechworth stuttered, holding up his hands.

The Grand Vizier sneered as he stepped close to Beechworth. "I can find someone who can both finish the machines *and* follow orders without question if you are not up to the task."

Angelique stepped forward. "Forgive my brother, Pasha. He is simply tired. Of course we can. However..."

Hasan's glare became angrier as he turned it to her. "However?"

"It is nothing major, I can assure you. We will simply need additional hands."

"We can spare no other engineers. You will have to make do."

"Oh, we have plenty of engineers, Pasha. What we could use more of, however, are general labourers. Men to do the heavy lifting, which, as you might imagine, not all engineers are suited for. Our increased work pace has rather worn these poor chaps out, I'm afraid, and their expertise cannot be best put to use due to that."

Hasan considered the men, then the airship. "Done. I will have someone—"

"No need, Pasha," she said, smiling. "One of the men knows just the able bodies who can assist us, who are also currently in need of employ. All we would require is the funds and they can be here today."

Hasan narrowed his eyes at her. "What of the gold and jewels we sent for your work?"

"Ah... Yes that. I'm afraid I rather used it all." She held up a hand to stop the tirade she anticipated. As she did, she walked to another rubberised silk cloth, this one black. "A test sheet," she said in response to his frown. "It came in very handy." The sheet billowed as she snatched it back to reveal a dazzling gilded aeolipede.

"The Sultan's machine!" Hasan was so shocked the anger slid from his face as quickly as the coated silk cloth had from the metal monster.

And monster it was. It stood longer than the original, its gnarled wheels also larger, covered with a thick layer of the red rubber. Its body was inset with jewels, and on the Greek Fire tank—which was now moved mid body before the rider and contained an exposed glass canister which shone—was the hand etched *tuğra* of the Sultan.

"Sultan Orhan will be—" The vizier had no words. All he could do was stare and shake his head.

"If he is rendered as mute as you are, Pasha, that will be more than enough for me," Angelique said, smirking lopsidedly.

Hasan walked around the machine, surveying its every inch. "It is ready to be presented to him, then?"

"Er... not quite," Beechworth said, sheepish.

Hasan glanced up. "Is it not operational?"

"We believe so," Angelique said. "I'm afraid we've not tested it."

The Vizier's brows crashed together. "What?"

"To test it we would need to ride it," she said.

"And we weren't at all sure we should," Beechworth added.

Hasan snorted through his nose in anger. "You cannot expect the Sultan to ride this first. What if it should explode? Unacceptable! I demand you test it at once."

"At once?" Angelique said, the corner of her mouth hitching ever so slightly higher.

The two vehicles roared around the steamworks building, emitting the sound of a thousand angry tigers. Hasan rode the original—though now heavily modified—aeolipede while Angelique, who laughed like a madwoman in the clutches of an opiated rapture, took the newer. She'd had to convince Hasan to allow her, saying there were features that needed checking to ensure it was safe.

As they came to a stop, Hasan had forgotten all his arguments to the contrary, harrowed and out of breath as he lifted the protective workman's goggles she'd given him from his eyes.

"*Allahım!*" Hasan said, calling out for his god, head and hands shaking. "That is the scariest and most exhilarating thing I have ever done!"

"Exhilarating, yes," Angelique said, fighting to keep the larger golden machine upright.

Beechworth ran to assist, holding it as she lowered a stand to hold the thing standing. She kicked her foot over the machine, turning to sit side-saddle.

"Imagine what an army could do with a fleet of these!" Hasan said, eyes wide and face blank as he stared at the thing beneath him.

Beechworth and Angelique shared a look of concern.

"I'm sure once Sultan Orhan sees it and rides it for himself, he will be of the same mind," Beechworth ventured.

Hasan drew himself from his reverie. "I'm certain he will." With a quick glance and a kick of a booted foot, he had the stand for his own aeolipede down and was dismounting. He pulled the goggles off completely and swatted them into his palm repeatedly in deep thought. "A pity that Remzi Ağa could not be here to see it," he said, the words pointedly directed at them.

"A pity indeed." Angelique's words held not a bit of remorse, and she had to fight to not smile.

"Has there been any news of the poor man's whereabouts?" Beechworth said, inserting himself verbally between the two. "Any advancement in the search for him, or the blighters that killed all those men?"

Hasan's eyes didn't move as he observed Beechworth. "Nothing. No. News has been surprisingly lax of late."

"It does seem that the seats of power in the Ottoman empire are rather dangerous places to be," Angelique said. "Do you not think so, Pasha?"

Now the man's piercing stare shifted to Angelique. "It would appear that way. Though, there are seats which are not directly in the path of danger."

Angelique returned the man's intense scrutiny. "Hidden seats, you mean?" She feigned alarm. "Surely not."

Hasan's lips split in a leery smile. "It would be wise to not speak openly of such things, Miss Farnsworth. There are those that would... take affront."

She fluttered her eyelashes. "Perish the thought."

Hasan took a step forward. "And those that take affront are wont to take drastic measures."

Beechworth puffed up, his face wrinkling. "Hasan Pasha, I'm not at all sure what you are—"

The vizier held up a finger, straight as an iron rod, his face just as implacable. "I know," he said in a whisper. Donning his goggles, Hasan threw his leg over the aeolipede and dropped onto its seat. He reached for the handles and turned to them. "I know!" he said again, now with an angry growl. "Watch your steps."

With that, the machine leapt to life and he sped off in a cloud of dust and steam for the large doors of the steelworks.

"That's it," Beechworth exclaimed. "We're done for."

"You really are one for histrionics, James."

"Histri— Did you not hear the madman? A threat, as plain as day. As plain as..." He threw his hand up in search.

"The moustache on your face?" Angelique offered.

"Is now really the time for glib remarks?" Beechworth's frustration overflowed. "What are we to do?" he said, voice gruff.

"I agree, he was being rather open with his threats. And yet..."

Beechworth's face underwent several convulsions as he waited for her to continue, breath streaming ragged from his nostrils. "Yes?" he blurted. "And yet?"

She turned on him in exasperation. Then turned again and kicked the golden monstrosity behind her, loosing a tirade of invectives in both French and Japanese, sometimes intertwined. "This is not what I imagined my revenge would be! Stranded in this land with insurmountable odds!"

Taking a deep breath, Beechworth released it in a hissing sigh. "I rather thought you enjoyed playing such games," he said, mustering as much mirth as he could.

She threw her head back and gave a sharp laugh before letting her face fall with a sigh of her own, hands limp at her waist. "You know me too well. Too well by far." Placing her hands on the cushioned seat, she kicked her leg over and leapt aboard. As she set the machine thundering back to the steamworks, she called over her shoulder. "If Hasan doesn't kill us first for knowing too much, I may well have to do you in myself for it."

"At least wait until after my wedding, eh?" he called as he jogged after her, causing her to laugh louder.

Crestfallen, they saw the Vizier and his men off and resumed work on the airship. Beechworth had made the analogy that her seemingly limitless reserves of energy had diminished, dimming like a lantern low on oil.

"Thank you for not taking the metaphor to its logical conclusion of a guttering flame," she said, to which he had no response.

Both their dispositions improved as the general labourers appeared, bringing with them carts of supplies. They were so overjoyed, in fact, that they went down and shook hands with every single man, bantering with joyful reinvigoration.

"Jolly good of you to come," Beechworth said, firmly gripping the hand of the large man leading the group.

"Yes," Angelique said, smiling. "We really do need all the help we can get."

Yunus' hulking, muscular, barrel of a chest shook as he chuckled. "We ready to work," Yunus said, indicating the rest of the Asena men around him.

"Excellent," Angelique said. "Let the games begin."

CHAPTER TWENTY-TWO

As work on the airship neared completion—Yunus and his men providing the much needed physical prowess the majority of engineers lacked, and at the ready to engage on their true purpose at a moment's notice—Angelique seemed to become melancholic and prone to silent deliberations. When Beechworth queried Hideyoshi on the matter, the young man nodded.

"This means far more to Tenshi than a mere mission or simple revenge. Things are coming to a head, and without the personal closure she so desperately seeks."

At first, Beechworth had wholeheartedly agreed with that diagnosis. Who better to know than her adoptive brother, he had thought. And, he assumed with a high degree of certainty, that would be a great portion of her ruminations. Yet he could not help but feel that something else weighed heavily on her.

When he found her at night smoking a cigarette she had obtained from somewhere, stood on the highest rail of their platform, hand gracefully placed on the corner beam for balance and staring at the dirigible, he knew he had been right.

"I would offer you a penny for your thoughts," he said, "but I rather think you've pennies enough for every man here tucked away and it would be of little use to you."

Her face shifted slightly at his humour, a corner of her mouth lifting ever so slightly. "One can never have enough pennies, James," she said. Pitching the remnant of the cigarette to spiral away, she held up her thumb and finger and closed one eye to peer through the gap. "I've observed a small hole in the hull of the gondola where two brass panels don't quite meet. A penny would be just the right size to patch it."

Beechworth heard the metallic slosh of liquid in a small container and was surprised when she offered him a flask. With a few contemplative blinks, he took the liquor and had several draughts before handing it back. "Whiskey?"

"The Ottomans may control their borders tightly, but hardly hermetically."

"But where in the devil did you— Actually, I rather prefer not to know."

"A wise choice." After a small laugh, her demeanour became dour once more.

"Whatever is the matter?" Beechworth said with no little annoyance.

Tilting back the drink, she clamped shut her eyes from the burn, then shook her head. "Why, I don't know what you mean. There is absolutely nothing—"

Exhaling sharply, Beechworth mounted the bottom of the three bars forming the barrier built to prevent the long drop down onto tools, sharp and blunt alike.

"What *are* you doing, Beechworth?" she said, exasperated.

"Each time you lie to me, I shall climb one rung higher. Whether I fall and spill my brains on that anvil—" he pointed his chin at the large wedge of metal, "—or impale myself on those pipes—" he proffered his head at the items, "—is entirely up to you. So I ask once more—"

"You are a most irritating fellow, you know? I feel nothing but sympathy, and just as much *empathy*, for your wife-to-be. There is nothing at all wrong with—"

He stepped higher, tottering as his knees pressed against the topmost rail. She stared back at him, scoffing in surprise and shaking her head

"Last chance," he said.

"I don't believe for a moment that you would—"

He raised his left foot, planting his shoe firmly with a ring of metal, and eased his weight onto it. As his lowermost foot began to lift, she leapt deftly down and pulled him back.

"You are incorrigible!" she said in a low voice, her face red. "You know nothing of what you are saying, yet you insist on—"

"You are afraid," he said, his volume even lower. "Afraid you will fail, of course, that is a given. But, mostly, you are afraid that you will *succeed*."

Her mouth had become a dancing O of incredulity.

He continued before she could interject. "Because once we succeed —and mark my words, by God we will—you are afraid that you will need to become a functioning member of society. Another lamb on the straight and narrow road, following the herd, with nothing to differentiate you from the bleating masses."

The O closed to a steely line. She blinked her eyes at him violently, possibly wishing him ill because—and he knew this to be so by her murderous stare alone—he had her measure.

Her eyes fell from his. "Get some sleep, James. I feel our adventure will conclude very soon. One way or another."

Beechworth awoke to silence, which had not been the norm for in as many weeks as he could remember. Awakening stiff of muscle and aching of bone, however, was. As his eyes struggled to acclimate to the bright light, and his body creaked like a lumbering machine in need of lubrication, he felt a waft of fresh, aromatic wind on his cheek and a strange thrum in the air.

The aroma of trees, flowers, and a fresh cooked breakfast.

"If you've quite finished salivating in your sleep..." Angelique smirked at him. "We've rather got to get on with the maiden voyage."

He sat up and straightened his clothing, doing his best to surreptitiously wipe his chin. "I most certainly was *not* sali—" He ceased his emphatic denial and stood as the blood drained from his face. "I'm sorry, did you say maiden voyage?"

She turned him about by his arm, his body grudgingly following. Angelique pointed out to where the airship had been, then above them. Beechworth craned his head to take in the scene, the rush of the wind and blood in his ears somehow increasing.

A colossal aperture now stood open in the ceiling of the workshop. It was the source of the brilliant light and breeze he had noted upon awakening. Far more disconcerting, however, it was the source of the now calamitous and nightmare inducing *basso vibrato* that assaulted his ears. That sound was married with something the likes of the drone of a thousand beehives as something moved to block the sun.

"The airship!" Beechworth said in breathless wonder as it drifted into view.

The sound ceased as it manoeuvred to the centre of the large opening and proceeded to gently, but all to quickly for Beechworth's peace of mind, fall toward the dusty floor.

Whooping triumphantly, the engineers, joined by Yunus and his Asena men, ran into the building, taking up ropes that dropped from the fore and aft of the gondola to tether the thing to the stone floor.

Angelique led Beechworth down the stairs as his feet became increasingly leaden the closer they got to the infernal conveyance. "I thought long and hard on what you said last night," she said, "and you were quite correct."

"Was I?" he said with little animation, his eyes locked on the gondola and an opening door on its side.

"Yes. I *am* afraid. I've no wish for a pedestrian life. Difficult as my lot has been, I have led many grand chases and more than a little excitement. To slow down now would be anathema, and contrary to my identity."

"Indeed," he muttered. "Anathema." They were now halfway down the staircase and his stomach fluttered.

"I've also come to the conclusion," she continued, "that I have absolutely no wish to die a matronly spinster."

"Jolly good," Beechworth said, eyeing the belly of the beast.

"Neither do I have a wish to die young. To that end—" she stopped on the penultimate step and turned to face him. "I will *not* die here in Istanbul! I will also not allow you or my *other* brother to throw your lives away. I do not know how you managed it, but you measured me up. And I thank you for it." She peered at his face as he strained to looked over her shoulder at the airship. "Are you listening to me, James?"

"Eh?" He turned to her, blinking rapidly. "Yes. Yes, of course," he said, recollecting himself. "I'm awfully glad to hear you say it. And you are most very welcome."

She frowned at him. "You are mocking me."

He felt a sudden heat on his face. "Why on God's green Earth would I mock you!"

Her head rose higher and she peered down her nose at him. "You had best not be."

"Damnation, woman! Who in their right mind would mock the most dangerous person in the building?" He stepped down and turned arms crossed. "Now... are you going to take me flying in this bloody death machine before I lose my nerve?"

She grinned, then joined him and thrust her arm back into his to lead him around and face the ship. "You really are a big baby, James Nathaniel *Farns*worth."

He sighed. "You fooled me in attempt to make me braver, didn't you?"

"Fear not science, James, but instead fear the hand of man." She pointed with tip of her head to the large double doors at the front of the steamworks as, with a putter and a hissing cloud, several steam cars raced toward it.

A door on the lead steam car flew open before it lurched to a stop and Hasan climbed out to immediately stride with purpose toward them, flanked by soldiers. "What do you think—"

Angelique turned on the man. "We were merely ensuring the airship—"

"You do not have the authority to fly this vessel without—"

"And, we were not aboard it, sir!" Angelique shouted.

Hasan drew his sword, the lines ingrained in the Japanese steel flashing. Yunus rushed toward the man from the rear, though the Janissary grabbed him first and thrust him to the floor, yelling at other men as they leapt forward.

All became silent as the barrel of Hasan Pasha's pistol stopped inches from Angelique's pale forehead, and his blade at her throat.

Her eyes were as cold and hard as the steel as she pushed forward, the blade kissing her skin. "Do you intend to shoot me, Pasha, or take my head?"

"Silence," Hasan hissed, voice low and jaw clenched. Eyes not leaving hers, he waved his pistol and barked in Turkish.

Yunus began to speak, but one of the Janissary cut him short with a boot to his side. It barely moved him, and had not seemed to hurt him, but it earned his silence. The same man pointed to one of the engineers, who answered promptly.

Angelique smiled as Hasan lowered his weapons. "As I was attempting to inform you," she said, "it was *your* engineers who flew the airship. It *had* to be tested to ensure the integrity of both the balloon and its systems before its first flight proper."

"Is it finished?" Hasan snapped, his voice carrying equal amounts of threat and suspicion.

"Once we confirm there are no leaks and every connection is firmly in place—"

"Is it finished?" he all but shouted, not breaking their stare.

"Yes," Angelique conceded.

Beechworth swallowed despite the dryness of his mouth.

Finally, Hasan nodded, a smile growing on his lips. His demeanour changed once more as he barked orders around him. Soldiers and engineers alike slowly quit the building, a great many glancing back in concern, though none dared stop or question. Beechworth was not so certain about Yunus and his men, however. Though the Asena leader went quietly, he shot a confused frown at the Vizier, which gave Beechworth pause.

Hasan trained his pistol back on Angelique and indicated the open door of the airship with a flourish of the devilishly lambent pistol. "It is time for us to bring things to a close... *Mademoiselle!*"

Beechworth turned to her sharply. He knew!

"I couldn't agree more, *mon amie*," Angelique said as they were led into the gondola at gunpoint.

Never at any point in his years had the sight of plain sand been as welcome as it was now to Beechworth. His fear only grew as trees, buildings and people grew larger through the large glass portal at the fore of the craft where he was shackled to a polished brass railing. Behind him, Angelique had the controls of the airship. And behind her stood the madman Hasan—proven now without a shadow of a doubt to be their long sought out adversary—with his damnable pistol still trained on her and sword in hand.

He did not allow them to speak, as much as she had tried to engage Hasan and have him answer her questions. Although that was not entirely true. The Vizier had spoken once, threatening to throw her from the doorway if she persisted. She of course had. At which Hasan had then threatened to throw Beechworth from it instead.

The man seemed absolutely capable of committing cold, bloody murder of such a terrible degree. Though a person, Beechworth surmised as he watched the ground looming ever faster, was more liable to die of fright than the impact. As slow as they now descended, the end result was to be just as likely. Their untimely demise.

"Land inside the walls," Hasan commanded Angelique, flicking the pistol in his hand at their location.

"*Baş üstüne*," Angelique replied in Turkish with correct inflection, smirking as she turned the wheel and adjusted valves and levers. "Quite an ironic location to bring us," she said of the stadium with its ruined wall. "Unoriginal... but ironic all the same."

Hasan ignored her.

Contrary to his initial thoughts, Beechworth found the nearer their proximity to the rough floor of the stadium, the more anxiety he felt. A muted squeak escaped his fingers where they worried at the polished brass bar that ran the entire length of the window, and he clutched it as the impact of their landing shook the vessel.

"Stay where you are, Miss Morreaux," Hasan ordered, moving

around her to Beechworth. He trained the weapon on him now, and undid the shackles. "Be so kind as to open the door, Constable."

Beechworth walked around the perimeter to the door, eyeing the man warily. "How long have you known?"

"Not long enough. No more talk. Move, now!"

He closed the distance to Angelique with quick steps and manhandled her into position beside Beechworth, the Greek Fire pistol in his hand pressed to her ribs. He pushed them both from the cabin and looked about the ruins. They were alone.

Hasan did not appear to much care as he pointed his sword at the churned soil in the shadow of the balloon. "Kneel," he commanded, then sharply lifted the Greek Fire pistol to bear on Angelique. "Not you." Beechworth lowered himself warily, but he needn't have worried. Hasan's weapons were affixed on her. "Remove whatever weapons you have concealed beneath your skirts, Miss Moureaux. Toss them far away."

Angelique leant to reach under her dress. She stopped at the scrape of Hasan's boot on the sand. Hasan's pistol was aimed at her head.

"Slowly!" he said.

She eased the cord to hoist her dress, fixed it in place, produced a knife and her tiny pistol and threw them aside. Hasan motioned with the weapon and she lowered herself to join Beechworth in the dirt.

"I do not trust you," Hasan said. "Especially you, Miss Moureaux. So keep your hands up where I can see them."

"You'll get nothing from us, Hasan," she said, straightening her back. "You may as well dispatch us both here and now."

Hasan grinned, taking several steps back and forth. "Do not be so sure. I have people that will make you tell me everything from your grandmother's name to your inner most desires."

"I was rather hoping we could avoid torture," Beechworth said, attempting to jest despite the cold perspiration building at his back.

Hasan's face suddenly shifted into an animalistic rage that was out of proportion with the innocuous comment. "I told you not to move!" he shouted, his voice echoing from the walls.

Beechworth glanced to his side and saw Angelique's hand creeping into her dress.

Hasan's pacing widened, taking him out of the shadow of the airship. As he did, a bright spot of sunlight was trained on his face. He raised his sword hand, its blade flashing as he covered his face and stepped away. He spun about and blinked the blinding light from his eyes as a figure repelled from the ropes tethering the massive balloon to the gondola.

Hideyoshi kicked against the balloon and used it to spring at Hasan, his own blade in hand. But too late. Hasan had recovered, and as skilled as Hideyoshi was, it appeared he had underestimated Hasan. With great skill, the Vizier turned and swung his sword.

Hideyoshi fell to the ground into a roll, a great slash across his chest, his curved sword tumbling from his grasp.

Hasan leapt back as Angelique charged in, driving him back with a wheeling kick, and in the same moment taking up her brother's blade, a murderous glint in her eyes as she vaulted over the prostrate Hideyoshi, leaving Beechworth to tend to him.

Their swords rang as they clashed, Hasan clearly surprised by both Angelique's skill and ferocity as she drove him back, almost having his measure more than once. So much so that he sought to bring the encounter to a swift resolution. Hasan's hand was lightning as it rose, the fire spitting pistol pointed at Angelique's face. With a swift swipe, she directed the shot into the burnt remains of the stadium seats, and disarmed him of the weapon. The pistol skidded through the loose dust and both of them glanced at the thing, but it was evident from the darkening soil beneath it the fuel source had been ruptured.

They clashed again, exchanging parries before parting several paces from one another. They circled slowly, their feet almost gliding across the soil.

Hideyoshi had been right in the meyhane—*this* was Angelique's dance.

"You've studied *bujutsu*," Angelique said. "Impressive."

"*Tenshin Shōden Katori Shintō-ryū*," Hasan said proudly. "And you?"

"*Iga-ryū*." One of her shoulders hitched a quick shrug. "Amongst others."

Hasan nodded. "I thought I recognised the Iga style at the root. Possibly some form of *gōngfu* thrown in. Effective, if sloppy."

Perhaps thinking to use the sleight as an opening, Hasan attacked once more, the thrust of his blade deflected by Angelique who quickly followed with a well-placed kick to his leg, followed by a heel kick to his kidney which caused Hasan to fall back.

Hasan clutched his side, face shrivelled in pain and rage. "I will not allow you, a mere foreign girl, to sully the Ottoman empire!"

Angelique scoffed. "A bold statement coming from one such as yourself. In any case, this is also my empire!"

Hasan had the look of a man who had been forced to eat something wholly wretched. "You cannot be so mad as to believe that, whatever it was the British and Americans promised you."

"Promised?" Angelique lifted her chin. "It is my birthright!"

Beechworth glanced up at Angelique's proclamation. "Eh?"

Hasan appeared to be just as confused, not knowing whether to laugh or spit in her face.

Angelique drew out her amulet and slipped it off to hold aloft. It was now fully cleaned of its covering layer and shone brilliantly, as it had in Beechworth's nightmare. The tuğra on its surface gleamed, quite evident.

Hasan's face was etched in rage as he pointed his sword at the locket. "Thief! Where did you steal that from?"

"Steal? It was passed down to me from my mother, who received it as a parting gift from my erstwhile father, an Ottoman soldier in Japan where she was held captive. Hardly conclusive proof, I know, but nothing else fits."

Hasan's face was a mix of emotions as he ran at her, though his sword was pointed at the ground.

"Hold!" she yelled, her sword tip inches from his heart as he slid to a stop.

Ever so slowly, Hasan sheathed his blade and raised his hands, reaching one out. "May I?" She eyed him uncertainly but tossed the locket to him. Hasan inspected it minutely, shaking his head. "It is not possible!" he said, incredulous.

"And yet, there it is in your hands. And if you would be so kind?" Angelique held her hand out, and caught the chain as he threw it back. Slipping it on, she tucked it out of sight once more.

Hasan loosened the top of his shirt and drew on a chain to produce the very likeness of Angelique's pendant.

Beechworth stared in awe. "You're... also a member of the Ottoman family?"

Hasan's face was full of his internal conflict as he gave a nod.

"Then please do explain, sir," Angelique said, waving a dismissive hand in the air. "How you could *possibly* allow yourself to be the leader of the Iron Clockwork?"

"Iron Clockwork?" Hasan said, almost spitting the words. "I am not in their damnable ranks, let alone their leader! I am the leader of Asena!"

"What?" Beechworth's eyes grew wide as he leapt to his feet. "That's impossible!" he exclaimed, pointing, though Angelique and Hasan's eyes were locked on one another.

"Beechworth! My brother's wounds are—"

"Look!" Beechworth shouted, stabbing his finger at the figure entering the stadium.

Hasan and Angelique turned as Janissary streamed in to surround them. In a break through their ranks came a man atop a horse. A man Beechworth had not thought to see again, at least on this mortal coil.

"At last, I have found you, Asena dog!" the man said, spitting at Hasan's feet from his mount.

Beechworth stammered, still pointing. "K-K-Kerim Agha?"

CHAPTER TWENTY-THREE

Angelique watched Kerim as he paced with his hands behind his back before the four of them knelt on the ground, his manner officious.

"Beechworth," she said, using his real name now the jig was up. She smirked at the man parading above them. "I thought you said he was dead."

Beechworth shook his head in dismay as he held Hideyoshi up by his shoulders. "I do not understand, Kerim Ağa."

Her brother had not been mortally wounded, though the diagonal cut across his chest would leave its mark and risked infection if not treated.

"*Paşa!*" Kerim bellowed. "Kerim *Paşa!*"

"Whatever your title, I— I saw you die! Run through and through!"

Kerim leered down his hawkish nose. "All a part of my ruse to use you in aiding *Demir Düzenek* to root out the traitorous Asena. And for this, I thank you."

"You are the traitor!" Hasan spat the words at the man. "*Demir Düzenek* and the Janissary are controlling the empire. Hiding behind a boy who is not even of *Osmanlı* blood, like the cowards that you are!"

"*Osmanlı?*" Kerim smirked. "What do we care of that? What do the people of the empire even *know* of that? Whoever we say is the Sultan *is* the Sultan!" Kerim strode to Hasan and crouched to meet him eye to eye. He spied the amulet about his neck and took it up with a scoff. "Unlike you, who will never sit in *Topkapı*." Kerim stood, lifting the chain as he went. "I will bury you facing the palace, so your ghost can forever see what you could not attain."

Hasan sneered. "Then I will haunt you until you join me in the grave."

"I look forward to it," Kerim said, grinning wider. "Though I suspect you will be waiting a very long time."

"I don't suppose you will be allowing us to return to England unscathed?" Angelique said.

"I'm afraid not, Miss Morreaux," Kerim said.

"Your skills are failing you, *onee-chan*," Hideyoshi said with a grimace inducing chuckle, the pain of his most recent wound evident on his expression. "Everyone seems to know who you are."

"I also know who you are, Ishinari Hideyoshi." Kerim nodded, the grin on his lips growing with every utterance. "The Iga, and your father, will owe us a *great* many debts for your return."

With a flick of his head, Kerim's men lifted Hideyoshi and pulled him from Beechworth's grip, manacling both his wrists and ankles, clearly aware of how dangerous he was.

"He will also want our family sword returned," Hideyoshi said with a nod to the man who was slicing the air and testing its weight, obviously having set his sights on it as a prize.

Kerim thought on that a moment. "Of course. Something to sweeten the deal."

With another nod, the man with the blade reluctantly retrieved its scabbard from Hideyoshi's waist and slid the thing home, holding it in a white knuckled grip.

Hideyoshi glanced at Angelique, and she gave him a smile and a nod. "Send my regards to your father, *otōto*."

Hideyoshi's eyes wavered, shimmering in the sunlight. He made to respond, but the words caught in his throat as he swallowed.

"Touching," Kerim said, and drew his own blade. "She will be the first, then." Kerim strode to her side as a guard shoved her forward and slapped away her hair to expose her neck.

"One last dying wish?" she said quickly, craning her head sidelong to Kerim who had raised the instrument of her demise.

"Ask," he said curtly.

"I know, of course, that there must have been a traitor somewhere on our journey here outside the Ottoman empire, who told you our identities and intentions. That much is clear to me now. But tell me, how on earth did you stage your death? Beechworth and I both saw it."

Kerim swelled with pride and stayed his hand. "A device of my own design. A spring mounted retracting blade, atop a bladder of animal blood."

"Very clever," Angelique said. "I assume the darkened library was also beneficial to selling the illusion."

"Naturally," Kerim said, conceding the point. "Upon close inspection, one would have easily ascertained both the cut in my clothing and the springs and mounting plate. Given the circumstances, and my men waiting close at hand, however, there was no such time."

"Blast my inattentiveness!" Beechworth exclaimed, drawing all their gazes. "You had a blade through you when you fell, but... the assassin still had his in hand!"

"Indeed," Kerim said, expression darkening. "I noted that too, and I will be having words with our *Kōga* vassals. Perhaps it is wiser we instead utilise the Iga assassins, however given Ishinari's involvement in these matters..."

Hideyoshi squared his shoulders and glared at their captor. "*Kōga* or not, cut me free and I will show you who is a vassal."

Kerim's teeth flashed and he raised his hands to indicate their surrounds. "You are in no position to make threats! I have the upper hand."

"You really are quite ingenious, *Paşa*," Angelique said. "You engineered the time you required to better orchestrate the workings of the Iron Clockwork from the shadows."

"Precisely."

Angelique nodded. "One more thing I must know. The wives and children of that contemptible child, Orhan?"

"Families of soldiers and other *paşa* captured to ensure their continued loyalty to the cause."

She nodded once more. She had suspected as much. The woman she had questioned in the gardens, Yasemin, had shown no little animosity and fear when they'd spoken.

"We, of course, had given him some girls with which to... entertain himself. You yourself know how easy it is to manipulate men with baser, carnal desires."

"Much like Remzi, you mean?"

Kerim's triumphant grin faltered. "Remzi was both a fool and a mistake. He allowed himself to be taken over by such trivial needs, believing himself to be beyond any reproach. At least Asena spared me from having to take care of the man myself."

"He would be very disappointed to hear you say that," Angelique said, smirking.

Kerim's smile slipped once more. "What?"

"Oh, my apologies. Yes, Remzi is very much alive and well with our friends." Angelique turned her head to Hasan. "Which brings me to... Had you and Yunus communicated better, you'd have known that, and that we were in collusion!"

Hasan winced. "We limited communication for safety."

"Safety?" Angelique said. "You could have killed Hideyoshi. I should—"

"Enough!" Kerim shouted.

"Quite right," she said. "I think this is entirely more than enough."

The crazed man looked down at her in confusion, his head snapping about to the arched entrance as a hellish sound echoed from its mouth, disgorging the source in short order with a spray of dust. Yunus rode in on Angelique's aeolipede, one of his men behind him on the original, and both followed by armed Asena men shouting battle cries.

It proved to be more than enough of a distraction.

Pivoting on her knee, ignoring the detritus digging into her flesh, she flung a handful of sand into the face of the man holding her down. The Janissary stumbled, clutching his face. Kerim had recovered from his shock and raised his sword once more, only to be met by her palm strike to his solar plexus as she stood. As he stumbled, she turned back to the Janissary guard, who had finished clawing sand from his eyes and peered through a stream of muddy tears as he brought his Greek Fire pistol to bear.

She twisted her torso, right palm blocking the man's wrist, left hand trapping it and pulling as she jabbed her knee into the cleft of his widespread thighs. Her body continued its motion, the weapon now in her hands, and she brought its thick stock onto the man's temple and brought him down. Not stopping her movement, she shot another man bearing down on Beechworth square in the chest. She turned once more and fired. A man Hideyoshi was wrestling with, his shackle chain around the soldier's throat, fell limp.

"*Tenshi!*" Hideyoshi's bound hands rose to point.

Kerim was fleeing on horseback while his men fought Asena. Angelique grit her teeth and made to run for her aeolipede.

"*Oi!*" Hideyoshi shouted.

She turned to her brother, and caught the sheathed Ishinari family sword one handed. She nodded to him and dashed through the melee, pistol raised. Two more Janissary fell, one of whom had been tussling with Hasan.

"Kerim's escaping!" she shouted at him.

Hasan turned to see the man getting away, and cursed.

"Follow me," she barked.

He took off after her, his frustration turning to hope as they ran through the skirmish and she vaulted into the seat of the original, much improved aeolipede. She lashed the scabbard on the front of the handles, stowed the pistol in a holster to the side, and set the machine thundering forward, mowing down several of the enemy under her wheels as she went.

She detected a shrill whistle from Hasan on the golden, dust covered facsimile of the machine. His fingers fell from his lips as he shot down a road to her left as she thundered past.

"*Merde.*"

Too late for her to turn about, she continued on to the next junction and attempted to take the corner at high velocity, which she managed only barely, and only owing to the cobblestones being covered in sand, their every pitted surface and fissures between the stones filled with it.

The rear wheel slipped on the sand, and Angelique felt the disproportionate lateral movement as its vulcanised surface slipped beneath her. She dropped her foot to the ground in order to stay upright, the sole and heel of her boot catching every protuberance and setting bone shuddering vibrations up her stiff leg and no doubt ruining the footwear. She briefly imagined attempting to explain the damage to a cobbler. She also imagined that, should she indeed survive this ordeal, she would need to fit the aeolipede with some sort of whistle device, perhaps like those on the *Pony* and *Silk Road Express*. She had barely heard Hasan over the roar of the aeolipedes.

That, and she was now facing a busy market street teeming with people.

The sound of the engines did an excellent job of announcing her presence, but the startled people became paralysed rather than flee, forcing her to slow. There was another road to her right and, hoping it was uninhabited, she turned into it, slowing to a respectable pace so as not to send herself flying. As hoped, she found the street empty and sped through.

Angelique cursed her luck at having lost her way, though her spirits improved when the palace rose in the distance through a gap in buildings and she navigated her way toward it and onto a main boulevard. She grit her teeth in elation as she saw Hasan and Kerim galloping up the road and over the crest of a hill, and frustration that she could not increase her speed.

When she reached the crest over which they had disappeared, she spied them well away from her and nearing the railed bridge that had taken her and Beechworth toward the palace so long ago. She also spied a contingent of Janissary closing ranks on the bridge, aiming Greek Fire rifles at Hasan but unable to fire for fear of hitting their commander as their target cut a zigzag close behind.

Angelique would have no such shield and would have to rely on the elements of surprise and momentum.

The Janissary turned to follow Kerim and Hasan as they passed. Try as she might, though, Angelique could not produce the speed she wished of the machine, nor think of a way to obtain it. With a curse, she lay forward and hoped it would suffice. Sure enough, with her body no longer catching the air, she was moving more briskly, and her new position had the added benefit that she posed less of a target.

The rush of the wind and vehicle shifted in tone as she left the valley of the buildings and shot into the open, shifting again as she flew onto the bridge, its pillars echoing back the roar of the Greek Fire engine in a rhythmic pattern. She gripped the handles tight and shuttered her eyes against the wind, tears streaming from them.

She passed the first man, whose shout was shortly followed by the hissing report of his weapon. Emulating Hasan's evasive actions, several other shots peeled around her, though she felt no impact or pain as she continued, the speed of her heart matching the sounds of her advance until she could no longer tell one from the other.

There was ting of metal. A shot hit the body of the aeolipede, splashing onto her dress and burning the cotton. Then, she was across the channel and thundering away from the men.

Ahead, Hasan disappeared through the gates to the palace and she raced to follow. Angelique was surprised to find the gatehouse and the ramparts bare, fearing that all of the men would be waiting within to put an end to their pursuit. She found her fears to be unfounded, however, and slowed her pace. Rushing headlong into an ambush now would assist no one. And, if she found Hasan in such a bind, getting herself likewise ensnared would only seal both their fates.

Angelique eyed every tree and outbuilding as she proceeded, and finally reached an inner courtyard of the palace to find Hasan taking cover behind stonework, his aeolipede on its side some way ahead of him, steam belching from its flank, one of its rubberised orb wheels still spinning. He waved at her and she dismounted behind a wall and dropped her own vehicle.

"You think to take the empire from me?" Kerim shouted in Turkish from a position Angelique could not make out. His words were followed by a sharp staccato rattling that brought with it a rain of projectiles. They tore into the stricken aeolipede and sent a shower of debris bursting from the ground about it, then the stonework Hasan was using for protection.

Risking a glance, she saw the device that was causing such carnage.

A thick gauge steel pipe jutted from a large box as thick and long as a man's thigh. This was mounted on a heavy tripod on the back of a steam car. From the device itself jutted two large canisters of brass encased glass, one containing water and the other Greek Fire. With each shot, a burst of fire followed by a puff of steam was ejected from the side of the weapon. Kerim stood at its back, one hand on a handle aiming it, and another clutching a handle that he cranked, his reddened face a rictus of rage. Reddened unnaturally. He had to have used a Greek Fire injector.

She ducked back from view before she could be seen, and signalled to Hasan to occupy the madman.

He nodded. "*I will take my family's throne back and personally feed your head to the birds, Kerim!*" Hasan yelled.

Kerim's response came after another volley of fire, and as Angelique busied herself in preparation for her assault.

"*Face me like a man, Kerim, instead of cowering behind a machine!*" Hasan said.

"*Come out, Hasan, and we'll discuss it like men.*" Kerim laughed, setting the repeating cannon chattering as he waved it about erratically in Hasan's general direction. Even as Angelique watched, he took out another Greek Fire injector and stabbed it into his chest, bellowing as it worked on his body.

Hasan shrank down as stone shards flew and bit at his exposed flesh, his arm protecting his eyes. His protection was limited from the infernal weapon, and his patience growing thin. He lifted his head and scanned about quickly only to pull down in haste as the weapon chattered once more and debris lashed his forehead.

Hasan dropped to sit and looked about, then closed his eyes and fists tight. "*Surrender, Kerim,*" Hasan shouted. "*I will spare your life if you fall on my mercy.*"

Kerim's chortling grew to an uproarious volume. "*You'll forgive me if I decline and don't extend the same offer of clemency, I hope.*"

"*Last chance, Kerim,*" he called, voice hoarse as Angelique got into position.

She rose to her feet and ran full speed atop the high wall she had climbed dressed much as she had been in the British Museum—in her underclothes. Her legs were bare but for the cotton she had torn from her dress and wrapped around her feet. The same cloth bound her hair, fluttering behind her. In one hand was Hideyoshi's sword, and in the other, a swaddled item.

"And you have no chances, Hasan, for now I am going to—" Kerim turned to Angelique as she came, a split glass vial of Greek Fire and water in his hand that he had been about to throw it at Hasan. *"What?"*

He quickly recovered and threw aside the incendiary device to grab at the nightmare weapon. In his Greek Fire fuelled rage, he ignored the explosion nearby to the vehicle and raised the ugly snout of the repeating cannon and fired.

At the same moment, Angelique leapt from the wall and swung the swaddled item forward sharply by its knot. The bundle of stones flew at her target just as intended, striking the repeating cannons glass canisters with a sharp crack.

"What?!" Kerim shouted once more as Greek Fire and water sprung forth.

Angelique rolled as she hit the ground and began to dash away. There was a rush of air and light as Kerim half ran, half flew off the back of the steam car platform, and she threw herself to the ground as resounding cracks sounded at random from all about the courtyard as the weapon exploded. The repeating cannon sat on fire, and steam issued from the steam car, its windows shattered and body full of penny sized holed. Then, everything was on fire as the steam car exploded.

Angelique fell back, hand to her face from the intense blinding heat. As she gathered herself and worked to find her feet, a sword tip appeared at her throat.

"Come out, Hasan, or I kill her," Kerim called out, in English for her benefit Angelique presumed.

Hasan emerged, hands held aloft. "I'm here, Kerim, let the girl go."

Kerim shook his head. "Only when you are both being held by my men. Guards!" Kerim called several times before men appeared and surrounded them. "Now what will you do, Hasan *Paşa*? Or should I say, Sultan Hasan?" Kerim laughed.

Hasan took in the men surrounding them, and he nodded.

"Resigned to your fate already?" "Seize them" he barked at the Janissary. The men about them did not move. "What are you waiting for, fools? Take him into custody! He is the leader of Asena, a traitor to the empire colluding with this whore of a spy!"

The men still did not move.

"Take him," Hasan said, and the men moved as one and worked to subdue the Greek Fire-incensed Kerim and relieve him of his weapons.

"My, you have been busy," Angelique said. They were, to a man, loyal to Hasan. He had obviously spent much of his time in the capital recruiting.

Hasan nodded. "Not being a tyrant with only their own interest at heart has its benefits." He stepped forward to retrieve his family amulet from Kerim as his men held him.

"This is not the end, Hasan," Kerim said. "Mark my words, it is not over!"

Hasan took Kerim's sword and held it casually, nodding for the men to prepare him. "For acts of treason against the Ottoman empire, Kerim *Ağa*, I sentence you to immediate death." Hasan raised the sword.

"Kerim *Paşa*," the man spat with venom, his face and eyes almost the same colour as the blood that flowed when his head rolled.

CHAPTER TWENTY-FOUR

The journey back to England, when it finally came, was far less circuitous, arduous and perilous than the one leading them to Istanbul. Angelique and Beechworth stayed on to see out the transition of the empire and rooting out of further Iron Clockwork dissidents and other violent dissenters. It took much convincing, time, and many a proclamation to spread the word of the new Sultan of the Ottoman empire and a new era, not to mention putting right the misinformation spread about Asena.

One of the solutions that helped to expedite the news actually came from Beechworth, however unintentionally, complaining of the call to prayer recording cylinder players one morning as he had attempted to finally sleep in.

"Far be it from me to stop a man from his worship, however these blasted things only play the same blasted sounds day in day out. Why can't they be used for something else? Reading my morning paper to me while I breakfast, for instance."

The cylinders had been cast as quickly as they could and spread throughout the land.

Missives had been dispatched to all port cities near and far, boxes of them to hand out to ships to take the news to foreign corners. The

Ottomans were inviting emissaries to re-open trade and travel alike, and re-opening their lands to peoples of all creeds and religions as they had in the days of old. It was to be their new renaissance.

Beechworth had also sent word of their success to England, and asked that Scotland Yard would in turn advise his constabulary and Abbie of his remaining alive.

During the intervening time they spent in Istanbul, Angelique had learnt as much of Greek Fire and steamworks as she could, putting that knowledge to great use on the airship and aeolipedes, the badly damaged golden machine having to be rebuilt completely.

The rest of her time was spent learning more of her past and her distant cousin, Hasan. He, too, had grown far from his homeland in exile, though his father had contrived to sneak them back into that distant arm of the Ottomans, the Japanese provinces of mainland China, which was where Hasan had learnt his martial skills, and also where he had hatched his own plot of revenge and to work back into the palace from the outside as a low ranking soldier proving his worth.

Their genealogical investigations led them to believe that they were both related to Sultan Ahmed the Third, deposed by his nephew Osman the Third who instigated the steam age and the empire's prodigious second rise, aided by the collusion of the Janissary who he also brought to power. They also concluded that Osman may have in fact started the Iron Clockwork society to ensure the empire's continuance after his demise, albeit of his own design.

It was all rather dizzying, even now as Angelique stood at the prow of a steamboat carrying them away from Turkey, gazing out across the waves. So much so that Angelique was lost in thought and did not notice Beechworth sidle up to the rail.

"You look as though you've had news of a terrible and personal nature," he said softly.

She couldn't help but smirk, but did not reply beyond that.

He nodded knowingly. They had indeed become good friends and close allies. Indeed, she could not fathom *not* working with him any longer, though she supposed after the time they'd had he would be resigned to a far quieter married life. With a substantial promotion to boot, given the acclaim their success would no doubt afford him. Perhaps it was that which troubled her.

"Whatever is it?" he said in feigned exasperation. "We rooted out the culprit with our skins intact. Well, mostly intact. We are on our way back to England. You uncovered your family history and had some measure of revenge on that front." Her lashes flickered as he said the last, and she averted her gaze. "So that's it."

"My revenge is only half done," she said. "And this portion of it, however large, has left me utterly exhausted."

"Is that the extent of it? Or is it because the remainder involves Hideyoshi?"

Angelique frowned as she gazed across the vessel at her brother where he sat, swaying in his seat after taking a small dose of the brown powders in order to mitigate the sickness brought on by their voyage. "Despite that I find myself with some distant blood relation now, however extended, Hideyoshi is still my brother. I fear, as you suspect, that he would..." She let the words trail. "I'm not averse, nor a stranger, to loneliness. But I do not at all relish that particular void my actions would inflict."

"Then forget the thing," Beechworth said sternly, though not unkindly. "Revenge is like that damnable Greek Fire you now love so much. It may at first blush appear bright and fantastic, but it will burn you through to touch it, and all those around you."

"Wise words, as always, Beechworth. But I simply cannot forgive Ishinari Hideo, nor forget."

"Then don't! But if you value your relationship with your brother as you say, then leave the wretched man alone. Leave him to be judged by God."

Scoffing at the words, she turned from the ocean. "That particular rose is of no use with this nail. Though perhaps you are right. Perhaps revenge is not the way forward and I should be done with it."

"Well, you needn't sound *quite* so surprised that I might be right. It has happened before, as you well know."

She looked at him in annoyance. "Smugness does not at all become you, James."

He gave a snorting scoff. "Well, as you're no longer obliged to feign my being your family, why should you listen to me."

"Indeed," she said, turning back to the waves. "Though I'm afraid you're still due a thorough punishment."

"Eh, what?" he said, gripping the rails tightly.

"Oh yes. You're quite stuck with me, I'm afraid," she said turning to him. "You too are now as dear to me as a brother. Or perhaps, a cousin? No! A distant uncle!"

Beechworth gave her a wide smile. "How very kind of you, mademoiselle. Uncle, indeed." He chuckled with her as he relaxed against the railing. "We must be getting close now. It's beginning to smell like home."

Home. It was a concept that had never been a part of her being. No matter where she had gone or been, locations were measured simply by the amount of time she had spent there.

As crates were unloaded at the dock in the fading light, curious warehouse workers and sailors alike gathered at a safe distance to see the arrived Ottoman vessels. Others quickly joined them as men ran from the scene then returned with colleagues and perhaps even strangers from the street.

Angelique waved and blew them a kiss when they continued to gape long after the sun had set, then resumed working at the crate for her aeolipede by the light of Greek Fire lamps from the ships.

"Jolly good of you to give us all this equipment and books, your highness," Beechworth said to Hasan.

The now Sultan was dressed as a simple sailor so as not to attract attention. "It was the least I could do, James. And to open peace with the rest of the world, we will need to share this great knowledge. No one nation should hold so much power again. I have seen firsthand what can happen when men become too ambitious."

"And the formula for Greek Fire?" Angelique said.

"Will be provided to the authorities. In due course."

She smirked. "But not at all diluted or tampered with, naturally?"

"Naturally," Hasan said, a sly grin stretching across his face.

Hasan had already expressed as much to her privately. The danger in hoarding such power was great, yes. But there was also danger in handing it over to the masses without proper care being given. She had agreed, certain that Hasan was a man of his word and integrity. Or at least more than most men she had met.

She was musing about the fact that the people now closest to her were all men—Hideyoshi, Beechworth and now Hasan—when one of them interrupted her.

"What is that sound?" Hideyoshi complained angrily, clutching his head.

"I told you, *otōto*," Angelique said, admonishing him. "You used too much of the powder."

"No," Beechworth said, confused. "I— I hear it too."

"You've *both* been on the ship too long," she said, dismissing them with a wave. "The engine noise is still on your minds, no doubt, and your brine-soaked brains are—"

"Mary mother of God!" someone in the still gathered crowd yelled.

Angelique climbed atop the aeolipede crate and raced toward its open end. There, in the dark sky, something glowed. She squinted in an attempt to make it out, then her eyes widened as clouds parted and the all too familiar profile of a gondola and large crimson balloon became visible.

The Ottoman airship—*her* airship—cleared the angled roof of the nearest building. The crowd went scrambling as flames erupted from the roof of the warehouse below the airship, scattering further as a fire bursts the same colour as the balloon exploded about the wharf with crashes of glass. They were dropping Greek Fire and water cannisters from it.

Men from Hasan's steam ships fired on the balloon, but their Greek Fire shots were ineffectual against the brass body and rubberised silk. Angelique screamed at them to stop. They were wasting both time and ammunition.

They soon had no choice in the matter as the nightmare chatter of a repeating cannon sounded from on high, mowing down the men on the ship who had no chance of escape. During the battle with Kerim, she had not had the chance to inspect the destroyed weapon. However they had found drawings for the thing, along with documents planning the mass production of it for, and for Ottoman expansion. Unlike the pistols and rifles used by Hasan's men, the repeating cannon fired iron bearings driven and surrounded by explosive shots of Greek Fire, making it doubly lethal.

Angelique leapt from the aeolipede crate and ran for the comparative safety of a brick warehouse wall. The airship had floated overhead and would have to come about to fire its deadly weapon once more. Beechworth, Hideyoshi and Hasan joined her, fire spreading around them as buildings went up. Then the situation worsened as more canisters were dropped on the Ottoman ships. Men caught alight, screaming in agony and jumping into the water, but that too lit up, and the full harrowing potential of true Greek Fire warfare was made clear.

They were trapped

"This is just like my nightmare!" Beechworth intoned, eyes wide in shock.

"Who is up in there?" demanded Hideyoshi of Hasan.

"I don't know! It must be someone from *Demir Düzenek* we missed seeking revenge. Somehow they have stolen the airship and followed us!"

"How could someone steal the airship?" Hideyoshi argued, giving Hasan an accusatory stare.

"I had no part in this. I am in as much danger as you."

"There's no time to argue," Angelique snapped. "We'll soon be in their sights once more, whoever they are, and..."

But the ship did not turn. Instead, it continued on straight, over the snaking River Thames.

"It's heading for London," Beechworth muttered in horror, recoiling as a fresh burst of fire lit the night. "We must do something!"

"The aeolipedes!" Angelique darted for the first crate and Beechworth ran with her.

Hasan collected as many of his men that he could, leaving some to douse the flames of their burning ships with the Greek Fire extinguishers and others to clear a path in the wall of flames nearby.

Angelique took hold of the wooden roof of the crate and pushed with all her might, Beechworth joining her soon after. With a crack and creak of bending nails, they threw the crate lid back and climbed aboard the aeolipede, Angelique immediately setting it leaping forward. Looking back, she saw Hasan and Hideyoshi boarding the larger golden machine and surge after them.

Angelique yanked on the steering handle as they turned onto a main road toward the airship and the heart of London, and the aeolipede thundered forth.

"Navigate for me, Beechworth," she yelled over her shoulder.

"Slow down for God's sake!" he shouted in her ear. "It's too dark."

"If we slow, we'll never catch—"

"Left! Left!" The machine swerved at his instruction. "Dear God in heaven! We won't catch them if you break our necks either!" Buildings in the distance lit up once more. "They're... headed for Buckingham Palace!"

Angelique swore. If an Ottoman airship destroyed the seat of the British monarchy, it would mean outright war the likes of which the world had never seen. That was what the Iron Clockwork was relying on, using Hasan's absence from Istanbul. If they could show he was present in London at the same time... It was dastardly clever.

"Where are Hasan and Hideyoshi?" she yelled.

Beechworth released his iron grip on her to turn. "Close."

Her mind raced. "Get us to Scotland Yard in the straightest route possible!"

"Whatever for?"

"Just do it, Beechworth!"

Beechworth was silent in thought, then his arm flew out. "Here! Right!" He quickly clasped his hand back to her torso as the aeolipede listed. "Then left up ahead and straight on."

Taking the turn at a perilous speed and angle, Angelique leant into the machine. Part of her adjustments and additions to the machines during their sabbatical in Istanbul was an increase in speed and efficiency, as well as a steam driven whistle, though she now regretted that lamps were not among those changes as she never imagined having to ever ride through the night.

They must have appeared as demons from hell as they tore through the street, steam whistle blowing and cloth flying. She was thankful that it was not a busy night, most people home and about their supper, and was able to weave amongst the cabs and horses that trotted through the street.

Soon their course brought them back in line with the river and they were running along it.

"Where are they?" Angelique shouted.

Beechworth scanned the sky. "There! We're ahead of them, but only just."

"*Merde*! How much farther to The Yard?"

"Not far enough."

She swore again, then leant to the right of the aeolipede and signalled at Hasan, pointing at the side of the machine. A sudden constriction on her chest confused her when she could not breathe. A carriage rushed past where her head had moments ago been and Beechworth released the back of her dress. She did not stop to thank him for pulling her back, instead leant back down and grabbed hold of a valve lever. "Hold on tightly, Beechworth," she bellowed, and pulled.

Compressed hydrogen gas stored within a cylinder used to start the vehicle released into the Greek Fire and water chambers, giving the vehicle a sudden and violent kick in speed with a roar and hiss of steam and smoke. They now easily outpaced the airship, Westminster Palace looming as they neared it. The vibration from the cobblestones and the heat radiating through the rubber coated orbs threatened to unravel metal and flesh alike.

Nearing Westminster Bridge, Angelique shut the valve and struggled to bring the aeolipede to a stop, its spheroid front wheel shuddering, sizzling and smoking rubber hanging in flaps from the wheels. She peered up at the re-construction work on the parliament building, scaffolding encompassing it like a second skin after it had gone up in flames years prior. If they did not stop the airship, it would likely be destroyed completely.

Hasan and Hideyoshi stopped beside them and she looked to her brother and barked something in Japanese. With a nod, the young man leapt from behind Hasan and ran into the darkness toward the palace.

"What on earth is he going to do?" Beechworth said, incredulous.

"Never mind Hideyoshi," she said. "We need to keep the airship occupied until help can arrive."

He instructed her on to Scotland Yard, now only a short distance away, while Hasan waited on the bridge. As they reached the building, Beechworth leapt off before they had come to a full stop and took the stairs two at a time while Angelique waited breathlessly, her fingers tightening on the handles with each passing moment.

After what seemed an age, he crashed out of the doors, several weapons in hand and slung over his shoulders, a handful of London constabulary behind him as he and sprinted back to her and mounted. The men would not arrive at either the bridge or palace in time, but if Angelique and the others were unsuccessful in stopping the airship, they would provide a last line of defence.

The aeolipede shuddered violently back onto Westminster Bridge and Beechworth abandoned it early as they arrived beside Hasan. He handed him a rifle, and they both got to work loading the weapons from the bandoliers he'd also brought.

The airship grew larger over the Thames, and the aeolipede went sliding on its side as Angelique dropped it, the machine grinding and bumping over the rough street as she ran to Beechworth and grabbed up a loaded rifle. "Spread out," she shouted. "Aim for the balloon, it's our only chance."

She took aim, fighting to slow her breath and heartbeat, and pulled the trigger.

Another crack followed, she shot a glance to her side and tossed Beechworth the spent rifle, a loaded one flying back to her. He then repeated the process with Hasan, and they fired again. They were not given a third opportunity.

The repeating cannon opened fire and they took cover. Her back to the bridge's stonework, Angelique threw her spent rifle down, accepting another from Beechworth as he came crawling.

"We've only time for one more shot!" he yelled above the din of the airship and its cannon.

"Then let us make them count. Wait until the ship is overhead."

Their breaths were ragged as they half lay against the stone bannister, and waited. Angelique was not sure if it was a second, or a minute, but the crimson tip of the balloon finally showed above them. "Fire!" she shouted. They stood as one and released a volley.

The occupants of the airship returned the attack, Greek Fire canisters falling from on high.

"Look out!" Beechworth yelled, diving toward Hasan as a blinding red plume engulfed the street and obliterated the night.

Overhead, the airship drifted on.

CHAPTER TWENTY-FIVE

"No!" Hideyoshi yelled as Angelique disappeared in sheets of flame. He was unable to determine whether they had consumed her, or merely the sight of her. His eyes flashed with the after image of the burst of light that seared like the petals of an exotic flower on his vision.

"Angelique?" he heard Beechworth yell. He was shielding his eyes and face from the flames on the bridge, fighting to search for her as Hasan pulled him away on his rear.

Even from Hideyoshi's vantage point, she was nowhere to be seen. The bright heart of the flames filled his vision. Seething with rage, Hideyoshi turned to the airship as it drew alongside him, slowly descending as it made its way toward its target. The figures in the gondola meant nothing to him. All he saw was red.

The airship was not low enough or close enough for him to leap atop it, as he had planned to do, and by the time it was, it would be out of reach. But Hideyoshi had a secondary plan to stop the thing.

He whirled a rope with a weighty makeshift hook he had taken from the scaffolding around the clock tower of Westminster Palace. The metal fastening and rod flew, the rope playing through his fingers, its coarse fibres burning his palm. The rope was only long enough for the makeshift hook to make it two thirds of the way up the expanse of the balloon, and he thought for a moment he would not have time to try again, and there was no room on the scaffolding to give chase.

The rod hit the balloon and slid down, filling Hideyoshi with dread. He had failed his sister and everyone. But then it tangled in the ropes that bound the balloon to the gondola, and the rope quickly stretched taut. Grinning in triumph, he wound the rope about the wooden beams of the scaffold several times, crossing it over and, with no time to secure the cord more permanently, placed a foot on the beam and pulled it tight.

The scaffold and rope creaked and groaned, the rope biting into itself as the line let out a tearing sound as it stretched to its limits. Fear gripped him by the throat once more as he thought the scaffold or anchoring rope would snap, but his fear was unfounded. He released a whoop of joy as the airship came to a halting stop, angling toward the building and scaffolding as the rope held the airship in place.

The ship's engines cut, and it fell back then surged forward once more.

Hideyoshi's celebratory calls were cut short as the platform he stood on rocked forward, the whole length of the connected frame undulating before falling back as the engines once again fell silent, only for the procedure to repeat.

The scaffold tilted, but stopped short of toppling, and the engines stopped once more, but the scaffolding did not return to its previous place. "*Chikushō*," Hideyoshi muttered as the airship pulled forward.

A loud ripping came from the airship balloon as broken scaffolding tore into it, a great hole appearing in its side. Cloth flapped as gas escaped and the airship tilted, pulling away from Westminster Palace and tipping earthward.

Hideyoshi whispered what he thought might be his last utterance. "Tenshi..."

The scaffolding creaked, then cracked as it, along with Hideyoshi, tumbled into the darkness below.

CHAPTER TWENTY-SIX

Beechworth watched Hideyoshi's battle with the airship in abject terror, unable to move from the spot. He knew he should search for Angelique, but if her brother failed then there would be no point. She would not admonish him for thinking in such a manner, he knew. To the contrary, she would not let him hear the end of it if he did not.

He had celebrated along with the young man when he had put a halt to the flying vessels advance, Beechworth's fist pumping in the air with a grunt of grim satisfaction. As he had started to jog to fetch as many of his constabulary colleagues as he could find to finish the job, he had put her to the back of his mind.

The great rending of wood and rope stopped him, and he ran back and gasped in horror at the destruction and the plummeting airship, afraid for what had become of Hideyoshi. Then, his dread doubled as he saw where the plummeting ship was bound for.

"Hurry, Hasan!" he called for the Sultan, all thought of formality lost in the dire situation.

"Go, James!" he yelled, his voice strained.

Beechworth looked back briefly to see the Ottoman liege limping, a large hole the size of an apple in his right trouser leg at the knee.

Judging by the melted edges of the cloth, the Greek Fire thrown from the airship had struck him. From everything Beechworth knew of the material, Hasan would not be running any time soon, and the destruction wrought by Hideyoshi had blocked the road for the aeolipede, not that it was in much shape for use.

Beechworth doubled his effort as he ran from Westminster Bridge after the stricken vessel, praying he was wrong about where it would fall. But as he turned the corner after picking his way through debris, he found that he had been chillingly correct.

"Dear God in Heaven, help us," he uttered the small prayer, his voice wavering, before resuming his pursuit.

As he sprinted, the end of Hideyoshi's rope fluttered in the breeze behind the still falling, damnable ship—the airship *he* had helped to build—but there was no sign of the man who had engineered its demise. He lost all thought of his companions as his legs faltered at the hopelessness of the situation. There would be no avoiding it. There was nothing he, nor anyone, could do to stop the airship now.

He watched and, God forgive him, hoped that the ship would hit the first target presented to it and come to a halt. But it did not.

With a sound like the heavens themselves screaming, the brass bottom of the gondola scraped atop the tower of St Margaret's Church. It seemed to bounce, gaining some little altitude, and Beechworth thought that divine intervention had played its hand. But then the thing dropped, and ploughed straight into the heart of the great northern rose window of Westminster Abbey with a cacophony of crashing glass, falling masonry and rending metal.

Wide-eyed and helpless, Beechworth fell to his knees, staring as the body of the thing disappeared into that snaggle-toothed stained glass maw, groaning and squealing as glass and stone clawed metal and the balloon deflated.

Then it stopped.

With a third of the gondola sticking from the church, it actually stopped.

Screaming people fled from the now opened doors of the Abbey, the penitent who had stopped to pray—perhaps doing so every night— and men of the cloth. They stopped, turning about to inspect the monstrous site and damage done to their most beloved place of worship.

Then they walked back.

"No," Beechworth said to himself, shaking his head. He rose to yell, hand outstretched, beseeching.

But too late, and too far away to make any difference.

Balloon and rope and whatever else that had been keeping the thing aloft gave way, and it slipped once, twice, and then a final time—the screams it emit as it did like the laughter of Lucifer himself. Then the airship slipped from view entirely, leaving a ragged blood-red flag left to wave in its wake.

There was an almighty crash, followed by a terrible din as the wreck settled. Then, after a brief and deceiving silence, hell opened its mouth and sent forth its flames to consume the consecrated ground.

CHAPTER TWENTY-SEVEN

Angelique crawled angrily from the Thames at Hungerford Bridge in her underclothes and climbed the steps to the street. She had been forced to strip out of her ruined outer clothing in the filthy water as it had been splashed by Greek Fire. She was all but certain that her body had been scarred for life, but she had no time to either confirm or dispel the suspicion.

Falling on hand and knee as soon as she was above the river walls, she purged her stomach by forcing her fingers into the back of her throat. She had seen enough of London to know what went into that particular soup, and would have none of it. She was not about to survive returning to Japan, Istanbul and the Iron Clockwork to only to die from filthy water. The irony would be far too great.

As she spat the foulness from her mouth and began to run, she saw a gentleman and lady walking arm in arm. Or at least they had been until she had fallen in their path looking like a half-drowned strumpet.

"Evenin', guv. Missus," she said, putting on more common airs and giving them both a nod and a wink before setting off at a run. Behind her, the woman admonished her husband for not averting his gaze from the 'wanton, Godless woman'.

Angelique barely had time to think before sounds of destruction ahead spurred her on. She arrived at almost the same place she had entered the Thames, and briefly looked over the downed scaffolding around Parliament before someone making their way through the debris came into view. She ran to the figure and found it was Hasan.

"What happened? Where are Hideyoshi and Beechworth?"

"Your brother happened," Hasan said, with a grin that turned to a pained grimace. "He brought down the airship, but..." Hasan shook his head. "We did not see what happened to him. James ran ahead as the ship went down. I—"

Shouting came from some distance, and the night was rocked by an explosion. When they ran toward it, they saw a stream of smoke lit with bright red fire.

"The airship!" Hasan said. "Only one thing can stop the fire now."

Angelique tore her gaze from the hellishly lit sky. "Can you—"

He grabbed her hand. "I will fetch *all* our ships. Go!"

As Hasan turned back and limped for his aeolipede, Angelique ran to the source of the commotion, eyes widening as Westminster Abbey came into view. It was aflame, though the brightness of the flames and black smoke reduced visibility greatly. The roar of the inferno and cracks of splintering wood and glass also served to confuse her. She thought she detected voices. Some calling for water. Others calling for help.

And... calling for her!

"Tenshi!"

Hideyoshi's voice was loud and clear, and she halted, glancing at where it had come from. Dishevelled and bleeding from cuts on his face, favouring his left leg and arm as he limped along, his right arm tucked hard against his ribs, Hideyoshi stopped as she turned to him and all but collapsed. She ran to his side and propped him up. As she did so, he gave a guttural grunt of agony.

"What happened to you?" she said.

He smiled, giving a coughing bark cut short by his more than likely broken ribs. "I brought down the flying demon, Tenshi. Grandfather would have been proud. But in so doing, I was dragged through the heavens." His eyes widened in terror, their glassy surface reflecting the fire in the abbey. "And now hell is upon us!"

"You've taken more of the powder," she said sternly. It was more than likely the only thing keeping him conscious at that point, else the pain would have been too great. "Stay here and rest, *otōto*. I have to find Beechworth and see what I can do to help." She made to run, but his iron grip stayed her.

His fixed eyes grew wide in terror. "Beware the demon, Tenshi!"

She grabbed his hand and attempted to pry it off, but his opiated fear induced strength in him, and she could not. "I must go, Hideyoshi," she said, easing her own grasp and laying her hand gently atop his.

"Promise me you will avoid the demon," he said, voice quiet yet strong, all but cracking, as if he were once again a little boy.

She stood up straighter, lifting her head. "I am Tenshi!" she said proudly. "The demon should be avoiding me!"

This mollified him and, with an idiot smile, he unfastened his sword and thrust it into her hand, eyes locked on hers. She inspected his wounds quickly and decided he would be able to await her return, and in so making up her mind, nodded at him and ran for the abbey.

She slung the sword over her shoulder and tied it on as she went, it's length and weight making it too ungainly for her to maintain a high speed. She would not be in need of it in any case, and had only taken it to appease Hideyoshi's addled mind.

The roar of the flames and the heat increased as she neared the inferno. A dishevelled suited figure with its back to her emerged as a whirl of smoke was whisked away by the wind the heat created, pulled aside like a curtain to reveal them.

"Beechworth?" she yelled as she neared the man, calling again as she closed rank with him, but he did not turn, the noise and sight of the fire overpowering. She clasped his shoulder and turned the man about.

It was not Beechworth.

The man was in obvious shock, his face soot and smoke grimed, eyes streaming and red. "It's on fire," he said simply, his voice like a lost child's.

"You need to get back, sir," she told the man sternly.

"Westminster Abbey," he continued in the same fashion. "It's on fire."

She grabbed him by the shoulders again and gave him a firm shake. "Then either help those in need, or get your useless arse out of the way!" The man blinked back at her, not seeming to know what to do, so she pushed past him with a firm shove. "Beechworth?" she called out, the acrid smoke stinging the back of her throat and her eyes as she searched.

How she wished she had a pair of sturdy work goggles now and a good—

Her feet faltered. She took hold of a layer of her clothing and yanked, cursing the well-tailored undergarment when it would not give. Reaching behind her, she struggled to pull the katana free, thanking her stars she was not in battle. The razor edge easily cut a notch in the cloth allowing her to tear a length that was good eight inches wide. She folded it diagonally to produce a long triangular mask, then fastened it around her face, the still damp cloth aiding her somewhat in her breathing.

She saw several other forms about and ran to them, working the sword back into place as she went, but they turned out to be constabulary. Knowing they were likely his colleagues, she asked after Beechworth. The first few had not seen him but had come from their posts on the route to the palace when they had heard the destruction. Others of them reported seeing him, but not recently, saying he had been assisting those stricken by debris or the flames.

"Good man," she muttered to herself. She now knew where to continue her search, nearer the centre of the chaos.

Along the way, she stopped at one of many water barrels with hand-drawn pumps that had been placed about the area after the fire that had burnt down the original Westminster Palace and Parliament, now threatened again by the crazed and suicidal Iron Clockwork. She washed her face in the water, ensuring that her mask and as much of her clothing as possible was doused, for all the good that it would do. Her arms, legs and head were bare, and the moisture in the scant amount she wore would evaporate quickly.

Without another thought on the matter, she ran toward the Abbey.

As she drew closer to the heat and light, figures from her left emerged carrying what appeared at first to be ropes. It was not until those lengths expanded along their length, filling to become rigid as they did, and emit a stream of foaming liquid that she realised they were hoses. Nearing them, she made out the Ottoman garb of the men, and heard the shouts in Turkish of their leader as he limped around the corner.

Hasan opened his mouth to call out to her, but another shout—one that rose above the howling wind of fire and echoed around the space —stopped them both.

All eyes fell on the figure that emerged from the smoke and steam now issuing from the abbey, almost as if they had walked out of the very flames themselves. In fact, it was not one figure, but two, the larger carrying the other, though carrying was a gross misnomer.

Beechworth's eyes bulged as the fingers that wrapped about his neck from the rear held him aloft, his boot toes scrabbling against the cobbling to keep from hanging himself, hands clutching at his captor's iron-like arm.

"Hasaaaaaan!" the imposing man screamed once more.

Now at her side, both Hasan's and Angelique's eyes widened in recognition.

"Ali *Paşa*?" Angelique said.

The man had a grin on his face like the devil himself, looking every bit the part lit by the burning church, though that was only part of the similarity. His chest and arms were bare as was his head, bereft of the brass fez he had always worn without fail. As her eyes travelled up the man's body, she could scarce believe what they reported to her brain.

The flesh of the once vizier's chest was ragged red, veined and stone-like in places, as if roughly carved from crimson quartz. Lending greater comparison to that mineral were the irregular, jagged crystalline protrusions jutting from his torso. The shoulder of his arm that held Beechworth was likewise a mass of the crystals, though the arm itself was equally as fantastical as the man. A brass pauldron was riveted directly to his stony flesh, and affixed to this was an intricate arrangement of rods, gears and pulleys that approximated a human arm, the very mirror of his own flesh and blood limb.

But the miracle abomination did not cease there and was not even the most horrid of his deformations. The top of Ali *Paşa*'s head was a construction of curved glass panels and bronze, giving full view to the man's brain, which like his chest and other parts was a mass of crystals. However, where she could tell his breast was red, she could only assume the same of his brain, for the tank it was contained in was filled with a Greek Fire solution, which gave a soft glow despite the nearby flames.

"How?" Hasan said, in total disbelief. "You died!"

"Died? I have now survived not one, but *two* airship crashes!" Ali *Paşa* laughed.

"*You* are the true leader of the Iron Clockwork," Angelique said brusquely, tone full of accusation.

"The leader?" the madman said, voice full of scorn and eyes taking on a fervour the likes of which she had never seen. "I am so much more than that, little girl!"

"Give up," Hasan shouted, anger flowing out like the heat of the flames. "We discovered and took the heads of most of your men, the rest of them are rotting in the dungeons awaiting the same fate. You have no hope, Ali *Paşa*, of ever—"

"Ali? *Paşa*?" The man said, his mocking sneer full of untold secrets. "No." He stood taller and puffed up. "I am Sultan Osman!"

CHAPTER TWENTY-EIGHT

Confusion built as Angelique repeated the name in a whisper. "Osman?" The implication of what the madman was saying rose, as did her brow. "Surely you don't mean... Sultan Osman the Third?"

The man's maniacal grin grew. "The one and the same."

"That's impossible!" Hasan shouted. "That would make you well over a century old!"

"Having survived that," Ali—or, as he claimed to be, Osman—said, pointing at the burning abbey, "you still doubt? Perhaps I should walk into the heart of the flames themselves to prove it? Of course—" He gave Beechworth a shake, who grunted in alarm, "—your friend will not be as fortunate as myself."

"No!" Angelique shouted. "What is it that you want?"

"Hasan!" he said, hissing through his clenched teeth. "I have worked too long and hard to have it all undone now by the likes of him!"

"It's over, Ali... or Osman, or whoever you claim to be," Hasan shouted.

"*I* will say when it is over!" The crazed man-machine bellowed, Beechworth issuing a cry of pain as the metal hand clenched around his neck. "I should have killed both your grandmothers when I had the chance. But instead, like the weak fool I was, I sent them into servitude. Or they fled when I had my uncle Ahmed executed. A mistake that I will never repeat again!"

"He's mad," Hasan muttered, eyes wide, shaking his head in disbelief.

"Mad?" the man shouted, impossibly having heard the utterance. "I will show you who is mad! For too long I have waited to conquer Europe, moving into Asia instead so as not to repeat past errors of the *Osmanlı* empire. Too long did I wait to grow *my* empire's strength. As ingenious a step as it was, bolstering our dwindling numbers with our Muslim brothers in China, freeing them from their infidel leaders who sought to oppress them... and by allying ourselves with the Japanese, tapping their spies and resources, creating a wall to fend off the contemptible Americans... Yes, far too long. I should have acted sooner."

"And now?" Angelique shouted. "You will rebuild your Iron Clockwork to take over the world, continuing to rule from behind the curtain?"

"I've no further use for the *Demir Düzenek*. It served its purpose. And I have you to thank for assisting me in dealing with their few troublesome leaders. No, now I will reveal myself and rule from Topkapi as I once did!"

"Men," Angelique scoffed. "Always threatening to reveal themselves to prove their dominance. Shall I give you some small advice?" She leant forward, almost conspiratorially. "They are not that imposing."

"Enough!" Osman barked. "You are a prime example of the salacious and sinful influences of the Western world that must be stamped out!"

"Oh, I had forgotten," Angelique said, glancing at Hasan and chuckling. "You are afraid of women. You had them banned from the palace, wearing iron shoes so they would think you were a big, scary man, when you were merely a little boy."

Osman smirked. "You think to anger me with your insults? Catch me unguarded? I have lived three lifetimes and met your like many times over."

"Yes, how did that come about exactly, your immortality?" Angelique said, her curiosity genuinely piqued. Insane fabrication or not, it would at the very least grant them some much needed time. "At least that little fact about you is not disinteresting. I can surmise from the reading material I had access to that it was you who discovered the secrets of Greek Fire in long lost vaults, probably during your incarceration as a young man in the palaces. But how did that lead to the Iron Clockwork and..." She indicated his body with a wave of her hand. "Your *condition*."

"As you say, I found a secret cache of Greek Fire and manuscripts containing the formula, brought to Istanbul centuries before that by a secret order from Alexandria. They had spent hundreds of years perfecting and studying it before fleeing when the city was sacked by my ancestors. There were also works produced by Leonardo da Vinci, and the work of others who attempted to decipher his inane code, the key to which he took to his grave.

"That great ancestor of mine, Sultan *Süleyman*, had recognised the importance of the research and had attempted to obtain diplomatically, by forming alliances with France, works of the artist which he believed he might have taken with him from Istanbul, or penned after his time there, and put many great thinkers to the task. But he was unsuccessful, and sealed the secrets away."

"Until *Süleyman* found the works from Alexandria in Pergamum," Angelique said.

Osman gave her a conceding nod and sneer. "You are a clever one. Our blood is strong in you, despite its *taint*." She gave him a bitter smile. "Yes, *Bergama* is where the work had been kept since it had left Alexandria a millennium before that."

"All very interesting," Angelique said, glancing behind the man as several shadows moved—men from Scotland Yard, slowly making their way toward him. "But that still does not explain your transformation and longevity," she said, hoping he would talk at length.

"When I happened on those works, I was so captivated with the stuff, and frequently in its presence with my most trusted men as they worked in secret. There was an accident. A fire. Many of my chief engineers perished, and I myself did not escape its touch, losing my arm...

and more. In such an infirm state, I could not appear either in public or in my duties, and rumours of Janissary dissent arose."

"And that's why you formed the *Demir Düzenek*," Hasan said, seemingly no longer a sceptic.

"And also how *you* came about the discovery of injecting your men with Greek Fire, and those injectors," Angelique added.

"Indeed. I placed a loyal young man in my place as my mouthpiece, then over the years replaced him with others. As you said, I was never one for women and had no offspring. After my accident, I could not even if I wished to. And having disposed of my brother, uncle, their wives and children, I had to ensure at least my ideas continued. Though somehow, I lived, despite the prognoses of all my doctors.

"More than that, I grew stronger! The Greek Fire fused with my flesh and began to transform it. It was then that I began to experiment with living tissue and..." His free hand indicated his body. "Alas, it seems Allah has ordained that only his chosen may benefit from it. While the creatures and men I tested on had certain benefits, they were temporary, and resulted in their eventual deaths. Still, a useful tool for the oncoming expansion of the empire.

"And now, I believe I have let you stroke my ego more than enough in the hopes of distracting me."

In so saying, the man turned and flung Beechworth at the constabulary who had been silently flanking the demon, rifles at the ready. Several of them were bowled over, the others setting off their weapons. Osman raised his clockwork arm to his eyes and charged, taking several shots to the torso and legs without affect. With an incredible kick, he sent one man tumbling back, the man clearly dead as he soared a great distance, limbs loose, like a rag doll thrown by a petulant child. With a ratcheting sound, a steel blade sprang from Osman's clockwork arm and he dispatched several other men in quick order.

Those that could fled, but he had lost interest in them. Turning, Osman charged at Angelique and Hasan with a bellowing roar.

Hasan pulled a Greek Fire pistol from his belt and fired at the approaching, wide-eyed monstrosity. The flying orbs of the normally lethal material ran from his flesh with no affect, only his trousers burning where the stuff dripped.

The men manning the hoses turned the streams on Osman, slowing him briefly and diverting him from their Sultan. He changed his course to deal with them. He ran the first of them through, using such force that the blade pierced the man behind also. With a gout of blood, he pulled the blade free and slashed at a third and fourth, who had released the hoses to fire their own weapons at the dripping, leering figure.

Osman turned back to Hasan and Angelique once more, and walked on without a care of harm, arms stretched out by his hips as he came. "You cannot stop me! You cannot kill me! Allah has blessed me and works through me!"

It was even worse than Angelique had first thought. Not only was he a madman, but he was a madman on a self-deluded holy mission. Every time she had met such people, be they Christian or Shinto or Muslim, they were dangerous in their own twisted way. Enticing the faithful to palm over gold. Influencing lawmakers to ease their way. Enforcing girls and women to become servile slaves and accept their lot. With fear mongering, fear of burning for eternity, of their angry masters on high. The worst were those who pulled puppet strings from the dark, as Osman had done with his empire. And those who were true believers, committing unspeakable acts in the name of their gods or leaders with no second thought or regret.

Acts like killing their own families and sending their women and children into slavery.

One way or another, Osman had to die.

And, so thinking, she scarcely remembered moving to attack, unaware of how she had so deftly pulled the sword at her back free. She sprinted at Osman, and steel met steel, though he more than easily pushed her and her attacks away with his bladed arm, almost batting her away with a single swipe and sending her into a spin.

Angelique renewed her attack, but was again repelled. Following directly after her, Hasan took up the charge, teeth bared as he fought both the madman and his own injury valiantly, though he fared no better. The two of them exchanged places, as if in a dance, one swinging or thrusting to be parried violently away, the other rushing in to take their place as quickly. And, just as quickly as if they had been engaged in such a lively jig, they soon grew weary, the added weight of their swords adding to their fatigue.

Sword fighting was not a sport, she had been reminded many times in the Iga village by her adoptive grandfather. A sword may be beautiful, but it was not a piece of art. It was a weapon. Its purpose was to kill, as swiftly and efficiently as possible, no matter the size or shape. Osman, on the other hand, was making a game of it, wearing them down and gloating. Goading them on with open glee on his face. Angelique's arms burnt, her muscles aching and slowing, Hasan in much the same condition and worse, his scorched leg dragging.

If the Mechanical Turk had wanted them dead, he could have done so already many times over, and it seemed he was now moving towards that end and had grown weary of his game, Angelique and Hasan proving to be less than worthy adversaries.

Angelique broke off to one side and settled in a squat to rest her arms, Hasan joining her, panting with exertion and clutching his thigh. During the altercations they had both also sustained cuts and bruises, although all minor. With the soiling of their skin from the soot in the air, sweat and water, they both appeared as though they had stepped straight from a battlefield onto London's streets.

Osman, meanwhile, trod to the fallen Ottoman soldiers and raided their corpses, pulling ampules of Greek Fire from their coats and ammunition belts. Angelique and Hasan watched in confused fascination as he went casually about his business. Activating some mechanism within his arm, a needle of some three inches protruded from his wrist. As they observed, he pierced the ampules one by one on the needle and tossed the empty glass capsules away. Fascination turned to dread as he revealed more of himself.

His blade sunk through the cloth of his trousers and cut them away with a few swipes. Both those limbs were also mechanical, the right leg to the thigh and the left to the knee. He faced them, activating some other part of the clockwork arm. A burst of steam escaped from its length. He had refuelled, and was now ready to finish their fight.

Osman strolled, and they met him halfway and resumed their assault with new vigour after momentarily regaining some of their own strength. But it did not last. Osman now doubled his own efforts and was no longer toying with them as he once was. The cuts they sustained were longer and deeper, the intermittent kicks, while not at the strength at which he had dispatched the poor constable, formidable. All of it served to sap them of what little energy they had recovered, so much so that Angelique doubted she could raise her arms.

Raise them she did, only to have her sword wrenched from her grip by the terrifying force from the flat of Osman's blade, followed by a sweep of its razor edge diagonally across her stomach, slicing her thin garment and severing the cord of the scabbard she had forgotten on her back. She caught the thing by the cord as her hand clasped the cut.

Osman then repeated the attack with Hasan.

Summoning her energy, Angelique pulled the iron and hardwood sheath by its cord. It weighed on her limbs as if it were solid steel, and on any normal man would be just as deadly. Regardless, it was the only weapon she had. With a death cry escaping her lips, she brought the thing down overhead with the last of her strength.

The curved length connected with Osman's artificial skull with a loud crack. He slowly raised his metal hand and gripped the scabbard. With a whir of gears and creak of wires, he crushed it like it was nothing and wrenched it from her hands to toss it aside. Osman sneered down his nose at her. A crimson droplet arced over the bridge of his nose, then hung on its tip before falling into his moustache.

There was a jagged crack in the glass around his brain, and it was leaking its Greek Fire fluid.

Osman swung his flesh-and-blood arm and backhanded Angelique across the face, sending her sprawling. Osman stomped toward her, kicking Hasan away, then raised his bladed arm, his face a knot of rage, lips pulled back like a snarling animal baring its teeth.

Angelique shuffled back on her rear, expecting the worst as he closed on her. If this was the end, however, she would meet it head on. She lifted her chin and, pushing out her chest, invited death.

Osman eased down in a squat, lip quivering as his arm eased back, the tip of his blade pointed at her heart and poised to strike.

They were both interrupted by the call of her guardian angel.

Angelique rolled aside as, with a roar and a whooshing steam whistle, her clattering aeolipede rushed past and into Osman's gawking face. Machine and man-machine alike disappeared in a crash of metal and sparks and were consumed by the billowing black smoke from Westminster Abbey.

"Tenshi!" Hideyoshi yelled as he limped forward to fall at her side.

"Hideyoshi!" she shouted, and threw her arms around him. "*Arigato, otōto,*" she said, squeezing him tight.

"*Did you see, Tenshi?*" he said, excited. "*I slew the demon!*"

"*Yes, I saw, Hideyoshi. Well done.*"

Hasan limped to join them, Hideyoshi's fallen sword in hand. He shook his head as he passed Angelique the weapon, and looked about to say something, but was stopped by the sound of creaking metal accompanied by a clank, then scrape. Clank scrape, clank scrape, the sound approached from the smoke, metal groaning as it came.

"I told you!" Osman screamed as he stepped from the roiling black cloud, dripping blood and Greek Fire from his broken face. "I. Cannot. *Die!*"

High over his head, held impossibly aloft, the equally broken aeolipede bled. Pure Greek Fire splashed down his skull, face and chest, to no effect. Only a small amount of the red liquid remained sloshing around his brain, yet still he came. The muscles in his chest and human arm stood out, the smashed yet still functioning parts of his mechanical arm complaining as they took the weight. Gears rumbled as he readied to toss the machine at the three weary figures.

"Excuse me, old chap," a familiar, if hoarse, voice called.

Osman's head snapped around.

Beechworth stood, worse for wear with his smoke soiled clothes and flesh, throat black and blue. He had a pistol pointed at the once-Sultan.

"Do your worst, English dog! I cannot—"

"Yes," Beechworth said, his tone thoroughly fed up. "So you say." Beechworth pulled the trigger.

The glass dome of Osman's skull shattered. The Mechanical Turk faltered, but did not fall. He grinned madly and his arms tensed in preparation of throwing the aeolipede.

Angelique had already moved. She ran at Osman, Hideyoshi's blade angled down by her side as she flew. The blade struck as she flew past him, as intended. It had missed the man-machine himself entirely. It did, however, strike the puddle of Greek Fire at his feet. Or, more importantly, the stone beneath it.

The spark of metal on stone blossomed into flame and the Greek Fire roared to life, rushing up Osman's body like a living creature to fill his mouth. It shone through his bloody, broken face and continued upward, leaping into his glass cranium and lighting his head like a demonic torch.

Osman screamed until either flesh or metal could no longer hold, and the heavy aeolipede crashed atop him, adding to the conflagration and pinning him down.

The Mechanical Turk burned long into the night.

CHAPTER TWENTY-NINE

On The Strand, not far from the fateful fire of Westminster Abbey, a young woman sat sipping tea in the Twining's tea room, her face pinched and uncertain. She said not a word as she listened to the accounts related to her, of thievery in underwear, of royal commissions to America and "Oriental lands". Of spying and near-death encounters, danger and murder, duplicity and threats to both London and the world the likes of which she had likely only ever read in penny bloods.

"I don't quite know how to react to all this," Abbie finally said, sitting up straighter after a long silence. She turned first to Angelique, her eyes lingering only briefly before becoming affixed on Beechworth.

It must have been terribly difficult for her to finally see the man she had been betrothed to, after months of absence and heartache and doubt of his return... to see him in such a new light. Abbie had said that the constabulary had alerted her to Beechworth's untimely absence, but nothing more.

All the poor girl could do was shake her head at his tale.

Beechworth opened and closed his mouth several times, reminding Angelique of koi in a pond from the Iga village. "You could begin by telling Beechworth you missed him terribly," Angelique said, "and stop feigning shock to hide the excitement you feel."

Both Beechworth and Abbie turned slowly to stare at her.

Beechworth cleared his throat. "I'm awfully sorry, Abbie. She has a tendency to speak her mind." Abbie's mouth still hung open. "Although, I have found that she is quite often correct." He gave Abbie a small smile. "Annoying, though correct."

Abbie turned to her fiancé, her cheeks and neck flushing. But she did not deny it.

"Your man is a hero, Abbie," Angelique said. "You don't mind me calling you Abbie, do you?" Abbie opened her mouth, but she was not given a chance to speak. "Not that you can brag about it, of course, being all very hush hush and what not. But a hero, nonetheless. Why, he saved my life and the lives of countless others by dispatching a truly evil villain from this world."

"I don't think Abbie needs to hear—" Beechworth began.

"Burnt him from the face of the Earth like the blight he was!" Angelique added, her face hardening at the mere thought of the man.

Abbie's eyes opened wide in horror, along with others in the tea room.

"You're upsetting my fiancée, Angelique!" Beechworth said brusquely.

"Yes... Well... Quite!" was all Abbie could muster to say.

"I'm terribly sorry," Angelique said, though her tone did not reflect apology. "I forget myself sometimes. Perhaps... Yes, I've overstayed my welcome." She stood from the table. "I should leave you to... re-acquaint yourselves."

"Yes!" Beechworth rose from his chair sharply, knocking the table and rattling teacups. He fussed at the cups, then composed himself, clearing his throat. "Perhaps that would be for the best," he said in a lower tone.

"No need to stand on formality for me, Beechworth," Angelique said. "We're too close for such things. I'm quite capable of seeing myself—"

"Yes! Time for you to go. Look at that—" Beechworth fumbled at his pocket watch. "You had that... appointment to keep, yes? Oh look, a Hansom cab!"

"Oh?" Angelique turned to the window, then back to Abbie. "Awfully lovely to meet you, *ma chère*. Beechworth mentioned you so very often, why I almost know you! Though, he failed to mention quite how attractive you are." Abbie's face flushed a deeper crimson. "Good for you, Beechworth," she said, and his face almost matched Abbie's.

As Angelique stepped around him, he turned to nod at her. "You are insufferable," he muttered, keeping a cordial smile on his lips.

"You have nothing to fear from me, my dear Abbie," Angelique said, turning back. "Beechworth is as a brother to me. I know that he will be a very good husband for you. And I am certain you will not mind if I borrow him for an evening or two here and there." She waved cheerily at them both. "*Salut!*"

Abbie watched her leave, suspicion plain in her eyes, and when she thought Angelique was out of earshot, said, "Borrow you?"

Beechworth turned to Abbie, and took a deep breath as he sat.

Just as Angelique was certain she would never have what Beechworth and Abbie shared, she knew their relationship would burn far longer and brighter than any Greek Fire.

The Hansom arrived at the docks and Angelique alighted to the usual glances and leers. And, as quickly, those men averted their gazes or doffed their shabby woollen caps when they recognised her.

"Good morning, lads," she said to the nearest of the men, who grunted their responses as respectfully as possible as she passed them.

"Should I even attempt to embrace you," a voice that seemingly came from nowhere said, "or will you threaten to give me a place for a peg leg and hook hand too?"

Angelique came to a halt and turned to a stack of crates, grinning. "With your arm and ribs broken as they are, *otōto*, I would not advise it."

Hideyoshi emerged from behind the crates, returning her smile.

"Remember when Grandfather would have us fight with one hand tied behind our backs?"

She rolled her eyes. "Do I! You used to always win!"

His teeth flashed as he laughed, the corners of his eyes wrinkling. "Because you let me."

"Perhaps at first. But as you grew and became more skilled..."

His expression slowly soured. "I'm not sure I am ready to return to the village."

"Oh? Did that swordsmith I send you to not repair the scabbard?"

Frowning, Hideyoshi opened his coat to show the sword, nestled in its place. "No. He was very good. But..." He raised his head, holding her eyes. "Some damage can never be repaired."

She went to him and took his hand. "You will be fine. Some rest, fresh air and exercise... Right as rain, as the English say."

Hideyoshi grunted. "And what of you?"

She shrugged. "What of me?"

"Is your revenge done? Or—"

"Osman is dead. The Iron Clockwork done and reparations being made. What more could I want?" His eyes darted back and forth, searching hers. "Do not look at me in that manner."

"What manner is that, Tenshi?"

"In the manner that says you do not believe me."

With a deep sigh, Hideyoshi stood taller. "If you say it is so..."

"I do. Why, I even have some local business to attend to, so you can safely board your ship and—"

His eyes narrowed in suspicion. "Business?"

CHAPTER THIRTY

"E re, you sure you want to be out 'ere, at this time o' night, Guv?"

Beechworth looked around, frowning. "Not at all sure, no. But needs must."

He paid the cab driver and watched in trepidation as he pulled away, leaving him alone. The hour was late, and the place deserted. Glancing about furtively, he made his way to the warehouse he had been instructed to attend.

The docks had been rebuilt with the assistance of Ottoman steam machinery, as way of reparation for the attack, yet the area still reeked of damp, burnt wood. He wrinkled his nostrils, more at the memory than the smell itself. Though there was another far less palatable odour under the remnants of fire which made him wish he had not lingered.

He reached the location and wasn't at all sure he was in the right place. The warehouse appeared as if had been abandoned, and for quite some time. He pulled a slip of paper with the address from his pocket and confirmed he had it right, then the time from his pocket watch. All correct.

With a sigh of resignation, he entered the dark and cavernous space within through a side door. In the back corner of the warehouse, a lone light shone through the window of an office.

"Once more into the breach," he muttered and soldiered on, his footfalls echoing in the dank, dusty space as he closed on the structure.

He did not bother knocking. Though he was expected, after everything he had been through, he was always prepared for subterfuge. When he entered the office, however, he was hit in the face not by a weapon or fist, but pipe and cigarette smoke.

"Inspector Kaylock?" Beechworth said of the Scotland Yard man, lounging in an old chair.

"Ah, Beechworth, old man." Kaylock didn't rise, and sounded anything but pleased to be there.

"What a surprise it is to see you here." Beechworth's eyes met Angelique's, who gave nothing away as she smoked where she stood behind a beaten and scratched wooden desk.

"Well, I was rather intrigued to receive a summons to come to an old, abandoned warehouse in the cover of darkness," Kaylock said around his pipe, smirking. "How could one refuse, eh?"

"How indeed," Beechworth said.

"Sherry?" was all Angelique said.

Both Kaylock and Beechworth took one.

Beechworth raised his slightly. "What are we drinking to?"

Angelique eyed Kaylock. "How about... a job well done." She tipped back the liqueur in one go.

"Ah! I expect you would like *this?*" the inspector said after his own draught. With a sly grin, he held up the sapphire he had promised to Angelique what seemed an aeon ago. Though he was reluctant—theatrically so—to hand it over.

"But of course," Angelique said. "We kept our part of the bargain. We even managed to fulfil both tasks you set for us."

"Did you now?"

"You know very well we did," Beechworth said brusquely.

"Surely you do not intend on dishonouring our agreement, Inspector," Angelique said slowly.

"The thing is..." Kaylock stood and placed the sherry on a cabinet, then picked up his coat from the back of his chair and placed it over his arm. He lifted the gem to the light and peered at it. "Well, with agreements made between respectable people and criminals, the respectable people have all the credibility, while the degenerates have only mud to their name. Quite right, eh, Beechw—"

The man did not get a chance to finish his words as he was struck in the face, coat, pipe and sapphire slipping from his grasp. Beechworth, stood above him, fists at the ready in a pugilist's stance.

Kaylock scrambled to sit, his tongue flicking at his split lip. "What in the hell do you think you're—"

Angelique joined Beechworth and picked up the sapphire, lauding her prize. "This," she said with venom, "is a treasure of the family of Osman, whose bloodline I am a direct descendant of. Not to mention close personal friends with my distant cousin, *Sultan Hasan Han Hazretleri*. You would not want to explain to His Majesty of England why it is that the waters eastward, only newly opened, were closed again would you, Inspector?"

The man picked himself off the ground, fuming. "I'll have you both clapped in irons before the day is—"

"You *also* might not want to explain to His Majesty and your superiors at Scotland Yard," Angelique said, cutting him short once more, "what it was you were doing colluding with the man who set fire to London from an airship."

Kaylock's eyes narrowed a fraction. "You've no proof."

"No," Beechworth said. "We do not. But you are the most likely suspect."

"And, I note, you are not at all denying it," Angelique said.

Kaylock grabbed up his coat and pipe, and stormed from the office, turning to Beechworth and Angelique as they followed him out and through the warehouse to the outer door. He brandished the pipe's stem at them. "You're through, Beechworth! I'll tarnish your name from here to all the bloody colonies! Do you hear me? Through!" Kaylock threw open the door, marched out, turned on his heel and jabbed the pipe stem at Angelique. "As for you, you heathen harlot—"

Angelique pulled a cloth affixed to the warehouse door as she closed it, uncovering a plaque and silencing the man. Kaylock's face became ashen in the moonlight as he read the embossed lettering. Beechworth hadn't even noticed it when he'd arrived.

MORREAUX AND BEECHWORTH
SPECIAL INVESTIGATORS
AND ROYAL STEAMWORKS ENGINEERS
BY APPOINTMENT TO
H.R.H. KING GEORGE III
AND
SULTAN HASAN HAN HAZRETLERI

Muttering threats, Kaylock disappeared into the night.

"Special Investigator and Royal Steamworks Engineer, eh?" Beechworth said. "Strange, I don't recall accepting any such position."

Angelique rolled her eyes, and made her way to an external staircase around the corner that led to the roof. "Don't be such a baby, Beechworth. How else are you to make a living now you've had the can from Scotland Yard?"

"And you can pay me handsomely, can you?" Beechworth said, looking about the rundown warehouse in confusion, wondering where she was leading him now.

"Not immediately, no. Though, I've a sneaking suspicion that an abundant sum of money will soon be coming our way from..." She fluttered her hand over the railing at the night. "Not to mention the work afforded to such lauded, and might I add experienced, persons."

"And what if my fiancée has objections to this... endeavour?"

"Well, then she would be rather contrary."

He frowned. "Eh? Why would she..." Angelique did not respond, or even acknowledge the question. "Because, of course, you've already spoken with her and she will be joining us."

"My, you catch on fast, Beechworth. You might make a good investigator yet."

"Hmm," was all he said, though it hardly expressed the rising joy in his chest. It was short lived as confusion returned, brought on by a growing burbling, and fluttering. "Pigeons?" he said as his head cleared the roof.

Cage upon cage filled with scores of the things lined the roof. Nearby to them were five large crates, two of which he recognised in size as belonging to the aeolipedes. She ignored those and bent to open a hatch on one of the coops, caught up a pigeon, and handed it to him.

He grimaced when the bird moved as he turned it about. "There's... a scroll on its leg?" He untied the roll and released the pigeon, and began to read as it flapped about then landed atop the coop. "Free for all, the secrets to... Ottoman Greek Fire? At your national institutes of science and libraries?" He lifted his head sharply. "But how? Why?"

"Let us say a little birdie told them. As to the why? This will ensure that no one person or nation ever has the stuff for themselves alone. No more secrets. No more controlling with power and fear. No more despots."

Beechworth nodded as he lowered the scroll and looked out over the London cityscape. "Do you at all think that Ali Pasha's preposterous claim was true? That he was Sultan Osman the Third?"

"There was a time that I would have categorically said no. After the experiences we had in Istanbul, however, I'm no longer at all sure."

"No more secrets, indeed."

"Quite. Though, having said... I think I'll just keep the full-strength formula to myself." She gave him a wink.

"You little—"

She smiled. "Well, one of us has to make sure you keep that pretty little Abigail of yours fed and properly clothed."

Beechworth rolled his eyes at her. "Pretty little Abigail? Good grief, woman. Anyone would think you're—" He blinked several times, aghast. "You're not..." Angelique laughed. "*Are* you?"

"If you're going to continue being such a prude, James Nathaniel Beechworth, I may have to reconsider my offer. It entirely spoils all the fun."

He let out a sigh, then waved the curled slip of paper in his hand at the crates. "Are we to begin with opening an aeolipede factory?"

With a grin, she made her way to containers, placing her hands affectionately on two that were side by side. "No. As much as the world needs Greek Fire, I'm not at all sure they are quite ready for that much speed and power."

He frowned, indicating the other three boxes. "Then…"

Angelique took hold of the long edge of one and pulled it easily, Beechworth noting bent nails indicating it had already been opened.

His brow rose as the machine parts within were revealed. "Why, that's—"

"The Mechanical Turk, yes. Hasan kindly shipped the pieces over at my request. A memento, if you will. I'll be rebuilding it and housing it here in my home."

"Surely you're not planning on living in a warehouse!"

Her shoulder hitched. "And why not?" She indicated another of the large crates. "My personal effects are already here, and I grew somewhat accustomed to it in Istanbul. I told you, Beechworth, I am wholly invested in this."

Beechworth's lips pressed tightly. "Admirable, but…" He glanced around the pigeon dropping covered roof of the warehouse.

"Oh, do not concern yourself. I already have workmen arriving come Monday to construct both a steamworks and a residence with an office befitting a woman of my new stature."

"My, you have thought of everything, haven't you?" His eyes stopped on the last wooden box, smaller than the others, though somewhat ominously the size of a casket. "And what of that? Should I expect Mister Hideyoshi to pop out of it?"

Angelique laughed gaily. "That would be something, would it not? But, no."

"Another memento?"

"Oh, very much so." She moved to the crate, picking up an iron pry bar and handing it to him as he followed. "If you would be so kind."

Beechworth sighed as he removed his jacket and rolled up his sleeves. "I wouldn't have worn one of my best suits if I knew I was in for manual labour."

She looked his clothing over and cocked her head dismissively and hummed.

He snatched up the pry bar and got to working the lid off. The lid cracked as he loosened it, then moved to the head of the box and around until it was loose enough to pull back toward himself.

Beechworth stepped sharply away as the contents of the box came into view, his eyes widening in terror. "That's—"

Angelique nodded and stepped to the head, both figuratively and literally. She reached out and her hand hovered over the remains of Sultan Osman. All flesh had been burnt clean off in the fire, though his Greek Fire crystal infused bones remained. Much of his metal and glass skull had melted, though his clockwork limbs appeared to have escaped the brunt of the intense fire, and had been cleaned.

"The *other* Mechanical Turk, yes," Angelique said.

He stepped closer, holding his head high. "And what do you intend to do with... *it*."

Angelique's face tipped up from gazing at the monstrous skeleton, a grin across her face.

Beechworth sighed and gripped the bridge of his nose. "Blast. There's *that* damnable smile again," he said, and prepared to steel himself for whatever was to come next.

THE WARD SERIES

Stacey Trampler came home from work to find her boyfriend Paul and girlfriend Jasper missing. In their place, a strange man claiming to be a Ward — whatever the hell that is — and the creatures they protect Earth from ... the Umbra. To save Paul, Jasper and her own life, Stacey will need to join the Wards in their battle ... and face the Shadow Man, who seems fixated on Stacey, though neither she nor the Wards know why.

The Ward Series is intense dark fantasy full of action, sci-fi elements and a whole lot of sarcasm.

Read on for links and an exclusive offer

THE WARD SERIES

Stacey Trampler came home to find her boyfriend Paul and girlfriend Jasper missing. In their place, a strange man claiming to be a "Ward" and the creatures they protect Earth from ... the Umbra. Then the Umbra evolved. The Wards were forced to evolve with them ... but with new enemies rising up, some from within, their mission will never be the same again.

Stacey does her best to stay out of trouble, but when that consists of kicking as much arse as she can to stop it, it kinda seems to keep hunting her down.

The Ward Series is intense dark fantasy full of action, sci-fi elements and a whole lot of sarcasm.

THE ENLIGHTENED

Melbourne, Australia – 1996

When Private investigator James O'Donnell is hired by Cassie Lawler to find a missing person, he thinks it's an easy job to pay the rent. But somehow his missing person, Nathan Mortimer, escaped from a secure psychiatric facility.

O'Donnell is quickly sucked into a world of the supernatural — ghosts, reincarnation cults, visions ... and murders.

If O'Donnell can survive long enough while holding on to his sanity he might be able to find Nathan, who's the key to unlocking all the answers. The answers to the murders. To who the mysterious and alluring Cassie Lawler is.

The answers to The Enlightened.

ABOUT THE AUTHOR

Cem Bilici is an author of supernatural thrillers and fantasy adventures.

Born in Adelaide, South Australia and of Turkish heritage, Cem lives with 1 dog — Bucky the beaglier — and 0 cats (that will likely never change), and a couple of humans. Cem currently lives in Melbourne with said dog and humans — Australia, not Florida.

Cem is also an avid fan of horror films, video games, and heavy metal.

You can connect with Cem on various social media platforms. Or sign up to his newsletter at cembilici.com/signup to keep updated on new releases and specials and **receive an exclusive FREE ebook collection of short stories** set in the Ward Universe, *Wild Turkey and Fanta*.

goodreads.com/cembilici
bookbub.com/authors/cem-bilici
facebook.com/CemBiliciWriter
instagram.com/fullmetalwritechemist
twitter.com/CemBiliciWriter

www.ingramcontent.com/pod-product-compliance
Lightning Source LLC
Chambersburg PA
CBHW060851250626
47159CB00008B/2684